Unanimous Praise for *Mozart's Ghost*

"Heartbreakingly funny." – **Erica Jong**

"Pleasing and deft… a blithely spirited and romantic tale that seems destined for a movie adaptation." – ***Booklist***

"A sweet little love story… Cameron's engaging style puts these characters through their paces with style. With humor and heart, Cameron gives us a host of flawed characters and the subtly hilarious situations." – ***San Francisco Chronicle***

"Delightful." – ***Publishers Weekly***

"Sweet… its words and feelings go down quick and neat, like glib wine. Cameron has real talent for painting a character with a few telling words. She's funny, and clearly has affection for [her characters]." – ***The Santa Fe New Mexican***

"As smart and funny as it is meltingly romantic. A real charmer." – ***Sullivan County Democrat***

"Wonderfully sly… beautifully realized… a delicious love story. This is a delightful novel." – **Tim Farrington, author of** ***The Monk Downstairs***

"Captivating… musically evocative, tenderly funny, and hauntingly erotic. Moving and delicious… a spellbinding novel." – **Judy Collins**

"A sly love story." – ***Deseret Morning News***

"Enchanting. Charming. Anyone who goes to a psychic or has been tempted to try a medium will love reading about Julia Cameron's spirit talker and Mozart's ghost." – **Sophy Burnham, author of *A Book of Angels***

"Authentic and entrancing... *Mozart's Ghost* has successfully captured the challenge and humor of living a spirit-filled life in the secular world. I loved her happy ending."
– **Sonia Choquette, bestselling author of *The Psychic Pathway***

"A grand little tale, worthy of Mozart's love and joy... a great symphonette." – **Don Campbell, author of *The Mozart Effect***

"A charming, festive novel that has kick. Well written and awake... We now have a fine tale from the author of *The Artist's Way*." – **Natalie Goldberg, author of *Writing Down the Bones***

Mozart's Ghost

Also by Julia Cameron

BOOKS IN THE ARTIST'S WAY SERIES
The Artist's Way
Walking in This World
Finding Water

OTHER BOOKS ON CREATIVITY
The Right to Write
The Sound of Paper
The Vein of Gold
The Artist's Way Morning
    Pages Journal
The Artist's Date Book
How to Avoid Making Art (or
    Anything Else You Enjoy)
Supplies: A Troubleshooting
    Guide for Creative
    Difficulties
Inspirations: Meditations from
    The Artist's Way
The Writer's Life: Insights from
    The Right to Write
The Artist's Way at Work
Money Drunk, Money Sober

PRAYER BOOKS
Answered Prayers
Heart Steps
Blessings
Transitions

BOOKS ON SPIRITUALITY
Prayers from a Nonbeliever
Letters to a Young Artist
God Is No Laughing Matter
God Is Dog Spelled Backwards

MEMOIR
Floor Sample: A Creative
    Memoir

FICTION
Popcorn: Hollywood Stories
The Dark Room

Mozart's Ghost

JULIA CAMERON

HAY HOUSE

Australia • Canada • Hong Kong • India
South Africa • United Kingdom • United States

First published in the United States of America by St. Martin's Press,
a division of Macmillan.

First published and distributed in the United Kingdom by:
Hay House UK Ltd, 292B Kensal Rd, London W10 5BE. Tel.: (44) 20 8962 1230;
Fax: (44) 20 8962 1239. www.hayhouse.co.uk

Published and distributed in Australia by:
Hay House Australia Ltd, 18/36 Ralph St, Alexandria NSW 2015.
Tel.: (61) 2 9669 4299; Fax: (61) 2 9669 4144. www.hayhouse.com.au

Published and distributed in the Republic of South Africa by:
Hay House SA (Pty), Ltd, PO Box 990, Witkoppen 2068. Tel./Fax: (27) 11 467 8904.
www.hayhouse.co.za

Published and distributed in India by:
Hay House Publishers India, Muskaan Complex, Plot No.3, B-2, Vasant Kunj,
New Delhi – 110 070. Tel.: (91) 11 4176 1620; Fax: (91) 11 4176 1630.
www.hayhouse.co.in

A catalogue record for this book is available from the British Library.

ISBN 978-1-8485-0226-0

Printed and bound in Great Britain by CPI Bookmarque, Croydon, CR0 4TD.

For Tim Farrington, a writer's writer

Acknowledgments

Sophy Burnham, for her meticulous craft.

Christopher Cameron, for his marine biology.

Domenica Cameron-Scorcese, for her clarity.

Carolina Casperson, for her romanticism.

Sonia Choquette, for her keen vision.

Judy Collins, for her inspiration.

Joel Fotinos, for his faith.

Natalie Goldberg, for her companionship.

Gerald Hackett, for his insight.

Linda Kahn, for her assistance.

Ben Lively, for all that jazz.

Emma Lively, for her musicality.

Larry Lonergan, a medium at large.

Marcia Markland, for her deft guidance.

H.O.F., for his artistry.

Susan Raihofer, for her persistence.

Ed Towle, for his stubborn belief.

Chapter 1

S he was late. She had cut it too close again. Someday, she told herself, she was going to arrive at her classroom early—refreshed, relaxed and grounded. But someday was not today. The ancient elevator in her apartment building chugged its way slowly toward the lobby. Anna tapped an impatient foot. When the elevator door slid open, she found her exit squarely blocked. A gargantuan beetle-black grand piano was wedged sideways into the minuscule lobby. Short of crawling on her hands and knees, she could not get past it.

"Hey! Some people need to get out of here," she called out. "Please! Somebody!"

Alec, the superintendent, who was supervising the moving of the piano, saw her plight. "Ride back up," he suggested. "Take the stairs back down."

"But I'm late!"

That's when the tall, redheaded stranger spoke up. He had been standing just to one side with two uniformed moving men.

"We tried to wait until everybody had gone to work," he said. "This won't take much longer."

"Well, it's taking too long for me. Oh, never mind!" Anna stabbed at the elevator buttons. As the door slid shut, she caught one last glimpse of the redhead. He smiled apologetically. Was it her imagination? Despite his frizz of red hair and his Buddy Holly glasses, he looked quite attractive.

The elevator door slid shut and that is when she heard the voice, scolding her in heavily accented English. *"You could have been more civil to him. You could have made him feel welcome."*

"Well, he's not welcome," Anna explained, aware that she was arguing mentally with a ghost. *"This building is lovely and quiet, which is necessary for my work. The last thing I need is someone pounding on a grand piano at all hours of the day and night."* A quick glance around the elevator told her the ghost was settling for an auditory appearance only.

"Pounding?" The ghost sounded outraged. *"His music is sublime—and I should know."*

"Well, it's not welcome," Anna persisted. *"And neither are you!"*

"You could have pretended," the ghost pressed on. *"What's wrong with a little feminine grace?"*

"I'm late," Anna announced the obvious. *"And he's making me even later. And besides, what business is it of yours? You're a ghost."*

"Don't remind me," the ghost sighed. *"His happiness is my business. His comfort. His ease. I want the best for him, you see—and I intend to see that he gets it."*

"Well, count me out of your plans," Anna retorted as the elevator stopped. *"And if you're going to visit me, do it when I am working."*

"Let me get this straight," the ghost sputtered. *"Kings vied for my attention. The pope himself knighted me. With you, I need to make an appointment?"* Clearly, the ghost was used to getting its way.

"That's absolutely right. I'll speak to you during business hours."

With that, the elevator door opened and Anna hurled herself toward the stairs, leaving the ghost behind.

Chapter 2

Was it her midwestern imagination or were New Yorkers' faces inherently more interesting, perhaps more craggy or clearly etched than the vaguely Scandinavian ovals of her Michigan childhood? It was in part to escape a fate wed to a Scandinavian oval that Anna had come to New York. In Ann Arbor, she would have ended up as someone's eccentric, misfit wife. New York offered a chance to be loved for her entire self, or, since the city was filled with single women, a chance to be loveless without shame. In Ann Arbor, she was a spinster. In New York, she was single.

At age thirty-two, Anna lived in a one-room apartment on Manhattan's Upper West Side. Her studio was on the fifth floor of a prewar building erected in the twenties. From her two north-facing windows, she enjoyed a view across rooftops where her neighbors, slightly miniaturized, held barbecues and sunned themselves on tiny rooftop decks.

If Anna leaned far out of her fire escape window, she could catch a leafy sliver of Central Park—that was as close to the trees of Ann Arbor as she ever wanted to get again.

Like so many other New York transplants, Anna had been a misfit where she came from. With its welcoming anonymity, New York was a mecca for oddballs longing to blend in. Back home in Ann Arbor, she had not blended in. There, in the conventional and conservative Midwest, her interest in the paranormal had branded her an outcast, although her peers regarded her with a wary fascination.

Under the careful guidance of a spiritualist teacher, Bernice Murphy, she had honed her skills—but also achieved an unwelcome notoriety. "Teen Ghostbuster Helps Police," one unfortunate headline had trumpeted. Anna was torn between the thrill of practicing her gifts and her longing to be a teenager amid teenagers. To add to her woes, her twin brother, Alan, seemed to dine out on her escapades. He would initiate conversations with remarks like, "Let me tell you about my weird sister." Indeed, as the "weird sister," Anna had been only too glad to escape to New York.

If Alan, back in Michigan, asked her about her work, Anna kept it vague. She knew he pictured crystal balls and tilting tables, and envisioned her wearing a turban—as many of the storefront psychics along lower Broadway in fact did. She had long since tired of trying to make her brother understand that to her, ghosts were simply a fact of life.

The first time it had happened, Anna was five years old. She was staying at her grandmother's house and she had been tucked into bed early. "Don't let the bed bugs bite," her grandma said, kissing her forehead, smoothing her covers, shutting the door.

What bed bugs? Anna wondered, staring at the ceiling where something hazy and bluish seemed to be floating. She squinted and the shape took on form. It was a woman, with her hair in ringlets around her face, wearing a high-collared dress that was clearly etched, although after the bodice, the dress trailed into nothingness.

Anna observed the ghost with astonishment. Handkerchief

pressed to its lips, it appeared to be viewing her the same way. She should have been scared, but what she felt was curiosity. She watched with fascination to see what would happen next. She knew enough to know it was a ghost, but it didn't seem threatening in any way. It coughed into its lace handkerchief.

Anna reached a hand from beneath the covers and extended it over to the night table where her grandmother had left a small bell—"A sick bell, for emergencies or if you need me." Anna rang the bell. The apparition smiled regretfully and started to fade. By the time her grandmother opened the door, it had vanished.

As an introduction to the paranormal, it had felt, well, *normal*, but how would her brother feel if he knew that most Sunday afternoons, as a thirty-something adult, she attended a tiny spiritualist church where a diehard band of six to eight worshippers gathered together and tried to receive messages from the other side? This prospect was made problematic since the "church" was actually a tiny rented rehearsal hall, mirrored along one wall, with a rickety stand-up piano on which the minister, with her minimal piano skills, pecked and pounded out nineteenth-century hymns. The ragged congregation raised its communal voice in scraggly song, but rarely succeeded in drowning out the opera singer who rented a rehearsal space two doors down.

Anna attended out of affection for Miss Carolina, the wizened Jamaican woman with her crooked walk and more crooked wig who presided over her dwindling flock. Despite herself, sometimes Anna felt foolish, riding up to the fourth floor in a tiny jammed elevator prone to distressing lurches, often in the company of Zoreida the Magnificent who taught a belly dancing class just down the hall.

"Pretty girl like you, you should learn to belly dance," Zoreida often urged her.

"No, no. I'm here for church," Anna always answered.

Once, under the shepherding of its late charismatic founder, Doctor Lucian, the church had been robust and healthy. Now, a decade after Dr. Lucian's death, a mere handful of followers remained. Anna worried that the lamp of their faith would flicker out entirely without Miss Carolina's sad and lilting sermons, without her cryptic but often astoundingly precise messages from the other side.

"You have the gift," Miss Carolina had confronted Anna after her initial service.

"Yes." Anna saw no point in denial.

"But you fight it." Miss Carolina went on, sounding gently dismayed.

"I try to cooperate," Anna protested. "I *do* cooperate."

"Exactly. You 'cooperate' instead of celebrate. It's a gift. A rare and wonderful gift, but you don't like being 'different.' Ah, well, it's hard when you're young."

"I'm thirty-two. Not so young," Anna argued. But Miss Carolina had correctly nailed her private conflict. As much as she loved her contacts with the other side—and she did love them—normal had always seemed eminently desirable to her, just impossibly out of reach.

"Well, it feels good to be around others, doesn't it?" Miss Carolina clucked sympathetically. Anna had to admit that it did and so for the admitted pleasure of "being around others," she became a regular at the tiny, ailing church.

No, Anna did not share this aspect of her life with Alan. Of course, Alan had his own weirdnesses, but Anna was loath to point them out. They were, after all, fraternal twins, two very different beings who had once swum together peaceably in their mother's womb. Twins had to count for something, Anna felt.

"Let Alan be weird," she often lectured herself. Let him live in Kalamazoo, Michigan, building handcrafted violins in his garage, poring over his obscure mathematical calculations, certain that he would eventually rival Stradivarius. Who was she to disabuse him—or anyone—of an obscure obsession, an eccentric ruling passion? No, Anna held her tongue.

Chapter 3

If she held her tongue with Alan, Anna did not hold it that afternoon with her new musical neighbor. Waiting for the elevator, in what was no longer the quiet and cavelike lobby, she found her attention snagged by a rising crescendo of notes. The piece of music was turbulent and impassioned. It dragged her attention in its stormy wake.

An invisible presence loudly cleared its throat. *"Magnificent, don't you think? It's almost like hearing myself play."* The ghost was back.

"What are you doing loitering in my lobby?" Anna accused.

"Loitering? I am enjoying the concert. Anyone but a philistine would recognize the opportunity."

"Do not call me a philistine. Scat!" Anna waved a hand at empty air. She distinctly heard a derisive snicker but with that, the ghost was blessedly gone.

The elevator was as slow as always at arriving. While she

waited, her "concert" played on. The notes rose in drama and pitch. They unfurled with greater and greater velocity and intensity. An inexorable climax was clearly building. Anna felt a sympathetic anxiety rising in her chest despite her attempts to focus her thoughts calmly. When the elevator door wheezed open, she was only too glad to escape.

I chose this building for its peace and quiet. I need to be able to hear myself think! If I'm distracted, I can't make contact. If I can't make contact, I can't make a living...

Anna's thoughts churned upward, floor by floor. She was slightly panicked. Distractions endangered her livelihood, which depended on her ability to focus on subtle vibrations. She had trained herself to listen through sirens and jackhammers, the rolling surf of the city, but this music was far more intrusive. Its very beauty held far more danger. How would she hear the other world when this one so compelled her consciousness?

The elevator door slid slowly open on her floor. The music greeted her again. Clearly it climbed straight up the stairwell. It was softer than it had been down below but still quite audible. Opening her apartment door, Anna found that a wave of music met her as she stepped inside. She had left a window open for ventilation and now the music leaped straight over the sill. Anna marched to the window. She leaned out and shouted down, "Will you *please* be quiet?" Into a rising crescendo of notes, she shouted again, "Please shut up, would you?" She found herself near tears with frustration.

The music continued unabated, and a now familiar, quarrelsome voice spoke out. *"Shut up? Is that what you said to him?"* Now the ghost was right in her apartment and determined to have her ear. *"You must admit that he is talented. Listen to his phrasing! Listen to his expressiveness! It's a privilege to live within earshot. You're a very lucky young woman."* The ghost rattled on.

But Anna did not feel lucky. She felt hurried and harried, trying hurriedly to put away clothes and straighten pillows. She liked her home to be a serene and neutral environment for her to work. She scolded the ghost. *"Get out! You can't just come here willy-nilly. Please leave! And don't come back without an invitation!"*

But the ghost did not leave. In an outraged voice, it went on. *"Not invited by you, perhaps! Marie Antoinette welcomed me. And Louis the Fifteenth. Or, if you prefer the English crowd, George the Third. I assure you, that pianist would greet me with respect. Just listen to him, would you? What rhapsody! Surely you can hear it! Just listen to his musicality!"*

"No, I will not listen to him. And I will not listen to you, either!" Anna retorted. She grabbed for a rattle and shook it vigorously just as her mentor, Mrs. Murphy, had taught her.

As a rule, ghosts hate the sound of a rattle and this ghost was no exception. It sputtered a final protest. *"Very well then, I'm leaving. But you could try to be civil. He's very sensitive and even if he didn't hear you this time, I did, and next time he just might. I can't have him getting discouraged."*

With that, the ghost was gone. Anna spritzed lavender water to clear the air of his obnoxious presence. She slumped into a chair, waiting for her buzzer to sound. She had an appointment scheduled in moments. The music pounded on.

Chapter 4

Dear Mr. and Mrs. Oliver,

I am writing to thank you (as always) for your generous help. You cannot imagine—or perhaps you can—exactly how much pressure you have taken off of me. And, in another sense, how much pressure you have put on me. A year's free rent! Time to practice! The leisure to actually prepare for competitions! I am one lucky fellow. My friends all think I am living on air or have come into a secret inheritance. As you requested, I have told no one of your scholarship or stake or "bet," whatever you want to call your generosity. Again, I am grateful.

Let me try to give you a picture of my apartment. It is on 86th Street near Central Park, on the ground floor of an old prewar building. Since it is a rental, they allow pianos. My friends tell me many New York co-op boards are hard on musicians. They consider our practicing mere noise. I suppose it is to some ears—not, thankfully, yours.

Where was I?

The apartment has ample room for my piano and enough extra for a futon and the desk I am writing you on. Don't get me wrong. To me, it feels like a penthouse. The ceiling is high. There are two windows looking north onto—you'd say an alley—but there is a tree out there and the leaves are just barely turning as I imagine they already have at home in Maine. (Pardon my writing. It's rusty and tiny. I am used to jotting notation.) New York is hot one day and cool the next. If I keep a window cracked, I get a nice breeze.

Mrs. Oliver, thank you for your suggestion. I'll try a geranium. I am afraid I have a black thumb. Not gangrene. (Just kidding.) I know you worry about my hands. They are fine.

Mr. Oliver, the landlord says he will accept checks from any postal zone, as long as they are on time. As I am sure they will be, don't get me wrong.

I play a little better every day. (Not in my personal opinion, of course, but I try to ignore that.) What I am trying to say is that I am working hard to live up to your faith in me. I will keep you posted.

Sincerely yours,
Edward

P.S. I am working a little on the Schumann. That, the Bartók, the Bach, and pretty much the kitchen sink. The Rachmaninoff, the Chopin, the Liszt, and the Mozart, of course. I am getting ready. Four months and counting until the competition. If I win, it's a year's living money, three years' worth of concerts and a CD. That would certainly be a good launch for anyone's career. Let's just hope I win.
P.P.S. Sorry I am such a self-conscious correspondent.

Chapter 5

When Anna first moved to New York, she endured a series of sublets, hopscotching around the city, learning its neighborhoods and moods, before settling on the middle-class bohemia of the Upper West Side. When she finally rented her studio there, she was evasive on her landlord's questionnaire. On the slot that listed "occupation," she did not write "medium" as her business cards read. There was no point in inviting questions, so she simply wrote "teacher." This was stretching the truth, but not too far. For her work reference, she listed her friend Harold, a grammar school principal, who understood her employment dilemma and consented to speak on her behalf—provided she actually do some substitute teaching for him. She did, to help cover her exorbitant, ever-escalating rent.

21

Harold was a gay man in his early fifties. He was carefully preserved and could pass for fifteen years younger. Trying to look wholesome for her job interview with him, she had worn her most dowdy and conservative outfit. "Oh well," she thought to herself, observing the effect, "Lassie's mother." She loved vintage clothes but there was a fine line between vintage and frumpy. For the sake of her interview, she had crossed it. She wanted the job and was determined to appear "normal." When her business card spilled onto Harold's floor and he snatched it up, she braced herself for the inevitable rejection of her teacher's application. "Medium" the card said in plain black and white. So much for "normal."

"What does this mean, 'medium'?" Harold did not return the card but fingered it curiously as if it might nip at his fingers.

"Ah, just a little sideline," Anna ventured, grabbing for her card.

"Not so fast," Harold said. "This is all very interesting." He motioned her to a chair and took his own seat behind an imposing wooden desk. He slid her business card under the edge of his desk calendar. "We all have our little secrets, don't we?" he asked.

Anna felt a moment of panic. People, men especially, often reacted badly to the news of her profession. Take the matter of romance. One date, two, sooner or later her profession would come out—often with her brother's help—and the invitations for dinner or a drink would promptly stop. She expected such rejection from Harold.

"Look," Anna managed defensively, "you don't have to give me a job. I can make ends meet without being a substitute teacher. I can type. I can wait tables. I'm an adequate salesperson. I'm good with plants. I can walk dogs, although I'd prefer not to. I have lots of skills." Even to her own ear, she sounded defiant.

"And you can see ghosts," Harold said. He fingered a pen.

"Something like that, yes," Anna answered.

Harold chuckled. "Maybe that would come in handy too. All your other specialties make you sound like an ideal candidate." He wrote "yes" on a small lined tablet. He used block-style kindergarten letters.

Anna saw that he had a fat sheaf of papers in front of him. Her resumé and paperwork, she presumed. It was harder to get a substitute teacher's job than it was to work for the CIA.

"You don't smoke? You don't have a drinking problem?" Harold looked at her with a genuine twinkle.

"I amuse you?" Anna asked.

"You interest me, not amuse," he said.

"You make me sound like a science project." Anna sounded as defensive as she felt.

"I suppose it is a science." Harold nodded to himself. "Yes, I suppose it is."

"What is?"

"Parapsychology of course."

"Oh, of course."

"But let's quite quibbling about semantics—you're hired."

Chapter 6

Westside Aquarium occupied the basement and ground floors of a vintage brownstone on 74th Street between Columbus and Amsterdam. It was just a block out of her way walking home from school and Anna stopped there most afternoons. The basement was freshwater fish. The ground floor was saltwater. Anna preferred the basement.

"You again," the clerk greeted her each day as she arrived. His name was Tommy. He had elaborate tattoos running up both of his arms. His head was shaved and featured pierced ears, nose and lower lip. Despite his fierce appearance, he remained very handsome and he seemed like a sweet young man.

"Me again." Anna smiled as she made her way to the back of the store past the neon tetras and the cichlids, past the angelfish and red-tailed sharks, to her favorites, the swordtails. "Swords," as she called them, were good swimmers, quick and zippy. When she approached the tank, they spun in unison and headed to the rear, behind the coral formation. If she waited patiently, they ventured back out.

"I got a new shipment of angels," Tommy interrupted her viewing. "Want to see them?" Anna felt an unfamiliar spark. He was watching her with his piercing blue eyes.

"I don't really like angels. They're too aggressive for me," Anna volunteered.

"I got a pair of blacks. They're really cool. I've named them 'Darth Vader' and 'Lady Macbeth.' What do you think?"

"That sounds sinister enough," Anna said. Was it her imagination or was he staring at her? She glanced quickly away. Tommy was in a talkative mood and he had stories to tell.

"I kacked a whole tank full of zebra danios," he told her morosely. "I think I overcleaned the tank and screwed up their nitrogen cycle. I came in this morning to a whole tank of floaters."

"That's too bad."

"Not as bad as when I was working upstairs and kacked the puffer fish. That was a real mess."

"I remember."

"I almost lost my job over that one."

"Almost as bad as when the cat got the marble hatchet fish," Anna sympathized.

"Yeah, I came in for work and found Barney enjoying some sushi," Tommy chuckled and reached a hand out to stroke Barney's orange coat. "They ask for it, though, those fish swim right on the surface. All he had to do was dip a paw in and scoop one out."

"Yeah. Our Barney is quite the cannibal," Anna agreed. She reached out a hand to scratch Barney behind one ear and her fingers brushed Tommy's. He didn't pull back.

"I am getting more swords," he volunteered. "They're really cool. Black and white translucent ones with black fins and swords."

"A little like tiger barbs?" Anna asked. She could talk fish for hours.

"Not quite as flashy. No red but the same general idea."

"I can't wait."

"So, how was school? Want a Reese's Peanut Butter Cup?" Tommy offered her the candy from a basket on the counter. He was flirting. She took a candy.

"Why not? School was okay. I've only got three troublemakers."

"I suppose it's just like here. Never put two male betas in the same tank."

"It's something like that," Anna laughed. "It's all a matter of who's compatible."

"Say, you wouldn't want to see a movie Sunday night, would you? 'Bluewater, White Death' is being revived."

"No kidding. What a great movie. It's great that they're bringing it back," Anna said enthusiastically.

"We could meet here, grab a bite, see the early show and you'd be home before you turned into a pumpkin." Tommy was coaxing her now. Was he asking her on a date? Anna stalled for time. She had always assumed Tommy was gay. Evidently not.

"Sure. That sounds great." Anna could tell she didn't sound convincing. She tried again. "I'd love to. Sunday night."

"Great," said Tommy. "Now let me show you my new corydoras."

Chapter 7

Anna was never sure what made Harold trust her—either as a substitute teacher or as a medium. He had watched her closely during her early days at his school. She would be shepherding her students to a bathroom break or lunch and there would be Harold, looming at her from behind lockers or the stacks in the student library. Chestnut-haired, mustachioed, and prone to wearing theatrical red suspenders, he reminded her of the Cheshire cat. Not that she said so.

Harold-the-Cat, she had come to think of him, because sometimes his plump, rounded shape *did* bare an uncanny resemblance to the Cheshire cat. Whenever she would catch him at it—spying on her—he would give her a big benevolent grin. One morning, one of her students, Jeremy, came to school armed with a water pistol and roundly drenched two classmates, Abby and Dylan, who shrieked and retaliated with kicks and punches. Anna was trying unsuccessfully to break them up when Harold loomed out at her from behind the classroom door—grinning.

"Trouble?" Harold asked.

"I can handle it," Anna said, grabbing Jeremy in a nonpolitically correct head lock.

"I see that you can," Harold said. "But come see me on your break."

And so, expecting to be fired or suspended, Anna made her way to his office. He produced a chicken salad sandwich on pumpernickel bread and a thermos of coffee from a bottom desk drawer.

"What do you think?" he asked.

"It's a great school," she said. "Really first-rate. In my opinion, that is."

"I meant what did you think about the chicken salad? It's my mother's recipe. She got it from her mother. I add a dash of chutney. Well?"

"Well, I, it's…" Anna needed a napkin. Harold produced one, cloth, from a different drawer. "It's delicious—and so's the bread."

"I think so," Harold said with satisfaction. "Coffee?"

"Love some," she admitted. Harold's coffee was rich and strong and caffeine was her one remaining vice.

"So. Listen. I've decided I'd like to make an appointment."

"I thought this was an appointment," Anna said. "Can't we talk now, over lunch?" Fired was fired, wasn't it?

Anna *did* love teaching at Harold's school, and hoped she would not have to find another venue. An administrator could call any name on an entire roster of New York subs. She wanted Harold to keep calling her. (Not to mention that she was acquiring a fondness for some of her pupils, the naughty ones in particular.)

"An appointment with *you*, to talk to someone. You see, my

27

partner has passed on." He held up her business card, sliding it out from under his blotter.

"You're hiring me, not firing me! ... Don't tell me anything more," Anna shushed him. "It's best that I know as little as possible. That way, you won't feel duped."

"I see."

"Sorry to be such a stickler, but it's really for the best."

"When then?" Harold was eager to close the deal. Anna took out her daybook. They set an appointment for two days later, after school.

"I shouldn't bring anything? A photo? His watch?"

"That won't be necessary," Anna assured him. "You're the draw."

Anna's studio had a loft bed and she had trained philodendrons to climb the four-by-fours that held it up. Inside the leafy bower this created, she had established her reading area: an overstuffed love seat graced by a few needlepoint pillows she'd made herself, a velvet Victorian chair rescued from the sidewalk and carefully repaired, and a small table flanked by a wrought-iron chair. She sat at the table. The love seat and the Victorian were for guests who needed something to make them feel comfortable. As a rule, she offered them a nonalcoholic drink. ("No spirits except the ones you invite," Mrs. Murphy phrased her anti-alcohol rule.)

"I'm just curious; I don't *really* believe in any of this," Harold said as she closed the door behind him. She was used to such protestations. They were almost routine. "*He* believed," Harold continued, but Anna held up a stern warning hand. She had been carefully taught to not allow clients to divulge any information about those they were trying to contact.

"I don't want to know," she told Harold. "The more I know in advance, the less you'll trust me, the more you'll suspect a hoax." Anna tried for a casual, matter-of-fact air. She knew how nervous her clients were, how much the contact they were seeking to make meant to them.

"I see your point," Harold allowed.

Anna closed her eyes. She laid her palms flat upon the table.

"Will it move?" Harold asked.

"What?" she had lost her focus.

"The table," Harold explained.

"You've seen a lot of movies, haven't you?" Anna asked. Clients' questions seldom annoyed her, but the music drifting upward through the open window did. *It was as bad as life with Alan.* She had spent her entire—*their* entire—adolescence with a sound track. Was she doomed to having one always? Couldn't he play more softly?

"Excuse me," she said and got up to close the window. Maybe in winter she wouldn't hear him. The window was swollen in its frame and she could not get it totally closed. She managed to shut it all but a crack.

"It was pretty," Harold objected, "Schubert, I think. Maybe Schumann."

"I wouldn't know," Anna sniffed, which startled Harold a little. Maybe he was expecting her to be a little more "spiritual"? Oh, well. Mrs. Murphy had assured her that sainthood wasn't a necessity. Anna closed her eyes to regain her focus. The music still distracted her. She frowned.

"What is it?" Harold worried. "Oh dear, is he all right?" Anna held a finger to her lips. She was beginning to get an impression.

Harold's "Andrew" came to her first as a voice saying clearly, *"Hello, darling."* She repeated the greeting to Harold. Next, she "saw" Andrew in her mind's eye as a tall, well-dressed man with silver hair and a ruddy complexion. She had an impression of good humor and considerable erudition. He muttered something in Latin that she didn't understand. She repeated it carefully, a syllable at a time. *"Non illegitimi te carborundum,"* she enunciated slowly.

Harold sucked in his breath. "We were together thirty years." Tears sprang to his eyes. After he composed himself he explained, "It means 'Don't let the bastards get you down.' Andrew always said it to me after a rough day at school. Oh, dear. Oh, dear God." Anna offered Harold the box of Kleenex that sat between them on the table.

"I suppose you see this sort of thing all the time," Harold said.

"I'm prepared," Anna told him. "But I am afraid Andrew is fading out."

"Tell him I love him!"

"He can hear you. He just can't transmit anymore. The first contact can take a lot."

"I love you, dear," Harold breathed into the ethers.

"It's mutual," Anna recounted Andrew's fading voice.

"It must be wonderful, witnessing reunions," Harold insisted after a long moment during which the music played delicately.

"It is wonderful," Anna admitted. "Really wonderful." Although she often longed to be normal, there were moments like these when her gift did feel like a gift.

After that first session, Harold set a regular appointment, weekly at five on Fridays. "Happy Hour," he called it. Anna felt glad to be a bridge.

Chapter 8

The newly installed pianist practiced for hours daily and his scales, his études, his sonatas, concertos and other musical intricacies floated straight up to Anna's open windows. It was like catching a faint but distracting whiff of perfume. She could concentrate only with the greatest difficulty. Sometimes her clients noticed her distraction. Perhaps Mrs. Murphy would have some advice.

Placing a call to Mrs. Murphy, back in Ann Arbor, Anna always felt a mix of gratitude and embarrassment. Having a mentor was a wonderful thing, but shouldn't she be able by now to figure things out for herself? She had certainly been carefully taught. But Mrs. Murphy was always glad to hear from her, so glad that it occurred to Anna she might be a little bit lonely. Mr. Murphy had passed on the year before.

"It's me, Anna. Am I interrupting anything? Are you in the middle of things?" She always asked, just to be polite.

"No, dear. Of course not. How good to hear your voice. Tell me, what is it this time?" Anna pictured Mrs. Murphy settling in on her velvet Victorian love seat, perhaps reaching for a butterscotch.

"It's this pianist," Anna launched into her complaint. "He moved in downstairs and he plays all the time. I mean *all* the time."

"Is he any good?" Mrs. Murphy sounded amused.

"That's not the point," Anna insisted. "He's annoying. I can't hear myself think when I am with a client and he's pounding away."

"He pounds?" Mrs. Murphy sounded sympathetic and Anna felt a flash of guilt.

"He doesn't actually pound. It just strikes me that way. I mean, I can't hear myself think when he's playing. I can't focus. I start to hear someone and then I find myself following a melody line instead and completely lose track of what I am doing."

"That *is* a problem," Mrs. Murphy clucked softly. "You need to be able to concentrate. How are you doing with your meditation?"

"What does my meditation have to do with his playing?" Anna could tell she was about to be taught yet another of Mrs. Murphy's lessons.

"Meditation helps you to focus. A little more meditation and his playing might not bother you. It sounds like your powers of concentration are wobbly."

"So you're saying it's my fault?" Anna felt herself bridling. Did her teacher always have to make her feel so young?

"I am saying that you have a solution. Isn't that good to know?"

"I suppose so," Anna said reluctantly.

"So tell me, are you getting out a little?" Mrs. Murphy snooped gently.

"I try."

"You're not lonely are you?" Mrs. Murphy sounded concerned. "You're not isolating?"

"I'm okay, really. I teach. I do my readings." Why did she sound so wan?

"Well, I just like to picture you having some good adventures. New York is just full of them. You're young and beautiful, let's not forget. And do try an extra dose of meditation. It does me worlds of good."

Mrs. Murphy's upbeat advice left Anna feeling less than

satisfied. She got off the phone with a prescription she felt reluctant to fill: more meditation. *Any* meditation felt hard enough.

Anna knew that meditation was a spiritual staple and she knew that Mrs. Murphy was probably right—she needed it. Still, meditating made her feel restless—so fidgety and full of nonspiritual thoughts that she actually came away from her meditations feeling less spiritual, less serene and less grounded than before. Maybe there was such a thing as a cleaning meditation. Domesticity in its many homely forms gave her a welcome feeling of humility. Yes, cleaning was definitely spiritual. She loved the calming smell of lemon Pledge and swabbing the dust off of her bookcases and window shelves always gave her a sense of well-being.

Chapter 9

"I'm glad you decided to come out with me. I could tell you didn't want to," Tommy announced just after they had finished placing their orders. They were sharing a sidewalk table at French Roast on a busy stretch of Broadway.

"What do you mean?" Anna stalled. Was she that transparent?

"I know your self-image: spinster-in-the-making. Well, I guess I blew your cover, didn't I?" Tommy teased.

"I guess you did." Anna admitted, laughing at herself.

"Most people think I'm gay." Tommy reached for a breadstick.

"Yes, well, I—" Anna broke off.

"It's okay. I wouldn't mind being gay. I think it would be a little simpler than—"

"Oh, heterosexuality is not all that simple," Anna blurted out.

"Compared to being bi, I'm sure it's a snap. It confuses people when they know you're bi. I'm confusing you right now, aren't I?" Tommy offered her the bread basket. She took a raisin roll.

"Actually, I find you sort of refreshing."

"That wears off." Tommy laughed.

"Well then."

"Wine?" Tommy offered.

"No thanks."

"You're not in the program?"

"The program?" Anna was at a loss.

"AA. Usually when you meet someone and they don't drink they're in AA."

"Oh. Well, I'm not."

"Why not then? A little Chablis? Some merlot? Do I sound like a wine salesman? I used to work in a wine shop. They've got some nice stuff by the glass."

"You go ahead." Anna sipped at her water.

"No, seriously, why not? Tell me." Tommy leaned closer so she could whisper.

"You should have been a detective. All these questions." Anna swatted at him. "You're not hiding something are you? That would be exciting."

"Tommy—"

But the waiter arrived then bringing Anna's rare hamburger and Tommy's Gruyère omelette. Anna was glad for the distraction. She hadn't really wanted to explain her occupation and just why it was that alcohol was generally off-limits.

"I should tell you that I already know," Tommy started up again.

"You know what?"

"You know. What you do." He grinned mischievously.

"And how do you know that?" Anna was curious, more than offended.

"I saw your business card."

"You did?"

"Actually, I snooped. You left your purse on the counter and, well—"

"Tommy!" Anna reached across to pinch him.

"So what's it like?"

"What? Give me a minute. I just found out you went through my purse."

"Only a little. And just because you left it there. You probably wanted me to find out."

"I did not!" Anna took a furious bite of her hamburger. Were their voices raised?

"It must be fun." Tommy was like a dog with a bone.

"You're a handful." Anna hoped to rein him in—no such luck.

"Thank you. It's nice to be appreciated. How's your burger?"

"Great, actually." Tommy was eying her like she was dessert.

"You don't really have to talk about it if you don't want to, although I do think it would be fascinating to hear about it straight from the horse's mouth."

"It's just that it's hard being the resident weirdo." Anna caught herself full of annoyance.

"I'm afraid that position is taken." Tommy grinned at her then and gave her hand a friendly little pat. "Don't worry. You'll get used to me."

Later, sitting in the darkened theater, watching the great white sharks lunge at divers protected only by flimsy cages, Anna caught herself smiling.

"Hold my hand. I'm terrified!" Tommy whispered. Anna held his hand.

Chapter 10

When Anna got home, she found her professional line blinking. She punched play. "My name is Rachel," the caller began. "I'd like an appointment to see you as soon as possible, like immediately. Tonight, if you can." The caller left a phone number, but Anna did not return her call immediately. Mrs. Murphy had carefully taught her not to be bullied or guilt-tripped by her clients into granting sessions on the spur of the moment or at times that were inconvenient to her. On the other hand, rent was coming due, and she could definitely use the money. Determined to be neither bullied nor manipulated, Anna returned Rachel's call around nine P.M. Not too late to call.

"Thank God you called," Rachel answered. "I've been waiting by the phone. I *really* need your help with something." She made Anna sound like a cleaning service, and she supposed, in some sense she was. "Where do you live?" Rachel demanded. Caught off guard, Anna gave her address. "And the apartment number?" Anna complied again. Rachel was a bulldozer, and she was being bulldozed. *You do need the money*, Anna reminded herself.

A half hour later, Anna had just had time to manically clean her apartment and spritz the air with a light lavender scent she found refreshing. "What's that smell?" Rachel demanded, entering.

If, at five-foot-three, Anna was short, Rachel was even shorter. In fact, she was nearly miniature, for which she was obviously compensating with a larger-than-life personality the size of a modest tornado. "Is it incense? Because if it is, I'm allergic to incense, and you'll have to put it out."

"It's not incense," Anna said defensively. "It's lavender."

"Well, I don't like it," Rachel announced. "Where am I supposed to sit?"

"Either place," Anna answered. Rachel promptly tried the velvet Victorian chair.

"It's too stiff," she announced, "and my feet don't reach the ground." This was true. Anna looked at Rachel apprehensively.

"Try the love seat," Anna suggested. Rachel did.

"Is there a loose spring or something?" she asked.

"Try the other cushion." Anna attempted a solution. There *was* a loose spring, and she had been meaning to fix it—or have Alan fix it the next time he visited.

"What about your nice little chair?" Rachel asked, jumping to her tiny feet.

"I usually sit here," Anna answered. "It's not really very comfortable."

"Then why do you sit there?" Rachel demanded suspiciously. "Let me try it." Caught off guard again, Anna yielded her chair. "This is perfect," Rachel announced. "Don't you have any tea or bottled water?"

"I was just about to offer you something," Anna lied. She was delighted to dive into the tiny alcove that passed for her kitchen. She stood at the refrigerator door, fuming. *I should dump it on her head*, she thought, as she hefted her pitcher of mint tea. She poured Rachel a tall glass, and poured another for herself.

Returning to her reading area, she set Rachel's glass on her reading table and settled herself on her love seat, avoiding the spring.

"What I want to know," Rachel said, "Is should I marry him?"

"Marry who?" Anna asked.

"Isn't that something you should know?" Rachel demanded. "I mean, isn't that your job? Isn't that why I'm paying you? Isn't that why I'm here?" Anna considered the possibility that Rachel was crazy with grief, that perhaps she had just lost a fiancé to a terrible accident.

"Did you lose someone recently?" she asked gently.

"That's another thing you ought to be able to tell," Rachel insisted. "I mean, something like that would certainly show up, wouldn't it? If you're any good, that is." Anna felt anger ripple through her like a surge through a surge protector. She was too well trained to bite Rachel's head off, but she did want to slap her. *Where exactly*, Anna wondered, *did some people get their sense of entitlement? Maybe from her perfect petite Ann Taylor wardrobe.* They were clothes Anna recognized but could not afford.

"Look," Rachel said querulously, "if you're charging me by the minute, we'd better get started." Anna was trying to get started, but between Rachel's attitude and the onslaught of scales that had started below her, she found it difficult to concentrate.

"I'm not getting anything," she reluctantly told Rachel. No one was coming through. *Of course,* Anna reflected, *she herself would have died just to get away from Rachel, since marriage to her clearly would have been a fate worse than death.*

"What do you mean you're not getting anything? What kind of a psychic are you?" Rachel burst out in a petulant tone. Anna felt a wave of relief. *So that was it. A simple misunderstanding.*

"I'm a medium," she explained to Rachel. "Not a psychic."

"Medium, psychic, what's the difference?" Rachel retorted. "I knew it was all claptrap." She took an angry sip of her tea.

Anna explained. "I deal with the past," she said. "Not with the future. I don't see things coming; I talk to people who are gone."

"You mean *ghosts?* Dead people?" Rachel exclaimed incredulously. "Now I've heard everything! And just for your information, my fiancé is very much alive." Scraping back her chair, mustering her full five-foot-one height, Rachel made for the door.

"Just a minute," Anna said. "Aren't you forgetting something?" She had been trained by Mrs. Murphy to bill for her time, not her success. Charging for her services helped her clients to value them. Not to mention that it prevented them from using her like a phone sex habit to speak to the dead.

"I don't owe you a thing," Rachel said. "You owe me an apology, passing yourself off as some kind of expert. Well, you won't be getting any recommendations from me, and you won't be getting any money, either." With that, Rachel opened the door and was gone.

What a stink bomb, Anna thought to herself. *What a little shrew.* She spritzed the apartment one more time with lavender, and took a long, Epsom salt bath to drain away her irritation. Then she climbed the ladder to her loft, and went to bed. Thankfully, the piano racket had stopped.

Chapter 11

Every Sunday at four P.M. New York time, she phoned Alan in Kalamazoo. Sitting in her reading chair, next to her non-fire escape window, she would wait out his message and keep talking until he heard her voice and picked up. You would think he would catch onto the pattern—Sundays at four, three his time—but not Alan. His message was always the same, a jazz great playing something he loved, and then Alan's fake DJ voice identifying Charlie Parker, say, or John Coltrane or Dizzy Gillespie.

"Alan, are you there? It's me. Your sister. Pick up. Are you gluing a violin or something?"

"Actually, I was," Alan told her, followed by the Kalamazoo weather report just so she would know what she was missing. Phoning Alan was like listening to NPR talk radio. It was nearly as bad on the phone as it was in person.

Some Thanksgivings, every Christmas, and sporadic Easters, she flew out of LaGuardia to visit her brother Alan in Kalamazoo and then be driven from there to their parents' house. Sometimes they drove through snowstorms, listening to Alan's jazz tapes; sometimes they drove along bare winter roads listening to Alan himself. He had missed his calling as a DJ.

"But enough about you," he would jokingly interrupt Anna, changing the subject to his newest jazz icon. Alan could talk at stupefying length about people Anna had never heard of. His conversation resembled a long jazz solo, complex and interminable.

"If I lived in New York, I'd be out in a club every night," he would lecture her. "You never get out, do you?" Anna wanted to protest but it was largely true. By day she taught school and by night she saw clients. Wasn't that adventure enough? Anna had long since abandoned trying to explain that her listening experience was often interrupted by the sight of dead jazz greats putting in surprise guest appearances somewhere up near the ceiling.

"How are you?" she barely had time to ask when he picked up. She suspected he worked as he talked. She could picture him with the phone cocked against his shoulder, mouthpiece sliding sideways while he did some minute calibration or applied the one hundredth coat of painstaking varnish. Alan made about four instruments a year, sometimes fewer, hardly enough to make a living by, but he said that was beside the point, sometimes pricing his favorites so high no one would ever buy them. This afternoon, Alan was on a tear about acquiring some rare wood from the same forest that Stradivarius had used. Anna tuned out and began to paint her toenails bright red, balancing them on her windowsill, perching the open bottle on the arm of her chair—a maneuver as intricate as anything of Alan's.

So why did she call him? She called him because it was grounding. They had communicated like this for years, occupying their parallel, distinct universes.

"What do you think of that?" Alan concluded. "Neat, huh?"

Did he mean the varnish? She hadn't meant to tune out so completely.

"You're doing your fingernails, aren't you?" Alan accused her. As twins, they had always displayed astounding ESP. Then again, they knew each other very well.

"My toenails," she confessed.

Alan snorted, "I'm impressed."

"Oh, goddamn it. Let me close the window. Some piano player

41

has moved in somewhere."

Instantly, Alan was all ears. "A piano player!" He sounded like she'd struck gold. "What's he playing?"

"How should I know? Something." Clearly, in Alan's fevered imagination she now lived near some obscure New York jazz great—as she very well might. She had once spotted a plaque on an apartment building announcing that Gershwin had lived there while writing *Rhapsody in Blue*. She knew that Leonard Bernstein had lived for years in the Dakota, fourteen blocks south of her apartment. New York was studded with apartment buildings where the greats lived in relative anonymity. Her offending pianist could be one of them. She cocked an ear. Sure enough, he was going at it somewhere below her.

"What's he playing?" Alan sounded ready to hop on a plane. For once she had his total attention.

"I don't know. Scales. Or now, maybe something classical. It's pretty fast—Oh, Alan, just turn up your own sound system," Anna teased. She was referring to Alan's self-devised, motion-sensitive omnipresent sound system. He had rigged it somehow to turn on as he moved from room to room and on and off as he opened and closed the door to his garage/studio. She didn't understand it. *Why couldn't he just flick a switch like everybody else?* No, she didn't understand Alan, but she loved him. *Wasn't he at least as weird as she was? Wasn't he, too, merely passing for normal? If making violins in your garage while listening to obscure jazz greats could be called "normal."*

She supposed, compared to what she did for a living, it could.

"Oh, Alan, you don't understand. I feel like I'm losing my mind, not to mention my connection to Spirit. It's just so distracting! I try to focus on my work but I keep following the melody line." Maybe she *did* need more meditation.

"Well, of course you do. You're supposed follow the melody line."

"Alan, I can't afford Music Appreciation 101 right in my own apartment."

"It sounds pretty great to me."

"You're just romanticizing it. Trust me. It's a problem."

"You're the problem," her brother said. Had he been talking with Mrs. Murphy?

Chapter 12

When the alarm shrilled, Anna moaned in her sleep. She wasn't a lark, one of those people who meet the rising day with good cheer. No, most days she yearned for more sleep, but she also yearned to be a better medium, and if Mrs. Murphy felt she should meditate more, meditate she would.

"It doesn't have to be anything fancy," Mrs. Murphy told her. "Simply choose a lovely image and think about that."

For her "lovely image," Anna chose a koi pond. Lying in bed, careful not to drift back to sleep, Anna pictured the lightly rippling surface of the water, the shadowy shapes of the peaceful fish swimming below. There was a white fish and a gold fish and a white-and-gold fish. Over by a rock, there was a dark fish and a silver fish. In her imagination, the fish kept multiplying. Now, in her mind's eye, Anna saw herself strolling slowly onto a small wooden bridge. Staring over the railing, she began to count the fish as they slid silently past. One, two, three...

By the time she had counted twenty fish, Anna could feel herself relaxing. She felt a calm stealing into her heart, a sense of well-being and connection. This was probably what Mrs. Murphy experienced most of the time. "Conscious contact," she called it and when Anna asked her, "With what?" she only laughed lightly, saying, "With whatever you choose to call it."

Anna knew that Mrs. Murphy believed in a benevolent something. She knew, too, that her brief and fleeting contact with this "something" brought to her turbulent temperament a rare peace and calm. "Why am I so cranky?" she had once asked Mrs. Murphy. Her personality exasperated even herself.

"Why, it's because you are frightened, of course," Mrs. Murphy had replied. Anna didn't like to think of herself as frightened. Mrs. Murphy had gone on, "Anyone could tell that you're just defensive. You desperately want to be loved and you're afraid you're not lovable. You act fierce but actually you are very gentle. That is what you don't want anyone to know. That is your secret."

"It's not true!" Anna protested. "I think I'm rather feisty. Alan calls me a 'handful.'"

"A handful of fluff," Mrs. Murphy insisted. "And I think I know you as well as anyone."

"And I don't just want love."

"Nonsense. That's why you moved to New York." Anna had to admit that this was true.

Chapter 13

E very Tuesday night, Anna met her friend, Stacy, at the Greek diner at six P.M. Stacy, like herself, loved the diner where they both had a fondness for spanakopita and a weakness for BLTs with extra mayonnaise. Her fatal flaw, Stacy believed. Her *only* flaw, as near as Anna could tell. Stacy was a tall, willowy Colorado blonde with cornflower blue eyes and droves of "eligible" men all eager to take her out. Stacy was vaguely Protestant, while Anna was definitely lapsed Catholic and a little date-phobic.

She and Stacy were unlikely friends. Their worlds were utterly different—only the diner and its superior BLTs had brought them together. Theirs was a case of opposites attract. Stacy inhabited the world of high finance. Anna lived in the world of making ends meet. She had to both teach and do readings in order to make her rent. Then, too, there were their differing opinions on appropriate disclosures. Self-disclosure was healthy, Stacy believed. Dr. Rich, her newly acquired therapist, was merely the newest outcropping of Stacy's self-improvement mania. Perfect already, she was always perfecting herself further, in any way money could buy. This meant therapists, yoga classes, self-help seminars, and sessions at Radu's gym—where the supermodels went. Above all, it meant disclosing many things Anna felt were better off not examined.

As part of a girl-bonding ritual, Stacy had insisted they divulge their romantic histories. Anna's was brief; Stacy's was dark with the shadows of too many choices. She had always had to beat men off with a stick, it seemed.

"It must be *awful*," Anna jokingly commiserated with Stacy, who had dates with ardent bachelors, breakfast, lunch and dinner.

"Boring," Stacy intoned.

"Men avoid me like the plague," Anna told Stacy—and then she told her the exact nature of her vocation.

"You talk to ghosts! How fascinating! Why, I think any man would be riveted!" Stacy had exclaimed.

"Trust me," Anna answered. "It's the intellectual equivalent of a flat chest. Men are not interested." She gave Stacy a mercifully brief description of her short-lived romantic attachments—not that there were many, and certainly not anything that she could dignify as "love." No, based on her experience romance was nothing she was interested in. She believed in investing where there was some healthy return. Certainly as a banker Stacy could understand her position.

"We'll change all that!" Stacy, with the bit in her teeth, was not easily stopped. She had "friends" and "friends of friends," cousins and neighbors, all for Anna to meet.

"I'm not doing it," Anna told her firmly. "Been there, done that. Men are a dead end."

"No way! You can't mean that!" Stacy had protested. "You're not dead. You're young, you're beautiful—in an old-fashioned sort of way. You're—"

"I am a medium."

Anna did not elaborate. She had long since learned that most people regarded her career choice as something dubious at best. To most people, Anna's claim to talk with the dead caused them to think she was a borderline personality. But Stacy was not to be deterred.

"You've got to be lonely." Stacy's blue eyes were lakes of sympathy.

"I've gotten over lonely. I recently went on one date and he turned out to be a bi-sexual."

"Uh-oh. I'd be careful."

"I'm careful—I'm nothing if not careful—but I'm definitely over lonely."

"Nobody gets over lonely."

"Well, I have. First I got over Roger, then I got over lonely."

"Roger?"

"Two years ago. Before your time. I thought he could handle knowing about my secret life—wrong, wrong, wrong."

"Tell me about Roger."

Anna had dated Roger when she first got to New York. The loss of Roger had been a real learning curve for her. With Roger, who had seemed open-minded and curious, she had tried to be frank about her gifts. One evening, feeling the effect of several Long Island ice teas, she had tried to point out to him the ghost she clearly saw lingering above the keys in the piano bar they were enjoying. Roger saw no ghost. When several of his friends dropped by their table, he regaled them with the fact that she, Anna, saw a ghost. The result of not being able to hold her liquor, Roger jokingly suggested. Everyone except Anna laughed uproariously. "But I always see them," Anna protested. "I always have." Roger looked guarded. A joke was a joke but she had carried it a step too far. That evening was their final date—and Anna had liked Roger.

"He wasn't good enough for you," Stacy loyally declared.

"He didn't like ghosts," Anna said firmly. She signaled for the check.

Early the next morning, the music started again. Lying in her loft bed, unable to believe he could be at it so early, Anna listened as the notes seemed to float across her ceiling like tiny sparkling lights, *like fireflies, exactly like fireflies*, she thought. Was it Mozart? It was way too early for such an outburst of energy. She resolved to ask Alec, the superintendent, for help with closing her windows. Meanwhile, the notes flew upward like larks ascending. Anna buried her head in her pillow.

A few hours later, when Alec came to help her with an overhead light bulb and her stubborn windows, he turned a deaf ear to Anna's complaints. "They have to live somewhere," he said, and Anna got the distinct impression he actively enjoyed the near-constant serenade. He jimmied her stuck window so that it slid more easily. But he left it open a crack, she noticed.

"I hear it too, when I'm down in the basement in my workroom," Alec informed her. "I keep the window open. Wonderful. Wonderful."

No help here, Anna thought. Alec went on to say that the music reminded him of home, Warsaw, evidently a mecca of culture for all concerned, "in the old days," that is. Alec waxed rhapsodic in his heavily accented English. In Warsaw, he told her, music wafted in the air, through the city parks, down the streets. *It sounds like a nightmare*, Anna thought, but since she had never explained to Alec, or anyone else in her building for that matter, the exact nature of her work, she could hardly complain about its interruptions. She could hardly say, "You see, I'm tuned to higher realms, and the music simply keeps intruding." No, music was the higher realm. She was clearly a philistine and now Alec knew it, simple as that.

Chapter 14

Dear Mr. and Mrs. Oliver,

Again, thank you so much for your generosity. I love New York. (Of course, I love Maine, too, but this place seems somehow "home" to me.) Does that sound grandiose? Maybe you have to be grandiose to think you can beat out one hundred eighty other pianists. I am certainly going to try.

As you asked, I will tell you all's well with my doctoral studies, too. (Although I sometimes think my thesis topic, "Haydn's influence on Mozart," could really be summed up in three words: "They were friends.") Classes are good and I try to get to one or two of them—just joking. When I'm not at the piano I *am* at the books, don't worry.

I do think I have lucked out with my teacher. He demands technical brilliance—I am working on that—but he never takes the focus off of the composer's intention. Every day I ask myself, "What did Mozart want?" That seems to me to be the million-dollar question. If you have any thoughts on this, let me know.

Yours gratefully,
Edward

P.S. You were right that New York traffic is fierce, Mrs. Oliver, but a good old-fashioned bike is really fast—fast enough even for Manhattan—where the rest of the bike riders seem to be delivering Chinese food. I *am* careful, though, so don't worry. And I'm saving money by not taking the subway.

Chapter 15

Anna kept two phone lines. One for her professional persona, and a personal line for Alan, her parents and her friends. On the days she was subbing, she called home for messages from the one pay phone in the school's main lobby. She had to do it on her lunch hour, and if a whole gaggle of children went past on their way to the playground, it meant she couldn't hear. Then there was the fact that her callers were frequently nervous, or grieved. Sometimes their grief made their messages hard to decipher, even with all her practice.

"Anything I need to know?" Harold would sometimes tease her when he caught her using the pay phone.

"That I'm too cheap to own a cell phone," she once joked back, but there was truth in her joke. Her rent was high and her budget limited. A cell phone seemed extravagant.

"You're not just cheap, you're old-fashioned," Harold teased her—and she had to admit that he was right. Cell phones struck her as an intrusion on her privacy.

"Now if you'll excuse me," she would plead. Harold knew she was phoning home for messages. He could tell by her concentrated frown and her rapid scribbling in the little black leather book she carried for phone numbers and appointments.

"Shhh," she would signal, straining to hear her messages. They were becoming real friends but not so intimate that she ignored Harold when he tapped his watch and waggled his eyebrows toward her classroom.

Although her mother had been right that her master's in

education, wasted money she'd felt at the time, did give her something to fall back on, some days "falling back" felt more like falling, period. There were occasions when the high spirits of her living students were harder to deal with than the spirits of the dead. Such as the day Abby decided to eat her Play Doh. She had to have her stomach pumped and her parents, litigious New Yorkers, had threatened Harold with a lawsuit.

By Friday night she was exhausted and doing the laundry was a calming ritual she looked forward to. She aimed for quiet, restorative weekends. She might walk in Central Park, visiting Turtle Pond. She might browse, solo, a neighborhood flea market. "Filling the well," she called it.

At Harold's insistence, she had watched several episodes of *Sex and the City*. It wasn't the New York she knew, and she couldn't imagine herself indulging in any of their hedonistic adventures. If Mrs. Murphy were right and she had moved to New York for love, that was her one, single bold step. She sometimes wished her rapport with this world were as easy as her rapport with the next. She might wish she could use her gifts to find a soul mate but her gifts were not so easily manipulated. No, she might be a matchmaker for others but not herself.

Something of a Mother Hen, Harold had quickly tuned in on her dateless weekend availability. Filling out her social calendar had become a project for him. He would often call her with weekend agendas. Would she care to visit the plant district? There were some wonderful bargains. What about a trip to Chinatown? He needed a fresh supply of chopsticks. Did she want to help him look for a faux oriental rug? It would mean a sortie to lower Broadway. Was she up for lunch in Koreatown? He knew a wonderful restaurant where they would be the only Caucasian diners ...

"If I weren't gay, I'd be madly in love with you," Harold had one day teased her.

"But you are gay," Anna pointed out the obvious.

"Yes, but you're still fascinating."

"To you, Harold. Just to you." Still, the attention was flattering and Harold's adventures were often fun. It was nice to have a little masculine attention, from any source.

Chapter 16

Anna did her laundry every Friday night right after Harold's standing appointment. The laundry in Anna's building was in the basement, a space she always found spooky, although whatever she expected to pop out at her was not a ghost. Perhaps an ax murderer? She laughed at herself. No matter what her mother thought of New York, what were the odds of that? She found that Friday nights the laundry room was close to deserted— everyone, or almost everyone, was out on dates, indulging in one of the countless, sophisticated doings listed in *Time Out New York*. Anna herself was indulging in Tide, a midwestern staple.

Fluffing and folding, usually with her nose half in a tabloid, Anna tried to make her weekly laundry as pain free as possible. She found that if she bought the tabloids when they were fresh on the stand each Thursday and saved them until Friday, she could indulge in an hour or two of mindless soap opera, studying the colorful, and probably exaggerated, trials and tribulations of the rich, famous, or merely hapless. She loved to read about lurid

Hollywood affairs while breathing in the comforting scent of gently drying laundry. She loved to sit alone, listening to the rhythmic thump of her tennis shoes as they spun around in the dryer, never entirely muffled by her load of towels. She got so lost in her tabloids she forgot about ax murderers—after all, they were safely on the page.

This Friday night began like any other, riding down five flights and then one more, balancing her tabloids, her laundry basket, her Tide. In the lobby, she heard a snatch of the piano music before the elevator door slid shut and she began her descent to the basement, that heart of darkness. Setting up on the big plywood table, Anna swiftly sorted dark and light, added her tennis shoes to the towels, and set a load of light to wash.

She settled in on the stained, chintz-covered floral couch, underneath the fluorescent lights, which heightened the tabloids' garish effects. That's when she noticed the music that seemed to be pouring in through an open window somewhere. She wasn't about to explore. What was it about this incessant sound that caught her ear so acutely? Why couldn't she just tune it out?

Focus, she told herself, frowning in concentration over a story of plastic surgery disasters amid noted Hollywood stars. The music stopped. She read on peacefully, flicking her pages with a lick of her index finger, a nasty habit she shared with Alan. The music started up again, this time faster and more furious. Anna thought about exploring the basement's bowels to find the offending window. Instead, she read on, trying to tune out the music, as insistent as a June bug bouncing against the screen door of her parents' summer cabin on Mackinac Island.

"*Damn it!*" she finally snapped, angrily reloading the washer and switching her lights to the dryer. The fluorescent light above the folding table flickered ominously. She sank back onto the couch, which she noticed smelled of mildew. She closed her eyes and began counting to ten. She found she couldn't count and focus on the music at the same time. That was probably the trick meditation was supposed to turn for her. The music stopped. After a few minutes, she heard the elevator descending to the basement. She waited for the intruder impatiently, not even bothering to hide her tabloids. *Let whoever this is think I am a functional illiterate*, she fumed.

The elevator door opened and disgorged two precariously balanced baskets of laundry perched on a pair of very long legs, bare, or at least in shorts, with dorky white socks and soiled, stained sneakers. Anna made out the face peering around the edge of his box of Tide. It was the pianist's.

"Hello," the pianist muttered. "Hope I'm not disturbing you." That's when the baskets of laundry toppled over and fell to the floor. Despite herself, Anna laughed. The pianist flushed. His glasses were knocked awry on the bridge of his nose. The Tide had exploded into a small sand dune at his feet. He was not only tall, he was heronlike, Anna noticed, watching him balance on one foot as he dumped the Tide out of his other shoe. He sported nerdy glasses and a tangled red briar patch of hair. *A geek*, she concluded. *An intellectual, probably a closet snob who reads Nietzsche and Schopenhauer.* She had known the type at school. In fact, that type always looked down on her—or seemed to. She resumed reading her tabloids and left the pianist to struggle with his mountain of sorting.

"Would you mind if we alternated machines?" he asked in a sonorous and deep voice. His voice caught her off guard. The timbre was so seductive, she almost said yes, they *could* share the machines, but then she came to her senses. Why share her washing machine? Only one washer was working. He was already on her time and territory.

"No," she said. "That is, yes, I do mind. You'll have to wait." And then, because she had sounded so patently rude, she offered a quick white lie, "I've got a date."

"Then mind if I read one of these?" He reached for her stack of tabloids and selected the one she had just finished. *Why argue about everything?* she thought. The pianist glanced up. "We're neighbors. I just moved in," he told her, as if he had to explain his presence.

"I know. You trapped me in the elevator, remember?" Anna still had her resentment, simmering now for several weeks.

"I hope you weren't late to work." His voice was good-humored.

"I was." Anna was not about to be charmed. Let him think she was crabby. She *was* crabby and it was his fault. If only he didn't need to practice, but he did.

"Then I hope no one noticed." He towered over her like a friendly giraffe. He was at least six feet two, but prone to stooping—or maybe he was just trying to meet her eyes. As he loomed close to her, Anna felt a little off center. Like his music, he was disconcerting.

"I'm afraid my whole classroom noticed," Anna said stiffly.

"You're a teacher. That's great." He certainly seemed to be stretching the conversation out.

"Some days," Anna cut him off.

After that, they both buried their noses in tabloids.

Chapter 17

Dear Mr. and Mrs. Oliver,

I'm writing you while my laundry dries. Thank you for inquiring about my New York "friends." I am afraid I don't have many of those yet. I'm sure you can understand I'm focusing more on the Mozart than my social life. Mozart is just so mysterious. He didn't leave us a lot of markings like Mahler did to indicate his intentions. I do my best to intuit what he meant but it's all guesswork, really. It's no wonder people race through his compositions. I used to but my teacher has put a halt to all of that. He's still talking about 'finding the composer's intention.' I just keep asking myself, "What was Mozart's?"

School continues to go well and the people in my building so far have not complained about my practice. I understand this is a rarity. My teacher told me a story about having had a crazy downstairs neighbor who complained every time he played. He'd sit down on the piano stool and she would tap her ceiling, his floor, with a broom handle or something. Eventually after months of this he tried practicing on an electric keyboard with headphones but then she complained—knocking at his door—that she still could hear the tiny clicks. Some people do have very acute hearing. I sometimes wonder if it's a misplaced musical gift. What do you suppose?

Again, Mrs. Oliver, thank you for inquiring. I am eating. I keep peanut butter, apples and Velveeta for cheese sandwiches. Of course there is also some great New York pizza if I get out of the house— when I do get out. I do. I ride my bike.

Sincerely,
Edward

Chapter 18

Anna's business line was blinking when she got back from the laundry room. Its one red eye flashed open and shut. She punched Rewind and then Play. It was probably just Harold saying thank you for his afternoon visit with Andrew. But no, it was a new client, a referral from Harold it turned out.

"This is Mary Peterson," the voice, high and slightly Irish, began. "I understand you can communicate—" The voice broke off. "I lost my husband two months ago." Anna took down Mrs. Peterson's number in her little black book. She would call her back after she ate. She had learned that initial contact was often the most upsetting, so she was careful to do it on a full stomach, when she herself felt alert and grounded. She could run downstairs to the Greek diner. On Fridays she liked to have spanakopita and Greek salad.

He must have done his laundry in record time, she thought when she saw the tall, red-haired figure slouched over a book and papers in the back booth. *Her* favorite booth, *the good one*, she thought peevishly even as George, her favorite waiter, was offering his own apologies that her spot was taken.

"Me again," the redhead offered her by way of greeting.

"You again," Anna joked, wondering how badly she was blushing, caught in an outright lie. Where was the date she had fabricated?

"I guess it wasn't a dinner date," the redhead echoed her thoughts. He seemed to be looking at her with an unusual intensity.

"No, it's the other kind," Anna answered and then blushed

57

deeper, realizing exactly what kind of date that would be. George came to her rescue.

"Spanakopita and salad?" he asked her, his thick Greek accent belying his American name. She nodded yes and slid into the one remaining empty booth. Now she remembered. She'd settled on the back booth not just because it was the most private but also because the leather seat in this one was taped and the sharp edges always pricked her thighs. "I'll be right back," she told George and went out to the corner newsstand where she bought a nice fat *New York Post* which she carried back inside. The pianist looked up and their eyes met again briefly. They both looked away, then both looked back. Anna felt a ripple of electricity. *Nonsense*, she told herself, as she quickly brushed it aside. *Without the nerdy glasses he might be cute*, she decided. She selected the gossip pages and sat on the rest of the paper. That made the seat much better. The spanakopita was delicious, as usual, and afterwards she went upstairs to return Mrs. Peterson's call.

Chapter 19

Dear Mr. and Mrs. Oliver, continued,
This was to be a brief note. Now I am writing to you from the back booth at a Greek diner where I am, yes, eating and also trying to study. As you predicted, Mrs. Oliver, my dissertation is at least as challenging as the upcoming competition. Worse, my dissertation is boring—or at least it is compared to the music. Maybe that's just resistance. I know how to practice through resistance but how do you write through it? I know what you're going to say, Mrs. Oliver,

"the same way."

Mr. Oliver, you asked me if my stipend was "sufficient." It's quite adequate. You're very generous, as I hope you know. Also, pizza is $1.50 a slice at Garlic Bob's, the joint across the street and down from the Greek diner. I prefer the Greek diner where they make an astoundingly good BLT. (And I thought that distinction belonged to the Irving's truck stop up home in Wilton.)

Thank you for wondering, Mrs. Oliver, but no, I am not homesick. You forget I got away—I mean went away—for college and for my masters, not to mention Aspen, Marlboro, Tanglewood and Ravinia— the summer festivals. I was only back briefly in the summers to help out at home, not that anything much could have helped out at home, as you once pointed out to me. I think you called me "the petunia in the onion patch," Mrs. Oliver, but it wasn't that bad. Lots of people come from tough backgrounds, but not a lot of people have supporters like you two.

Sincerely,
Edward

Chapter 20

On Saturday nights, as if to emphasize her dateless status, her mother would faithfully call. This Saturday the expected phone call came as usual.

"What are you doing home?" her mother asked as always, acting tactfully surprised to find her daughter in. And in the big city!

"Let me close the window; I can't hear you," Anna complained. The pianist below was at it again. "Oh for God's sake! Shut up!" she yelled in frustration into a crescendo of rising notes. The window would not close; the music continued unfazed.

"I didn't know you had a stereo, dear," her mother commented when she got back on the line. "Did Alan send you something?"

"A postcard," Anna joked. "Wished I were there."

There was a pained silence on the other end. Her mother always hated it when Anna was "snippy." For that matter, Anna hated that her mother got to her.

"No, mother, Alan didn't send me anything," Anna said finally.

Her mother taught grammar school English as *her* mother had before her. Anna and Alan came from a long line of teachers, and both were well educated to make the line longer still. Alan had so far resisted this calling, as Anna herself had resisted it for years. "It's in your blood," her mother said, perhaps rightly.

Anna knew that her mother wished that, since he wouldn't teach, Alan would use his facility with electronics, computers among them, "to make good money." To her, violin-making was a dead end, which it probably was. Still, it was an improvement over whatever it was Anna claimed to do, which her mother refused to discuss. She was thrilled when Anna started substitute teaching, feeling, obviously, that Anna had finally come to her senses.

"And how is your teaching going?" her mother would ask every week.

"Fine, fine," Anna would reply, aware she was placating her mother.

Her mother loved agreement and harmony. She achieved it in her "Teacher of the Year" classroom, if not in her family, where she had her husband to cope with.

"Can I speak to my father?" Anna asked. Her mother liked to put this off as long as possible, feeling that Anna and her father "egged each other on," not that her father took much egging. A former professor of comparative religion, Anna's father was a secretly zany man. He had given up teaching and was now a university dean, a figure of some authority. Little did his students know of his many private antics—all family fables.

"Your father," her mother replied, "is right here. Did I tell you he got birding binoculars? He claims he's using them on the co-ed dorms. That man."

Anna's father got on the phone. "How are you and all your companions?" he inquired. He had always called her ghosts "companions."

"I'm fine. They're fine," Anna reported. "Actually, school is what wears me out. So does Mom, for that matter. And this pianist has moved in. It's driving me crazy—I wake up to music. I fall asleep to music. It's like living with a sound track. I just hate him."

"He's no good?" her father inquired sympathetically.

"Oh, who knows? He's probably very good. He's just distracting. Mrs. Murphy wants me to meditate more so I will have the concentration necessary to tune him out. I resent meditating in the first place. Meditate more? What a drag. Why does it always have to come back to me?"

"Alan drove over for dinner last night," her father reported in a whisper. "Your mother wants him to get a part-time computer job."

"Or use his history degree for teaching," Anna put in.

Where Anna had chosen English literature, Alan claimed history was like story hour, the most painless way he could ever go along with his mother's wishes. Of course, Alan's version of history was long on inventors and gadgets—Edison, Marconi, the irrefutable Mr. Bell without whom they would not be talking.

"Need money? I could send you some for postage," her father asked. Every so often he mailed her a little something extra, flouting his wife's insistence on financial independence.

"No thanks, Dad. I'm fine." Anna did not want him worrying about how closely she watched her budget. Every expenditure had to be carefully weighed.

"Is that 'barely'?" her father persisted.

"I didn't say it. Really, I'm okay."

She knew he'd mail her a little cash—plain cash in an envelope. His wife would be horrified if she knew but without a check, he left no trail.

Chapter 21

"As you can imagine," Harold told Anna as they rode the number 1 train south, he "owed" his expansive social calendar to his deceased partner Andrew, a trader, whose many acquaintances had been varied and colorful. Andrew was much more vibrant than he, Harold, which Harold thought she certainly must sense even in Andrew's current diluted form.

"Spirits are not 'diluted,'" she disagreed. To her, spirits were as real and as vibrant as anyone made of flesh and blood.

Squishing closer to accommodate the Saturday night crowd at Times Square, Harold continued. He absolutely trusted her, Harold said, which was why he had invited her to tonight's birthday party, a surprise birthday party for someone named Arthur, whose special birthday guest was a stunning brunette transsexual named Havoc, not someone that a person in Harold's responsible position ought to know.

"Havoc," Anna repeated dimly, thinking that at least Alan would now be satisfied that she was having a genuine New York adventure right in Greenwich Village. In the two years since she had moved to New York as a thirtieth birthday present to herself, her real life adventures had not lived up to Alan's expectations. And her adventures with the afterlife were not something they could share.

"You just brought me along so that you would have your own portable conversation piece," Anna accused Harold as they emerged from the subway. "This is my weird friend Anna. She talks to ghosts…"

"I don't think you're weird," Harold countered. "I think you're very normal, for a medium, that is." He gave her his Cheshire grin.

The party was being held in an old church, renovated into a theater space and available for nightly rentals as well. Anna wondered briefly if the God who had been worshipped there cast an understanding eye on the shenanigans now unfolding. When they entered the church, Anna saw it had been decorated with balloons, one of them an inflatable six-foot penis that was sacrilegiously placed near what once had been the pulpit. It tee-tered there precariously, bobbing gently and therefore giving the disconcerting impression that it was alive and real. Harold seemed to take it in stride. Anna tried to and hoped she wasn't staring at it or anyone else.

Dragging her by her arm as if he were tugging along a re-luctant terrier, Harold led her directly to the communion rail on which Havoc was perched in a black sequined dress showing a disconcerting amount of thigh. He (she?) had very good legs,

Anna noted.

"Havoc, darling," Harold kissed the transsexual drag queen on a perfectly sculpted cheek. "You look *marvelous*."

"Of course, darling," Havoc replied, looking Anna up and down. She had worn one of her vintage dresses, a navy gabardine with cranberry piping. By comparison with Havoc, she suddenly felt like a plain brown wren. Why were transsexuals so much more feminine than real women?

"This is Anna, she's a medium," Harold promptly announced despite all promises he wouldn't.

"A medium?" Havoc perked up with interest. "I'm a six, eight, or ten, depending on the designer, of course. Some of them like to make you feel good by making their small sizes just a little larger. In Halston, I was always a four. Just like Liza."

Anna was stunned and then relieved to realize she was being interpreted within Havoc's own universe. That's when she noticed the first ghost. It was a faint bluish haze, like cigarette smoke, hovering near what once would have been the choir loft. *Oh, dear*, Anna thought, looking further up. High among the arching rafters, near the stained-glass windows, spirits were thick as bats. To Anna, they were clearly visible. Of course, no one noticed except for her. She just hoped none of them would make contact.

Harold was tugging at her arm again, this time towing her toward the party's focus, a tall, good-looking man who bore a startling resemblance to Paul Newman in his celluloid prime. His name was Arthur—"he hates 'Art,'" Harold whispered as he thrust Anna forward to be met.

"How do you do?" Arthur greeted her, kissing the air near Harold, "They really shouldn't have. I think a half a century— me!—should have been allowed to pass in peace."

Mozart's Ghost

"He hates aging," Harold hissed to Anna.

"So unlike the rest of us," Arthur sniped. Harold looked briefly chastened.

Anna took advantage of their tiny spat to survey the crowd: buff bodies in expensive Barney's suits. It looked like a convention for *Gentleman's Quarterly*.

"Ah, Alexander!" Harold was exclaiming, shoving Anna forward to meet a small round man wearing a diamond earring so large Anna guessed it might be a cubic zirconium. Alexander stood out almost as much as Havoc did. He wore a tight purple T-shirt and blue jeans. The T-shirt emphasized his protuberant round belly, jolly as St. Nick's.

"You two might have a lot in common," Harold announced. "Alexander is a very good psychic. He and his late, and I might say estranged, partner own a metaphysical shop on Houston Street." To Alexander, he stage-whispered, "Anna is a medium."

Like everyone else, Alexander looked Anna up and down. "And about to experience the love of her life," Alexander predicted.

"I don't think love's all it's cracked up to be," Anna retorted. Was that her denial talking? She supposed it was.

"He's very near," Alexander persisted. "I hear music. How does the wedding march go?"

Harold helpfully hummed a few bars of "Here Comes the Bride."

"Harold, stop it!" Anna protested. She swatted his arm.

Harold chortled. "What else do you see? Give Anna her money's worth."

"Choices to be made," Alexander giggled unpleasantly. "Choices to be made."

"Maybe we should keep my private life private," Anna huffed.

"It isn't very comfortable to be spied on."

"As you prefer!" Alexander, offended, turned on his tiny heel.

Meanwhile, for the second time, Anna glanced a little apprehensively upward. Churches were often full of spirits, but this one was even worse than usual. Perhaps the party brought them out. Was it her imagination or was one of the ghosts eyeing her back? If word got out there was a medium present, she could be inundated.

"Let's go, Harold," she pleaded, but Harold was accepting champagne from a passing tray held by a very good-looking young waiter.

"I'm leaving, Harold," Anna said firmly, declining her own glass of champagne. The last thing she needed was to feel any more off center than she already did.

"Harold, I'm going. I'll get myself home." Harold was oblivious. Anna quietly took her leave. Outside on the chilly street, she could clearly smell autumn despite the city's smoke and fumes.

Why was autumn so poignant? Anna wondered. Did it speak to everyone of decline and decay? Or was she simply getting older? Once, autumn had meant new beginnings, the start of her academic calendar, but it didn't mean beginnings any longer. *I'm still a young woman*, Anna told herself resolutely, but she felt something different. Was it her profession as a medium that encouraged in her a certain sage detachment, an elegiac overview of human affairs? In her role as medium, she was often able to offer wise counsel. It was only in her own life that she felt ill at ease.

"Is everyone part of a couple?" Anna grumbled to herself as her subway car seemed to fill with more and more young couples, both gay and straight. *Was the whole world in love? I have nothing against young love, whatever its sexual orientation*, she told herself firmly as loving glances and soulful kisses were exchanged all around her.

I am not repressed, not prudish. I have simply chosen to be single, she reminded herself. *Men, at least the ones I've met so far, are put off by my profession. Even when I try to break it to them gently, it's too much for them. Or maybe their skepticism is just too much for me.* By the time she reached her stop at 86th Street, Anna felt distinctly depressed. New York was no longer her grand, madcap adventure. It was a large and crowded city in which she lived alone.

Chapter 22

Dear Mr. and Mrs. Oliver,

Thank you for the box of fudge, lest I forget. I'm afraid I ate nearly all of it for breakfast.

Mrs. Oliver, thank you also for the pressed fall leaf. The trees down here aren't turning yet but Wilton must be beautiful as always. Maine is a tourist state for a reason, I guess.

Mr. Oliver, tell your wife not to worry. I am very careful in traffic on my bike. I do use it in Central Park when I need a little break from the piano. In answer to your question about friends again, Mrs. Oliver, I am too busy to be lonely, and remember, New York is crowded. (A little joke.) I did buy a geranium for my windowsill and so far I haven't killed it from neglect. Maybe it likes Mozart. They say plants do thrive on classical music. I am thinking of buying some goldfish. Their feeding schedule would remind me to check the humidifier for the piano.

Sincerely,
Edward

Chapter 23

He was at it again. Naturally, he started up just as Anna was expecting Mrs. Peterson. At first there were a few quick trilling notes, the kind a songbird might make if startled into flight. After that, incessant waves of music, cascades of music that floated upward on the afternoon's early-autumn breeze. Anna tried to slam her windows closed, but lingering summer humidity made them stick in their frames. She was in for a concert, like it or not.

He would start now, she thought with exasperation. *Now* meaning on someone's initial grieving appointment. She wondered if the superintendent would tell her the apartment number of their noisy new tenant so she could register a personal complaint. A dangerous snake on the loose, that pianist's sound, slithering everywhere—curling around her very philodendrons. The noise could probably climb right up into her loft bed the same way. Thank God he was not, yet, playing late at night.

Mrs. Peterson buzzed from the lobby. Even on the intercom, she sounded nervous, nearly panicked—so many of the grieving did—and Anna could certainly understand it. By this point, she was long accustomed to the spirit world and the way it overarched our own. To the average client, however, communication with the dead seemed like a half-baked theory or, worse yet, a hoax. Anna always had to remind herself of their understandable doubts. After all, even Alan still remained a skeptic.

Often at a death, especially an unexpected one, there were so many things left unsaid, a simple "I love you" chief among them.

Alan could scoff, but Anna still felt a thrill when she was able to facilitate the loving exchange of a final farewell. Maybe Mrs. Murphy was right and Anna was sweeter and more sentimental than she cared to let on.

There was a knock at her door. Anna opened it to Mrs. Peterson, a tiny birdlike woman who entered timidly. As she hobbled in, Mrs. Peterson looked apprehensive, peering around as if she were entering a witch's lair. Anna was used to this and did try to keep her reading area as matter-of-fact and nonesoteric as possible. Assuring herself that it might be "safe," Mrs. Peterson entered the room. She paused and took in her surroundings. *Like a cautious sparrow*, Anna thought. "Oh," she breathed quietly, "what lovely music. Howard just loved music. It's Mozart, isn't it?" Mrs. Peterson cocked her head toward Anna's still-open windows where the damnable music poured over the sills.

"Can I get you anything? Tea or coffee?" Anna offered. Mrs. Peterson declined. Anna motioned her to the love seat and moved to her own position at the little table. When Mrs. Peterson was settled, Anna asked, "So, we are trying to contact 'Howard'?" At the mention of his name Mrs. Peterson jumped.

"How did you know his name?" she chirruped.

"You mentioned it when you commented about the music," Anna reassured her.

Mrs. Peterson sank back, her small figure nearly lost amid the pillows.

"Howard was my husband. We were married forty-three years. He died, passed over, two and a half months ago."

Anna held up a palm. She spoke softly but firmly. "That's enough now, Mrs. Peterson. The less I know the better, otherwise later you will think that I made it all up because you gave me the clues."

"I see," Mrs. Peterson said, settling her delicate hands primly on her knees like an expectant child. There was something child-like and innocent about her, Anna thought, and then she felt the familiar little shove as her own thoughts and perceptions were pushed out of the way.

"Was your husband an extremely tall man with very white hair?" Anna asked now.

"That's Howard!" Mrs. Peterson answered. "I always told him he looked like a mountain peak covered in snow. Oh, dear, you said no clues."

"No clues. I need to listen. Do you want to write things down? There's a pen and paper there on the couch-side table—or I could take notes for you."

Mrs. Peterson took up the paper and pen from the table near the love seat. "I'm ready," she whispered. Anna smiled to herself at Mrs. Peterson's sense of drama. It seemed to her that often, clients wished for the heightened atmosphere of hocus-pocus and all the paraphernalia—crystal balls, tilting tables and the like—that they were familiar with from the movies. No such luck. Anna had been taught to treat the afterlife as simple and matter-of-fact. Mrs. Peterson might be disappointed, but she could not feel herself to have been conned.

Anna started, as she had to start, with the odd bits of infor-mation Howard was communicating. It didn't seem likely, Mrs. Peterson was so mild, but there it was, a fight between them. After listening for a beat, Anna said, "Howard wants you to stop beating yourself up about that fight. He says everybody has a fight once in a while."

"We did have a fight," Mrs. Peterson gasped. Anna thought she saw a wave of relief wash over her features. "It was over the sandwiches. I always made him his lunch and he wanted chicken salad and I made him tuna fish. He got quite cross. In fact, he blew up at me. I wondered if that caused the stroke."

Anna strained to listen. It was difficult since half of her ear seemed to be following the music, rather celestial now, like a sound track for Howard and the other world. Anna frowned, concentrating to hear accurately through the increasingly rhapsodic melody.

"Why are you frowning?" Mrs. Peterson asked anxiously. "Is Howard in trouble?"

Anna reassured her. "Howard is doing fine. He says he's sorry he was crabby about the sandwich. He says your tuna fish is good, too. He was just being a cranky old bastard."

Mrs. Peterson looked startled. Anna hoped she had got the message right. She had heard "cranky old bastard," hadn't she?

"Did your husband swear?" she asked.

"Oh, yes," Mrs. Peterson chimed up. "Howard loved to swear but he never apologized, not when he was living."

Anna held a finger to her lips. Howard was finally "talking up" in her mind's ear. True, the damn music kept intruding—so beautiful now, but still like a fly buzzing in her ear. Anna reached for her own tablet and pen. Sometimes writing down the messages helped her to focus and Howard was so newly dead he might not have a lot of energy for sending. She scribbled down exactly what Howard said. He sounded both miffed and concerned. Anna laid down her pen when he went silent. It all seemed so unlikely, but she had learned to set her own skepticism aside.

"What did he say?" Mrs. Peterson demanded a little jealously. "I thought I might hear him."

Well, there was no getting around it, so Anna plunged in.

She told Mrs. Peterson exactly what her dead husband had said. According to Howard, his widow had taken up with a new lover, a younger, smooth-talking con. "Are you seeing someone new? He's after your money." Mrs. Peterson blushed hot pink to the roots of her white wispy hair.

Bingo, Anna thought. Just as Howard had said, Mrs. Peterson *was* seeing a new man, a gold digger after her money.

"I knew Howard would disapprove," Mrs. Peterson said defensively. "He was always so jealous." It was not without pride that she spoke of her husband's possessiveness, the way he had always sought to rein her in on social occasions where male attention was present.

Anna spoke up, "He says that's true but this is simple reality. Fall for him and you'll lose everything we had. That's what he said."

"Oh dear," Mrs. Peterson murmured, smoothing her demure print dress over her slender legs. "I hate to think he's right. Jerry is so..." She stared dreamily into space, clearly smitten.

"Persuasive?" Anna suggested at Howard's nudging. "Smooth?"

"Oh, dear," Mrs. Peterson reached for her purse.

Here we go again, Anna thought. *Shoot the messenger.* Mrs. Peterson was glaring at her now with a bird's bright and hostile beady eyes. In any case, Howard was fading. Anna lost first his impression and then his voice. The visit had taken a lot out of him, she thought.

"We'll just have to see about Jerry," Mrs. Peterson said icily rising to her feet. "Howard was always very suspicious. Still, I'm glad he apologized. That was a first. Here's your check. Shall I show myself out?"

Anna hopped to her feet and crossed to the door. She held it open for Mrs. Peterson who had quite a temper of her own, Anna thought, closing the door behind her. So often, the grieving are so vulnerable, she thought, remembering her experiences over the years, the tales of swindlers and con men preying on her clientele who seldom wanted to hear the unvarnished truth even from the afterworld.

The Mozart—was it Mozart? Anna thought perhaps, yes, but she really had no idea—spilled sympathetically into the room. Anna saw the note Mrs. Peterson had scribbled and forgotten. "Howard says he's sorry and to be careful," she had written in a fine, scratchy hand.

After Mrs. Peterson, Anna felt exhausted and crabby. Howard had certainly come through, loud and clear, but she doubted that his wife would heed his warning. Sometimes Anna felt powerless to really help her clients. Say what she might, there was still free will involved and they often chose against their own best interests. *Scoundrels prey on widows and children*, Anna thought angrily as she grabbed for a sweater and contemplated meatloaf and mashed potatoes. That was the Saturday special at the Greek diner, and even though the meatloaf tasted faintly Greek, she liked it.

Chapter 24

Dear Mr. and Mrs. Oliver,
Thanks for your endless kindness. I got the cookies, although they got crumbled up a bit in the mailing process. Still, I'm not complaining. I put them over vanilla Häagen-Dazs and they were just delicious. I can only imagine how great they were fresh and whole.

Mr. Oliver, the Mozart goes fine, more or less. I am having a little understandable difficulty with the tricky third movement but I am sure I will figure it out. You were right about the Schumann and Liszt coming to me more easily. And the Rachmaninoff is really showboating, don't you think? I mean, it sounds so much harder than it is. The Mozart, on the other hand, *is* demanding, but closer to my heart. I just wish he had left us some operating instructions. Mahler practically left us footnotes!

What else? So far, that back of the neck tension I get isn't freezing me up, although of course it's always there, lurking. I think I aggravated it last time I was home from trying a hook shot playing basketball with my brother. Well, lesson learned.

Mrs. Oliver, I hate to say this, but I am not sure I really have time for "friends." I understand you think I need them and perhaps I do, but I think of preparing for a big competition a lot like being in training. Try to picture asking Muhammad Ali or Magic Johnson if they have friends. Does that sound too pretentious? I just mean I have to concentrate, and besides, with cookies like yours, who could hunger for anything more?

Yours,
Edward

Chapter 25

Anna loved the fall days. When she got home early enough from school, she headed straight for Central Park, entering at 86th Street. On more than one occasion she had spotted a rat scurrying for cover in the thick carpet of ground cover banking the park's entrance, but rats didn't really scare her, snakes did. Luckily, she had never seen a snake in Central Park but she knew there were some.

This afternoon, Anna spotted no rats, just a small, energetic Westie digging with her owner's full approval at the edge of the ground cover where it clearly smelled a rat.

"Cute dog," Anna remarked.

"Her name is Charlotte," responded the owner, a sleek, aloof-looking blonde who proved to be far friendlier than she initially looked. As a near-daily walker in the park, Anna had come to recognize many fellow users. Anna bent down to greet the little dog, which responded by leaping up to kiss Anna's hand.

"You really rate," the owner smiled. "Usually when she's after a 'Ratty' she's too busy to say hello."

"I'm flattered," Anna laughed. Charlotte, seeming to understand, kissed Anna's hand once more before returning to her pursuit.

"Goodbye, Charlotte," Anna remarked to the preoccupied dog as she struck out toward the bridle path that ringed the reservoir. She eschewed the running track around the reservoir with its busy hordes of yuppies improving their already excellent shapes. No, she preferred the quiet crunch of the black cinders, the traffic mainly elderly dog walkers and the occasional rented horse.

Today the fall leaves seemed at their zenith, a wonderful bird-filled and colorful canopy over her head. She almost—that is *almost*—missed tree-laden Ann Arbor on days like this. When she was a child, her second-story bedroom window had opened straight into the arms of a large sugar maple, resplendent in gold and crimson every autumn. *It was practically like living in a tree house*, Anna thought fondly, until she caught herself.

New York is much, much better. She snapped herself back to reality, just as a bicycle almost mowed her down. She jumped into the bushes. The rider went careening head first, ending up in a little pile holding his hands aloft like a surgeon. It was the pianist from her building.

"Don't you know bikes aren't allowed on this trail?" Anna yelped, before realizing he might be hurt and she wasn't.

His glasses lay on the cinders. His lake blue eyes blinked at her myopically. He *was* almost good-looking, she registered, except for that mop of carrot-colored hair. What was he doing holding his hands in the air? Did he think he was under arrest?

"I'm sorry," he muttered. "I didn't read the sign." He was trying to untangle his long legs from the bicycle. His baggy pants were torn at both knees where two spots of bright red skin showed through, to Anna's horror. So he was hurt, the idiot.

"Do you need a hand?" she asked.

"It's not too bad. If I can just find my glasses." Now he was flexing his hands; he looked ridiculous, like he was squeezing invisible tennis balls floating in the air.

"Your glasses are under your left knee," Anna directed, "and what are you doing with your hands?"

"That's right. His hands. His hands," Anna distinctly heard the heavily accented voice issuing from nowhere. *That ghost? Here in Central Park?* It was possible, just unusual. *"Yes. Yes. He must guard his hands. Certainly you could be more careful, young lady!"* the voice spoke again.

"What?" Anna asked. According to the ghost, the accident was *her* fault.

"I'm a pianist," the bicyclist offered mildly, as if that explained everything, which it did. "My name is Edward," he added, as if they could *possibly* be friends.

"Be nice to him," the ghost admonished. *"My wife was always charming."*

"Are your glasses okay?" Anna asked.

"They're fine." He settled them back on his face. Now he looked Anna up and down.

"Encourage him," the ghost urged. *"Flirt a little. Go on!"*

"Well, I'm glad you're okay. You are okay, aren't you?" Anna asked.

"Just clumsy." He shrugged self-consciously. He tilted his head from side to side as if testing to be sure he still had a neck.

"Just clumsy," Anna echoed, aware that she was letting down the ghost. But who was that ghost to offer her advice?

"I'm glad you're okay. You are okay, aren't you?" The redhead swept Anna's figure head to toe with a lingering gaze. She felt herself flush.

"I'm okay. I'm fine. You can stop staring. I'm all in one piece."

"Well, if you're okay then—" Limping slightly, he made his departure.

Chapter 26

Officially, there was no access to the roof of Anna's building. Unofficially, the brave at heart simply shoved open the door marked FIRE EXIT ONLY, and there you were. Anna liked to climb to the roof at twilight, just as the sun was busy gilding the buildings to the west. Looking down 86th Street, she could see the Hudson. In all the times that Anna had come to the roof, she had never encountered anyone else. She had come to think of the roof as her private kingdom, a sort of grand terrace that was hers alone. She had to admit that, to her, the roof was a romantic spot. If she had allowed herself fantasies, she might have imagined being kissed there. As it was, it remained one of her favorite retreats.

"Ah, we meet again, my young lady," This time, the speaker was courtly. Anna jumped at the sound of the voice. She spun in a quick circle but no one was in sight. Clearly, the voice was a ghost's. A certain ghost's.

"Where are you?" Anna demanded. *"Show yourself."* She waited for the ghost to materialize, but nothing happened. Clearly, her authority as a medium carried no weight.

"I'm right here," the heavily-accented voice replied, chuckling a little. *"Right by your side. And I prefer a little anonymity."*

"You don't belong up here," Anna protested. *"And you didn't belong in the elevator, or my apartment, either. The rules are really very simple. You come when you're called."*

"Whose rules are those?" the voice asked. *"Not mine. You're as bad as a crown prince, thinking everyone is in your service."*

"I'm not going to argue with thin air. Show yourself!" Anna demanded. *"Ah, but I choose not to,"* the ghost responded. *"I do have free will, you know."* For just an instant, Anna felt frightened. She was, after all, alone. The ghost was not what she would really call friendly. Clearing her throat, she drew herself up to her full height and authority. *"You could have the respect to come to me when I am working, not in my time off."* she protested.

"Why would you think I came to see you? I came, like you did, for the view. Lovely, isn't it?" Now the ghost chuckled in earnest.

"You have no right to be here." Anna fumed. *"It's not your roof."*

"I have every right. It's my own private concert. Have you even been listening?"

"What are you talking about?" But even as she spoke, Anna heard the music rising up from far below. It was the pianist. There was no mistaking him. The music he was playing was intricate as lace.

"He's quite good, isn't he?" inquired the ghost. *"I find him very expressive, don't you? The interpretation is so subtle."*

"I have no idea," Anna retorted. *"His music drives me crazy. He's at it at all hours of the day and night. It's like living with a radio."*

"Tut. Tut. Tut. I would have thought he would command more respect. He's quite the virtuoso."

"Maybe to you, but to me it's like Muzak."

"Now you offend me," the ghost said hotly. *"He is my protégé! Surely you can hear he is an artist!"*

"What I hear is the end of my peace and quiet. As you may have noticed, I am a medium and a certain amount of peace and quiet is quite necessary to my work. As a ghost, you should appreciate that." Even to her own ear, Anna sounded stuffy.

"He's what I appreciate." The ghost was baiting her.

"Well, that makes one of us. Now if you don't mind—" Anna brushed her hands in the air. The ghost, invisible, simply dodged them.

"But I do mind. I mind very much." The ghost was nothing if not stubborn.

"Well then, I'll leave. Enjoy your concert." So much for her tranquil moment of solitude. With that, Anna left, noting with regret that she was missing a particularly beautiful sunset.

Chapter 27

A nna passed a restless evening. The pianist practiced until nearly midnight. His turbulent music matched her mood. He finally stopped, but she was awake again at two A.M. and once again at four. At six, she admitted she was in a little over her head. At seven, she phoned Mrs. Murphy who rose early to meditate. As a medium, she was used to encountering ghosts in her work sessions, but it was another thing entirely to run into a ghost on her roof, or, for that matter, at the park. To be frank, such encounters spooked her. There had to be some protocol that Mrs. Murphy might know, something that would render such encounters less unsettling.

"I hate to bother you," Anna began. "But there's this ghost that is following me."

"Someone sticking around after you've made contact? Usually some Epsom salts and green fire will take care of that." Mrs. Murphy offered Anna her tried-and-true housecleaning advice: take a deep pot, add one cup Epsom salts, light on fire. Anna had used it before to clear out pesky, lingering spirits.

"No, no," Anna explained. "It's not someone from a reading. It's just a random ghost. A really pushy ghost. He seems to have attached himself to that pianist I told you about. I keep running into the two of them together. Yesterday, it was in the middle of Central Park. The ghost was lecturing and meddling as if—" Anna had been about to say "as if I were a regular person," but Mrs. Murphy disapproved of such shows of ego.

"I'd disregard it," Mrs. Murphy said tartly. "Simply turn a blind eye to its shenanigans. Not all ghosts are our business."

"I'd love to be able to disregard him," Anna shot back, a little bit miffed at being chastised. "But he seems bent on telling me what I should do."

"Well, then, just ignore him. That shouldn't be too difficult."

"He's always telling me what to do. He's always balling me out." Anna heard herself whining. That ghost had really gotten under her skin.

"Why didn't you say so? Your ego is involved." Mrs. Murphy pounced on Anna's vulnerability. "Ego" had no business in spiritual affairs.

"Not my ego," Anna protested. "More my sense of professionalism. This ghost has no boundaries."

"No, I'm afraid some of them don't," Mrs. Murphy laughed. "Some of them are real troublemakers. Boundaries are up to you. You must really spell it out, just what you will tolerate. Most ghosts are very teachable. They're so glad to have someone to talk to."

"I don't think this ghost is very teachable," Anna retorted. "He's just full of his own opinions."

"With which you disagree?" Mrs. Murphy sounded distinctly amused.

"Actually? Yes. He keeps on and on about the pianist." Anna could hear herself complaining. "How I should respect him. How I should treat him with more courtesy and grace. How I should flirt with him."

"As perhaps you should. Is the pianist attractive to you?"

"Of course not! He's disturbing to me. Why do you have to take his side? I called you to help me."

"I'm trying to help you, dear," Mrs. Murphy interjected. "I am simply trying to be objective—and you might want to try the same thing."

"I'll be objective when he's objective," Anna burst out. "Isn't there some way to banish him or something?"

"Are you talking about the ghost, the pianist or both, my dear? We can't control other people and events. Only our own reactions to them. Frankly? This pianist of yours sounds interesting and this ghost has gotten your goat."

"But that's why I called you!"

"The autumn leaves are lovely this year." Mrs. Murphy's tone was high-minded.

"You're changing the subject!" Anna moaned.

"Yes, I am. The autumn leaves are lovely and if you tried focusing more on the positive, you might meet with better results." Mrs. Murphy had on her teacher's voice and there was no evading her perceptions, or her "chin-up" clichés.

"So you're saying the fact that this ghost bothers me is my fault, my negativity, something like that?" Anna felt, and sounded, more than a little huffy.

"I am saying that a little humor and a little detachment can go a long, long way."

"I'll try telling that to the ghost."

"Don't be so sensitive, dear. And have a wonderful day."

On that note, Mrs. Murphy ended their call.

Chapter 28

When Anna got to the Greek diner, Stacy was waiting for her just outside the door. "I don't think we should eat here," Stacy announced.

"But why?" Anna protested. "We met each other here. We always eat here. You love it here." Not to mention, it fit safely into Anna's budget.

Stacy explained. "Dr. Rich says I should act at all times like a woman with high self-esteem." Dr. Rich was Stacy's intrusive therapist. She hung on his every word. Anna wanted to just plain hang him.

"Yes?" Anna prompted. "And?"

"Would a woman with any self-esteem eat in a dump like this?" Stacy asked. Her dismissive wave clearly signaled the appropriate answer: no, never. The shabby but clean and cheery little diner did not pass muster. Its Edward Hopper charm was lost on Stacy.

"Where do you *want* to go?" Anna whined. She hated having their routine, and her budget, disrupted. She loved the Greek diner. It felt sweet and normal. Otherwise, the neighborhood was filled with pricey, swinging-singles restaurants.

"The Popover Café," Stacy prescribed. "It's cozy, it's delicious, it's close, and it has all those cute teddy bears on all the ledges." Dr. Rich had also been urging Stacy to embrace her inner child lately. That's where the teddy bears came in. Anna, who spent her days with children, wished Stacy would embrace her inner adult instead. But no, it was to be the Popover Café.

"Come on, you'll love it," Stacy urged, and Anna allowed

herself to be dragged into the street, where her friend towered over her. *We look like Mutt and Jeff together*, Anna thought. *And I'm the mutt.* Tall Stacy wore her sleek, skintight riding clothes. Diminutive Anna bundled herself into the distinctive heavy tweed coat that she had bought at a village vintage shop, thinking it looked vaguely British and suitable for romantic walks across the moors. What it looked, compared to Stacy, was dumpy. *Yes*, Anna thought, almost bitterly, *the odd couple.*

As a sensible lapsed-Catholic midwesterner—and she was, aside from her capacity to talk to ghosts—Anna had a built-in mistrust for therapy and its central premise: disclosure. Weren't some things better left private and unsaid? Anna had an introvert's distrust of too easy admissions. Stacy felt differently. She was the sunny extrovert.

Stacy believed in "healthy self-disclosure" and a number of other concepts, like "boundaries" and "confrontation." Since Anna herself, like her family, trusted strategies like tactful evasion and deflective humor, she often felt her friendship with Stacy was like her tabloid habit, a peek into a very foreign world. Confrontation was not in Anna's vocabulary. Stacy was forever urging Anna on outgoing courses of action she couldn't begin to consider. Casual dating was only one of them.

"David was really terrible," Stacy broke into her thoughts. "Very withholding sexually. I confronted him on that."

Anna winced, imagining the confrontation. David was the most recent of Stacy's boyfriend-wannabes. Stacy sorted men the way Anna sorted socks: "Is this one a match?" Stacy had very demanding standards sexually, and she was not above giving her sex partners a bad review.

"Terrible how?" Anna picked up her end of the conversation,

not certain she wanted to know.

"In bed, of course," Stacy answered. "He didn't even know about kissing thighs." Anna was staring at her plate. "Are you listening to me or the afterlife?"

"Very funny." But Anna did enjoy Stacy's casual acceptance of her after-hours vocation. "I'm listening," Anna protested now, "You were telling me about David."

"Oh, enough about David," Stacy snorted contemptuously. "He's over with." Anna knew from long experience that once a man was "over with," there was no going back. Stacy believed in such things as "moving on," and "cutting your losses." As far as men were concerned, Stacy had a definite attention deficit disorder, as Anna would have diagnosed it in a student. She simply couldn't concentrate on one for very long.

Dr. Rich had interpreted this as "low self-worth." To him, it represented a pathological inability to commit. Anna tended to think of it less pathologically. To her eye, Stacy was a self-improvement junkie in all things. Men were simply one field among many. Each man was a small stepping-stone toward Mr. Right. They walked the long block from Columbus to Amsterdam, and the even longer distance psychologically from the Greek diner to the Popover Café.

"I can't do our usual Tuesday date next week," Stacy said, once they were settled into a cozy booth at the Popover. "I'm going to an art opening that night, unless you'd like to go with."

"Mmmm," Anna responded noncommittally. She had learned that social invitations from Stacy tended to be opportunities to feel like a wallflower. "Where is it?" she asked, stalling. She didn't like trekking all over the city at night, especially if it involved places like SoHo and too many train transfers. (Stacy blithely took cabs.)

Anna wasn't sure of the precise difference in their incomes, but she guessed it was considerable. Stacy had once told her that entry-level pay for someone of her training was $95,000 a year, and Stacy was not at entry level. Banking was still a male-dominated field, and men tended to like and promote her.

Anna scanned the menu. There was nothing she could really afford except a bowl of soup and a popover. *Why couldn't they have stayed at the diner?* Anna fumed. *Why did Dr. Rich have to consider diners to be slumming?*

"He has a game plan for me—Dr. Rich, that is," Stacy continued, adding, "I'm treating you, and I always will when we come here." That was Stacy's insensitive form of sensitivity.

"Thank you," Anna responded, a little guiltily. She might be a lapsed Catholic, but her guilt factor had never quite managed to lapse along with her church attendance. Stacy was a blithe Protestant, and suffered few hangovers of remorse. This fact fascinated Anna, and slightly repelled her. Sometimes she found herself studying her friend like an exotic plant, a Venus flytrap, to be precise, with men her hapless prey.

"Dr. Rich wants me to go for the gold," Stacy continued. To Anna's ear, this made life sound a little too much like a triathlon, but then, Stacy was a natural athlete—out of bed as well as in. Stacy ordered a blackened shrimp salad, the most expensive thing on the menu. Anna settled for the more modest Waldorf.

"Dr. Rich says I simply should not settle," Stacy went on, "that settling is simple masochism. He feels I may have hidden masochistic tendencies, that's why I can't commit." Stacy unspooled more therapeutic theory. To Anna it sounded dubious at best, yet he had Stacy hooked. By the time Stacy was through, Dr. Rich would certainly live up to his name. Her psyche would pay for his country home.

"I thought you didn't like any of them," Anna interjected. "I thought they were boring, in bed or out."

"That's just it," Stacy continued. "Men like David *are* boring."

"He sounded perfectly nice," Anna observed as their popovers arrived. "Okay, maybe a little dull, a little cookie-cutter, but I thought that was just how you liked them."

Privately, Anna felt compassion for some of Stacy's conquests. Dating Stacy, Anna suspected, might tend to resemble a close-order drill. Over the year-plus of their friendship, Anna had heard men described in roughly the same terms as Stacy's dressage mounts, who was well-muscled, and more. Still, well-muscled as some of them were, none of Stacy's wannabes ever held her attention.

"What about it?" Stacy wanted to know. "Do you want to go to that opening? I'm sure there will be scads of men there."

"Scads of men is not my idea of heaven," Anna protested. "To the contrary."

"Oh, come *on*," Stacy urged. And then, "Maybe you should see Dr. Rich. You know it's just denial. What's-his-name. That guy two years ago, Roger? He hurt your feelings and you've been sulking ever since."

"I am not sulking," Anna sulked. "And besides, unlike some people, I have an entire history of romantic disaster. Maybe enough is just enough. No, you go."

Now it was Stacy's turn to sulk. She hated getting no for an answer. And, in fact, she seldom did.

Chapter 29

The phone rang as Anna walked in the door. It was her mother, calling just to "give her a few thoughts." Her mother had thoughts about her health, about her holiday plans, and, it developed, about her love life.

"I am wondering if you've considered the Internet?" her mother asked. "I know it isn't conventional but you are living in New York. I have been reading about something called Match.com. Have you heard of it?"

"I've heard of it." And she had, from Stacy. Stacy, too, thought it might be a good idea.

"Of course it's not as good as an old-fashioned introduction but we live in modern times, don't we? You might find someone who shares your interests."

"You mean I might find someone who didn't think I was weird?" Anna knew precisely how to get her mother's goat.

"Must you be so—" Her mother broke off.

"Rude? Cranky? Brattish? If you're going to go pestering me about my love life, I am afraid so, Mother."

"I just thought it sounded like a reasonable idea. Very safe really, they see to that." Now her mother sounded wheedling.

"Mother, I do not want to have a cyberrelationship." Anna spoke with force.

"You make it sound so ugly." Her mother sounded like a petulant little girl.

"Well, just remember it was your idea."

"Your father and I just thought—" Her mother broke off again.

"Don't drag Daddy into this."

"All right. I just thought you could be so much happier."

"I am not unhappy, Mother. I'm just single. I'll tell you what makes me unhappy. Dating makes me unhappy. Remember Roger? I do."

"Roger was a limited man." Her mother's dismissal was absolute.

"Roger was normal. I'm not."

"Must you say such things?"

"Yes, Mother. Evidently so. Now if you don't mind, I'd love to get some sleep."

Hanging up from her mother, she scooped together her wash. She fished some already-read tabloids from out of the trash. *Was that low self-esteem, in Stacy's phrase?* she wondered.

They were down to one washing machine again, as usual, and it was rocking back and forth alarmingly. Someone, a missing someone, had clearly overloaded it and then left. *How thoughtless,* Anna thought, *to leave your laundry unattended.* On more than one occasion she had removed a soggy armload from an available washer, dumping the sodden heap onto the folding table or, if she was feeling charitable, sacrificing fifty cents to start the offending mess to dry in an available dryer.

"I ran out of Tide. I had to go get some more," a deep male voice behind her said apologetically. The pianist entered with a family-size orange box of Tide cradled in his arms. He set the Tide on the folding table.

"Well, you're probably too late. It's gone through rinse already and now it's on spin," Anna lectured him crossly. He walked a little stiffly, she noticed, like his knees still hurt from his—their—accident.

89

"Oh, that load I had just enough for, I hope," he said politely. Anna felt like a shrew.

"Well you overloaded it anyhow," Anna went on. Something in this man—*everything* in this man—brought out her very worst.

The pianist limped to the washer and tried to open its lid. Didn't he know anything?

"It automatically locks on spin dry," Anna informed him.

"You must be very domestic," he observed.

"No, I'm not. Don't get your hopes up." Anna barked at him. With horror, she heard herself spinning straight out of control. Where was her detachment? Wasn't that what Mrs. Murphy advised? Where was her objectivity? "Find yourself some other groupie—" she burst out.

"Groupie?" he looked blank.

That's when she heard the by now familiar voice. *"You're on thin ice,"* the voice warned her. *"He's not some rock star. Try to keep a civil tongue in your head."* Anna ignored the voice. It only made her angrier.

"A groupie for your piano playing," Anna lit into the pianist. Clearly, she was on a tear. After all, she had been dying to complain for what seemed like—and *was*—some weeks now.

"My piano playing?" he sputtered, once again knocking over the Tide, a snowdrift this time, all over the table and floor. Anna did not feel pity.

"You confuse him," the ghost accused her. *"He's so well meaning and you're so difficult."* Anna resolved to ignore its comments.

"Yes, your piano playing," she went on. "Don't act so innocent. You're the one with the Mozart, or whatever it is, right?" She sounded like a shrew. A shrew and a philistine.

"You're going to get him all worked up," the ghost complained.

"I am trying to keep him nice and calm, but how can anyone be calm with you?"

As if to refute the ghost's words, Edward answered Anna calmly. "Mainly Mozart, some Liszt, some Schumann, some Bartók, Bach, Rachmaninoff and Chopin," he responded carefully. Anna thought she had seen a flash of fire when she sneered at Mozart but behind those nerdy glasses she couldn't be sure. Did he think he was Clark Kent? Why couldn't he get contacts like everyone else? Then he'd be out from hiding, except of course, for the Einstein tangle of vivid hair. He must have gotten teased about that.

"Hey, Red. Hey, Bozo," Anna could just imagine the cruelty he must have endured. She pictured him suddenly as a carrot-topped, skinny nine-year-old trying to hold his own on the playground. The poor thing. The poor little thing. Despite herself, Anna smiled up at him. He seemed somehow so naïve and innocent. If she thought of him as an overgrown child—

He was explaining something with preternatural patience, articulating carefully, as she sometimes did to her slowest students. He was explaining, oh dear, exactly what he was playing, which works, for some competition. It was all Greek to her. Where many people had an education in classical music, she had an embarrassing void. Her knowledge was zilch, except for one course in college and her mother's lingering piano skills. She snapped out of her thoughts just as the redhead explained that for pianists, some competitions were rather like athletic events—the NBA finals or the World Series. *Great*, she thought, *as it nears he will be playing more than ever*. She swigged hastily on a Diet Coke. She knew she was frowning again.

"You're cute when you're mad," Edward suddenly said, looking as startled at his words as she was. His big line fell flat. "I know it's a cliché. Sorry."

Against her will, Anna laughed.

"That's better," the ghost said approvingly.

Chapter 30

Dear Mr. and Mrs. Oliver,
Well, here's the field report. I think I am beginning to get a handle on that tricky third movement I told you about. I tackled it at length this morning and I do feel I've cracked the spine of it—what a terrible expression.

Mrs. Oliver, I regret to tell you I do not think I am making friends in this building. On the contrary, just as I feared my practicing can be overheard and it's driving at least one tenant crazy. I know music has charms to soothe a savage beast but those charms are evidently not in my repertoire. My irate neighbor, to satisfy your curiosity, is a woman who looks about my own age. Both my laundry technique and my piano technique leave something to be desired in her eyes. Personally, I thought she was rather cute, except for her attitude of course. Who could hate Mozart?

Yours sincerely,
Edward

Chapter 31

"I am glad to see you're not avoiding me," Tommy greeted Anna as she entered the aquarium store. "I've got a new angelicus catfish that has to be seen to be believed. You might want to check out the African dwarf cichlids. I got a huge shipment. They're so cool, like checkerboards. Who was it wore a checked zoot suit? Chubby Checker?"

"Maybe." Anna stopped to admire a tank full of zebra danios. "These characters are pretty racey, black and gold stripes!"

"Yeh, well, Barney's got his eye on them." Tommy came out from behind the counter, rag in one hand, Windex in the other.

"They do swim near the surface." Anna paused to take in their antics.

"Right. But they're a lot faster than the marble hatchet fish." Tommy began swiping at the tank fronts, scrubbing off finger-prints and random smears.

Anna made her way back through the shadowy aisles to her fa-vorites, the swordtails. She let out a little whoop of delight. "Hey, when did you get all of these colors? I like the orange and green." As soon as she spoke, the swordtails zipped behind their coral.

"Well, they like you, too. Just the other day as I was cleaning the tank, they asked me, 'Where's our Anna?' I told them I scared you off, going through your purse and all."

"That wasn't your finest moment," Anna teased.

"Say, I've been meaning to ask you. Can you get anybody? Anybody dead, that is?"

"It doesn't work like a search warrant. I talk with those who want to talk. It's kind of like I dial the telephone but they don't have to answer."

"I wonder if he would."

"Do you want to tell me he 'who'?" By now Anna had given up on the idea of a quiet, meditative visit. Clearly, Tommy had been waiting for her appearance.

"His name is Hughie," Tommy volunteered. "What else do you need to know?"

"It's better if you don't tell me anything else."

"I get it. So you can't pull a fast one."

"Something like that."

The flotilla of swordtails was beginning to come forward from behind their coral formation. Anna counted more than a dozen.

"So what do I do? Make an appointment or something?" Tommy was swabbing at the front of a tank full of tiger barbs.

"Sure. We could do that. Here, this time it's legitimate." Anna fished in her purse for a business card. "Just give me a call at this number."

"Just give you a call. That simple."

"It is simple, really."

"That's what I like about you. No hocus pocus." Tommy swirled his rag midair.

"No, I'm afraid not."

"And not much small talk, either."

"No."

"So why don't I leave you alone?"

"Yes. I do come here to calm down."

"That is not a compliment." Tommy shook his head and winked. "I'll let you be."

Chapter 32

It was Alan. He wanted to know how Anna was, suspiciously not self-preoccupied. He wanted something. She could always see Alan coming—just before he ran her over like a truck, that is. This time, Alan wanted to come to New York and sleep in a sleeping roll on her studio floor. It seemed some jazz great, something or other Didier, a protégé of Stéphane Grappelli, was coming to New York.

"For just one night at the Village Vanguard," Alan assured her. He'd be no trouble.

Anna listened cautiously. Earlier in the year, Alan had come for a night and stayed for three weeks, running all over New York attending every single musical listing in *Time Out*, it seemed to her. Should she let him come back? For that matter, could she stop him? Nothing stood between Alan and his jazz obsession. He'd sleep in Central Park if he had to. She couldn't let that happen to her own brother, or could she?

"One night?" she asked warily. "I suppose you already have your ticket?" Meaning for his flight.

"Actually, I do," Alan confessed, "and I've got my airline ticket too."

That certainly put things into perspective.

"I'll stay less than a week this time." A threat or a promise?

When she got off the phone, having said a reluctant "yes," Anna checked her calendar. On the night Alan had mentioned, for once she was relieved to see a penciled-in invitation from Harold, a book signing for a friend of his in the back garden space of some obscure metaphysical shop on Houston Street. They'd probably freeze their asses off, Anna thought, but being dragged along by Harold seemed imminently preferable to being dragged along by Alan to some tiny, smoky club with dead jazz men populating the ceiling.

The wonderful thing about having Alan for a brother, Anna thought, watering her philodendrons, was that as "weird" as her vocation was, he was overtly weirder. After all, how many people had brothers on farms in Kalamazoo? Crafting handmade violins? How many people had brothers who could quote Charlie Parker or Miles Davis, chapter and verse? What was it Alan always quoted from Miles Davis? "Don't fear mistakes, there are none"? Anna still feared that it had been a mistake to tell Alan "yes" about his visit. Not that she really had much choice.

Alan's visits tended to be exhausting. Alan, too, tended to be exhausting. This was his, what, sixth visit in two years? (She, stupidly, had sent him a subscription to *Time Out New York*.) "Why don't you just move here?" she needled him.

"Kalamazoo is cheaper," Alan always retorted. "Why should I leave here and pay fifteen hundred a month to live in a postage stamp, like you do? Do you know how many tickets fifteen hundred can buy? Besides, *you* live there." Alan had a point.

Anna prepared for his visit as for a military campaign crossing the Alps. Alan required rations. He was notoriously cheap, and so she bought a vat of peanut butter, a stash of his favorite seven-grain bread, a gallon of "natural" apple juice and almonds, peanuts and cashews for snacks. On Alan's previous visit—the long, extended one—he had pored over jazz listings like he was deciphering the Rosetta stone. He had stayed out all night, or nearly, creeping home at dawn, just as Anna was getting up to teach. (Jazz greats were night owls, she thoroughly learned.)

When Alan was visiting, any semblance of a personal schedule flew out the window. Anna knew she was supposed to have boundaries (she had learned that much from Stacy's therapy), but how do you set boundaries with someone who had floated with you, buck naked, in a shared womb? Besides, Alan would have to respect boundaries, which he didn't. No corner of her life was too obscure, too personal, for his scrutiny and scathing comments. She suspected him of listening to her messages when she was away at school and she toted her diary in her briefcase with her just in case. Yes, no doubt about it, Alan was coming and she was in for it.

Chapter 33

The pianist, Edward, was in her booth again downstairs at the Greek diner. He looked even nerdier than usual, sporting both glasses and a neck brace, snowy white and rigid. He was trying, with mixed success, to ladle soup into his mouth. It looked like split pea with ham. He glanced up as she entered. When he saw her frown—he did have her booth after all—he looked quickly back down, just as far down as the neck brace would allow him.

Might as well be civil, Anna chided herself. She quietly

approached his table, noting his soup-stained book—no, it was a musical score. Feeling her loom over him, the redhead jumped—a deer, or perhaps a moose, in the headlights.

"Hello," he managed.

"Is that thing from our accident?" Anna inquired.

"You mean the neck brace? I'm afraid maybe it is. I have this recurrent tension in the back of my neck. The accident seems to have set it off. I'm just being cautious," he petered off. "My name is Edward," he reminded her. "Appleton," he added. "Apartment One-E."

"I'm on five," Anna informed him, "and I can still hear you."

"I worried about that," Edward confessed.

"You did?"

This put a new wrinkle in things. Anna had assumed that as a pianist he would be like Alan, totally single-minded and self-obsessed, much too self-centered to think of anyone else and their inconvenience.

"It's nice that you worried about the noise," Anna said. Was it her imagination or did he wince at the word "noise?" Of course, his neck could simply be bothering him.

"I'm Anna, Anna Chester, Five-C," Anna said, belatedly remembering her manners, not that she wanted to be friends. Edward extended a large, bony hand. He gripped her much smaller one in a bone-crushing clench. *Piano hands*, she thought.

Just as she walked in the door, Anna's business machine clicked on. She heard her own soothing voice leaving explicit directions. "This is Anna," the voice said. "It is possible that I can help you reach out to, and be reached by, your dearly departed ones. Please leave your name and phone number, speaking slowly and carefully. Thank you."

As her machine clicked over to receive, she heard a distinctive clipped British voice. "This is Nathan Nettles," the voice began. "I'm calling you regarding my mother. You can return my call at 555-8585. That's area code 212. Oh yes, I'm a friend of your friend Harold."

Ordinarily, Anna would have returned the call, but she was in no ordinary mood.

She scowled at herself in the mirror. Her vintage dress looked suddenly frumpy. Was that it? Maybe she should cut her hair, a mass of pre-Raphaelite ringlets. With a more modern haircut might she not manage a more modern life? She'd practically bitten the pianist's head off.

Chapter 34

Dear Mr. and Mrs. Oliver,

I'm afraid that your fears were justified. I didn't want to tell you, but I did take a fall on my bike. Not in traffic, Mrs. Oliver, in Central Park. I actually ran over that neighbor I told you about, Anna, her name is. Don't worry, though, my hands are fine. Ditto wrists, arms, legs, etc. I'm afraid I did do something to my neck again though. As you know, not to mix metaphors, my neck is my Achilles heel. I am, however, still able to play and the awkwardness is actually helping my memory. Mrs. Oliver, there's your silver lining, I suppose.

Oh, Mrs. Oliver, thanks for the toffee. I'm afraid I ate almost the whole box at one sitting. I'd never heard of Enstrom's before but they really should be world famous. Their toffee was just delicious.

I'm saving all my receipts as you requested, Mr. Oliver. Do you want them more than once a month? I could get them to you weekly, if that would be better. I'm afraid most of them are from the Greek diner right next door. I can get three squares a day there for just under twenty, I hope you think that's reasonable.

Sincerely,
Edward

Chapter 35

R eturning home from school the next day, Anna walked in to hear her mother's voice speaking succinctly from her answering machine.

"Anna darling," her mother was saying, "you might want to give us a call. We've got news, I'm afraid."

Bad news, Anna supposed, diving for the telephone.

"Hello? Mom?"

"Don't panic, dear." As usual, Anna thought, her mother was managing everything, right down to acceptable emotions.

"What is it, Mom?" Anna cut to the chase. "Is it Dad? Alan? Are you all right?"

Anna heard her mother draw a breath, then exhale, slowly and evenly. She knew from experience that this meant it was some kind of emergency.

"Your father's going to be fine. He doesn't want you to come home. He says he'll talk to you soon."

Anna felt herself choking. Her father?

"Is he in the hospital?" she demanded to know. "Was it a stroke? A heart attack? A car accident?"

"He went in for a minor procedure and, it should have been minor, so he didn't want to bother you," her mother began.

Bit by bit, Anna dragged it out of her mother. A routine bit of minor surgery gone awry. Her father would be fine. He just couldn't get to the phone but he wanted her to know just in case.

"In case what?" Anna asked. Her mother paused, marshaling a sufficiently temperate low-key response. "Why, in case something happens," she finally mustered, ending the call with forced good cheer.

Getting off the phone, Anna noticed the little red box telling her she had another message. *Might as well get it over with*, she thought and pressed Play.

This time it was Alan, supposing she might already have heard from their mother. Dad would be fine, probably. Alan was on his way to the hospital. She should stay right where she was, New York, and he, Alan, would call her again, later. "Don't go off half-cocked," her brother rang off. Anna sat down on her floor with great hiccuping sobs.

Which hospital? Why didn't they want her to come home? She should call an airline but that would tie up the phone. Anna never called out on her business line and in her upset, she forgot that she could. Meanwhile, the business line shrilled, Anna heard her own calm voice followed by another, more agitated, message from Nathan. "I'm waiting to hear back from you," he nearly snarled.

Ever since she was little and the business of ghosts had started up, Anna's mother had considered Anna and her father to be two peas in a pod—not that her father also saw ghosts, merely that he suffered, in her mother's opinion, from a hyperactive imagination, not a seemly gift in a college dean. He was always up to some high jinks.

There was the matter of the red MG roadster for example. Her father had acquired it over her mother's dead body —not that Anna herself would have used that phrase. Her mother thought the roadster was far too racy for a man of his stature. She had lobbied strongly that their second car should be another sensible Volvo, this time gray. The roadster had won out.

"It's as bad as the ice boat and just as dangerous," her mother fumed, perhaps rightly.

When she was five, Anna's father built her an ice boat out of two boards, a sail and some old ice skates. He and Anna took it to a nearby lake—Michigan was dotted with tiny lakes no bigger than ponds. To her mother's horror, they had raced across the ice, belly flopped on the boards, steering with the sail and a foot. Anna had loved the swift ride. Her father had climbed off ashen.

For once he had taken his wife's scolding without a wry retort. "You must have been going sixty," she said. "Inches from the ice. You could have scraped your faces off."

With the MG roadster, her father tended toward a distinct lead-foot, pedal-to-the-metal technique and he often left their driveway spurting gravel. Anna loved it on the days her father drove them to high school. She rode shotgun in the passenger's seat. Alan folded his lanky frame into the tiny rear where he held on for dear life.

If Anna's father loved drama in all forms—he referred to his students' varied plights as his "personal soap opera"—Anna's mother worked very hard to keep a lid on it—and him.

"Don't encourage her," she hissed to him about Anna, who had her second encounter with a ghost in their summer cabin on Mackinac Island.

Anna had just turned eight, young enough that she and Alan still shared bunk beds in the same room. Again, it was bedtime. She was drifting off to sleep on the upper bunk when she saw him: a man this time, bearded, thirtyish, in rustic dress, a leather jacket with fringe and a coonskin hat. He was floating, or half of him was, right near the window by the pine tree.

"Alan, Alan, wake up!" Anna had hissed urgently. But Alan dreamed on while the apparition hovered scant feet above his sleeping head. As Anna watched, the Davy Crockett-clad ghost floated toward the window just as if peering out. It tapped at the glass with a strong but silent finger. To Anna's amusement the finger jabbed straight through the glass and when the figure left, a moment later, it calmly slid straight through the rough-hewn log walls. It had been a ghost, she knew it, and once again, she alone had had the chance to see it.

"Don't indulge her," Anna's mother had warned her father when she saw he was in danger of believing her about the ghost. "She has a very active imagination—just like someone else I might mention—and I think we would do best to let it settle straight back down."

Instead, Anna's father had driven her all the way to the county courthouse where together they had researched the cabin's previous owners. This gave them names. Next, in the bowels of the town's sole library, they had carefully turned the pages of soiled and moldy newspapers, some of which turned to powder in their hands. It was in a daguerreotype taken on his wedding day that

Anna recognized Ethan Gambler, sure enough the former owner and builder of their cabin.

"That's him," she had declared with excited satisfaction. "That's who I saw."

"Maybe your next ghost will be on microfilm," her father had observed.

His humor was always comforting. So was the scent of the lemon Pledge that Anna used as she turned manically to cleaning her tiny kingdom while waiting for the phone to ring with further news.

Chapter 36

It was three hours later when the personal line shrilled again, this time Alan. It had been an air bubble that traveled to the heart, Alan reported in. There had been a "minor" heart attack. For a while it was nip and tuck but their father would survive.

"The hospital nearly killed him," Alan fumed. "The procedure he went in for was supposed to be an outpatient, in and out, twenty-minute thing, some vein in his leg."

"Well it wasn't in and out," Anna said. "I'm coming home."

"But I'm coming *there*," Alan wailed. "I'm telling you Dad's okay, a little pale, maybe. But he's going to be fine. I just saw him. You don't need to come."

"I'm coming," Anna said.

"It's Didier Lockwood, for chrissake," Alan burst out. "He lives in France, just outside of Paris. It's a miracle we even got him over here."

"Well, I'm coming." Anna repeated herself.

"You would," Alan griped. Alan was more than frustrated with her, he was obsessed. Not even their father's heart attack—"minor, minor" Alan assured her—could come between him and a jazz great.

"I could leave a set of keys with the super," Anna reluctantly volunteered—anything to shut her brother up.

"Actually, you won't need to. I made a duplicate set on my last trip out," Alan confessed.

For a beat, Anna was angry about the keys, then she laughed. Alan was, after all, a jazz addict and nothing, certainly not a small thing like personal space and "boundaries," was going to stand in his way.

They probably passed in midair, Alan flying east, Anna flying west with a hastily assembled suitcase of clothes. She took a cab from the airport straight to the hospital—at least she'd managed to pry that much out of Alan.

When she entered his room, her father looked like something out of a science fiction movie, tubes and monitors everywhere, an ungainly glucose drip hanging in a bag from a pole near his head. Now that they'd nearly killed him, the hospital was doing its best to save him—and fend off a lawsuit, no doubt.

When she entered the room, dragging her carry-on bag behind her, her father was sleeping while her mother worked furiously on her newest needlepoint project, sitting close to him in the bedside chair.

"I knew you'd do something dramatic," she observed evenly as Anna slid into the room.

"Oh Mom, this *is* dramatic," Anna insisted as she kissed her mother's lightly scented cheek.

"He's going to be fine," her mother insisted, without looking up from her project. Anna looked more closely around the room. She saw the orange plastic chair Alan must have used at her father's far bedside. She noticed the view which featured some of Ann Arbor's fabled trees. She took in the abandoned cafeteria tray, doubtless her mother's. It still featured a blob of chocolate pudding in a small plastic dish.

"Sit down, dear," Anna's mother said very calmly in a low voice she used for immutable orders. "As long as you're here," she added.

Carefully, wincing at every small noise her suitcase made, Anna crossed the room to her place. There was just enough space between her father's hospital bed and the wall to maneuver the suitcase without incident. Anna sank into the plastic chair. Her mother set down her needlepoint, took pen and paper from her purse and carefully, across her father's chest, amid the tubes and contraptions, passed Anna a note. It read, "They can hear everything."

For a split second, Anna thought that her mother meant ghosts, then she realized "they" must mean patients, like her father. Was he in a coma? She had assumed he was just sleeping, his hands folded peacefully, but disconcertingly, across his chest.

"Hi, Dad," Anna ventured. Instantly, her mother set down her needlepoint and hissed, "He's sleeping!"

Anna's father stirred, ever so slightly. His eyelids fluttered. He turned his head toward the sound of her voice and opened his eyes.

"Hi, ghostbuster," he said. "I figured you'd be showing up any-time now."

To Anna's horror, hot wet tears slid down her cheeks. Her nose began running and she sniffled.

"Use a Kleenex," her mother insisted, handing one across the bed. By then Anna was clutching her father's folded hands and the Kleenex fluttered over them like a tiny shroud.

"I'm not dead yet," her father joked. "Or I'd probably be seeing more of you. Good flight?"

Anna nodded through tears, relieved beyond words that her father's humor was intact. Surely the rest of him might follow.

"You look like you've seen a ghost," she joked back. Their shared humor was a thorn in her mother's side, but at the moment Anna didn't care. Besides, her mother always had Alan to side with her.

"I'll be out in no time," her father informed her. "That's what I hear." Anna thought of her mother's note and wondered if her father *had* been in a coma, still tracking the nurses and doctors from some deep part of his mind, the way Houston—or was it Cape Canaveral?—had tracked the Apollo astronauts far out in space.

Her father squeezed her hand. His fingers were icy and clammy to the touch. *A very close call*, Anna thought. *A very close call.* Was there really any such thing as a "minor" heart attack? Anna hated such euphemisms—her mother's specialty.

"You're going to be just fine," her mother interrupted their moment. "He'll be up and around in no time," she advised Anna as if her father weren't in the room.

"So how the hell did they do this to him?" Anna finally boiled over. She wanted the whole story, and now.

Instantly, Anna's mother laid a finger to her lips and hissed, "Shhh." Arching her eyebrows meaningfully and jerking her head toward the busy hall, she again held up her note for Anna's scrutiny. "They can hear everything," Anna dutifully read. With a little jolt, Anna realized her mother meant the doctors, nurses and visitors in the corridor. *Great*, Anna thought harshly. *Even here she's doing it. What would the neighbors think?*

Appearances mattered greatly to Anna's mother. This extended into all areas of her domain. Their yard, for example, was always immaculately barbered. The trim on their house was kept freshly painted. They donated to the Girl Scouts on cookie drive and they always had an adequate candy supply for Halloween. Christmas decorations were artful and never overdone. No, no one was ever to judge them as anything but proper and conventional, which was why Anna's adolescence was a nightmare of scrutiny and control. The newspaper story relating her ghostbusting exploits was treated by her mother as an unfortunate blot on the family's good name. She took no pride in Anna's abilities. She didn't like anything that set them apart from the crowd.

And so, stationed at her husband's bedside, she undertook to control her family's public appearance. She knew well the dangers of gossip and she was determined that her family be spared. If only Anna would cooperate for once. That Anna! She was so—

"You might want to let your father rest."

"C'mon, Mom. I'm not bothering him."

"Well, you're bothering me. We need some peace and quiet after everything that's gone on." Her mother's fine hazel eyes flashed angrily.

"You're telling me they just botched things?" Anna dug for the truth like a terrier after a bone.

"I am telling you no such thing!" Anna's mother burst out, then she pantomimed "zip the lip."

Defeated, Anna kissed her father's cheek and left the room.

Chapter 37

Mrs. Bernice Murphy lived in a two-story stucco house that had seen better days in a section of Ann Arbor that had seen better years. The late Mr. Murphy had kept it in higher repair, but it still had a certain dignity, like a once beautiful woman still dressed in her faded finery, as Mrs. Murphy was herself. Opening her front door to Anna, Mrs. Murphy wore an old Chanel suit and a carefully lipsticked welcoming smile.

"Hello, my dear, and come in," she said.

Anna stepped into the familiar sitting room, taking her place on the Victorian love seat where she had sat so many Saturday afternoons. Just being in Mrs. Murphy's atmosphere, Anna felt better, and the first symptom of her recovery was anger.

"She's got him under armed guard," Anna began. "She's got him right where she always wanted him. Under her thumb."

"Yes, yes. I can imagine," Mrs. Murphy put in. She offered Anna a butterscotch.

"There's no need to imagine. You could go to the hospital and see for yourself, although I am certain you wouldn't be welcome, either."

"Your father still must have been glad to see you." Mrs. Murphy was well aware of Anna's family dynamics. She was practically her surrogate mother throughout her rocky adolescence.

"Oh, maybe. Not that he wants to rock the boat with Mom." Anna could feel her rage siphoning off into irony.

"It's a difficult dynamic,' Mrs. Murphy stated, her attention caught by a cardinal at her bird feeder.

"Difficult? It's impossible. Have you ever wondered why Alan and I are so relationship phobic?" Still vexed, Anna had the bit in her teeth and Mrs. Murphy seemed content to let her vent. "I'll tell you why. Life with our parents is exhausting. I know I make Mom out to be the villain, but Dad is just as bad as she is. They have agreed to disagree. It's their deal. One says north and the other says south." Anna reached for a butterscotch.

"I'm glad you see it's not personal," Mrs. Murphy commented. She reached into a table drawer for the bag of butterscotch. She poured a goodly amount into a little crystal dish and offered it to Anna.

"That's just it. There's nothing personal about it. Alan and I are just pawns in their game." Anna fumed but she could feel her irritation sputtering out and turning to amusement. Mrs. Murphy's bemused detachment was blessedly contagious.

"For a mere pawn you are looking very well. I am gathering that New York agrees with you." Mrs. Murphy now steered the conversation to smoother waters.

"Oh, it does." Anna savored her butterscotch as she thought fondly of her New York life.

"And tell me about your practice? Is that ghost still bothering you?"

"When he shows up, he's very bothersome—and I can never tell when he's going to show up."

"You said he seemed to be attached to that pianist who bothers you, does he still bother you?" Mrs. Murphy eyed Anna with kindly curiosity. Anna felt herself flushing.

"He seems okay," she hedged. "He actually worries about making a racket."

"Ah. I was hoping that maybe it would grow on you."

"The racket?"

"The music. Now then, tell me about your practice?"

Anna had to admit that her practice was flourishing. She described her routine, teacher by day, medium by night, and tried to give Mrs. Murphy some notion of her clientele. After all, it was to her long years of training that Anna owed her livelihood. It felt good to thank Mrs. Murphy in person, not just as a disembodied voice over the phone.

"So it sounds like you're doing quite well then," Mrs. Murphy summed up. As was her habit, she had sought out the overview. Anna's current difficulties were just bumps along the path, nothing serious, nothing to get wound up about. Anna accepted another butterscotch.

"I'm doing pretty well," she admitted. "I've had a few stink bomb clients but nothing too dramatic."

"You can always call," Mrs. Murphy reminded her. "And are you meditating like I told you?"

"Yes. At least I am trying. After all this time, I've got your voice in my head. I can well imagine what you would say most of the time."

"Then imagine me saying I am proud of you and just let your mother's antics slide off your back. After all, you've made good your escape."

"I have, haven't I," Anna agreed.

"You have. You certainly have," Mrs. Murphy assured her.

That night, after a difficult dinner with her mother in the hospital cafeteria and a ten-minute cab ride home, Anna stared at the ceiling of her childhood bedroom. She saw no ghosts there. Instead she lay awake as her mind again unspooled memories of her mother and father's marriage, one manic optimist (her father), one depressed "realist" (her mother). As she lay under the purple checked coverlet waiting for sleep, it seemed to Anna that her parents had occupied, from time immemorial, two separate poles of existence. Her zany father was always coming up with plots, plans and inventions like the ice boat. Her mother, the conservative, was always coming up with second thoughts, doubts and considerations about why her father's harebrained schemes would never work out.

They enjoy the dialectic; the argument amuses them, Anna told herself as she considered counting sheep. And, truth be told, they probably did. Despite their squabbling, theirs was a happy, solid marriage. *I am on to something here*, Anna told herself as she mulled over her remarks to Mrs. Murphy. *I am absolutely right about this one*. The reason she and Alan had not married to date was because they simply lacked the adrenaline to undertake the debate that their parents' marriage had modeled.

Somewhere in the two hundreds, the sheep worked. Anna slept deeply but fitfully. Her mother had insisted she herself occupy the cot that they placed in her father's hospital room next to his bed. Anna's last conscious thought, just before she began the sheep and drifted to sleep, was that her mother finally had her father exactly where she had always wanted him, firmly and help-lessly under her control.

Chapter 38

Dear Mr. and Mrs. Oliver,
First let me report in that I do have a friend, or at least an acquaintance. His name is Alan. I met him at the Greek diner when all the booths were full and we were seated next to each other at the counter. He's an interesting guy; his sister is the girl I nearly ran over on my bike. Her name is Anna as I may have told you. Alan is a jazz buff and he's in town to catch some guy named Didier Lockwood. He couldn't believe I'd never heard of him, being a fellow musician. I explained that I was a classical musician and that most of our greats are dead.

Mrs. Oliver, you are right, I am afraid the neck is giving me a little trouble. I probably look like Frankenstein at the keys in my neck brace, but who is there to see it? And at least I have kept on playing and the hands still work. Unfortunately, Alan says he can hear me from his sister's apartment on the fifth floor. Is that possible? I know I have a big sound, but...maybe I should put towels by the windows or something over the piano. I can't hear myself accurately if I play with the mute pedal on.

Thank you, Mr. Oliver, for offering to pay for me to see a specialist. I'm not sure I'll need one, and besides I hear they are all madmen who want to operate. A member of the violin faculty who teaches at my school can't play at all anymore because some hotshot cut the nerves in his arms to "remedy" his tendonitis.

Mrs. Oliver, the leaves in the park are finally turning. It's almost Halloween and jack-o'-lanterns are turning up on stoops, fire escapes and in some apartment windows, I don't know how they afford the pumpkins. I saw a little one for $15.99 at the Korean greengrocers on the corner of Columbus and 83rd. Maybe people will go to any lengths, even financial ones, to remember their roots.

Sincerely yours, and gratefully!
Edward

P.S. Alan thinks it is extremely weird that I write you "old-fashioned" letters. What's wrong with e-mail? he wants to know. What's wrong with calling? I say letters give you something to hold on to.

Chapter 39

Anna planned on staying home at least over the rest of the weekend and longer if needed, but that plan was promptly nixed almost as soon as she drove her father's MG roadster into the hospital parking lot the next morning.

"He's-doing-very-well-and-is-scheduled-to-go-home-in-just-a-few-days," Anna's mother announced slowly and distinctly as if her father were now a learning-impaired child. From the bed, her father quietly winked at her as Anna hovered in his hospital room's doorway. He did look back from death's door. His color was better and he was sitting up. But he was still sprouting tubes and monitors everywhere.

"It was a minor, minor heart attack," Anna's mother emphasized. "Dr. Hackett—he's the one I really listen to, the head of the team—Dr. Hackett tells me a little physical therapy and your father will be as good as new, even better." She nodded brightly as she did to her second-grade classroom.

Anna knew better than to argue with her mother, who clearly had the reins firmly in hand.

"You could catch a flight tonight," her mother suggested. "You know how you and your father always get each other so wound up."

I get it, Anna thought, *now I am a medical liability, a life threat.* Again her father winked from the bed and gave a tiny shrug. It was always like this, when push came to shove her parents always sided with each other despite their differences. Her mother reached over to stroke her father's brow. He closed his eyes like a cat being stroked. *He's enjoying this*, Anna realized with a little start. *He likes having the attention, being the cosseted baby.* Oh well, who could blame him? At least he wasn't pulling out his IVs and insisting he immediately go home.

From the bedside phone, Anna booked a return flight to New York. She would just have time to drive home, get her suitcase, call a cab and make her flight. Her mother, and perhaps her father, looked instantly relieved.

When Anna, exhausted, let herself into her apartment, she found Alan and the pianist seated cross-legged on her floor passing a set of headphones back and forth between them as if sharing a joint. Maybe they'd done that, too. What was his name? Edward? He got to his feet stiffly—almost as stiff as his neck in its snowy white brace. When he stood up, he yanked the headphones off sharply giving his neck what looked like another painful twist. His glasses flew to the floor. Alan worried at once about the headphones and quickly checked them to see if they still worked, which they did.

"We were just listening to some music," the redhead stated the obvious. "I guess this is your apartment. It's very nice. Mine's more of a cave."

"Don't move. Your glasses are right by your left foot," Anna told him. He promptly shifted a large foot and stepped squarely onto his glasses. They broke with a sickening crunch.

"Hey, now you're both blind and deaf." Alan made one of his bad jokes. "I told him anybody with ears should know about Didier Lockwood."

Anna felt an unexpected wave of pity. The redhead stood like a flamingo, lifting the offending foot to balance on one thin but well-muscled leg. The biking, probably.

"Let me get your glasses," she volunteered. "What's left of them. Do you have an extra pair?"

"I'm afraid not," the redhead muttered miserably, sounding on the verge of panic. "Maybe I can tape them or something."

By this point, Anna had retrieved the glasses and held the mangled offending article dangling between her fingers. A lens popped out and plopped to the ground where it skittered across the hardwood floor and came to rest under the radiator.

"They're really wrecked," Alan observed. "You won't be able to see a note until you get some replacements."

Even in childhood, Alan had always cracked lame jokes whenever he was nervous—and he was nervous now, plainly. Late to the party, he realized that his sister might not like having a stranger in her apartment, perhaps listening to her messages. Alan knew she kept her profession a well-guarded secret from her neighbors.

Right on cue, Anna's professional line rang and her message began. Anna dove for the machine, and shoved down the volume, lest it instantly divulge her occupation. Listening closely, she could still make out the message. It was Nathan calling her for the third time. Now he sounded snappish and irascible. "Listen," he said on her machine, "time may be different on the other side but you could at least have the civility to call me back. My mother, or something, is driving me crazy and you're the only medium I know."

The beans are certainly spilled now, Anna thought, glaring at Alan. At least they would have been if Edward weren't too stunned to pay attention. The redhead was standing on two feet now, blinking into space. He did look stunned. And his eyes were remarkably blue. Edward seemed to be in shock, focused on the catastrophe of his broken glasses. Perhaps her secret life was secret after all.

Anna spoke calmly and evenly, exactly like their mother, she observed in passing. First, she directed Edward to the love seat normally reserved for clients. Second, she told Alan to shut up or go back to listening to his goddamn music. Third, she set the mangled glasses on her little reading table and reached under the radiator for the missing lens.

"Goddamn it. Goddamn it," she exclaimed, emerging from under the radiator with a burn on her now soiled arm. She would have to use the Dust Buster more often, she thought. Her arm stung.

"I-am-going-to-try-to-tape-your-glasses," she explained to the redhead in remedial English just as her mother had spoken to her father.

The redhead half nodded, although with that neck brace he couldn't do much of anything. "Good idea," he finally managed to spit out. *No one was mentioning anything about ghosts,* Anna noted with relief. *Perhaps she really had reached the machine in time. Perhaps the men were too preoccupied to hear it anyhow. Still, she could kill Alan.* She could just murder him. So much for her carefully guarded privacy.

The glasses proved quite a project. One side stuck far out at a skewed angle and she couldn't get the loose lens to pop securely back into its socket. The frame was broken. Working with the extra-wide tape from her plastic box of school supplies, Anna managed to achieve a goggles effect. When Edward slipped the glasses back on, again hiding his beautiful eyes, he looked like a scuba diver in a neck brace.

"I did the best I could," Anna said defensively.

"Hey. Don't sweat it. I can see out of one eye," Edward answered with some self-deprecating humor or chivalry.

"My sister could take you to get some new ones," Alan volunteered. "She wears contacts, you know, but she has glasses."

"Now he knows nearly everything," Anna hissed, shooting Alan a warning look to which he was clearly oblivious.

"I could take you to my optometrist late tomorrow afternoon," Anna caught herself volunteering, surprised as the words spilled out of her mouth. Was she up for sainthood?

"I'll need to do something, sooner rather than later. I know it's Halloween and you might already have plans. But I need to be able to read music."

"I'll pick you up in the lobby at three-thirty," she told Edward. The less she said to Alan right now, the better.

Chapter 40

The following day, Anna arrived home tired and crabby. Her classroom had been a zoo all day, the children keyed up from their costumes and the sugar highs they got from Halloween candy. Jeremy, Abby and Dylan brought to school a stash of candy corn which they shared among themselves—if pelting each other with candy could be called sharing. When they carved the class pumpkin, Jeremy slimed his nearest neighbor with pumpkin goo while Dylan and Abby shot sticky seeds at each other. Even without Harold peering through her classroom door, Anna had felt out of control.

On the walk home, it was worse than usual, trying to distinguish the genuine weirdos from the weirdos for a day. Yes, she was hot, she was bothered, she just wanted to go upstairs, listen to her messages and calm down. Then, a tranquil night of laundry—her guilty pleasure—far from the madding crowd. But first, her business with Edward. Now where was he? That was when Anna registered the music pumping unrelentingly into the lobby from underneath the door to apartment 1E. "E" as in "Edward," she thought, still thinking like her day job as teacher. *Hurry up, E as in Edward*, she thought peevishly, but the music continued. After five restless minutes she tried knocking at his door, to no avail. Defeated, she slumped onto the lobby's one worn velvet bench. She rested her head against the cool marble flank of the lobby's faded glory and she closed her eyes as she surrendered to the music washing over her. *He's really very good*, she thought reluctantly. Or maybe it was just the music itself, simultaneously playful and celestial. *Does the music of the spheres sound like this?* She wondered. *Do musicians, like mediums, live close to the veil?* And that's when the rhapsodic music suddenly stopped. After a moment or two, her eyes snapped open. There he was in the lobby, staring down at her, keys in hand. He was certainly tall.

"That was fast," she exclaimed defensively.

"You mean I'm late? I'm sorry. It's that tricky third movement," he trailed off. "Too late to apologize, I suppose," he tried again. "Were you waiting long?"

Anna drew in her breath. He'd caught her listening, or nearly. She could still feel a half smile on her lips. *Get a grip*, she lectured herself. *It's just music.* The redhead was saying something as she tuned back in.

"And I like the cat whiskers." He was definitely flirting.

The cat whiskers! She'd forgotten about the cat whiskers. She'd drawn them on to placate her third graders since she wasn't wearing a costume. How could she muster any dignity if all the time she was wearing cat whiskers? Furious, she rubbed at the whiskers with a balled up fist. She'd made them with eyeliner pencil in the little girl's room mirror. There were six of them, three on each side, straight as tiny pokers.

"Are they off?" she demanded.

"No," he said, "just smeared." And then he grinned, a lopsided antic smile. Anna scrubbed at the whiskers until Edward nodded they were gone.

Even with the scuba diver glasses perched on his nose, he looked charming in a cockeyed 1930s Jimmy Stewart sort of way. Anna loved old movies. She got her supply from Hollywood Video, right across the street, and from her perspective they were far more fun than dating. Give her Jimmy Stewart over some oversexed yuppie any day.

"You're staring," Edward said. "That is, I think you are." A large hand flew to his face where the glasses were dangling now at strange angles. "Your tape held up long enough for practice," he said.

Normally, Anna would not have held hands with a stranger but it seemed the simplest way. The glasses were beyond repair and he was blind without them. And so, as though he were one of her charges lost on the way to the bathroom, she simply took his hand and led him out onto the street.

"Just hold my hand and you'll be fine," she said.

"I'm sure I will be," he laughed. Anna almost snatched her hand from his but his piano hand clutched her much smaller one with a tensile strength.

At the subway turnstile—they went down the stairs at 86th and Broadway, Anna urging him to watch his step—the redhead insisted on paying. From a battered wallet, he took a MetroCard and swiped it once for each of them sending her ahead with a little shove, saying "Ladies first." Despite herself, Anna felt a little thrilled at Edward's chivalry. Accustomed as she was to Alan's thoughtlessness and Harold's agendas, it was touching in an old-fashioned, courtly way, to have a man extend even the smallest courtesy. *Anna, get a hold of yourself! It's just a subway fare, for God's sake, and you* are *doing him a favor.*

When the number 1 train came, they hurried aboard. The train was crowded with regular passengers and the occasional witch, vampire or monster dripping gore.

Edward and Anna clung to overhead handles. As the train lurched and jostled them, their bodies were thrown together. Anna got the distinct impression Edward was enjoying this. For that matter, so was she. It was a little bit like a high school mixer, the titillating sexual contact of a slow dance with a boy you barely knew. It was her overheated imagination, Anna was sure. Weren't classical musicians something like monks? Weren't all their passions focused on their instruments?

At Times Square, where the train converted to express and sent them hurtling south and against each other even faster, Anna had a sudden sexual fantasy. With his oversized piano hands, Edward was carefully unbuttoning her blouse. In her fantasy his hands knew exactly what to do, as if playing a sonata on her body.

Anna! I said, get a hold of yourself! She snapped out of it, but not before her face flushed and she was hurled against Edward's chest. He smelled of Dial soap.

"Sorry it's so intimate," she managed to sputter.

"Oh, I'm not," Edward blurted. He gave her a huge smile and started laughing. Was he laughing at himself? At her? Did he find her amusing? *Damn him, then.* Anna planted her feet more firmly and resolved not to be thrown against him.

They exited at the 14th Street stop, at 13th actually, across from what Harold had pointed out as the Gay and Lesbian Center. Clutching Edward's hand, Anna felt defiantly straight—and they certainly looked the part, holding hands like moonstruck lovers.

Her optometrist was on West 11th Street in a tiny shop sandwiched between a Korean grocer and a mystery bookshop.

"Here we are," she told Edward who surrendered her hand and stumbled as he held open the door.

"Edward, you are blind as a bat," her optometrist, Dr. Willis, announced cheerily. Anna favored him because he was blunt, direct and very reasonable—also fast.

"I am," Edward concurred.

"Sure you won't try contacts?" Dr. Willis asked. Dr. Willis was a mild, gray-haired man, as tall as Edward but stooped—perhaps from years of bending over patients.

"No thanks," Edward declined. "Just glasses, thank you. Do I need to pick a frame?"

With Anna's help, Edward picked a far less nerdy pair of glasses. Instead of black plastic—his ruined ones looked like Buddy Holly's—he selected a pair of gold-toned wire rims. They made him look distinguished, and perhaps a little intellectual.

Waiting for the glasses to be made up, Edward and Anna walked the few blocks to Tea and Sympathy, a popular "British" café on Greenwich Avenue. There, for the cost of a full meal at the Greek diner, they enjoyed two cups of tea in tiny China cups and one piece of carrot cake with gooey cream cheese frosting. Even when they sat down, Edward continued to hold her hand for dear life. Anna herself was near-sighted, slightly, but her contact lenses remedied that. Edward was both very near-sighted and very astigmatic. As Dr. Willis had so cheerily put it, "In any other age, you'd have been biologically selected out."

"Thanks," Edward had replied gamely.

Over Edward's straightforward cup of orange pekoe and her own more exotic Yorkshire gold, Anna learned he was from Wilton, Maine, did *not* come from a musical family, and that his neighbors, or his parents' neighbors, the Olivers, a childless couple, had allowed him to practice on their piano and had driven him the six-hour round-trip to Boston every Saturday for his more advanced lessons. They were still his greatest supporters, he reported, and had remained so through his college years and his performance master's. He was now working on his doctorate and finding the academic side, as opposed to the performance side, a real grind. Edward told her all this a little like an astronaut debriefing. Anna appreciated his candor and lack of guile although she supposed that, too, was a social strategy of sorts, a nonline, as it were.

While Edward held her hand a firm captive, Anna reflected that he really should invest in contacts. That, and a good haircut to tame his unruly red hair. Between the glasses and the wild fire-engine coiffure, he looked like a mad scientist. *Maybe classical musicians were even more like mad scientists than they were like monks*, Anna speculated. Edward certainly gripped her hand in a nonmonklike fashion.

When it came time for the check, Edward again insisted on paying, counting out the amount carefully in single dollar bills, calculating precisely a 15 percent tip and recording the final sum in a tiny pocketsized notepad that he evidently carried for just such purposes. In order to accomplish these transactions, Edward had to relinquish her hand. *Good*, Anna thought, *now we look less like a greeting card for young love in the city.* (She had been aware of the misleading look of them all through the carrot cake.) Edward seized her hand again and allowed her to lead him back into the street. They headed back to the optometrist's.

In his new wire-rimmed glasses, Edward looked like Strelnikov, the young Russian radical in *Dr. Zhivago*, one of Anna's favorite movies. The glasses disappeared into his well-boned face. He was suddenly handsome—not that he noticed. Edward was very busy testing the glasses out. He pulled a carefully folded piece of sheet music from his back pocket and scanned the tiny dense notes from several different angles. Then he read and reread the tiniest, finest print on the eye chart.

"I'm a pianist," he had explained to the optometrist. "I absolutely must be able to see."

"You musicians," Dr. Willis chuckled sympathetically. "I would tell you to try laser surgery but it's still too much of a risk."

"Beethoven was deaf, not blind," Edward joked. Dr. Willis went into an elaborate dissertation on focal planes, depth of field, high light, low light and contrasts. He and Edward might have been conversing in Mandarin Chinese.

"Try them for a few weeks," Dr. Willis finally advised, "come back if you need to." He had never made such an offer to Anna, whose contact lenses were a matter of simple vanity.

By the time they emerged from Dr. Willis's office, twilight had already settled. Jack-o'-lanterns glowed in apartment windows, gap-toothed, smiling pumpkins leered from store fronts. The streets were crowded with a high-pitched manic energy.

"Queen for a day," Edward surprised Anna by observing. He nodded toward the high-heeled gaggle of evident females clattering toward them. All wore showy outfits Liza Minnelli and Diana Ross would have envied. In fact, several of the drag queens did bear a striking resemblance to both Liza Minnelli and Diana Ross.

He's hipper than he looks, Anna thought to herself about Edward. Edward did look hip now, or nearly. With his newly restored sight, he had an intense hawklike quality. Anna found herself missing his former helplessness and docility. There was something cute about his being a little muddled instead of hyperfocused, as he was now. *They probably have to have extreme powers of concentration*, Anna found herself speculating, *in order to learn all that music.* Edward took her by the elbow and guided her across the Mardi Gras parade 6th Avenue had become.

Chapter 41

When she got home—she and Edward parted in the lobby; he all but plunged toward his piano to try out his new eyewear—Anna found a note from Alan posted on her front door for all to see. It read:

Dear Ghostbuster,

I have gone to the Village to hear Didier Lockwood. Too bad you kept Edward so long, I got him an extra ticket—on your mirror if he cares to use it.

I expect to be home before dawn. I know how you love those early wake-up calls.

Alan

Anna tore the note from her door. She hated, loathed, despised her brother's humor, inevitably at her expense. "Oh get off it," he would say whenever she complained. Speaking of which, she wanted to complain now. Edward's relentless music was flooding over her windowsill. Evidently the new glasses were working, maybe that and being out of the neck brace, mysteriously absent all afternoon.

Now that she had noticed it again, Anna found Edward's music extremely intrusive. *It isn't that he isn't good*, she thought. *Perhaps the problem is more that he is too good.* There was no not listening to him when he played. Even scales, which he set himself to now, seemed oddly compelling. There was something in the way he played that allowed her to hear the architecture of the music itself. *Oh my God*, she asked herself suddenly, *am I really beginning to have a crush on him?* The thought filled her with anxiety.

Yes, she was far better off without men, certainly more comfortable, and she believed this despite New York's multitude of attractive strangers, and despite her friend Stacy's pleas to the contrary. Speaking of Stacy, there had been a conspicuous radio silence. Stacy had not called her with her usual report of men conquered, dates accepted. Anna had called Stacy, but her voice mail always picked up. "Have you vanished," Anna had asked, "or have you finally met *him*? Call me." Radio silence had continued.

Anna carried Alan's note inside with her. There was the ticket, stuck in the frame of her bureau mirror. *I could take it down to Edward*, she caught herself thinking, and recoiled as from a hot stove. She would not chase a man.

One thing leads to another, she chided herself. Start being "thoughtful," and end up dying on the vine, pining over some impossible romance. No, she wouldn't do it. She could always use the ticket herself or offer it to Stacy—at the thought of a liaison between Alan and Stacy her mind froze. No, the less she did with

Alan's red-hot ticket the better. She had plans to do laundry and she would stick to her plans.

There was a knock at the door. It echoed loudly through her small studio's resounding silence. When had the music stopped? Were her own thoughts that loud? Was she that self-obsessed? Obviously, the answer was "yes."

It was Edward at the door. In his large piano hand, he clutched a note that matched hers from Alan.

I need to get a grip on myself, Anna thought. *He keeps getting more attractive. It was remarkable how beautiful even the most ordinary face could become when it belonged to someone you loved.* Often, on the street, Anna had noticed happy, but ill-matched pairs—the beautiful woman arm-in-arm with the stumpy man by no means handsome; the handsome man finding beauty in an unexpectedly plain consort. *Either Edward's looks are growing, or they're growing on me,* Anna realized. The thought alarmed her.

"You've got a ticket for me?" he asked.

Anna handed over the ticket and didn't say a word. As she closed the door on his newly attractive face, she realized he had said nothing to her all day about ghosts. *So he hadn't heard her telltale message clearly,* she thought. What he didn't know couldn't hurt her…

The personal line was blinking. Anna pushed Play and found Harold's last-ditch attempt to convince her to go partying. She did not call him back. Instead, Anna took advantage of the temporary lull of Alan's absence to call her father. For once, her father himself answered the phone. His voice sounded cheerful, and not at all forced. *He really must be feeling better*, Anna thought.

"So, what's new?" Anna asked.

"Oh, your mother's at it again," he replied. "She wants me to go back to church with her, back to being a practicing Catholic. Well, I practiced till I got it perfect, and then I quit. That's what I tell her, but she doesn't like my jokes. Maybe I'll go to midnight mass with her at Christmas, just to calm her down. She told me she almost got me the last rites when I was in the hospital. I told her that was dirty pool. A man has to have the courage of his evictions and I just don't like the pope's politics." Her father wound down. Anna was delighted to have heard him on a tear.

"I don't like the pope's politics either," she said. And she didn't. She didn't like the Vatican attitude on women and she certainly didn't know how to reconcile Catholicism with having a sex life.

"Can I say something terrible?" her father asked.

"Be my guest," Anna invited.

"Okay, it's this. I think your mother is having the time of her life having me as her official 'patient,'" Anna's father confided.

"You mean she's spoiling you rotten?" Anna asked.

"Oh, it's low-fat, low-cholesterol everything, but you know she does like to cook and she's bent on making me these special soups…"

"I get the picture," Anna said, "peace and harmony reigns."

"Exactly, I just may stay an invalid forever."

"Daddy," Anna protested, thinking he was just naughty enough to relish feigning an illness.

"How's your brother?" her father asked.

"The same as always." Anna answered.

"That bad?" her father joked.

"Maybe worse." She and her father laughed together over Alan's many foibles, just as they often laughed about Anna's mother, just not now in this honeymoon period her father was reporting.

"Where's Mom?" Anna asked. Not that she wanted to get her on the phone.

"She's gone to get some more supplies in. You will be coming home for Christmas?" Her father sounded wistful and Anna could tell he missed her.

"I miss you, Daddy," Anna said.

"I miss you, too. I'm sorry she sent you on your way so fast when you were home for a minute there, but it was probably for the best."

"Yes, I suppose it was," Anna conceded. She wasn't about to vent any hurt feelings. Not with her father still under the weather.

"So how's the ghostbusting business? Flourishing?" her father prodded.

"Oh, flourishing," Anna assured him. *I really should check my professional line*, Anna realized. "Look, Dad, I'll call you in a couple days and see if I am allowed to speak to you." Her father chuckled and hung up the phone.

The professional message light *was* blinking and Anna was sorry to discover Mrs. Peterson calling with a request for another talk with her husband. "It seems Howard was right," Mrs. Peterson whined, with more than a hint of self-pity and righteous anger in her tone. "I have gotten myself involved with quite a swindler. Maybe Howard can tell me how to get out of this mess, do you think so?" Anna didn't know the answer to that but she could give Mrs. Peterson another appointment and again try to make contact. Faithfully, she took the number down in her little black book. She would call her tomorrow.

Chapter 42

At five-thirty the next morning, Alan came clomping into her apartment. At the sound of the key in the lock, Anna was instantly awake and alarmed. *Get a grip*, she chastised herself, *burglars do not use keys*. Yes, she still had a midwesterner's bred-in-the-bone paranoia about life in New York.

"Rise and shine," Alan chirped manically. He was clearly prepared to give her a full blow-by-blow of his exciting evening. Anna had endured this pattern on Alan's previous visits. He came in at dawn, rousing her. He regaled her at length about the New York "she was missing," she went off to school, sleep deprived, while he slept all day, saving up chatter for when she got home. No doubt about it, Alan's "visits" were a sort of marathon, like sleep deprivation studies that hospitals sometimes conducted.

"What did you do all night?" Alan asked, not that he wanted to know.

"The laundry," Anna replied dourly, trying to climb down the ladder from her loft.

She had, in fact, really done the laundry. She had sorted, washed, fluffed and folded with Edward's features spinning on the face of the dryer. *Dear God, this is serious*, she told herself, alarmed. Meanwhile, some other, less serious, part of herself tracked Edward's probable whereabouts as he descended like Orpheus into the underground and emerged into the chaos of Greenwich Village. What if Alan used "between sets" to regale Edward with tales about his "weird" sister? She should have said something to Alan about his zipping the lip but she didn't want

131

to put any ideas in his head. No, she could only hope that Alan had been reticent for once. Maybe he had outgrown the phase where he needed to dine out on her adventures. Maybe he would discover some latent chivalry, a soupçon of tact. Maybe—

Anna was definitely distracted. She caught her nightgown on the bottom rung of her ladder and nearly went sprawling straight onto Alan who was just unrolling his bedroll in the unlikely event he intended to use it. (Anna knew that once she was at school, he slept in her bed.)

"So, how was it?" she asked, against her better judgment. All she really wanted to know was if Alan had blabbed any more of her private business. Of course, her query pressed the Play button.

"Lockwood was the greatest," Alan enthused. "He played three full sets just like they often do in Paris. His riffs were unbelievable, just fantastic." Even her friend Edward had seemed to dig him. *Her friend Edward.* And God knows what terrible snobs classical types could be. *Classical types?*

All Anna wanted to know was whether either he or Edward had brought up the issue of her mediumship. The problem was she didn't dare ask Alan directly for fear of starting a chain reaction. There was nothing worse than a triangle, Anna fumed, wondering why she herself was the one impaled by a point of it.

As Anna sipped her once-daily allotted cup of Starbucks espresso blend, Alan dropped tantalizing hints about Edward's reactions. He drank scotch, Anna learned, and nursed a single drink all night. Lockwood's inspired imagination reminded him of Mozart's inventiveness within a given form, but then, everything reminded him of Mozart and that he really should have stayed home playing.

"I get the impression the guy is really sort of like a monk, totally devoted to his music," Alan said. Anna wondered if he were really talking about Edward or indulging in a little wishful thinking about his own epithet.

If she lived on a shoestring, Alan was even cheaper, and he had remembered to buy bacon and eggs so Anna could cook him breakfast "for the duration" of his stay.

"How long is that?" Anna asked him as Alan slathered butter and apple butter on a piece of toast.

Alan grew vague. She saw he had *Time Out* beside him and had done some work with a Magic Marker circling events of interest. A lot of events, she noted with dread. While she loved her brother, she valued her privacy. And a studio apartment was a studio apartment.

"Look, Alan, I work for a living. I have this guy to see tonight, Nathan, and I'd appreciate it if you kept your stuff in one corner and gave me the house to myself from six until nine." Anna knew she sounded hostile, but it was "boundaries."

"Fine. I'll go visit Edward," Alan answered. Setting boundaries with Alan was never easy and setting them with Nathan, her prospective client, had proved not a lot easier. He had called six times in total and he sounded way too hysterical for her liking. Still, he *was* Harold's friend.

Chapter 43

Dear Mr. and Mrs. Oliver,

Last night I got down to Greenwich Village with a guy named Alan, the brother of that girl I wrote you about. We went to the Village Vanguard and heard a guy named Didier Lockwood. Next to classical music, I believe I am drawn to jazz.

Mrs. Oliver, you were right. It was good to take a little break from the piano. I do, as you know, tend to get a little obsessed when I am preparing for a competition. What did you compare me to? A monk? I hope I am a little more carnal than that. (Greenwich Village was carnal and a carnival last night, less said the better.)

Mr. Oliver, at your suggestion, I have dispensed with the Frankenstein neck brace. I suppose you are also right that it was the bike accident that reinjured my neck. Of course, I also have my share of bad playing habits that, as Mr. Mayakovsky theorizes, "might only exacerbate my condition." I think an artistic career is very much like an athlete's career. You need to handle injuries the way a marathoner learns to deal with shin splints. I'm probably a closet jock.

You'll notice among the week's receipts an expensive piece of carrot cake and two costly cups of tea at a place called Tea and Sympathy. (A "chick place" if you ask me.) It was a thank you to Anna who guided me like Diogenes in search of one honest man all the way through the subway system to get me some new glasses. Actually, they are very good. I tried them on some Mozart before I did my scales.

Sincerely yours,
Edward

P.S. I am not getting distracted, don't worry.

Chapter 44

A s she had feared, her early wake-up call had made her day's teaching an exercise in willed patience. She hated being cross with her students, and Harold had an uncanny nose for it, too. On this particular morning, he came upon her just as she was collaring Abby, who had maliciously tugged down Stephanie's shorts.

"That's enough from you, Abby," Anna had bellowed, catching her unruly student by the nape of her neck. She was tempted to dunk her at the water cooler but Harold popped out from behind a locker grinning his gotcha grin.

"Are we a little bit testy today?" he wondered at her over lunch break. Of course she was testy. She was phoning home for business messages and he was yapping away at her elbow. Couldn't he see she was concentrating?

"Shhh!" Harold raised an eyebrow just to remind her that on his turf he was boss. "Sorry," she mumbled. Harold moved a discreet distance off. There were six messages, three more of them from Nathan, wanting to move his appointment earlier. His hysteria was definitely escalating. His temper was on the march. She jotted his furious name and number, then jotted down the others.

"About this friend of yours, Nathan," Anna queried Harold before he had a chance to start in on her. She *was* tired—and crabby.

"A lovely man," Harold opened, "and quite undone since his mother passed away. I told him you worked miracles."

"Gee thanks," Anna replied.

In her experience, a big buildup was a sure recipe for disaster.

"Underpromise and overdeliver," she professed to follow Mayor Giuliani's advice. With Nathan, Harold had clearly overpromised.

When she arrived at her building after school, Anna spotted him immediately. He was perched dead center on the lobby's velvet bench. He was watching the door alertly and she just had time to think "It's Nathan," before he pounced on her, doubtless with the help of a description from Harold.

"I'm Nathan," he announced breathlessly. "I must say you're a little hard to get a hold of."

"I work," Anna said shortly. "I have a day job, with Harold?" She felt like adding, "and I have a life of my own to worry about," but did not.

She guessed Nathan to be in his mid-fifties, like Harold, but striving to look twenty years younger. He had an artificial tan, immaculately barbered hair, a small, slight moustache intended to be debonair. His shirt was crisply starched. His trousers sported knife-sharp pleats, and his shoes shone black and glossy as a new Porsche's paint job. In short, Nathan looked perfect, the precise impression he intended to project. Just looking at him, Anna felt exhausted. Nathan did not offer to carry her books.

Had Harold said it was Nathan's mother? Now she remembered. Harold had said it and so had Nathan's first relatively cogent message. Juggling her schoolbooks, far too many for a mere briefcase, Anna pushed the button for her floor.

"I expected someone older," Nathan said. "Are you sure you know what you're doing?"

Anna sometimes wondered that herself, but it was not the answer Nathan wanted.

"I've trained for years," Anna reassured him, not going into detail about her teenage years, when she had sought out every scrap of knowledge she could find in Ann Arbor, Michigan. As her sightings became more frequent, her worried father had joked, "I detect a trend," and he faithfully drove her to talk to anyone and everyone who might help her. Finally they had found Mrs. Murphy, a spiritualist of many years standing, who took Anna under her wing.

"So you're seeing ghosts, well, well, well," she had chuckled, looking Anna up and down, leaning intently on her pearl-handled walking stick. Mrs. Murphy had clear, light blue eyes in a serene, oval face. She wore her hair in a chignon like Grace Kelly during her Monaco years. Her Parisian suit was slightly dated, but still modish. Anna liked her immediately.

"I used to see ghosts. Matter of fact, I still do," Mrs. Murphy continued with an assessing glance at Anna's father. "We won't be needing you except to drive her over. She can come every Saturday from three to six," Mrs. Murphy dismissed him as superfluous.

"Three to six it is," her father gave his consent. The deal was struck almost without Anna's consent, and so it was for the next six years that Anna's Saturday afternoons were spoken for.

Mrs. Murphy tutored Anna carefully in what she referred to as "spiritual law." Anna quickly proved adroit at "receiving messages," and under Mrs. Murphy's watchful eye she learned the ethics of mediumship, and such basic survival techniques as how to get a good night's sleep.

"Spirits can be very bossy," Mrs. Murphy lectured. "They need to understand you're not just at their beck and call, willy-nilly at all hours of the day and night." And so, for the duration of her training, Anna set up a routine: a regular time daily to meditate and receive messages, an hour for study of spiritual materials, and an hour-long daily walk to keep her grounded.

After her initial glee at discovering her gifts—a period Anna later remembered as being like joyriding—Anna was grateful for the older woman's rules and regulations. They made her feel safe.

"You're the traffic cop," Mrs. Murphy often lectured her when she'd arrive at class bedraggled with fatigue. "You tell them when to come and go and not to all speak at once."

Mrs. Murphy treated the other side as a large and unwieldy kindergarten class. At first Anna was shocked, having assumed that spirits were, well, spiritual. Not necessarily so, Mrs. Murphy informed her. Not everybody learned from their mistakes. Some spirits were just as stubborn and wrongheaded in death as they had been in life—and equally demanding and bossy. Perhaps even more so since being "in spirit" gave them a certain leverage. Nathan's mother was one of those, Anna suspected.

When her building's antiquated elevator lurched to a halt at her floor, Nathan did not hold open the door for her to exit. No, the pair of them barely made it out as the elevator door slid shut behind them.

"You're early," Anna managed to say, fitting the key into her lock. "If you'd wait here…and give me a couple of minutes—" But Nathan had swept past her, entering her sanctum sanctorum with impunity. Seeing her studio through his eyes, Anna noticed the messy heap of Alan's belongings, the dead brown leaves on her philodendrons, the various stains and smudges on light switches, doorjambs, and the like. As if to say, "Well what did I expect?" Nathan heaved a deep and weary sigh. Anna hung her raincoat in the single closet. *Damn Alan*, she thought, nearly tripping over his unused bedroll. *My God, could he still be in her loft bed, sleeping?* She climbed awkwardly up the ladder clutching her skirt to her knees; the bed was empty. She and Nathan were alone—more or less. Climbing down the ladder, Anna already sensed a querulous and overbearing presence.

"Sylvia," a haughty voice announced. Anna had the mental picture of a small, imperious woman with luxuriant bouffant hair.

"I am getting the name, Sylvia," she said to Nathan who had settled stiffly into the well-stuffed Victorian chair.

"That's her," Nathan said with a mix of dolefulness, fear and excitement.

"She is small, with" —Anna searched for appropriate words— "with a lot of hair."

"It was a wig," Nathan stated flatly. "Although she always claimed she'd had wonderful hair until I was born. Do you know if it's true that some women lose their hair after pregnancy?"

Anna shrugged helplessly. "I have no experience in that realm."

"Well, she did," Nathan spat out.

"She says you're giving her dog the wrong flavor treats," Anna repeated what she heard. "Are you?"

"Well, actually, yes, she always gave him liver; I'm giving him chicken." Nathan answered defensively. "But it's just a treat. Maxie is lost without her."

Maxie was the deceased's lapdog, left in the careless custody of Nathan, Sylvia's surviving heir.

"If it's not one thing, it's another," Nathan complained. Since his mother's death, his house had been the site of what Anna would call "light poltergeist activity." Cups, saucers, dog bowls had scooted across counters and sailed through the air. There had been rappings and knockings and a nearly incessant stream of strong mental directives. Nathan's life was not his own. *No wonder he is undone*, Anna thought sympathetically.

"Your mother's quite a character," Anna said, understating it.

She got a quick mental picture of a cane. In her mind's eye, it was brandished like a weapon. "Was she crippled?"

"Not really," Nathan groused. "Or only when it served her. It took me years to figure that out."

"Mmm," Anna said, trying to be neutral. In the name of professionalism she strove not to take sides. Still, Nathan's mother was highly unpleasant, intrusive, clutchy, even domineering. She had run her son's life for years and she was determined to run it still.

"She's having a little trouble with her transition," Anna offered her professional opinion, stating the state of affairs mildly.

"You're telling me," Nathan snapped. "Do something about it."

Anna considered her options and settled on Spiritualism 101 according to Bernice Murphy.

"Tell her to stop," she said simply.

"What?" Nathan was incredulous.

"Set some boundaries," Anna suggested, quoting both Mrs. Murphy and Stacy.

Nathan looked at her as if she were suggesting he lift a semi-trailer with his pinky.

"It never worked when she was alive," he sighed. He suddenly looked every minute of his age.

"You're the traffic cop," Anna repeated what she'd learned from Mrs. Murphy.

"The traffic cop," Nathan repeated.

"It really is up to you. Simply ask her to stop."

"What about an exorcism?" Nathan asked. Anna felt his mother's irate ripple.

"I've never found it to be necessary," Anna reassured him. Nathan looked doubtful then briefly hopeful. He cleared his throat, scooting forward, hands on his knees.

"Mother, stop it," he said aloud. Then louder, "Mother, I said, 'Stop it.' So stop it. *Stop it.* You ran my life when you were alive, but now you're dead, and I'd appreciate it if you stayed that way. So leave me alone. Leave-me-alone!" Nathan's face was growing livid. A lifetime of repression was packed into very few words. Anna heard a mental door slam as his mother left in a huff.

"I'm sure she heard you," Anna interjected. "It's not like psychodrama. They do get it." The studio, and Anna herself, felt suddenly light and breezy.

"Do you have any water?" Nathan asked weakly. He, like Anna, could feel the atmosphere was clear.

Anna offered him a choice—water or the fresh mint tea she kept in a pitcher in the refrigerator. Nathan opted for tea. He even smiled at her, a shiny little boy's smile. Anna offered him Milano cookies—she loved the mint ones—and he accepted eagerly.

"My mother hated these," he said with glee.

Chapter 45

Anna was too tired and hungry to cook. What she wanted was a moment's quiet before she ventured out to the Greek diner. Naturally, quiet was not to be had. First came several sets of scales, like waves, and then, once he got warmed up, the showy and precise musical pyrotechnics she supposed must be Mozart. *Music is just like language*, Anna caught herself thinking. *Mozart was a man of many words*, Anna mused on, although whether she was thinking about Mozart or Edward himself was a moot question.

Alan used one of his bootleg keys to open the door. He came staggering in laden with an armload of LPs.

"I can't believe it," he said. "I found this guy on the street—" Alan set down an armload of old albums. The cover designs suggested the forties and fifties. "I bought practically his whole collection, Bird, Miles Davis, Dizzy Gillespie, Woody Herman, Lady Day, some Ellington—"

Perhaps noting her blank stare, Alan trailed off. "I'm starving," he said. "What's for dinner? Sounds great, doesn't he?" He hooked a thumb toward the open window where Edward's Mozart was still leaping over the sill.

Downstairs in the Greek diner, Alan continued his monologue. He stopped himself long enough to ask George the waiter what the special of the night was. The answer was liver and onions. Alan hated liver and onions. Anna ordered the special. Alan asked for moussaka. "After all, I'm in New York," he narrated his choice.

During Alan's voice-over of their evening meal, Anna learned in some detail that Edward was preparing for a competition for which he had to learn a repertoire of diverse composers, and that he was concentrating his hopes on some "finger shredding"— Alan's words—Mozart. There would be a field of more than one hundred eighty pianists. The rounds began with tapes, then if your tape got selected, as Edward's had, you made it to the second live, round; then if you were selected again, as Edward had been, you made it to the finals. And, of course, someone won. Edward?

"Like the Olympics," Anna sniffed. Competitions of all sorts

"I would have said pneumonia but he liked to be blunt. It was AIDS-related pneumonia, yes."

"He says to tell you he's quite comfortable. He says there's lots of good music."

"He loved music." Tommy was tearing up. Anna handed him her box of Kleenex. "What else does he say?"

"He says that we all go sooner or later and he wouldn't change a thing. Do you need some water?" Anna reached for the pitcher that she kept on a side table. She poured Tommy a tall glass. He sipped at it gratefully.

"I went a little crazy," Tommy finally said. "I didn't deal with things very well."

It was not the first time that Anna had been privy to a confession. Mrs. Murphy had schooled her in detachment. "Listen, don't judge," she had been taught. Now she tried to focus on the ghost, to be a clear channel for whatever it wished to convey.

"He says it was his time," Anna related. "That you just have to accept that. He says he knows you were afraid. He says he understands." Hughie, the ghost, felt calm and compassionate.

Tommy set down his glass. "Tell him I'd do it all differently if I could. I'd be more loving."

Anna conveyed the message. Then she frowned in concentration. "He's whistling something," she said. "It's from Rodgers and Hammerstein, I think."

"Oh, he just loved them." Tommy laughed through his tears. "You know how it goes, 'Whenever I feel afraid'? My father taught it to me."

"Yes, yes. That was one of his favorites! It's from *The King and I*."

"Well, he says you should cue up your CD of overtures and

147

lighten up a little. He's fine. He says he's dancing again.'"

"He's fine? Really?" Tommy swiped at his eyes with another Kleenex. "That would be so wonderful."

"Now he's singing, 'When you walk through a storm.'" Anna sang a snippet of the song. "He says, 'Don't be such a drama queen.'" The ghost was good-humored, not at all bitter or maudlin. Anna enjoyed Hughie's levity. He came through clear and warm-hearted.

"Tell him dying was dramatic." Despite himself, Tommy was smiling.

"And don't forget to watch the Tonys, he says."

"That was our favorite thing!" Tommy was sniffling happily.

"Don't forget to phone home. Don't forget to vacuum under the couch," Anna relayed the now fading messages.

"He always vacuumed," Tommy said. He took another long swig of water then reached for Anna's hand.

"Thank you," he said. "You can't know how much this meant to me." He did not surrender her hand. Instead, he lifted it to his mouth and kissed it. The little kiss felt surprisingly erotic.

"Tommy—" Anna tugged her hand free. "One thing at a time, all right? How can you even be thinking about sex at a time like this?"

"Oh, all right, but you are so cute. And I'm always thinking about sex."

"You are?"

"Doesn't everyone? I mean, if they would admit it."

Chapter 48

On Thursday, Harold sent for Anna and asked that she join him in his office during her free period. Crankily, she complied. Harold was being a high-maintenance friend lately. There were his weekly sessions with Andrew—those were professional—but also his frequent and untenable invitations. Did he really think Anna had no life of her own? *The truth is, I barely do,* Anna thought. *In between my readings, my teaching and the Greek diner, that's pretty much it. I might as well be cloistered. I'm just mad at Harold because he's called me on it.*

"How's my favorite spinster?" Harold greeted her with cheery passive aggression before she had closed the door behind her. "Or," he whispered sotto voce, "did you meet *him* yet?" Harold's eyes twinkled and her anger at him evaporated.

"Him who?" Anna countered. "Not everyone wants a *him*."

"The man of your dreams, the one my friend Alexander told you about," Harold stubbornly reminded her.

"Warned me about," Anna retorted. When she wasn't so cross, she did enjoy Harold's jibes. For that matter, she really did enjoy Harold, who now pulled two chocolate croissants from a lower desk drawer. "Tempt you?" he murmured.

Anna gave in to Harold's lure. She would never be thin, although she would never be truly fat, either. *I'm a medium, medium,* she joked to herself. She accepted a flaky pastry and a reconciliatory smile.

Harold regaled her for the next half hour with tales of the party she had missed and great costumes he had seen both at the party and afterward, on crowded 6th Avenue.

"The whole street was Men at Work," he exulted. "Men in uniforms—sailors and Boy Scouts, policemen and telephone repairmen—those might have been real."

Anna marveled at what Harold's imagination found erotic: "A whole posse of the Marlboro Man." Harold himself had gone as Gainsborough's *Blue Boy*, a choice so highbrow it was largely dismissed.

"Blue Boy with a mustache?" Anna demurred.

"I couldn't shave this thing for one day," Harold explained, stroking his thick moustache that emphasized his Cheshire cat smile.

Yes, Anna mused, nibbling on a croissant, the erotic imagination was quixotic. She caught herself thinking dreamily of Edward's piano hands and then felt a little guilty, mixing eroticism with art. And it wasn't just Edward's hands. There was the back of his neck where his orange curls curved tenderly. With a real haircut, Edward could be dangerously attractive. She was thinking about the raw material beneath his garish fluff of hair. Not to mention his legs. Anna flashed on his lean but well-muscled calves.

"Come back, come back, wherever you are," Harold broke into her thoughts. "You *have* met someone," he declared triumphantly. "You have that dreamy fuckable look on your face."

"I do not!" Anna yelped, but perhaps she did. Mercifully, the bell sounded and she went back to a classroom of less speculative students. She was trying to interest them in *Winnie-the-Pooh*, although Gerard, a colleague, had suggested she try comic books.

Chapter 49

For once, Stacy was having man trouble. It was a Tuesday night, the night Anna and Stacy ate dinner at the Popover Café and then walked over to Claremont where Anna watched Stacy's riding lesson. Truth be told, it was one of Anna's favorite times in her week. She would pull a chair up to the plate-glass viewing station window and watch as Stacy meticulously and balletically put some giant horse through its intricate paces. In dressage, the horse was cued by the tiniest and most imperceptible shifts of leg and hand. To the casual eye, Stacy sat still as a statue, her silken blonde hair caught in a snood under her helmet, her perfectly chiseled profile gleaming alabaster under the riding arena lights.

Stacy's man trouble was not her usual—too many men—but the fact that she herself had actually fallen for someone, "someone not suitable." By "suitable," Stacy meant well-heeled and well-dressed; rich, young and handsome—as most of her men were. To Anna they all looked and sounded alike, closely resembling the good-looking stag line in a thirties comedy about debutantes.

"Where do you find them?" Anna had teased Stacy. To a man, Stacy's admirers were eminently eligible, *GQ* attractive, and, more astonishing, straight.

"Oh you know, at openings, drinks after work, pretty much anywhere," Stacy answered. She was generally knee-deep in men and didn't much notice where they came from. As an investment banker in training, money lay all around her, not only in her past, but in her present and future. Maybe that explained her plethora of wealthy young men. But she had yet to explain her recent absence.

The problem was someone named Jeffrey. It seemed Stacy had gone to yet another opening and managed to fall for the actual artist and not one of his buyers.

Jeffrey was short—shorter than Stacy; balding—he wore a bandanna on his head; and tattooed—"Van Gogh," a youthful enthusiasm. He drank too much, he still smoked, and he wore filthy T-shirts and blue jeans. Stacy was totally smitten.

"I've never met anyone like him," she announced breathlessly as she bit into a crisp popover spread with strawberry butter.

"Mmm," Anna answered, carefully ladling a spoonful of three-bean soup into her mouth.

Jeffrey was a rebel. A free spirit. A married man with an open relationship, Stacy prattled on. Anna nearly choked on her soup.

"Jeffrey is a downtown cliché," she wanted to tell her friend, not that Stacy would have listened. As Harold would have noted, she was wearing "that dreamy fuckable look."

"What does Dr. Rich say about Jeffrey?" Anna fished, thinking for once she and the doctor might agree.

"Oh," said Stacy, as if she were sucking on a delicious candy. "Dr. Rich thinks Jeffrey is a wonderful idea; a real breakthrough."

"He *does*?" Anna asked, thunderstruck.

"Yes!" Stacy continued breathlessly. "He thinks it's very healthy that I finally care for someone."

Resigned to a rough six months or more while the relationship traveled its inexorable course, Anna listened to Jeffrey's virtues and thought about Edward's.

But did Edward really have any virtues over Jeffrey's? Presumably he was unmarried. But was evident celibacy preferable to promiscuity? Certainly he could give anyone a run for their money in terms of creative self-obsession. He did not, however, (at least to the best of Anna's slight knowledge) sport a Mozart tattoo.

Anna tuned back in. Stacy was still talking, oblivious to her inattention. Jeffrey had hit her like a car accident. He and Stacy had ended up in bed—"and you know I *never* do that"—on that very first night. Jeffrey's bed was located on the floor of an acre or so of expensive loft space in Tribeca. Jeffrey seemed to be an extremely successful artist. He certainly had been successful bedding Stacy. Anna considered the notion of mentioning Edward in the name of female bonding, but stopped herself. *Practice containment*, she advised herself. She was good at keeping secrets, and besides, Stacy would only load her down with unworkable theories and well-meaning, impossible-to-execute advice. No, she definitely would not mention Edward. Instead, she let Stacy rattle on, which she did at such length that Stacy had to leave cash on their table and race to her riding lesson.

Anna went home from her date with Stacy ever so slightly dispirited. She felt a little like the lumpy sidekick in a forties comedy. Not that she was lumpy, exactly. Just not as genetically tall and svelte as Stacy. Who was?

At the corner of 86th and Columbus, she heard her name. "Miss Anna, how are you? Not so good?" It was George the waiter, taking a cigarette break just outside of the diner.

"Hello, George. How are you?" He gave her a friendly smile and stubbed out his cigarette. For an instant, Anna wished that she smoked.

"Fine. Fine. Come inside, I give you a cup of tea."

Feeling like a stray puppy, Anna allowed herself to be ushered inside the diner. Her favorite booth was empty and, true to his word, George brought her a cup of hot tea.

She murmured a thank-you, but George hovered near her table, clearly wanting to talk.

"We all get lonely," he said.

"We do, don't we?" Anna answered. It seemed tactless to deny it.

"It's a big city," George went on.

"Yes, very," Anna agreed.

"It's good we have each other, a place to come," George continued. Anna knew he was recently widowed and that he missed his wife. *"Ask him for some soup,"* she heard a woman's voice in her head. *"He loves to bring you the soup,"* the voice urged.

"George, I'll have a bowl of the minestrone soup," Anna requested. She heard the voice again, *"Good for you. He's lonely."*

Spooning down the hot soup, Anna shared a quiet moment with George, who hovered nearby, not talking. As she went to pay her bill, George waved her aside. "My treat, Miss Anna." One last time, Anna heard the voice, clearly his wife's. *"Tell him it's good to have a friend,"* the voice prompted.

"Thank you, George," said Anna, slipping into her heavy coat. "It's good to have a friend."

Chapter 50

Dear Mr. and Mrs. Oliver,
First, Mrs. Oliver, I got the peanut brittle. It was delicious, not that it holds a candle to your own homemade fudge. Still, I'm not complain-

ing. I am afraid I pretty much devoured it although I did put the very last shards over vanilla Häagen Dazs this morning for breakfast. (I know. I know. But you know my sweet tooth.)

Mr. Oliver, regarding your inquiry, with Advil and acupuncture and some new playing postures, the neck is better. I shouldn't complain but the music is hard enough without worrying about my posture. My teacher, Mr. Mayakovsky, feels I am playing well and, with the help of extra Advil (which I eat like M&Ms), I am. We are now "nearly in the chute," as he says and he's stepped up my lessons, which are really elaborate coaching sessions. He said, last week, he felt like Burgess Meredith in *Rocky*. I took that to be a good sign.

No, Mrs. Oliver, I am not burning the candle at both ends. I've got a pretty solid regime, although Alan's adventures are very tempting. My sleep is good, or relatively, I'm getting in a lot of piano time and so far so good Alec, the superintendent, says about the neighbors. In some ways, he's like my personal Cerberus but he's guarding the piano, not the gates of Hell. He says the music brings the building back up a notch.

Mr. Oliver, I believe I have found a very good, and reasonable, technician to work on the piano. Again, how can I ever thank you for the use of this stupendous, truly beautiful instrument? The guy I found, named Theodor, is a Steinway specialist. I suspect he's giving me a considerable break on his fees. We spent four hours yesterday and the action is very much improved. The D above middle C remains ever so slightly troublesome.

Forging ahead,
Edward

P.S. Yes, Mrs. Oliver, I do have "a crush."

155

Chapter 51

A nna came home to Alan's wreckage—LPs in stacks on the floor—and a message light blinking on her personal line. She expected, and got, her mother's carefully modulated voice. It was a progress report on her father.

"I thought you and your brother would like to know that your father is coming along nicely," the message began. "He is feeling better and pestering me to play some chess. I think he misses Alan…"

Well, Anna thought, for once the guilt trip was aimed Alan's way. She saved the message in the slight hope that their mother's voice, and the prospect of chess with their father, would send Alan winging homeward.

Meanwhile, there was the matter of the LPs. They were fragile and should not be lying, as they were, in the middle of her studio floor. Anna began to methodically stack them along her longest wall, at a safe remove from traffic and the radiator.

Anita O'Day, she noted. John Coltrane, Freddie Hubbard, Lee Morgan, Charlie Parker, Dizzie Gillespie, Billie Holiday, Woody Hermann, Dave Brubeck, Miles Davis, and, of course, the violins, Stéphane Grappelli, Jean-Luc Ponty, "Stuff" Smith, Joe Vinuti and Regina Carter, a new "hot" jazz violinist Alan planned to see later that night. She found his note on top of the radiator.

Dear Ghostbuster,

I've gone to hear Regina Carter at Birdland. Hopefully with Edward who can't practice all the time. Home in time for breakfast.

Alan

But Edward had not gone to Birdland or, if he had, had left a credible imitator behind him. Music danced and sparkled throughout the studio's atmosphere.

No wonder I think about him, Anna thought crossly. *There's no getting away from him.* She tried closing the window but it stuck two inches from the sill. Music bubbled still through the crack— and then a man's voice cleared his throat, asking for her attention.

"I sound good, don't I?" inquired the now familiar ghost.

"He sounds good," Anna corrected him. *"Not you."*

"Yes. But he's playing my music," the ghost snapped. *"He plays it almost as well as I do myself. If you ever heard me play you wouldn't be such a philistine. I could win you over—perhaps I should."*

"Ego. This is really all about you and your ego, isn't it?" Anna demanded.

"It's not ego, the ghost argued. *It's inspiration. There are certain spiritual values to be found in music. When I was composing I felt myself in touch with some larger power. Traces of that contact survive in the music itself. Surely even you can hear it? Divine inspiration."*

"I hear noise," Anna said stubbornly. This wasn't quite true anymore, but she couldn't resist teasing the uppity ghost.

"Noise! You could listen to the angels singing and report that what you hear is noise!" The ghost was hopping mad and Anna enjoyed goading him.

"Why don't you go downstairs and talk to your protégé directly?" Anna teased. She suspected that this was a sore spot and she was right.

"That's my problem in a nutshell. You can see me and hear me. He can't. You can't imagine my frustration. Oh, he asks me

for inspiration but when I give it to him, he doesn't really think it comes from me. He discounts it. He thinks it's his imagination."

"He doesn't believe in you?" Anna prodded.

The ghost gave an audible sigh. *"Not like he did when he was little. Now I am just a historical figure to him. Once he knew I was alive but not any longer. Now I'm just a specter."*

"Well, you're certainly a bit more than that to me," Anna volunteered.

The ghost sighed again. *"Yes, your 'gifts' as you call it are very comforting."* This was the closest the ghost came to admitting any fondness for Anna herself. No, she was really just a convenience.

"If I could have some privacy?" Anna tried for a tone of authority and curt dismissal. To her delight, for once it worked.

"Oh, all right. As you wish." And with that the ghost was gone.

The studio was suddenly empty. She felt a little out of control. She would straighten up her apartment and then do her laundry. Putting things in order always calmed her mind.

Chapter 52

Down in the laundry, the concert continued, seeping in through an open window in Alec's workshop, Anna supposed. Sorting her lights from her darks, Anna thought she heard the tiniest fumble as Edward played one passage over and over, as if driving the phrase of melody into her head or his hands. Then, abruptly, the music stopped.

Anna, very uncharacteristically for her, had brought to the

laundry room a newly opened bottle of wine, "a creditable mer-lot," Alan had pronounced it. It was his house-warming gift—a sort of bribe—and she figured she might as well sip it as she dried towels and scrutinized her tabloids. Anna had made herself quite comfortable on the laundry room's sagging floral sofa. Wine, read-ing materials, her one good glass—

When she heard the elevator grinding closer and closer, she quickly swigged her wine and recorked the bottle, hiding the incriminating evidence in the bottom of her laundry basket. Edward, laundry first, entered the room on his basketball player legs. *Evidently,* Anna thought, *he likes to wear shorts, at least to do laundry.* Above his white socks and below his laundry, his well-shaped legs were naked again.

"You!" he exclaimed, before recovering himself, spilling his load of laundry onto the folding table. "I didn't think anybody would be here."

"No, I guess you didn't," Anna teased, gesturing toward Edward's bottle of Dewar's, clutched tightly in one piano hand.

"Want a shot?" Edward asked gallantly. "I've even got a glass. I'm trying to un-kink some tendonitis. The alcohol helps—in mod-eration." He materialized a shot glass from inside a sock.

"Great minds think alike," Anna smiled. She hated scotch but she liked wine. She pulled her bottle and glass out from its hiding place.

"Do you think everyone secretly drinks down here?" Edward wondered.

"This is my first time, I swear!" Anna responded. "I had a very hard day at school—I teach school—and Alan brought me this bottle, and so."

"That Alan," Edward chuckled as if he'd known Alan forever.

Then he added, "It's good to blow off steam once in a while, I think. But I don't do it very often."

He loaded his whites into the miraculously functioning second washer, added Tide, and then poured himself a carefully calibrated shot.

"Care to join me?" he asked.

"Not scotch," Anna answered, but she didn't see the harm in a second glass of wine.

Edward, disconcertingly close even at the far end of the sofa, settled in, drink in hand. He rested his stiff neck amid the pillows.

"Still hurt?" Anna asked, sipping at her wine in what she hoped was a ladylike fashion.

"Some," Edward replied.

"You don't think it was our accident?" Anna asked with a flash of guilt. It had been *his* fault, she reminded herself.

"Hard to tell," Edward answered. "It goes with the territory."

He went on to explain about playing injuries, the high rate of tendonitis, a professional risk, like carpal tunnel syndrome among computer operators. So far, he did best holistically—that and he popped a lot of Advil. Scotch helped, too, he added, but only in extreme moderation or he could feel a diminution in his motor skills the next day.

"It's called a hangover," Anna joked. He laughed at her joke. Feeling just a little like a lush, Anna poured herself a third glass of wine. Edward poured himself a second stiff shot. Through a glass darkly, everything looked brighter.

It was the alcohol, Anna thought half-gratefully when she reviewed

Alan rambled on about a jazz riff as Anna and Edward hurriedly pulled their clothes on—Anna used the bathroom, but Edward,
who grew up with a younger brother, dressed as casually as if he
were in a locker room. He didn't seem the least disconcerted by
Alan's intrusive presence. Anna had that privilege all to herself.

"Will you shut up!" she willed her brother silently, but no:
Regina Carter had been "just fantastic" and Birdland itself "a total
blast." Edward seemed interested, pulling on his geeky white
socks, tying up his sneakers.

"Are you going to make us bacon and eggs?" Alan wanted to
know. Did she look like a short-order cook? Not in her pink ve-
lour robe, which was intended to make its wearer look "cuddly as
a bunny," as its original tag had said.

"Sure," Anna said in a sullen tone. Edward flashed her a glance.
Anna couldn't quite decipher it. Was it conspiratorial or disapprov-
ing, and exactly who was he bonding with, her or her brother?
She could picture the two of them getting a hearty shared laugh
out of her paranormal activities. Edward was probably as skepti-
cal and tongue in cheek as Alan. They were certainly fast friends,
real buddies.

Just last night, Anna felt herself blushing to match her robe,
she and Edward had been the ones talking. They had talked so
easily and so well. Unlike Alan, Edward also knew how to listen.
Conversation had volleyed effortlessly back and forth—thanks to
the liquor, perhaps, and before the kiss. She was just about to arrive at the conclusion that she was a fool and a slut when Edward
unmistakably winked at her over Alan's talking head.

So he's okay with it, Anna thought, cracking the first of the
eggs. *I'm the neurotic one. Then again, I'm the girl and he's the
boy.*

Chapter 53

Dear Mr. and Mrs. Oliver,

The Mozart goes very well—that straight from my teacher's mouth, who delivered one of his rare compliments. I am figuring out that exasperating third movement. "A good strategy," I'll tell you my teacher's precise words. I remind myself that Mozart was a piano prodigy. My difficulty may have been easy for him. After all, he was playing concerts at age six! Not too mention writing duets for him and his sister Nannerl. What was it Emperor Franz Josef told him? "Too many notes"? Well, not for Mozart, just for the rest of us.

I'm sorry I wasn't in last night when you called. I was probably down doing my laundry. I am getting to know a few people in the building. Alan, and his sister I told you about, Anna. They are both very nice. Did I mention that Alan was just visiting? He actually lives in Kalamazoo, Michigan, where he makes violins. I picture Kalamazoo, or its outskirts, where he lives on a farm actually, to be a little bit like our own Wilton, Maine. Alan tells me it's rustic enough to make New York look very good. That sounds like Wilton, don't you think?

Yes, Mrs. Oliver, the trees in Central Park are almost "gone." There are Thanksgiving cutouts in the pharmacy window and my Greek diner has a big gobbler right on the door as you go in. "Turkey drumstick with all the fixings" has appeared on the specials menu and I think I'll try it.

I saw Mr. Choo again who said I had too much "chi"—that's life energy—stored in my back, arms, shoulders, and hands. I explained again that I was a pianist but I'm not sure it got across the bridge. In any case, the neck is better, although last night I may have slept on it funny.

Sincerely yours,
Edward

P.S. I do remember my vitamins, thank you, Mrs. Oliver.

Chapter 54

At first, Anna kept expecting that she'd run into him. In the laundry room (sigh), in the lobby, at the Greek diner. But after their indelible evening, Edward was nowhere to be seen—just heard. From first light until well past her bedtime, his music poured forth. She heard it when she waited for the elevator. She heard it in her apartment as she tried to focus on clients. One day passed, then another, and a third. Anna began to get paranoid. *He could call and say thank you—or something. Would "How are you" kill him?* She had remembered to give him her number, hadn't she? Yes, just as he was leaving, she had. She was certain. A fourth day passed, then a fifth. The music continued, and so did Edward's conspicuous silence. Anna's paranoia settled into a dire certainty.

At least he hasn't blown town, even if he's obviously avoiding me. Let him bury himself in his work; I can do the same thing, Anna thought caustically as the music from under the door of 1E-for-Edward serenaded her as she waited for the elevator.

At home, of course, there was no getting away from his music, even if he wasn't calling her, even if he didn't do her that fundamental courtesy, he was still, unmistakably, there. It was November. Her sticky window could now be closed, but there was the matter of ventilation and, perhaps, a certain masochistic fascination. A few days gathered into a week. Now Anna began to dread running into him. What would she say? Clearly, he wasn't interested in a relationship with her. Theirs had been a one-night stand, an alcohol-induced fling, nothing meaningful, as it had seemed at the time. Anna took particular care with her hair, with her dress—there was her pride, after all. In case she did run into him, she wanted to look her best. She never left her apartment without a careful glance in the mirror.

Mrs. Peterson arrived for her second appointment considerably chastened in manner. Still birdlike, she now looked like someone had doused her feathers. Without any guidance from Anna, whom she barely seemed to notice, she took her perch on the velvet Victorian chair and waited for her session to begin.

What was her husband's name?

"Howard," announced a voice in Anna's head. *"I'm her husband, or I was her husband, and my name's Howard."*

"He's here," Anna told Mrs. Peterson, "your husband Howard."

Mrs. Peterson stared at her hands. She twisted her wedding band and diamond engagement ring, which she still wore. After a minute, she said, still without looking up, "You tell Howard he was right. Without him I just went wild. He was always right about me. I never wanted to admit it. After he died, I just went a little crazy. Now I think I'm teetering on the brink of disaster."

"Give him the boot," Anna heard.

"He says to 'Give him the boot,'" she repeated.

Mrs. Peterson looked up. Hope flitted across her face. "Howard's speaking to me?" she asked.

"Evidently," said Anna.

"Tell her to lose the bastard," Howard snapped. *"She hasn't signed the papers, and she doesn't need to."*

"He says you don't need to sign the papers," Anna again translated. "Are there some papers?"

Mrs. Peterson flushed. Her hands twitched at her skirt. "Securities," she answered. "I was going to sign over our securities."

"Well, don't do it," Howard boomed. *"He's a son of a bitch. You deserve better."*

Anna repeated the message. Mrs. Peterson daubed her eyes with a Kleenex from the box on the table between them.

"Tell him where to get off," Howard ranted on. *"Tell him you're on to him. If you can't tell him that, tell him I'm on to him. Tell him he'll rue the day he went after you. Tell him I'll—"* Howard paused in his rampage.

"Your husband says he'll back you up," Anna summarized. "Just don't sign anything. He'll take care of the rest." Mrs. Peterson gave a coy smile of gratitude in the general direction of the air above Anna's head.

"It's okay, Doll Face," Anna heard. She repeated the endearment.

"He always called me that," Mrs. Peterson sighed happily. "So, I just don't sign?"

"Damn straight you don't sign." Anna relayed the adamant advice.

"All right then. Tell Howard I won't." This time, Mrs. Peterson accepted a glass of mint tea. "I'll just wet my beak," she told Anna. "Why, there's that lovely music again."

Was it her imagination, or unrequited love, that made Anna think his music sounded better than ever? Now the music pirouetted and curtsied, bowed and danced on. In her mind's eye, she could see it so clearly, the bewigged, bepowdered ladies and gentlemen of another era—so like her visitor of the other night: She had nearly forgotten about her visitor.

Well, she thought brimming with annoyance, *evidently sex with Edward is a spectator sport!* Still, her mind strayed to the slope of his shoulder, the way his crimson curls had curled tenderly around her arm. Hadn't she—she had—suggested he try a more dignified haircut? Yes. "That hair," she had drunkenly suggested. "I'm sure it detracts from your playing."

"My trademark," Edward had assured her.

My God, what else had she said?

Details of the evening kept coming back to her in flashes. On the subway, home from work, she had suddenly remembered the rosy hairs on Edward's forearm, the gentle way his piano hand... She had nearly missed her stop.

Get a grip, she lectured herself. *He's probably a very fine artist and you're mooning over him as a sex object*. It was not dignified. But then, dignity had been blessedly missing on the night they'd spent together. They had seemed so comfortable, so easy and "right" that she had almost told him about her calling. Almost, but not quite. Even drunk, or nearly, she had managed to hold her tongue about that topic. Why lose Edward when she so newly had him?

Chapter 55

In an attempt to distract herself and simultaneously placate Harold, Anna agreed to accompany him to his friend's metaphysical shop on Saturday, provided he accompany her to Jeffrey's show. She owed that much to Stacy, not to mention curiosity.

Harold and Anna sat close together as the train rocketed south. With each small lurch, their shoulders would press together. Harold's shoulder was soft and comforting, not all thrilling as Edward's chest had been. *Get over it*, she lectured herself. *He clearly has.*

Emerging at Houston Street, Harold and Anna set a brisk pace east. The nippy wind plucked at their clothing. Anna wished she had worn her frumpy tweed coat which had the advantage of being warm even if it weren't sleek enough for the denizens of ever so sleek SoHo. Instead, she had come dressed in a black all weather trench coat that she hoped could pass for anonymous sleek. *At least it was black.*

"First the metaphysical shop, then your show," Harold steered them according to his own agenda. "I cannot tell you how important it is that you and Alexander actually talk with each other."

"But I've met Alexander. And he didn't talk to me. He predicted at me," Anna protested. "He was at that birthday party, remember? He was the one with the cubic zirconium earring and the purple T-shirt—"

"That was a real diamond," Harold interrupted her. "Back in the golden days of their relationship, his partner gave it to him."

"It's bigger than an engagement diamond!" Anna exclaimed.

"Exactly," Harold said. "Jay got it for him just before their commitment ceremony. Here we are."

Harold plunged down a small flight of stairs into a dingy-looking basement-level shop. The doorway was hung with a Crescent Moon sign. "Incantations," it read in Gothic script. Anna followed Harold with some reluctance. The store's interior looked both dark and forbidding. The black-painted walls were hung with capes, swords and racks of metaphysically emblazoned T-shirts like the one Alexander was wearing as he stepped out from behind a glass display case to embrace Harold and give a quick nod to her. "The Goddess Rules," his T-shirt proclaimed. It featured a headless goddess holding aloft two arms twined with snakes. Anna suppressed a shudder.

"Hello, darling. Well, I finally got her here," Harold announced in full voice.

A curtain stirred at the back of the shop. A bald man with piercing eyes stuck his tattooed head out. "Please, he announced. "I am doing a reading." *Tarot cards*, Anna presumed. A hand-lettered sign announced that such readings were available.

"So, let me show you around," Alexander took up the lead. But where could he lead them? The shop was tiny.

"This is Anna," Harold said. "The friend I have been telling you about."

"You certainly have been," Alexander sniped. "But I think I'm doing very well on my own." He seemed every bit as eager to slough off their arranged marriage as Anna was.

"His partner died," Harold explained. "I thought perhaps you could make contact for him? Maybe he could give you a psychic reading back? You could barter. You could become friends, don't you see?"

Anna and Alexander both saw very clearly that Harold was up to his usual agenda of professional matchmaking. *He should have been a booking agent, not a principal.*

"He didn't die until he nearly killed me," whined Alexander, speaking evidently of the deceased partner. "Finally, we are headed in the right direction."

That direction, as far as Anna could tell, involved Wiccan religious practices. There were goddess bumper stickers plastered on the wall by the cash register. The glass display case featured pentacle necklaces, small but ornate goblets, and a selection of wavy bladed knives. "The kris, a ceremonial knife," Alexander explained. Anna thought of human sacrifices and ghastly Mayan ceremonies, but the goddess religion was actually "festive," Alexander explained. Dancing, Beltane fucking, the works.

The curtain stirred again. "Shhh. I said I was reading," hissed the bald-pated tarot reader. Anna felt sympathy for a fellow reader, but couldn't they at least whisper?

"I hate snakes," she whispered to Harold.

"Snakes did you say?" Alexander demonstrated keen ears or keen ESP. "Oh and I must introduce you to Isis. Why I have Isis right here." With that he lifted the lid off of a glass terrarium, dipping his hands inside to come back up with a large reptile. Handling her like a feather boa, he draped his neck with the hefty weight of a rosy python. "She's very sweet," Alexander continued. "She just needs a mouse or so a week. Don't you, girl?"

To Anna's horror, Isis flicked out her tongue and gave his cheek a snaky kiss.

"Harold, get me out of here." Anna stammered. "Harold, I am afraid of snakes!"

"She wouldn't hurt a fly," Alexander whispered, then corrected himself.

"Actually? She eats them, don't you, girl? Would you like to pet her?"

Isis stretched her neck, if she could be said to have such a thing, in the general direction of Harold. He gave her an obliging little pat. Harold evidently was not afraid of snakes. Meanwhile, Anna was turning white.

"I mean now, Harold," she said on a rising note. The snake turned its head slowly and began to stretch in Anna's direction. *Maybe snakes are like dogs*, Anna thought. *They can tell who fears them and they just have to come right over.*

"Dear God, Harold, I am leaving," Anna announced. Clutching at her coat, she grappled with the door and made good her escape.

"You've met him, haven't you?" Alexander caroled after her. "Your job now is not to botch it. You haven't botched it already, have you?"

Moments later, Harold joined her out on the street. Anna was heaving like a cart horse. "I hate predictions!" she panted. "I hate being spied on. It's *my* life."

"Are you having a panic attack?" Harold inquired. He seemed amused.

"Yes, Harold, I am. Or maybe it is pure rage," Anna answered.

"C'mon. Be a sport. Actually Isis is very sweet and so is Alexander."

"I'll bet," Anna said.

Hauling Harold by the arm of his navy blue cashmere coat, which gave him the effect of a pig in a blanket, Anna dragged him toward Lafayette Street and the address Stacy had given her for

Jeffrey's show. It was an industrial loft space turned to gallery use. When they got there, a spectrally thin young woman in fashionable black tatters buzzed them in. The tiny foyer was hung with some very fine line drawings—of men's urinals. *Well*, she thought, *at least Jeffrey and Stacy would have certain interests in common.* That is when Harold cleared his throat.

"Jeffrey-What's-His-Name's paintings are in here." He was holding up a postcard advertising Jeffrey's work. The card looked like a close-up of a gaping wound. Anna was positive she could not have gotten it right.

Ah, but she had.

In the cavernous ash-gray room where Jeffrey's paintings were hung—and "well hung" as Stacy might joke—Anna found a series of outsized paintings featuring gore of many descriptions. There were spatters of blood like a Jackson Pollock. There were dire headlines like a Rauschenberg knock-off.

"Wonderful, fantastic, aren't they?" the young Morticia opined. She hovered like a vampire in the shadows.

"Riveting," Harold agreed with her. "Compelling."

Anna chose not to comment.

Jeffrey veered from one style to another but never off of his subject—mayhem in its most appalling forms. Dismembered arms, decapitated heads leering down. Anna might have been watching CNN News or *Gladiator*.

"The show is about the evanescence of life," explained the young gallery assistant. "It courageously faces the fact that we all die and that we must find meaning in death itself, rather than seeking to hide out in transcendence." *Where did she dig that up?* Anna wondered.

"That explains it then. How fascinating," Harold volunteered, egging her on.

Encouraged, the waif went on. "The entire show is really a memento mori, a reminder that our time on earth is fleeting and we must find value in whatever we can. In the face of all around us we must find a sensitive, humane response. This series is the artist's plea for world peace." *Now why didn't I know that?* Anna mentally sneered.

"I prefer snakes," Harold hissed in her ear just low enough for Morticia to miss it.

"To tell you the truth?" Anna whispered back, "So do I."

Chapter 56

The personal message light was blinking when Anna let herself in. She punched Play and discovered Stacy, not surprisingly wanting to meet and discuss Jeffrey. "It's an emergency. I need your help," Stacy had told the machine. Anna returned her call and agreed to meet for coffee and baklava at the Greek diner. Stacy got there first.

On her way outside, Anna had lingered in the lobby like some starstruck groupie lusting after Edward, who was locked away with his music behind a firmly closed door. She could barely force herself to leave. *It's like abandoning a cloud of music*, she thought. A few stray notes, like a flock of tiny butterflies, followed her all the way to the diner.

Goddamn him, Anna fumed, *maybe all those stories about male artists and their narcissistic self-absorption are true. He doesn't want a girlfriend or a relationship. He wants a fan club, the adulation of applause.* Well, she would not give it to him, no matter how beautifully he played, no matter how deeply his damnable music had sunk into her soul. She headed for the diner, delighted it was once again on Stacy's list of "allowed."

Stacy was seated in what Anna now thought of as "Edward's booth." Was that a black eye or just smeared mascara? As she took her place across from Stacy, Anna was immensely relieved to discover that is was *not* a black eye.

"I think he's in love with his wife," Stacy revealed in misery. "Her picture is everywhere, even in his bathroom."

"You're kidding," Anna sympathized.

"I am not kidding." Stacy paused long enough to order a piece of baklava. Anna ordered the same.

Jeffrey and Stacy had been seeing each other nightly. The sex was wonderful, and accomplished chiefly in Stacy's own cherry-wood sleigh bed. They'd had blissful nights of honeymoon sex... In fact, they had pretty much had sex nonstop. This was the first day after the first night Stacy had been back to his loft. Her news brief was hot off the press.

"Everywhere, absolutely everywhere."

"The sex?" Anna could believe it.

"Her picture," Stacy fumed. "She was practically watching us as we made love!"

The baklava arrived, oozing golden honey. Stacy's sat untouched. She had an appetite for love and nothing else.

"I didn't remember all those pictures being there the first time I spent the night," Stacy moaned. She shook her silken head.

"Maybe he put them up to torture you or to get the upper

hand," Anna speculated. "Maybe that first night you were just too crazed to even notice." In three huge bites, Anna finished her baklava. *I'm sublimating*, she thought. *Edward had to go and wake up my sex drive.* Now she could identify when Stacy talked about missing great sex.

The sex must be it, Stacy agreed. She'd been too blinded by passion to notice. Jeffrey was much too sensitive to indulge in random cruelty. You could tell that from looking at his paintings— *which looked like bloody car wrecks*, Anna added to herself.

"How could I do this to myself?" Stacy was wondering as Anna wondered the same thing. Her friend was much too upset to do more than pick at the gooey baklava. Anna reached across and retrieved her friend's piece. It was as delicious as her own had been.

Jeffrey had an open relationship, Stacy explained for perhaps the tenth time. The deal was, he and his wife could both sleep with anyone, they just couldn't fall in love. She had missed that part, the fine print, at the beginning.

"So you're just a sex object?" Anna ventured, wanting to be sure she had the story straight, "And he's true love?" Anna signaled for a cup of tea. One for her, and a soothing cup for her friend.

"I think so," Stacy sniffed. Now she had matching raccoon eyes. Their tea arrived, and Stacy stared into the depths of her cup as if she could read her fortune there—or perhaps see Jeffrey's. Anna reached across the table and patted her hand.

Obviously, this was not the time or the place for Anna to bring up her dilemma with Edward. This night was about Stacy and her man troubles, not Anna's own. *Clearly, Edward was avoiding her.* Clearly, she was avoiding telling Stacy anything about him. Aside from female bonding, there was her pride to consider. It had been how long now since "The Night"? *Too long*, Anna thought.

Too long. She almost told Stacy, but her romantic interlude with Edward was turning into something more sordid—an ill-advised, one-night stand. *Why tell Stacy about that? Why tell anyone? No, let Stacy continue to think of her as her man-less friend. That was far less painful than the recent truth.* If she couldn't save face with Edward, she could at least save face with Stacy.

"You've heard enough about me. What about you? Any interesting ghosts lately?"

Stacy stirred her tea and waited for an answer. Anna loved that Stacy took her vocation so in stride.

"I met George's wife," Anna whispered. "She seemed very nice."

"Well, George is nice so it's no wonder," Stacy concurred. "Anything else? You look a little different to me—your makeup, maybe, and you're wearing heels."

"Not too much that I could tell you. There's client privilege, you know." Anna sounded a little stuffy but Mrs. Murphy had always stressed the importance of confidentiality.

"I wish I had someone for you to contact," Stacy said. "Of course that would mean they'd have to be dead and the only person I want dead right now is Jeffrey's wife."

Stacy laughed at herself and Anna laughed with her. It was shared laughter that bridged their differences and made them friends.

Chapter 57

He's as good as dead to me! Anna was furious with Edward, who still evidently talked to Alan and even shared meals with him, but she was more furious with herself. How could she be so stupid as to romanticize a one-night stand?

"Stop talking about your friend Edward," Anna snapped at Alan who thoughtlessly sought to regale her with another of their adventures in musical male bonding.

"What's wrong with Edward?" Alan wanted to know.

"Everything," Anna snapped back. "Everything."

"Okay, okay, but I like him. And you seemed to like him well enough the night I went out to hear Regina Carter." Alan cocked an eyebrow to signal she was crazy.

"Well I don't now!" Anna retorted. "So just keep me out of it."

What kind of tart, idiot, fool—the list went on—would fall for a patently unavailable man? Edward was shacked up with his beloved music. He was practicing day and night. His music-making bedeviled her during client sessions. Harold's last session with Andrew had been a case in point. With Edward's soundtrack slithering through the window—still open a crack for air—Anna could barely focus on the messages and impressions she was receiving.

"You seem a little distant today," Harold ventured.

She wasn't about to tell Harold about Edward. Maybe she should have, but she hadn't even told Stacy. At first, she hadn't wanted to discuss Edward like a sexual entrée, as Stacy so often did. Later, she was too embarrassed by her own ineptitude with men, not to mention her drunkenness. No, she hadn't told anyone.

What was there to tell, really? A fling? A roll in the hay? Containment was the only dignified course.

To Alan, she acted indifferent, the key word being "acted," whenever he mentioned Edward's name, which was still painfully often. *Didn't he have any sensitivity to her feelings? No, he did not.* Clearly, they were thick as thieves. *Birds of a feather*, Anna thought bitterly. *They deserve each other.*

But what did she deserve? Surely one phone call wouldn't kill Edward. Or maybe, here was a thought, Alan had decided to divulge the lurid details of her secret life. He had certainly done it before, repeatedly. And, too, Edward had overheard her entire muted professional message, if he hadn't been too distracted, or self-obsessed to listen. *As a musician, wouldn't he have excellent ears? Even more acute than average? And if he'd missed that message, to catch Alan's gossip, he wouldn't need good ears. Any ears would do.*

Yes, Alan had to be at least part of the problem. Was he trying to establish New York residency? A woman with any self-respect would have asked him to leave, but clearly, she didn't have that. And so, battling her resentments, Anna fought to hear higher realms.

"Andrew seems kind of distant, too," Harold said wistfully.

Great, Anna thought. *Now Edward is interfering with my professionalism.* With an effort, she dragged her consciousness back to the task at hand. Her impression of Andrew strengthened. She distinctly heard the words, *"Tell him not to invest."*

"Are you thinking of investing?" she asked Harold. "Andrew says not to."

Harold looked like a kid with his hand caught in the candy jar. His Cheshire grin took on a sly quality.

"Just thinking about it," he admitted. "There's this great opportunity. An incredible return on my investment—"

"Hah!" Andrew's basso profundo boomed in Anna's ear. Sometimes ghosts were not subtle.

"He caught you," Anna translated her impression.

Harold snickered self-consciously then he confessed: He had always had a weakness for get-rich-quick schemes of all stripes. Only Andrew's conservatism had kept them out of the poorhouse.

"We had a system of checks and balances," Harold joked. "I wrote the checks; Andrew checked the balances."

"Well," Anna said, "he says not to do it and so I hope, as your friend, that you won't." Did she sound like a priss? She felt like one.

"Isn't our hour up?" Harold suddenly suggested. Clearly he did not want to hear good sense from Andrew, her, or anyone else.

Harold belted up his handsome coat and knotted a cheery cherry red muffler at his throat. "Nearly the holidays," he announced brightly. "Will you be going back home?"

"Why should I?" Anna asked. Her parents were practically on a second honeymoon. "Alan's right here."

Chapter 58

The straw that broke the camel's back was Alan's expedition with Edward out to someplace called the Knitting Factory to see someone called Ron Carter who had once played bass for Miles Davis. Alan left in high spirits. Edward was taking the night off and together they were hopping the subway to God knows where.

"Have fun," Anna said. "But I don't want to hear anything about it. Obviously you and Edward are real pals. Remember, I don't want to hear anything about him, either." She resigned herself to yet another endless evening—thankfully sans sound track, for once.

First, she would clean the apartment. With Alan in residence and her own unremitting gloom, she had allowed dust balls the size of large mice to build up. She got out her Dust Buster and started poking under the radiator. That's when she nearly sucked up the tiny Post-it note on which Alan had scrawled, "**Call Edward back.**"

Call Edward back? Clearly this note had been meant for her. Of course it wasn't dated. Anna felt an astonishing shift in the axis of her emotional universe. The sun rose on her dark night of the soul. So he *had* called her, at least once. Anna manically vacuumed all other corners and crevices, but that was the only note.

He had called her. Perhaps not immediately, but sometime. Reality began to sink in. *He had called her and she had not called him back.* Alan, the dickhead, had never thought to convey the message. More likely, he enjoyed hoarding Edward to himself. It was just possible that Edward wasn't ignoring her; she was ignoring him!

Although she knew Stacy would have called instantly, making some light joke or telling the simple truth of the misplaced note, Anna did not immediately call Edward back. Rather, she savored the "fact" of his call like a cherry-flavored cough lozenge melting slowly on her tongue. *He'd called*, she thought dreamily. *So maybe he wasn't a moron or a dope, an idiot or a lady killer.*

Possibly, conceivably, he was a nice guy with decent manners and not a self-obsessed jerk like Alan. Maybe she had just been tarring him with the same brush. What was it called? "Demonizing"? Well, she had been. Maybe, now—

Now what? Anna wondered. Certainly too much time had passed for her to gracefully give him a call. The ball was in her court, but what to do with it? She could write him a letter. That might be the best tack. Yes, a letter.

In her head, Anna began devising a long and elaborate letter to Edward that would, with charming candor, divulge her past relationship history, and the way that she had understandably mistaken him for just one more…*No*, Anna thought, *that note is pathetic. Why go into her miserable past? Better to keep the note short and sweet… "Dear Edward, so sorry I haven't gotten back to you sooner. You see, my dickhead brother Alan, the one you've been male bonding with, never gave me your message."*

…That was not quite it, either… "Dear Edward, just got your lovely message, and so have realized that you are not a self-absorbed jerk"…No, no… "Dear Edward, big of you to phone—once. Obviously our 'encounter' was merely a drunken episode to you. Thanks for nothing."

Where did this well of anger come from? What had Edward really done to deserve it? He had called her. *He probably only called me out of a sense of duty.* Wouldn't a note from her just be chasing him? Stacy, she knew, would simply pick up the phone. Stacy, further, would be rating Edward's performance instead of worrying about her own. Why, Stacy…but she wasn't Stacy. She was Anna.

That night Anna slept fitfully, caught between this world and the next. In her dream life she was at a crowded club with Alan and Edward, but Mozart, not Ron Carter, was holding forth. In her dream, Mozart played a splendid pianoforte, unfurling the precise composition Anna recognized from Edward's practice sessions. Not only the composition, but the rendition of it—the playing itself sounded uncannily similar to Edward's own. "Bravo Maestro, bravo Maestro," the crowd cheered. Mozart finished the piece to resounding applause. Then, when taking his bows, he singled Anna out at her ringside table. "He does like you," Mozart declared.

Anna woke and shot bolt upright. Mozart's voice was still echoing in her head. No, it wasn't echoing. It was forming, quite distinctly, issuing from a solidifying vapor over near the fire escape window. Bewigged and dressed to the nines as he had been on the night she spent with Edward, it was the precise figure from her dream.

"You're Mozart!"

"I am!" The apparition nodded and grinned.

Mozart, Mozart himself! she now realized, and he was speaking directly to her, as she was safely tucked in her loft bed. *Mozart!* For a moment she felt dazzled, then dismayed. She should have realized it sooner, but it was her first visitation from a celebrity ghost and she yanked her covers up to her chin, half shy, half defiant at the trespass. This ghost was arrogant. Pushy. Even aggressive. Fame was no excuse for bad behavior.

"He likes you," the apparition said clearly. *"He likes you very much."*

"What makes that your business?" Anna retorted. As usual when caught off guard, defiance was her chosen defense.

"He's my business," Mozart replied. *"Not that I expect someone like you to understand, but he is my business."*

"More like mine," Anna argued, but Mozart's ghost only shrugged. *"You were spying on us,"* Anna scolded. *"There is such a thing as privacy."*

"Vastly overrated. No fun at all." The ghost tittered at its own humor.

"You could have a little decency," Anna retorted. *"Even now. You're intruding."*

"Perhaps you don't know who I am?" The apparition floated closer. He turned this way and that for her scrutiny. He was distinctly preening. He was also distinctly familiar. Mozart!

"Perhaps who you are doesn't matter to me. Decency is decency." Anna felt her cheeks flush. *"All right. I know you're Mozart but that doesn't give you the right to come barging in here."* Anna was pleased with herself that she was holding Mozart to some standards. She didn't want his celebrity to go to her head. No, better to be plainspoken.

"It gives me every right," the ghost insisted. *"You have no idea how important your young man is to me. I'm pleased he found a little night music."*

"A little night music!" Anna sat upright, shaking with indignation. Mozart chuckled to himself, floating just out of reach. Anna chided him, *"You're nothing but a glorified pervert, a voyeur! You should be ashamed of yourself."*

"I was never good at that," the ghost laughed. With a wink, it added, *"You're good for him. So he's a little shy. So it took him a while to call. Men don't always get things right. Why, I initially thought I was in love with my wife's sister! Give him another chance, what would it hurt?"* On that note, the ghost vanished.

Anna snapped on her tiny bedside light with the beaded shade. She stared, astounded, into the dark and empty space where Mozart had been. He was truly gone, just as he had been truly there. Mozart! Mozart himself. Mrs. Murphy had not prepared her for this. Why, even Mrs. Murphy might not believe her, might wonder if her "gifts" hadn't gone a little to her head. To be honest, Anna wondered that herself. She had always looked down on new-age channelers claiming to speak for entities sixteen thousand years old. Mozart was younger than that, but just as unbelievable. Accustomed as she was to ghosts, she wasn't accustomed to *this* one.

Alan's key turned in the latch. Anna was ready to let him have it about the note but caught herself laughing; she had bigger fish to fry. *Give him another chance, Mozart had said. She just might. Just as soon as she figured out how.*

"Is that you?" her brother asked incredulously. "Awake, in the flesh, and laughing?"

"It's me," Anna confirmed. Her tone was gay and welcoming.

"Usually you're just so self-obsessed lately," Alan accused her, a case of the pot calling the kettle black. "I won't tell you we had a good time."

It was four-thirty in the morning. Anna would be exhausted at school the next day but she didn't care. Scrambling down her loft bed ladder, she volunteered to make Alan eggs benedict, his favorite. He had thoughtfully purchased the ingredients as a very broad hint.

Chapter 59

Dear Mr. and Mrs. Oliver,
I did burn the candle at both ends. Last night, Anna's brother Alan took me out to this joint called the Knitting Factory. It was very hip and I even felt that way myself. It's strange to think how Mozart was maybe the Miles Davis of his time.

Mr. Oliver, the neck is okay right now. I wouldn't say great. I have been putting in some pretty long hours and that may set it off. The competition looms ahead of me and I am working to be ready. I have an appointment tomorrow with Mr. Choo and I have been doing those exercises your sports medicine man gave me. What a dope I was to try that hook shot and then not to give up the bike. (From now on, I'll let my brother be the jock.) Thank you for your patience with me.

Sincerely,
Edward

P.S. Mrs. Oliver, my friend Alan tells me there's a Miles Davis quote, "Don't fear mistakes, there are none," but I may have made one with Alan's sister Anna. Cross your fingers for me that it works out somehow.

Chapter 60

Anna spent her school day in distracted obsession. Instead of thinking about her lesson plans, she thought about Edward, Edward and Edward. *Too much time has passed now to return his call*, she worried. And yet, what kind of a slut would he now take her for, casually screwing him like some bad episode of *Sex and the City*? He was sensitive. *To play the way he does he has to be sensitive, doesn't he?* Anna thought. How, she wondered, could she have ever thought him otherwise? She'd been absurd, paranoid, desperately overreactive.

Of course I have, Anna thought with a passing flash of compassion for herself; her track record with men was both dismal and sketchy. Thoughts like these eddied through her head the entire day, leading a rambunctious classroom to slip inexorably out of her control. One of her colleagues must have complained about their noise level because Anna saw Harold's nose pressed curiously against the glass window of her classroom door. He waggled an eyebrow.

I'm going to get reprimanded, Anna thought, *and I don't care.*

That was when Jeremy, ever one of her more rebellious students, balanced on a desktop and went crashing to the floor, writhing in the aisle in what turned out, fortunately, to be mock agony.

"Into your seats; back at your desks," Anna ordered, but clearly the tide had turned against her. Her directions fell on deaf ears. Someone—Abby?—hurled an eraser. She would be lucky to make it out alive. Her class demanded every scrap of her attention. Clearly you couldn't balance even a soupçon of a romantic life, against a crowded classroom.

When she got home from school—the lobby was again filled with Edward's impassioned music—Anna found Alan just taping up the second of two large cartons intended for UPS.

"I'm going home," Alan announced. "I've run out of money and I'll see you in a few weeks anyhow."

It was the first time that Alan had seemed to notice her, other than as a short-order cook with a convenient crash pad.

"Why will I be seeing you?" Anna asked, stunned by the thought he might be going home to earn some money and then heading straight back.

"It's nearly Christmas," Alan informed her.

"What happened to Thanksgiving?" Anna countered. Where had the month gone? Could she have missed a major holiday?

"A low-rent, second-rate, uninspired-holiday," Alan opined. "Although I do like pumpkin pie. It's three days from now, earth-to-Anna and three weeks after that you usually fly home. Am I reaching you?"

"You're not being fair," Anna moaned. "You're the one who's normally in outer space."

"Sticks and stones can break my bones," Alan mocked. "But words can never hurt me."

Anna held her tongue. Alan always won their squabbles, managing to get the last, and most of the other, words anyway. He was launched now on one of his typical diatribes. She'd been moonstruck, Alan informed her. Sappy and out of it. Worse than usual, when she was simply communing with ghosts. She was bad enough, but Edward was worse. "Your sister," was how he began every third sentence, and this when he was telling Edward something important, some salient fact about the Marsalis family (Wynton, Branford and Ellis) for example. No, frankly, even if he hadn't run out of money, Alan had had six bags full of young love gone awry. Let her live her life. Let Edward lead his. He was going back to Michigan to build violins and practice the *art* of violin making—"Art," he recalled, was the name of someone else she had briefly dated. Alan ranted on and on, his scathing voice-over breaking over her head like gentle waves. *So Edward thought about me, actually talked about me,* Anna thought dreamily. Alan could have managed to tell her that much before now, but no.

"Would you care to tell me exactly why you never told me Edward *liked* me when you were seeing him all of those times?" Anna spoke carefully, aware that she was perilously close to one of Stacy's "confrontations"—aware, too, that her brother hated being cornered.

"I didn't tell you," Alan answered defensively, "because I didn't tell you. I mean, what's the big deal? You asked me not to talk about him." A family therapist would have had a field day with this piece of sabotage, but Alan himself seemed oblivious.

"I asked you not to talk about him since I was afraid he wasn't talking about me. Or that if he was talking about me, you were telling him all about my ghostbusting. You *do* have a big mouth when it comes to that."

"Oh, for God's sake, Peter was a jerk. Give me a little credit, would you?"

"What about Bud? What about Brendan?"

Alan smiled slyly. His eyes cut to one side. As usual, he deflected a head-on confrontation by deflecting her attention to another subject.

"I've called UPS. Alec will get these on the truck if you'd be so kind as to help me lug them down to the lobby," Alan said. He was stuffing his sleeping roll into a duffel bag, yanking at its extra-strength zipper. The subway to Grand Central, a shuttle to LaGuardia, a flight leaving in three hours. She could say good-bye to Edward for him or maybe he would knock on the door, not that Edward would hear him.

Ah, yes, the music! It cavorted near her ceiling like the scattered multihued reflections of a crystal catching the light. Edward was practicing. A good-bye would break his concentration. Didn't Alan have any respect for his privacy and need to focus? No, of course not. *My God, the music is sublime.*

Tugging and heaving, Anna managed to get one box of precious LPs to the studio's door and then out to the elevator where she punched the button. Alan was doing a last minute "idiot check." He came out the door with his duffel bag, the other box of LPs and a tattered, coffee-stained copy of *Time Out New York*, his bible. Together they rode down to the lobby where Alan went directly to the door of 1E. He pummeled the door with his fist. The music stopped. Anna stood frozen in her tracks. Thank God she had done her makeup. Edward swung open the door.

"Anna!" *Was Edward always so thin? He couldn't live on music alone*, she wondered with a little shock.

"Yes. Hello." Face to face with Edward, she found herself nearly mute.

"Yes?" Edward looked ghostly pale, an effect emphasized by his stiff white neck brace, incongruous over a ratty gray T-shirt and the torn-at-the-knees chinos that had survived his biking accident.

"I'm leaving," Alan announced.

"He's leaving," Anna echoed, wishing desperately she'd worn a different dress, or at least taken the time to comb her unruly hair. Frankly, she looked a little wild, but not, she thought, as wild as Edward. They stared at each other over Alan's shoulder. Alan gave Edward an awkward hug and pounded him manfully on his tender back. Edward winced, which Alan misinterpreted.

"Yes, I'm sorry to see me go, too," he told Edward. "But I'll be back and by then you might have a little more free time."

"Bye, man," Edward mustered, sounding surprisingly hip.

"Got to go," Alan cut him off. "Back to your salt mines." He helpfully slammed the door right on Edward's face. Anna stood frozen in place, stupefied by their encounter. On autopilot, she kissed her brother good-bye. Edward's slammed door rose like a canyon wall, towering and impassable. As she punched the button to ride back upstairs, the music started again.

"Now what?" Anna asked herself as she reentered her suddenly lonely apartment. As if cued, her professional line rang and her carefully modulated professional voice answered. "This is Anna…"

Chapter 61

Dear Mr. and Mrs. Oliver,
I'm afraid the neck is really a mess. My teacher is convinced that new playing habits are the answer. It seems he went through something similar himself. At any rate, he is coaching me on two fronts these days: my approach on the music for the competition and my approach to playing in general. I am really on countdown about the competition. Every day that passes is one less day "until." Maybe I shouldn't be taking such a make-it-or-break-it attitude, but I am afraid that I am. Winning would be a real miracle. The whole shebang is even going to be on the Internet. Do I sound a little daunted? "It all goes with the territory" is all Mr. Mayakovsky says. God knows he knows and I'm lucky to have him, stern taskmaster that he is.

Mrs. Oliver, since you asked, I am bored to death with work on my thesis. I'm afraid I've just lost interest. All I really want to do is play (the piano). Still, I will finish it somehow and your hints on writer's block are very helpful—just like Mr. Mayakovsky's hints about my neck.

Mr. Oliver, your sports medicine man says he is running out of options. Mr. Choo says approximately the same thing, although he does know a hypnotist whom he thinks might be able to help me. Maybe I can be hypnotized into playing without pain.

My friend Alan left yesterday. I think I really botched any chances for friendship with his sister Anna—you don't have to know the details. For a thirty-two-year-old man, I can act like a stupid kid.

Mrs. Oliver, do you think going into music so early may have stunted my psychological growth? Or did I do that myself without any help?

Sincerely,
Edward

Chapter 62

Mrs. Murphy answered on the fifth ring. The old lady's voice was elegant and welcoming. "Hello," she said, "this is Bernice Murphy and who are you?"

"It's Anna," Anna announced. "I think I need some advice. Do you have a minute?"

"For you, I've always got a minute, my dear. Now what seems to be troubling you?"

"Do I sound that bad? I suppose I could. I mean I guess I do. I mean, I think I have a crush on someone and I don't know what to do about it. Should I just be waiting for destiny?" Anna ran out of breath.

"A crush?" Mrs. Murphy sounded delighted, as if Anna had just given her a lovely present. "Why a crush is lovely. And a crush can certainly be part of destiny. Have you told me about the young man?"

"He's that pianist I told you about," Anna confessed. "The one who is driving me crazy."

"So he's still driving you crazy, just in a different sense?"

"Exactly." Anna felt relieved to be understood.

"What seems to be the problem?" Mrs. Murphy prodded gently. "You like him. He likes you."

"Yes."

"Am I missing something?" Mrs. Murphy was trying to be delicate in her questioning.

"He called me and now I am afraid to call him back. You see, I didn't get the message. Alan didn't tell me—"

"That Alan!"

"Yes. Alan didn't tell me and now forever has gone by and—"

"How long is 'forever'?"

"Maybe a week. I feel like an idiot. I mean I know I should just call him."

"Yes. That's the modern thing to do, I understand." Mrs. Murphy's voice trailed off suggestively.

"You mean I shouldn't?" Anna felt both relieved and upset. She didn't want to call, but if she didn't call, how would they ever get together?

"Why not let destiny play a hand?" Mrs. Murphy suggested mildly.

"Destiny?" Anna felt a surge of exasperation. She wanted to say she didn't believe in destiny. "Does destiny boil down to playing hard to get?"

"It's been known to work. Give it a try, dear." And with that, Mrs. Murphy rang off.

A long walk in the park did nothing to improve Anna's perspective. She looped the reservoir once, then angled south toward the rowing lake. She stood, forlorn and windblown, on Balcony Bridge and watched as a small flotilla of ducks made their way across the lake's surface. The ducks looked self-possessed and purposeful. Bundled into her tweed overcoat, Anna looked like Little Orphan Annie. Trying for a state of meditative calm, she only arrived at more confusion. She felt adolescent and completely out of her depth. She had now *seen* Edward but how, exactly, could she trust destiny to guide their affairs? And after so much time had lapsed? And exactly how could she, as Mozart suggested, give him another chance? By now she was certain he had had second, third, even fourth thoughts about her. If he had liked her at the beginning—and certainly her body had distinctly thought that he had—how could he like her now? No more enlightened than she had been when she set out, Anna headed back home.

Fortunately, just in time to distract her, her professional life was heating up. There was one request to visit a haunted house in Chester, Connecticut. That would be pretty much routine, she suspected. She could rent a car or take the train up on Saturday, even Friday. It was soon to be a long holiday weekend.

"This is Alexander," a second message began. "You may remember me. I am a friend of your friend Harold's…" Anna certainly did remember Alexander. Still, she had to hand it to Harold in the matter of referrals. Didn't he realize she'd stop teaching once her practice stabilized? Or maybe his referrals were a gentle hint that her teaching, master's degree not withstanding, left something to be desired?

A third message revealed a woman's breathy, little girl voice. She wanted an appointment as soon as possible. Was today or even Thanksgiving a possibility? It wasn't an emergency precisely but there was a matter of some urgency and she could really use all the help she could get. Oh, yes, her name was "Dizzy." Dizzy? Anna pressed Rewind and listened again to the soft, coy voice. The name was "Daisy."

Anna took down Daisy's number, the Connecticut information, and Alexander's in her little black leather book. She would bury her woes in her work, just like Edward in his music, she decided. Then she noticed that her family message light was blinking also.

"I thought you'd like to know your brother made it home safely," her mother's voice began. "Even as we speak he and your father are enjoying a game of chess in the family room. Your father is doing much better now that he is home. We could sue the hospital for malpractice but your father doesn't want to do that. You know him. He says that accidents happen..."

Never one to leave a brief message when a longer one would do, Anna's mother went into their Thanksgiving plans—she planned a turkey just for the two of them and, of course, Alan. Anna wondered if she detected a veiled guilt trip in her mother's report but then decided that Alan could do his part for a change, standing in for both of them. Besides, she had to earn a living and the Connecticut trip should be good money.

Taking a deep breath, Anna dialed the Connecticut number. She got a real estate office and, after a lengthy Muzaked transfer, she was connected to a Realtor named Phyllis. Phyllis explained that she had a hot sale in the offing and that Anna's services were required but merely a formality. The couple loved the house and were ready to sign but there was the little matter of the ghost— the possible ghost—to be cleared up. And that was where Anna entered the picture. Didn't she feel her $500 day fee plus travel expenses was a little steep? (No, she did not.) Perhaps it could be put to closing costs? Just a little joke but perhaps it could...

Anna did not much care for Phyllis, finding her, perhaps predictably, a little evasive about the details of the possible ghost. They settled on a Saturday visit. Anna would take the train up. Phyllis would magnanimously drive her back down.

"I myself have never seen the ghost," Phyllis explained. "But several potential buyers have sensed *something*..." she trailed off. Anna hung up the phone with a creeping sense of discomfort. Phyllis was a little bit smarmy. Not to mention vague.

Alexander, on the other hand, was anything but vague. She must remember him, he insisted, he was Harold's friend the psychic, the one with the shop, the one who had foreseen her meeting the man of her dreams? Had she yet? Anna found herself speculating about Alexander's X-ray vision the same way that people often speculated about hers. Could he, for example, ethereally detect a certain ill-tempered reticence in her about having her private affairs poked at? *Be professional*, Anna reminded herself. She booked Alexander for Wednesday evening, Thanksgiving eve. A fellow professional, he had not let slip, Anna noticed, anything about the nature of his call.

Dialing back Daisy, Anna looked over her calendar again and decided the holiday Friday could go to Daisy. That would leave only Thanksgiving proper to fill.

Chapter 63

Tuesday was Stacy night and Anna thought her friend looked like she was doing better. The Popover Café was crowded. Stacy had beat her to their rendezvous again and was sipping at a glass of white wine, looking cool and very much in possession of herself—except that she usually didn't drink before she rode. Anna slid into her waiting chair.

"So," she asked, but Stacy was off and running.

"Jeffrey is very understanding," she explained. "He can understand my feelings of vulnerability. In my shoes, he might have had such feelings himself, but as things stand, he says he has no plans of actually reconciling with his wife, Eva."

"He's quite content with matters as they lay?" Anna joked, but clearly Stacy was still vulnerable and beyond the reach of irony.

Anna ordered a Waldorf salad. Stacy chose the "nice dice" salad. She was actually dieting a little, doubtless to be even more perfect for Jeffrey. Eva, it seemed, was dark, Latin and very small, a sort of Frida Kahlo look-alike but without the eyebrow.

"And how are you?" Stacy asked with a sudden show of friendship. "You've been completely off my radar screen. How *are* you?"

Now was again the moment for girlish revelations. Now was the time to unveil perplexing Edward and her dilemma over The Phone Call. Stacy, after all, was a relative black belt in matters romantic. She was bound to have some advice. *Advice I couldn't possibly take; advice I couldn't possibly pull off*, Anna thought ruefully. If Mrs. Murphy's advice seemed impossible, Stacy's might seem even worse. Furthermore, Stacy was too close in. Mrs. Murphy at least was at a distance. No, she wouldn't ask Stacy for advice. As she had before, she let the moment pass.

Call it her sense of Catholic secrecy (there was a "seal" on the confessional after all), call it her conservative midwestern roots, call it her long training from Mrs. Murphy in "containment." She found herself curiously protective of her relationship, or whatever it was, with Edward. She didn't want his character, couth or lack of it, to become a matter for female speculation.

"I'm fine," Anna answered finally. "School is kind of wearing me out. The kids get all wound up around the holidays." Anna was ready to continue her workaday scholastic complaints, but she noticed that her friend wasn't listening.

"Mmm," Stacy replied, clearly still watching her inner movie, the soft porn one starring Jeffrey. "Do you think men ever change their type?" she more urgently wanted to know.

"Do you mean, if Eva is small and dark, could Jeffrey truly love you who are tall and blond?"

"Yes. What do you think?"

"On the one hand, I think leopards don't change their spots. On the other, you might be a refreshing change of pace."

And so it went. The dinner boiled down to "men"—meaning Jeffrey—and "their habits"—meaning Jeffrey's. Stacy had it bad, Anna thought as her friend ordered a second glass of white wine, then a half carafe, "If you don't mind. Just to unwind from work."

No doubt about it, Anna thought severely. Her friend was riding for a fall and not just on tonight's dressage mount. This Jeffrey sounded like a real piece of work, not that Anna voiced this opinion to Stacy.

For one thing, she had no credibility given her own bungling of matters with Edward. Then, too, Stacy's giggly report of her gymnastic sex life was intimidating. Jeffrey, it seemed, was into "playful S and M." He liked "light bondage," whatever that was. Anna had a brief but disconcerting image of her best friend trussed up like a Thanksgiving turkey.

"What do you think about that?" Anna asked, trying for delicacy. She didn't want to pry, but she wanted Stacy to have the chance to vent.

"I guess I think it's interesting," Stacy answered, flushed.

"'Interesting.' You don't mean painful?"

"No, no," Stacy exclaimed, perhaps too quickly. "Not painful. Just odd, you know."

"I'm afraid I don't know, but I can imagine."

Stacy laughed. "Please don't. It's weird enough as it is!"

After her dinner date with Stacy, Anna had a fitful night's sleep. In real life, she had dissuaded her tipsy friend from riding. In her dream life, Stacy wore a red silk dress and stood, balancing precariously, on the rounded rump of a white circus horse as it cantered around a ring. Jeffrey played the role of the ringmaster, whip in hand. Just as he lashed the horse's plump hindquarters, Anna woke gasping from her dream. She kept water by her bedside and now she reached for a tepid sip. There was still the matter of Edward to consider—and that predicament was good in itself for a sleepless night. She would be a real disaster area in the morning, Anna thought angrily. She turned on her stomach and buried her head in her pillow. Nonetheless, she distinctly heard the words, *"He needs you."*

Oh for chrissake, not now, not again, Anna thought, the

novelty of Mozart's ghost paling before her incipient insomnia. She opened one reluctant eye and peered toward the fire escape window. Yep. He was there. She squinted her eyes tightly closed, willing herself, "Sleep. Sleep. Sleep." No such luck.

"I'm talking to you," announced Mozart's ghost in a somewhat more elevated voice.

"Leave me alone," Anna grumped. *"Come back at a reasonable hour. I'm trying to get some sleep."* She turned her back on the ghost. It had worked before.

"I need to speak to you in private, and now's as good a time as any," Mozart's ghost countered. *"I need you to understand what I am doing with him. I need you to listen up."*

"What is it?" Anna growled, through clenched teeth. Rude was rude, after all. Perhaps as a celebrity ghost, he felt entitled. Reluctantly, she rolled back over.

"My dear young woman," Mozart's ghost scolded. He looked no older than Anna herself. *"This isn't personal. I don't really see quite what he sees in you, but love is blind."*

"Thanks a lot," Anna answered. Hurt, despite herself.

Mozart's ghost continued, musing aloud. *"No one really liked my wife Constanze, either. My father thought the whole Weber family was beneath us. My friends thought she was wild and profligate. Which, thankfully, she was. We were always in debt—not that it bothered me the way it should have. But I was talking about you. I really haven't got a leg to stand on. But he does need you. It helps the music."* By "it" Anna knew he meant sex.

"I see," Anna said. *"So this is not personal. It feels pretty personal to me."*

"Touchy, touchy. Try to take the long view."

"You really don't care about my feelings, do you?" Anna fumed.

"Should I?" inquired Mozart's ghost. *"I'm afraid all I care about is the music."* He sounded amused, both by his own temperament and by Anna's temper.

"The music is lovely," Anna conceded. Her comment opened a floodgate.

"He's really very good," the ghost rushed on. *"Unlike so many of them, he's onto what I actually meant. He's trying to play my intention—not some superimposed theory of his own. Do you know how rare that is? Why it's been years since I've heard my music played so truly. A century anyway. So you see, he's important to me. Why, if he won a few major competitions, he could start a trend in interpretation. That would be so refreshing. That would just be a dream for me. So, you be nice to him. Stop dilly-dallying,"* he finished.

"I am not dillydallying," Anna retorted. *"I am trying to behave with dignity."*

"Vastly overrated. No fun at all. Never believed in it myself."

"I've heard stories." Even as a music phobe Anna had heard of Mozart's profligate ways. His wife, Constanze, was said to have been incorrigible. Their sexual high jinks practically outshone his music.

"I tell you what. They're all true," he laughed. *"Just give him a chance. You could use a few jollies."* On that naughty note, the apparition blinked out.

Anna lay back, steaming. He *was* naughty. And immature. Mozart had died young, Anna remembered, and he well deserved to, she thought as she again buried her head in the pillow and willed herself, "Sleep. Sleep. Sleep."

Chapter 64

Dear Mr. and Mrs. Oliver,

You'll pardon my saying so, but the hypnotist seemed like a lot of bunk. First, I was to picture myself on an escalator, "riding down, down, down." Next, I was to "find myself," just before the injury. Going out the door with my brother to shoot hoops? Next I was to "undo" the injury, using my "visualization powers" to imagine a different outcome. Well, to be brief, I creamed my brother in my mind's eye, but when I rode back up the escalator to the hypnotist's office, my muscle tension was as tight and painful as ever. Still, I'm sure it was a good try. (At this point, I'd try anything and almost have.)

Mr. Mayakovsky let slip that I was doing well, considering. As he is pretty tightfisted with his praise, holding his students to his own standards, I took this as a rare compliment. He added, "Don't let that go to your head."

I am trying to live up to your faith in me.

Sincerely yours,
Edward

P.S. Alan called me "Edward Pianohands" after that movie "Edward Scissorhands." I'm not sure it played in Wilton.

Chapter 65

Harold summoned Anna to his office. This struck her a little like calling "time out" in a football game. The students were wild with the impending holiday. But then, so, evidently, was Harold. He had a cutout pilgrim posted on his office door. Once inside the room, Anna discovered that Harold had an entire Thanksgiving tableau: a cutout stand-up gobbler vied for space with a cornucopia and another pilgrim on Harold's desk. There was barely room for him to get his work done, or lay out one of his famous gourmet lunches.

"So you're going to see Alexander," Harold announced, gesturing for her to close the door behind her. "As you might suspect, I'm hoping you two will form a professional alliance." Harold always had his agendas.

"Don't tell me anything," Anna warned. "The less I know, the better." There were, after all, professional ethics to consider. Although she sometimes lapsed, Anna tried to live up to Mrs. Murphy's dictums.

"I'll zip the lip," Harold responded, making a zipper motion just under his considerable moustache.

"To what do I owe the honor, or am I on the carpet?" Anna inquired.

"No, no, you're doing fine—or almost. You've stuck it out longer than most," Harold told her. "You've almost got a handle on Dylan, Abby and Jeremy. Of course with parents like theirs..."

"I try."

"Well, try this." He wanted to show her a travel brochure. He produced it from his center drawer.

"Sail the Metaphysical Seas," the large print read. Anna skimmed a description of a weeklong Caribbean cruise featuring "psychics, tarot readers, numerologists and astrologers." Harold was thinking of going. The junket fell during their Christmas break. Was Anna interested?

"I don't think so, Harold," Anna answered him politely. She didn't mention her resentment at being so casually lumped in with the new-age crowd. Talking to spirits, after all, was a time-honored vocation. Mrs. Murphy had tutored Anna carefully on her spiritual lineage, drumming home the fact that her gift was no mere parlor game but rather a serious spiritual responsibility.

In most cultures throughout the world, the dead ancestors were honored and invoked. "Could so many people have deluded themselves for so long?" Mrs. Murphy asked Anna whenever Anna raised the possibility that her gift might just be an overactive imagination. "Impossible," Mrs. Murphy assured her, and over the years, as the accuracy and validity of Anna's messages were borne out, Anna, too had come to take seriously her gift. No, there would be no Metaphysical Cruise, no mediumship as oddity or entertainment. Mrs. Murphy would not approve of her taking part in a spiritual smorgasbord.

"It could be a break for you," Harold was insisting, his managerial tendencies getting a little out of line. "You could use a little publicity."

"No thanks, Harold," she demurred. "I deal in attraction rather than promotion."

"Have a sandwich then," he insisted. Harold dove into his "lunch" drawer. "It's my famous chicken salad on olive bread."

Anna accepted half a sandwich. Harold munched away jovially, beaming at her across his desk. He looked like the cat that had swallowed the canary, smugly smiling his trademark grin. Clearly, he had a secret.

"I know something you don't know," he finally burst out. "I know something you'd love to know."

"Let me guess; I get to monitor detention," Anna guessed dourly, adding, "Look, Harold, if your psychic pal has told you anything about me and my affairs, I don't want to hear it. For one thing, there are no affairs. For another, I value my privacy. Why do you think I moved to New York?"

As she hoped she had made clear, Anna had no appetite for second-hand, third-person psychic impressions. In fact, she resented the possibility that Harold might be snooping on her, if only on an astral plane.

"It's for me to know and you to find out, but you're just going to love Alexander," Harold hinted as the class bell blessedly sounded, drowning him out.

Anna was frankly exhausted. She would need to catch her second wind before she saw Alexander. Not to mention, she thought with a glance in the lobby mirror, her hair looked wild. She pushed the button for the elevator, slumped against the marble wall and closed her eyes. Edward certainly sounded good, she thought, as the music pumped into the lobby from under the door to 1E–as-in-Edward. *Oh, damn it*, she softly cursed. *If he can bury himself in his work; I can bury myself in mine.* Her phone did seem to ring incessantly. *I just need to welcome the distraction*, she thought.

What was it about holidays that set kids into wild elation and drove her straight to depression? Did she really miss family bonding? Her mother's rigidity could sometimes make holidays feel like a close-order drill. Well, at least she wouldn't see the kids again until Monday and Harold's friend Alexander might conceivably be fun.

As she slid her key into her lock, Anna felt someone already coming through. *For Chrissake. Let me at least get my coat off,* she mentally snapped. If she failed utterly at setting boundaries with Alan, she did slightly better with spirits. She could normally back them off until the twenty-minute meditation time she liked to have to herself before a client arrived. Meditation wasn't strictly necessary, any longer, but it certainly helped. For one thing, there was Anna's own temperament to contend with. She was so often restless, irritable and discontent. Meditation improved her equanimity and put her into a receptive state. It allowed her to pick up on subtle and elusive vibrations—not that whoever was waiting to talk with Alexander seemed either subtle or elusive. With or without meditation, she was receiving a stream of invective. *"Back off,"* Anna mentally ordered. Huffily, the spirit obeyed briefly, then the diatribe started up again. *"Back off,"* Anna demanded again. She settled herself in the velvet Victorian chair and focused her attention inward onto her calm pond of koi. There. That was certainly better.

Alexander, who was slightly breathless and flushed when he arrived, was exactly as Anna remembered him: pushy and artificially cheerful. With his short, plump figure and rounded jolly belly under his peacoat, he feigned the jocund air of one of Santa's helpers. In truth, his mood was far from jovial. He gave her apartment a cursory glance and headed straight to her reading area without being told.

"I'm an old hand at all this," his manner suggested. He settled his plump bottom onto her similarly plump love seat. He placed a velvet-backed needlepoint pillow squarely on his lap and folded his hands. Despite herself, Anna felt he was waiting to be impressed. *We'll just see about that*, she thought. She had had sessions where she was sadly unable to make contact at all, although this clearly did not promise to be one of them.

"Someone's been talking to me nonstop for fifteen minutes," Anna informed him. "Do you have a former business partner with a grudge?"

"I was afraid he was angry," Alexander admitted. "But I still think I'm right."

Anna braced herself. She frankly hated being the go-between in contentious matters. It was a little like being on a phone line filled with static. Nonetheless, it was her job.

"He says you're running the shop straight into the gutter with all of your occult nonsense," Anna replayed. She noted Alexander wore the outsized diamond earring. She noted, too, that he was picking at a corner of her handmade pillow where a tiny bit of stuffing showed through. She had meant to mend that.

"It's not nonsense," Alexander retorted belatedly, pausing to ask Anna, "Do you think it is?" He suspected as much, his look said. He picked again at the pillow.

"I do not take sides, and put that pillow down." Anna said firmly. "Jay—is that the entity's name?—feels what you're doing is very bad for business."

"It is not," Alexander hotly retorted. "You tell Jay that I'm sick of him," Alexander flared. "And tell him I was sick of him before he died. I'll tell you what's bad for business—a heart attack right in the middle of the store."

Oh, dear, Anna thought as Jay filled her mind with snappy comebacks which she faithfully relayed, thus escalating the fight.

"Once a diva, always a diva," Alexander huffed, rolling his eyes to summarize his attack. By now Anna had gathered that Jay and Alexander were onetime romantic partners with a volatile relationship that their co-ownership in a shop had done nothing to quell.

"Profits are up, tell him," Alexander directed Anna querulously. "He's not even missed. You tell him that."

Anna held up a warning hand. She did not like being used as a punching bag. Alexander and Jay would have to continue their fight without benefit of her as an inter-plane-interpreter. She called the session to a halt. Alexander was not satisfied. He wanted to continue.

"I'm willing to pay you," he whined.

"Money is not the issue," Anna replied.

"Well, it is for most of us," Alexander retorted. "And you could use a new love seat, too. I have a spring up my ass. No wonder your love life isn't working out. You blew it with him, didn't you?"

"Probably, yes," Anna confessed miserably, certain that Alexander could only be speaking of her debacle with Edward. "Now, if you'd let me get your coat."

"You know, you're not unattractive. You're actually pretty in an old-fashioned way."

"Thanks."

"You are pretty. You ought to be able to do better with men. It must be your personality that puts them off." Alexander struggled into his coat.

"Thanks a lot. Did you forget to take your tact pills?"

"Just a little honest feedback! Harold said you were touchy!"

"Let's leave Harold out of this!"

"Yes, let's. Thank you for your services."

"You don't have to make me sound like a call girl."

"Harold did say you were touchy!"

"Harold also said we would like each other!"

"Nobody bats a thousand." Alexander buttoned his peacoat. He turned up the collar as Anna showed him to the door. Her personal line was ringing.

Chapter 66

"Good of you to come out," Tommy said as he reached across and tucked her scarf more tightly under her chin. "I know it's cold but we've got our love to keep us warm."

"Tommy."

"Well, if I said we've got our lust you'd really be offended."

"Tommy!"

"Come on. Just be a good girl and hold my hand and we will have the tiniest little adventure. I love watching them get the floats ready. It's more exciting than the actual parade, if you ask me."

Tommy had Anna's hand in his and he piloted them south along Columbus Avenue, past the American Museum of Natural History to where the floats for the next day's Thanksgiving Day parade were being assembled on a side street. The scene resembled a traveling circus. A crowd of chilly New Yorkers had turned out to view it.

"It's too cold," Anna protested. "It's too windy. I'm miserable."

"You're just in a mood. I knew it the minute I picked you up. What happened? Did you have a stink bomb client? You must get a number of those."

"I do. I did. I mean, he was all right. I can't really talk about it." Anna was beginning to find the cold invigorating—or maybe it was Tommy's company.

"You can't? How thrilling."

"Yes, well confidentiality is an important part of my work. I have to be able to keep a secret."

"Well, you certainly can keep a secret if you ask me. Take right now. You've got a secret misery and you are not bending my ear about it." Tommy stooped closer so that his ear was at her mouth.

"I do not have a secret misery!" Anna protested.

"Liar! Anyone could tell you're obsessed about something. Of course, I am hoping that it is me."

"You are such a flirt."

"It's one of the best things about me. Relax and enjoy it. A little flirting is good for the soul."

"Oh, look!" Despite herself Anna was excited at the sight of a huge float towering thirty feet into the air.

"It's almost like seeing a dinosaur, isn't it?" Tommy asked her.

"I wouldn't have put it that way."

"Anna Banana! Lighten up. Don't you dare throw a wet blanket on my excursion."

"I'm sorry. I'm not trying to be glum. It's just…oh, never mind."

"There you go. 'Oh never mind.' That's you keeping a secret. Well, I can see that I might be confusing for you. As a confidante, I mean. I mean, I'm not exactly like a guy and I'm not exactly like a girl. I like to think I am the best of both."

"Tommy, you're perfect. It's just me." *Me and men*, Anna was thinking. The sidewalk around them was thronged with New Yorkers eager to get a peek at the floats.

"Anna!" She knew the voice instantly as Harold's. Sure enough, she turned and saw him making his way toward them his face alight with his large Cheshire grin.

"Harold, this is Tommy," Anna said, well aware that Tommy still held her hand captive. Reluctantly he relinquished it and offered Harold a manly handshake.

"So this is what you've been up to, isn't it?" Harold teased.

"Not really," Anna answered.

"We're shacked up," Tommy piped up. "She just won't admit it. You're Harold, her boss, aren't you? She's talked about you often enough."

"Her boss among other things," Harold allowed. "Are you really shacked up?"

"Harold, Tommy, that's plenty. Did you see that they are blowing up the Doughboy?"

"Oh, goodie. It's like something out of *Ghostbusters*," Tommy crowed. "You must be very familiar with that movie."

"Very familiar," Anna allowed.

"Let's go for a drink," Harold invited. "Anna, you don't mind a gay bar, do you?"

"I'm the shy one," Tommy said.

"I'm buying," Harold declared. "Come on. Sanctuary is mere steps away."

Anna followed Harold and Tommy as they made their way to a nearby bar. Once inside the doors, Anna realized she was the only woman there. *Think of it as an adventure*, she told herself.

"I'll have a Rusty Nail," Tommy told the bartender.

"Make that two," Harold offered. "And you, Anna?"

"Verona chocolate," Anna announced, as she gestured to the sign over the bar advertising Italian cocoa.

The bartender slid a drink towards Tommy and another toward Harold. "The cocoa takes a few minutes," he explained to Anna. "Would you like a club soda in the meanwhile?"

"Sure she would," Tommy answered for Anna. "And where are those good little bar nuts you usually serve?"

"So you're a regular here?" Harold asked with interest.

"I'm a known presence," Tommy allowed.

"Me, too," said Harold. "But I don't remember ever spotting you."

"I'm hard to miss," Tommy said.

"Well, I've never been here before," Anna volunteered. She was starting to feel slightly left out. Harold was grinning even more than usual and Tommy was basking in the attention. At his sociable best, Harold seemed far more attractive than he did at school.

"I haven't been in in a while," Tommy went on. "This was one of Hughie's watering holes. He was the regular."

"Hughie?" Harold inquired. He took a handful of the newly materialized bar nuts.

"My partner. Recently deceased."

"I'm so sorry," Harold said. "That puts us in the same boat."

"Yes, sometimes I think it's the *Titanic*," Tommy said. "Everybody has lost somebody."

"Ah, but you've found someone again." Harold nodded toward Anna.

"Harold," Anna interrupted. "I don't think you should go jumping to conclusions."

"I'm sorry. Am I jumping?"

"Hopefully not," Tommy put in. "I've told Anna I am hers for the taking."

"And?" Harold asked. "And?"

"To be continued," Tommy ventured. "In the long run, I am irresistible."

"I can see that," Harold said. He punched Tommy lightly on the arm.

Chapter 67

Thanksgiving Day dawned bright and chill. Accustomed to her school hours, Anna woke at six-thirty. Her apartment was already flooded with light. *If I were a true New Yorker,* she thought, *I'd take myself back down to 79th Street and watch them launch those floats.* But Anna didn't feel like a true New Yorker—leave that to Alan. She felt like a midwestern wannabe, hopelessly square and unhip, pining after her mother's orange-cranberry relish and the turkey that would even now be roasting.

At least he's up too, Anna thought as the opening bars of Edward's morning regime pole-vaulted over the sill. Was it her imagination, or did his playing sound subtly "off"? Perhaps he was feeling as sour and dispirited as she was. What was it Alan had quoted Charlie Parker as saying? Oh, yes: "If you don't live it, it cannot come out your horn." *Maybe the same applies to pianists. Maybe Edward is growing too enclosed, closeted as he is, with just his piano for company. Maybe Mozart had a point and she was good for him. Why didn't he just call her again?*

Yes, the morning's serenade sounded a bit rocky to her amateur ear. Edward's scales started and stopped, started and stopped. Anna was used to their cascading like a waterfall. His Liszt was listless, he might joke—although certainly, to Edward, an "off" piano day would be no laughing matter. Far from it. *He would be monitoring his performance like an athlete*, Anna thought, and then caught herself up short. She was thinking way too much about Edward and the musical variables that made up his monkish life.

I really should prune my philodendrons today, Anna mused as she mulled over her empty day. There was always a certain nasty satisfaction in pinching away the dead, brown leaves. Lying in her loft bed, listening to Edward's battle far below her, Anna considered her alternatives. Alexander probably was right that she'd blown it with him. And what did she *really* know about him anyway? That night with Edward in front of the washer-dryer, she'd told him a ghost-free version of her years in Ann Arbor and she suspected his rendition of life in Wilton, Maine, was equally sanitized. Music had been everything to him, Edward had confessed. Was that just some romantic pickup line? It made him sound "ungettable." Was that the lure that had gotten her "got"?

Anna climbed slowly down her loft bed ladder. She could spend the morning like a true recluse, reading the tabloids. She would, she decided. Throwing her black trench coat over her nightgown, she made a furtive dash to the corner newsstand. Even if it was Thanksgiving, it was Thursday—new tabloid day. She grabbed them, paid for them, and raced back inside. She did not see Edward, and Edward, mercifully, did not see her.

Safely back at home, allowing herself an extra holiday cup of her Starbucks espresso blend, she whipped into her tabloids in a caffeine-induced frenzy of concentration. When she looked up, it was already time for lunch. In Ann Arbor, the scent of turkey and stuffing would be wafting through the house, mixed with the heady perfume of her mother's excellent pumpkin pie. In Ann Arbor—*Oh, dear*, Anna thought. *Ann Arbor again. I must really be feeling low if I'm pining for Ann Arbor. The Greek diner suits me just fine.*

When she entered the Greek diner, Edward was seated in his booth. He looked up and their eyes met. Anna managed a sickly smile. Edward didn't do much better. He was wearing the neck brace again and his smile looked more like a wince.

"I'm having Tom Turkey," he volunteered loudly, speaking across the heads of the other diners. "With all the fixings. It says so right here." He tapped the special card that perched on the table. *Is this lowly meeting destiny?* Anna wondered. She smiled.

"Good to see you," Edward announced, encouraged.

"Is that an invitation?" Anna asked. In a split second, she had decided to go for broke, speaking straight back to Edward above the heads of the regulars.

"Yes. I guess so," Edward managed. He moved aside the score he was studying to make a place for her across from him. *Has Edward always been so pale?* She wondered. His eyes were darkly circled even under his glasses. He held his head at a skewed angle. Was that new? Anna slid into the booth. Her leg brushed against his and a bolt of sexual energy shot through her, flushing her cheeks. Her body remembered this man very clearly. Now Anna noticed his piano hands drumming on the Formica table. So she *wasn't* the only nervous one.

"And what for you? The Tom Turkey?" George the waiter

inserted a suggestion into the lull in their conversation.

"Yes, of course," Anna answered him. "Turkey with everything. Does everything mean cranberry relish?"

"It better," Edward spoke up. He winced a little as he spoke, though whether from shyness or pain, Anna was not quite certain.

"You're practicing a lot," Anna observed. Edward grimaced.

"But not well," Edward voiced her own suspicions. "My neck's acting up again. My playing sounds like crap, pardon me."

But there was nothing to pardon. Anna felt a tiny thrill at his language. She really had been thinking of him as a musical monk. And his voice—his voice was like a Steinway, full-bodied and resonant. *I've got it bad*, Anna thought, hopelessly. She and Edward both stared at the salt and pepper shakers with sudden fascination.

"So, Tom Turkey it is!" George exclaimed. He was still standing above Edward and Anna waiting to take their order.

"Tom Turkey sounds great, George," Anna murmured. He left them to their awkward devices.

"It's good to see you," Edward finally broke the ice. "I thought you were avoiding me."

"I thought you were avoiding me!" Anna burst out.

"I called you," Edward defended himself. "You never called me back."

"I never got the message," Anna lied stiffly. "Well, not in a timely fashion."

"You didn't?" Edward was incredulous. "But I talked to Alan. He took the message."

"Alan's a son of a bitch. He always screws up my relationships!" Anna boiled over.

"Always?" Edward sounded hurt.

"He *has*," Anna responded, flushing. She realized belatedly how "always" must sound.

"I thought you thought you'd made a terrible mistake," Edward confessed. "I thought perhaps you hadn't acted characteristically." Edward was tripping over his words.

"I hadn't," Anna admitted. "I mean, I'm not a slut."

"Too bad," Edward shot back, smiling. She bristled. It took Anna a beat to realize he was joking. "I had a good time," Edward volunteered lamely. "A wonderful time, really."

"Me, too." Her inner movie was starting up again, the one where she and Edward made love in soft focus. Anna felt herself flushing yet again. "I had a very good time," she finally managed to say.

"You did?" Edward still looked apprehensive, afraid, perhaps, of a bad review.

"Yes."

That single syllable, "yes," seemed to shift them to solid ground. *We like each other*, Anna realized. It was really that simple and that complex. Both of them were in over their heads.

George, both arms fully laden, arrived with their Thanksgiving meal. The turkey looked ashen. The gravy was gelid, the stuffing looked dry and the cranberry relish was a garish carnival red. Both Anna and Edward ate ravenously, eyes shyly meeting as they chewed.

"Your brother told me all about you," Edward volunteered as their pumpkin pie arrived.

"Oh goodie," Anna said dryly. She could only imagine just what.

"He's so grateful to you for your patience giving him a place to stay while he explores New York," explained Edward. Both Alan's gratitude and her own patience were news to her. Edward was continuing, "I guess as a teacher you need lots of patience."

Had Alan, for once, respected her privacy? No mention of ghosts so far. She may have been presented as she presented herself: a perfectly ordinary young woman, a good citizen who taught school.

"Yes, I do need patience," Anna belatedly responded. "But then, as a musician, so do you. All those scales."

"I knew they were annoying you," Edward apologized. "Alan told me you could hear me."

"But I *love* hearing you," Anna burst out. "At least I do now."

"My girlfriend, my ex-girlfriend that is, always said music was the other woman." Edward laid his cards on the table. His out-sized piano hands straightened the flatware. "She resented my practicing all the time. It drove her crazy, she said. I can see how it would do that, going over the same thing over and over..." he trailed off.

So I'm not the only one who carries liabilities, Anna thought with surprise. She had expected Edward to be snooty about his profession, not modestly apologetic.

"So you teach school," Edward prompted, between bites of pie.

"Yes, I do. By day," Anna answered.

"And what do you do by night?" Edward picked up her cue.

"Besides laundry, you mean?" Anna was stalling for time. She didn't really want to tell Edward she talked to ghosts. Couldn't she extend their sweet normalcy a beat longer? Draw the man out, the women's magazines would advise. Make small talk. Determined to try, Anna asked about his neck injury.

Old, old, old, Edward told her. Just reactivated. He described the recent fateful hook shot in a pickup game with his little brother. The neck had bothered him ever since, although, as he understood it now, it wasn't the neck per se but some trapezoidal muscles...He was boring her. He was sure. He broke off. His store of small talk seemed as pitiably small as Anna's own. "This must be boring you," he trailed off.

"But I'm not bored," Anna assured him.

Edward then launched back into the long history of his injury, the years he had already lived with it, the danger of its acting up when he was under stress and really had to play his best. "Like now," he added and explained to Anna his preparations for the gold medal competition, emphasizing both the odds against his winning and, a little proudly, the odds he had already faced down.

"There are one hundred eighty pianists at the very start. Then thirty-five. There will be six finalists and one winner. Hopefully, me."

"I knew you were that good," Anna told him. "I'm a music illiterate, really, but you play awfully well. It's like living with a sound track." Now Anna broke off. Did she sound stupid?

It had been easier with alcohol to grease the conversational wheels, but then one thing had led to another. Suddenly Anna remembered Edward's precise, accurate and thrilling touch. She could feel herself coloring. She met Edward's gaze, then broke away.

"I got carried away. We went too fast. We freaked ourselves out," Edward summarized their dilemma. He paused to gulp at his water, then he continued on a course of full disclosure. "It made me paranoid. I buried myself in work. It probably took me at least a week to call you. That probably made you paranoid. I can understand that. What about a drink on Sunday? About four? I'll need a break then, okay?"

"Coffee, not a drink," Anna countered.

"Coffee then," said Edward. "Shall we meet in the lobby at four?"

"Hello, you two," a sultry voice spoke. Anna looked up with dread. Just as she feared, it was Stacy, who eyed them both with interest. Anna felt herself flush. *How long has this been going on?* Anna could practically hear her friend thinking.

"What are you doing here?" Anna asked Stacy, meaning, *get out.*

"So you two are all alone on Thanksgiving, too," Stacy answered.

"We're not alone, we're together," Anna answered, trying to stake a territorial claim.

"Well, I'm alone," Stacy said. "Mind if I join you?" Anna did mind, she minded very much, but she cast a quick glance at Edward and saw that he, like all men, was falling under Stacy's golden spell.

"Please! Have a seat," Edward offered, making room for Stacy on his side of the table.

"How's the turkey?" Stacy asked. "I was just going to have a BLT."

"Really! A BLT?" Edward acted like this was the most fascinating news he had ever heard.

"I *love* BLTs, don't you?" Stacy crooned. "There's something delicious about all the contrasts. And I know I shouldn't, but I always get extra mayonnaise."

"Why shouldn't you?" Edward said. "With a figure like yours, you don't need to worry."

A figure like yours? Anna fumed. He had not said any such thing to her, and he certainly examined her figure more closely.

Fool, fool, fool, she chided herself.

"Cat got your tongue?" Stacy asked solicitously. Anna willed herself to find some manners. Even a scrap would do.

"Edward, this is Stacy. Stacy, this is Edward," Anna mustered.

"I gather you and Stacy are friends?" Edward asked.

"I gather you and Anna are friends," Stacy murmured. She had dropped her voice to a Jacqueline Onassis whisper. The man had to lean closer to hear her. It was a trick Anna had seen her use before.

For God's sakes, stop it! Anna snapped. *My God, had she said that out loud? No, she had not—not that she hadn't wanted to.* Edward was trying to convince Stacy to have a full Thanksgiving meal. "Although, frankly, it tasted like cardboard," he joked.

"I *love* cardboard," Stacy teased.

"So what do you want, a BLT or turkey?" Anna intruded. Stacy looked up, a little startled, as if she were surprised to find Anna still there at all. *And what am I doing here?* Anna thought miserably. *I had my moment in the sun. Obviously, Edward prefers Stacy. He responds to her like any other red-blooded male.* She signaled for the check. George materialized promptly, his eyes brimming with what Anna took to be pity.

"Just yours, Miss Anna?" he asked.

"Just mine," Anna answered. "They're not finished yet." She gathered her tweed coat around her shoulders and got to her feet. Edward looked alarmed. *Or guilty.* Was it her imagination?

"I'll see you Sunday at four," he muttered weakly.

"I've been having some trouble with my boyfriend," Anna heard Stacy confide as she headed for the door. Edward leaned sympathetically closer.

Chapter 68

I n Anna's dream, Stacy was dressed in a lavish wedding gown. She held an outsized bouquet of white roses and stephanotis and stood poised at the altar ready to take her vows. Exquisite music issued from somewhere in the choir loft and Anna realized at once that it was Edward at the keys. She herself was dressed in a bridesmaid's dress that looked every bit as frumpy and also-ran as bridesmaids' dresses typically did.

Everything was in order except for just one detail: Where the groom would normally stand, there was instead a long line of men, bachelors of every description. With a final flourish at the keys, the music suddenly stopped. Anna watched in horror as Edward joined the back of the line and the queue began inching forward. Stacy rejected the men one by one.

As the conveyor belt of wannabes moved forward, Edward moved closer and closer to Stacy's side. Would she choose him? On this cliff-hanging note, Anna awoke from her restless night's sleep. Her buzzer was shrilling.

Goddamn him, she thought. Then, *Goddamn her*. Then, *Goddamn both of them*. Abruptly, her buzzer sounded again. What time was it? Anna squinted at her clock. It was nearly ten-thirty. She had rotisseried in her bed of pain until four and then slept her deep but not dreamless sleep until now. *The buzzer, my God, the buzzer!* She threw back her covers and scrambled for the ladder. She pressed Talk and spoke carefully into the intercom to her client.

"This is Anna. I am just finishing up a few things. I will buzz you up in five minutes. There's a very nice Starbucks just across the street." *Was that rude?* She hoped not. *In any case, too late now.*

Anna flew to the bathroom to brush her teeth. She twisted her tangled hair into a barrette. The nightgown came off. The underwear and a demure vintage dress went on. Then mascara, then lipstick, now, coffee? She had to have at least a cup. Tripping over her slippers, she dove into the kitchen, took the coffee out of the freezer, poured a generous amount into a filter and set the pot to drip. The buzzer shrilled.

Deliberately, Anna crossed to the intercom, "You can come up now," she said cheerfully and buzzed Daisy in.

When she opened the door, Anna had the sudden feeling she was reading her tabloids. Daisy, a Double D platinum blonde known for her wild escapades stood smiling in her hallway. Her cartoon figure and Kewpie doll face were unmistakable. Anna blinked.

"That's right. It's me," Daisy confirmed. "I mean, I have as much right to be here as anyone else, don't I?" She peered curiously into Anna's studio. "I found you through my friend Eleanor. She knew about you through her friend Harold…" So it was Harold again.

"Why, of course you have a perfect right to be here," Anna assured her.

"Good. I was hoping you'd understand." Daisy stepped into the room. Her stiletto heels ticked on the hardwood floor. In person, as in print, she looked a little top heavy, like she just might tilt over at any second. Anna ushered her to the love seat as quickly as possible.

"Thank you for the tip about the Starbucks," Daisy went on, "but I just grabbed a doughnut at the little Greek diner. It's so cute. Oops. Is there a spring here?" Daisy delicately lifted a perfect haunch.

"I'm afraid so. You better try the other cushion or the chair," Anna advised her. *She's a lot nicer about that spring than Rachel or Alexander*, she thought.

"I'm fine. It just goosed me, that's all," Daisy giggled. "And I have been goosed before." She moved to the love seat's other cushion as her eyes took in Anna, sitting with willed composure in her reading chair. "You poor thing. I woke you up, didn't I? Did you get your cup of coffee?"

"Not quite," Anna answered truthfully.

"Well, why don't you just get it right now. I can wait. Now that I am here, I feel much, much better." Daisy snuggled back amid the pillows.

"Can I offer you anything? Some coffee yourself?" Anna was starting to relax. She felt the genuine calm of a good session starting to steal over her.

"No, that's all right," Daisy bubbled. "Tap water is fine. I mean, I still drink it, don't you?"

"Yes, I do," Anna answered. She had noticed the wedding band and fistful of diamonds on Daisy's left hand. She had also noticed the famous breasts. She suspected that for her, Daisy was dressed conservatively—in a trim black suit with a tiny skirt and a plunging neckline. Anna retreated to the kitchen. Of course, she knew the rudiments of Daisy's story from the tabloids.

A virginal young Texas stripper, Daisy had attracted the eye, and fortune, of a wealthy octogenarian oil baron. He had showered her with gifts, married her and then died, which was probably to be expected. What was not expected were the terms of his new will in which he left Daisy nearly all of his vast business empire, a fortune encompassing oil holdings, cattle ranches, several airplanes, a small herd of prize Arabian horses, and the wrath of his other heirs. Daisy and the heirs had been in court practically since the funeral. The will appeared airtight, and Daisy might yet win.

Reaching into the cupboard for a glass, Anna heard a thin yet gravelly old man's voice. *"She's a little sweetie, I'm telling you,"* the voice remarked.

Anna filled the glass at the tap, poured herself a steep cup of coffee and headed back to Daisy.

"How do we do this?" Daisy wanted to know. "I'm a little bit nervous. Thanks for the water."

"Tell her to just settle down," the voice directed Anna. *"And tell her that I like that little getup."*

"He says to settle down and that he likes your getup," Anna relayed.

"Getup? He said 'getup'?" Daisy giggled. "That's what he always called my outfits at the club," she explained, adding, "I used to be in the entertainment business but that was before I met Bunky."

"She always called me 'Bunky,'" the old man's voice confided to Anna's inner ear.

"He says you always called him 'Bunky,'" Anna relayed.

"Oh goodness," Daisy exclaimed. "Oh my goodness. Oh, this is just great. How is he?"

"Better off than you are," the voice answered in Anna's inner ear.

"He says he is better off than you are," Anna conveyed.

Daisy slapped a spectacular knee. "You tell Bunky I am just fine and not to worry," she told Anna.

"You can tell him yourself," Anna explained. "He can hear you.

I really just need to take care of his end of things."

"He can hear me?" Daisy's already large eyes grew round with wonder.

"Of course I can hear you," Bunky replied. Anna passed it on.

"Oh, Bunky. How are you? How do you like it? Are you having any fun?" Daisy took to the conversation with relish. "What does he say?" she asked Anna.

"Stick to your guns," Anna heard. She repeated the message.

"Oh, Bunky. I don't want to stick to my guns. They can just have the whole kit and caboodle," Daisy answered. "I miss you. And if they're such greedy guts they can just take the money."

"No," Bunky snapped, suddenly sounding like a querulous old man. *"They can't. They don't deserve my money. They were always after my money, always saying 'yes' to me no matter what they really thought. They are a bunch of spineless wonders. You'll do better with my money than they ever did."*

"Actually, I think I'm doing pretty well. I'm starting to catch on," Daisy volunteered. "I just do what I think you would have done and that seems to work out fine."

"I do like it that you listen," Bunky told Anna, who told Daisy.

"He does? I mean, You do? You mean you're guiding me?"

"Of course I'm guiding you, Sugar Pot." Anna repeated the message and the endearment. Daisy grew wide-eyed and tremulous at the concept of ongoing guidance. Many people did. *She's really very sweet, just like he said*, Anna caught herself thinking. Reading the tabloids, she had tended to side with the hapless heirs.

"Sugar Pot was his pet name for me," Daisy explained. "And a few other love names I would rather not go into."

"There's no need to go into them," Anna assured her, wondering at her own inability to muster more skepticism. But, no. True

Love was always a possibility. Anna had been present at many reunions and few held a candle to the evident affection of this one.

"You tell Bunky—" Daisy broke off. She reached for a Kleenex
and swiped at her eyes. "You tell Bunky I am just glad that he is
happy. I really miss him," she managed.

"We had a good run," Bunky's voice spoke up in Anna's inner
ear. *"You tell her to take care of herself and that I'll be doing some
watchdogging from up here."*

Anna repeated the message as Bunky started to fade.

"Is he gone?" Daisy asked her.

"It takes some effort for them to make contact," Anna explained.

Daisy insisted on taking her own glass to the kitchen, where
she stayed by herself for several moments before emerging with
the brave little smile that Anna knew so well from the tabloid
photos of her days in court.

After Daisy left, Anna placed a phone call to her father. As luck
would have it, her mother answered. "So what did you do with
your Thanksgiving?" she inquired. Anna did not quite feel she
could say, "Oh, gee, Mom, I spent it getting rejected and betrayed,"
Instead, she mustered a convincing lie, "I went to the country with
a girlfriend. Her parents have this wonderful house..."

"That's great, dear, was the turkey good? I must say ours was
delicious, even if I do say so myself."

"Actually, we had ham." Why did she enjoy lying to her mother? Why did she still like shocking her? *I just like keeping her at
arm's length from my life.*

"Ham?" her mother rose to the bait. "Well, I suppose some

people get by with ham. It's certainly much easier, but it's just not a turkey, is it?"

"It was delicious. I loved it," Anna goaded her on.

"We had stuffing, and yams, mashed potatoes and gravy, cheesed creamed onions, bean casserole, two kinds of cranberry relish, pumpkin, mince and cherry pies," her mother not-so-subtly bragged. "I told you father he could have one day off for good behavior."

"Where is Daddy?" Anna asked.

"I am afraid he's sleeping. I told him he had to lie down for a little nap after his big day yesterday," Anna's mother sounded pleased with herself—and that's when an extension picked up.

"Ghostbuster, is that you?" her father cheerily inquired.

"I'll be going, then, and let you two have your little visit," Anna's mother all but slammed down the phone.

"Daddy—" Anna began.

"You sound miserable," her father countered. Anna started to sniffle. "When we didn't hear from you yesterday—"

"Not miserable, not exactly, well sort of," she admitted.

"Lousy Thanksgiving?"

"Not too bad. I went to the Greek diner."

"I'll bet they have a way with turkey. Isn't that a neighboring nation?"

"Daddy!"

"Okay, okay. I won't try to cheer you up." Her father paused. It was Anna's cue to confide in him. She found herself stalling. *How exactly could you tell your father about a crush and a one-night stand? She couldn't. And if she tried confiding her insecurity about Stacy, he would only try to bolster her to no avail. No, she didn't want to talk with her father about her sex appeal quotient.*

"How are you?" she finally mustered.

"Better every day."

"Is that the official version, or yours?" Anna wanted to know, meaning, he sounded like her mother.

"A little of both," her father's tone grew level. "I still get worn out more than I should, I think. I do take naps just like your mother wants me to, but I'm gaining and the physical therapist is pleased."

"That's good. I am sorry I didn't make it home."

"I think that was for the best, really. Your mother is running a pretty tight ship."

"Meaning I am not welcome?" Anna couldn't help herself.

"Meaning I will see you at Christmas," her father said soothingly. "We'll build another ice boat and scare the hell out of your mother. How's your ghostbusting?"

"Fine." *It did take her mind off Edward and Stacy.*

"Your companions treating you okay?"

"If you mean the ghosts, yes." Anna enjoyed this ritual exchange.

"And if I mean anything else?" her father asked carefully. He was deliberately breaking their protocol to give her an opening, but she thought he sounded a little frail. There was no point, really, in making him worry about her. And certainly not about her love life, or lack of one.

"Everything's okay, Daddy. I am just a little tired. Why don't you take a nap for both of us." Anna hoped her tone sounded light. Her father was not easily fooled.

"I think I will," he said, a little wearily. "You're sure you're okay?"

The extension picked up. It was, of course, her mother. "You two still talking?" she wondered, meaning "time to get off."

"Just saying good-bye," Anna's father answered meekly.

"Good-bye, Daddy. Good-bye, Mom"—and so they rang off.

That left Anna with a full night's leisure to do nothing but roast over the budding romance between Stacy and Edward. Determined not to obsess—and obsessing anyway—she resolved to be productive. Laden with tabloids and hopes she kept hidden even from herself, Anna did a full Friday night's laundry. *I should be out on the town*, she chided herself. *I should find more to do with myself than my laundry.* Daisy was not in this week's editions. Edward was not in the laundry. His omnipresent sound track was missing as well. *Was he out consoling Stacy? Oh, probably. Make that definitely. What man could resist her wounded beauty routine?*

No, it was not a peaceful night.

Chapter 69

Phyllis, the Realtor, met Anna at the station in her red Volvo station wagon.

"I hope you had a nice trip up," she said, handing Anna into the car. "I'm glad we were able to retain your services. Radio okay?" Phyllis herself had an aggressive energy, like the frequently too-loud radio in a New York cab.

"No thanks, thank you. Quiet is better," Anna leaned back and closed her eyes. The train had been a nightmare of competing cell phones. Her seat mate had argued with her boyfriend all the way from New York to New Haven. Anna wanted to focus, to calm down and get centered. *Stop thinking about Stacy and Edward*, she willed herself. *He wasn't "yours." It's a free world. Get a handle on yourself, would you? Stacy was a force of nature, nothing she could compete with.*

"It's really merely a formality," Phyllis broke into her tormented reverie. "The sale is all but a done deal. They just want you to check out the vibes, so to speak." Resigned to a conversation, Anna opened her eyes. She glanced at Phyllis, whose speedy driving along the narrow, tree-lined Connecticut roads alarmed her. For that matter the roads themselves with their twisting turns alarmed her. Phyllis was a tall, immaculately coiffed brunette. She was dressed for success in layers of beige cashmere. Anna's day fee wouldn't have bought her sweater.

"It's purely routine," Phyllis continued, piloting them through an increasingly mazelike series of seemingly identical faux-country roads. "Absolutely routine," Phyllis repeated firmly, although as far as Anna knew, haunted houses were not a staple of the real estate market.

"They're really sold on the place," Phyllis went on. "And they should be. They're getting it for a steal."

Phyllis pulled into the driveway of a handsome fieldstone-and-shingle house that rambled with charming effect over half of a well-wooded acre, featuring a small duck pond and miniature Dutch windmill. A pair of stately willows guarded the entry.

"Beautiful, isn't it?" Phyllis stated more than asked. "Five bedrooms, five baths, pool in back, Jacuzzi in the master suite, very California for Connecticut. Belonged to a retired actress and she was very California, too, I gather. My buyers are theatre people. I guess you posted a card on the Equity bulletin board?"

Anna hadn't, but perhaps Harold had. He was always lobbying for her to get a more "interesting" clientele. Those he couldn't personally supply himself, he might steer in her direction by other means. Yes, it was probably Harold's handiwork.

"Now listen," Phyllis said, suddenly all business. She took Anna by the arm, a little too firmly. "It's a perfectly lovely house and I hope you tell them that. I want to make this sale."

Climbing the flagstone steps to the front door, Anna felt a wave of unease. The brightly lacquered red front door looked inviting enough, but there was something she couldn't quite finger. The prospective owners were waiting on a handsome wooden bench just to the right of the door.

"Marc and Mallory Rodgers, and our dog, Sparky," the husband introduced himself, his wife, and their small dog. He was a tall, whippet-thin figure with a lean and long-jawed face. His wife closely resembled the Cairn terrier she was carrying. Both sported tousled locks, and bright, shiny eyes peeping from beneath their bangs. As Daisy had, Mallory sported a showstopper diamond and on Sparky a matching rhinestone collar.

"Are we all ready?" Phyllis produced a key and swung open the attractive door. As Marc and Mallory stepped through into the foyer, Anna experienced a sudden skin-crawling chill. She stepped over the threshold with reluctance, finding herself in a central hallway where a carved wood banister curved upward to the second floor.

"It happened right here," she felt the words forming, and then she "saw" the crumpled figure lying on the floor near the bottom of the stairwell. As she watched, the figure seemed to stand, drifting lightly up the spiral stairs.

"There is a ghost," Anna said.

"Now, *really*," Phyllis put in, "just like that?"

"A woman's ghost," Anna continued.

"Oh, dear," said Mallory. Sparky whimpered, staring in the direction the ghost had ascended.

"Did she fall or was she murdered?" Marc wanted to know. "They found the body right at the foot of the stairs. There was talk of an intruder."

Anna could barely hear him. Her ears were filled with a high shriek and the loud pounding of a heart. She heard labored breath, a sudden gasp—involuntarily her hand flew to her throat. She felt suddenly dizzy. She rocked on her feet. Mrs. Murphy had warned her that on rare occasions, she might feel a ghost's emotions rather than merely receiving information. Clearly, this was one of those rare occasions. Knowing that didn't help. Her head was whirling. Her breath felt shallow. She felt a film of fearful perspiration forming like dew on her skin.

"Let me get you some water," Marc volunteered. Mallory's tiny dog, Sparky, had begun growling. Anna sank down on the final stair. She buried her face in her hands.

"I'm sure we can all be very dramatic," Phyllis intervened, "but it's a perfectly normal house with a bit of a history."

"I was pushed," Anna heard the words form distinctly in her head. *"I saw him at the last second. He pushed me."* Again, Anna felt the rush of terror, the shove and the push. Anna distinctly heard the words form in her head. She felt the tumbling fall. Mrs. Murphy *had* warned her about this. Although most of the time her ghosts would come to her as simple information and detached impressions—voices and visuals, so to speak— in rare and traumatic circumstances, they could also come as feelings. She couldn't say she had not been warned but this was her first

233

experience of the phenomena.

"It wasn't an accident, was it?" Mallory demanded. "Sparky here goes crazy whenever we come."

"That's nonsense," Phyllis pronounced sharply. "He just wants to get down and play. Don't you, Sparky?" she crooned menacingly at the tiny canine who showed her a small set of white and shiny teeth. "I don't feel a thing," Phyllis continued. "Nothing ominous. Never have, never will. Not everyone is susceptible." *Meaning gullible*, Anna thought.

"Are ghosts dangerous?" Mallory wondered aloud.

"As a rule, no," Anna answered. "In fact, most of the time, I find them almost jolly."

"There, I told you." Phyllis seized on this bit of information. "Nothing to fear except fear itself. An old lady fell downstairs. It happens all the time."

"Here you go," Marc said, handing Anna a tall glass of water. "Please forgive the expression, but you look like you've seen a ghost."

Anna smiled weakly. She hadn't merely seen a ghost, she'd felt one. She explained to Marc and Mallory that sometimes the spirits in violent deaths got caught at the scene of the crime.

"So it was violent," Marc suggested.

"Yes, I'd say so," answered Anna, aware of Phyllis's palpable anger but aware, too, of her job.

"Can't you do an exorcism or something?" Phyllis wanted to know.

"It's not my forte," Anna answered, feeling once again the cold and clammy chill, sensing that the ghost was again gathering itself in an attempt to speak. *"He pushed me,"* Anna heard the words clearly.

"He who?" she mentally queried. *"He who?"* But silence answered her back.

"Anything we should know?" Mallory asked fearfully.

"It wasn't an accident," Anna said carefully. "She was murdered, pushed down the stairs."

"This is ridiculous," Phyllis retorted. "Absolutely ridiculous."

"There is a ghost," Anna said stubbornly. "That's what you paid me to know."

"So get rid of it. Do something," Phyllis insisted.

"I told you, I can't, I don't," Anna explained.

"What good are you then?" Phyllis wanted to know. "What do you actually do? I thought you could get rid of ghosts."

"Actually," Anna answered. "I talk to them. I'm more like a telephone than anything else. Is it her heirs who are selling the house?"

"This is nonsense!" Phyllis snapped. "Her son put this house on the market because it was an expensive albatross for him."

Anna sipped at her water. Her strength was coming back as the ghost ebbed away. She felt steadier.

"I hate to say it," Anna spoke more to Marc than Mallory. "But I wouldn't buy it."

"New-age hogwash," Phyllis piped up. "Claptrap. Parlor tricks. Idiocy."

Anna didn't bother to retort. She didn't doubt the legitimacy of the old lady she had seen or the terror she had felt. Her own system felt poisoned by the adrenaline that had washed through it.

"I hope I was useful," she finally managed to say. Marc helped her to her wobbly feet. He volunteered to drive her back into the city himself. Anna accepted with relief. Phyllis locked the door behind them.

"Thank you for coming," she all but snarled. Anna did not say, "Anytime."

After Phyllis, Mallory, and Sparky pulled away in Phyllis's red Volvo, Anna allowed Marc to usher her to the passenger seat of his black BMW. "Comfy?" he asked.

"I'm fine," Anna answered. She slid into the glove leather seat and securely fastened her seat belt. "I could have used one of these in there," she joked lamely.

"That rough, eh?" Marc inquired sympathetically. He shifted smoothly, and the car sprang forward. To Anna's discomfort, Marc would prove an aggressive driver, promising her a ride back to the city nearly as harrowing as it might have been with Phyllis.

"Actually, yes, it was rough," Anna replied. "You see, usually, I just 'know,' but, very rarely, I feel. This time I felt the ghost's last moments."

"Too bad," Marc replied. "The house is a steal, and it's exactly what Mallory and I have been looking for. Isn't there something you can do about a ghost?" Anna began to get a clearer picture of Marc's personality. He was charming, rich, and used to having his own way.

"I usually just chat with them," Anna joked again. "Most of the time it's nothing like this." Was it his driving or her own equilibrium that made her woozy?

"But the ghost wasn't dangerous or violent itself, was it?" Marc wanted to know. Clearly, he was building his own case.

"Well, no," Anna answered. "The ghost—it was a she—was actually rather sweet. It's just that her death was so violent." Again, a wave of terror washed through her. Did he have to drive so fast?

"So if we moved in, we'd be moving in with someone nice?" Marc asked.

"Quite nice," Anna conceded. She found it difficult to swallow and her breath came in shallow pants and her chest was tight. Did he want to get them killed?

"And what did she look like?" Marc wanted to know. He was tailgating the car ahead of them.

"Pretty," Anna answered, "especially for such an old lady. She wore her hair up in a French twist and had beautiful eyes. Could we slow down?" Marc slowed down resentfully. "Mallory hates my driving too," he told her.

"Pretty, eh? That's how she looks on all her *Playbills*," Marc returned to their conversation excitedly. To Anna's discomfort, he was becoming more and more thrilled by the idea of cohabiting with the famous, or semi-famous, ghost of the lately deceased actress. It would give him yet another bit of social cachet. Just like his BMW, it would announce his specialness and importance. *Women wear jewelry; men wear cars*, Anna thought to herself.

"There are people who specialize in getting rid of ghosts," Anna volunteered. "I could try to find you one of those." She closed her eyes and resigned herself to a hell-for-leather ride. The unwelcome image of Stacy and Edward intricately intertwined flashed to mind.

"No, no, no exorcists," Marc demurred, cornering assertively on the dark, serpentine Connecticut roads. "You did a very good job, I thought. I'll just have to explain to Mallory the ghost is nice."

"And Sparky?" Anna asked. "What will you do about Sparky?"

"Sparky'll get used to it," Marc answered, with a sudden show of steel. It occurred to Anna that Marc would do exactly as he pleased. He was, after all, a theater producer. His real personality was as aggressive as his driving.

Chapter 70

Anna knew the drill. Mrs. Murphy had seen to that. When, as an ill-advised teenager, Anna had become involved with helping the police solve a violent crime, Mrs. Murphy had helped her to detox from the adrenaline of the crime scene—if not from the resultant publicity.

"Whenever you get thrown off-kilter, you need to put yourself back in balance," Mrs. Murphy would say. "Restoring your own spiritual equilibrium is putting first things first. There are a variety of tools you can use and, if you do use them, you will come right-sized again."

The drill Mrs. Murphy then taught her involved cleansing baths, prayers and rituals. Anna had seldom had to use it but she knew it by heart. First, there was the hot Epsom salt bath, as hot as she could stand it—that cleared her etheric bodies of negative influence. Next was the white candle to be lit, and prayers to be said for her own peace and the peace of the deceased. Sleep came next. *If she could only stop thinking about Edward and Stacy. Hadn't Stacy taken a seminar on tantric sex? Yes, she had, with what's-his-name—David. Why even now Stacy might be practicing her techniques on Edward. Anna pictured the two of them intricately intertwined. Edward's piano was ominously silent...* Mrs. Murphy strongly suggested saying a rosary instead of counting sheep. Sleep was essential. *Sleep to mend the raveled sleeve of care.*

Weary to the bone, even wearier after her hot salt bath, Anna climbed up to her loft bed, rosary in hand. *"It comes with the territory,"* she reminded herself, starting up her Hail Marys'. A bead at a time, she recited the comforting words, letting their pious syllables wash over her, feeling their ancient grace begin to bring to her a sense of safety.

It was so rare, really, to have an encounter like the one in Connecticut. So much of her gift was spent on benign, even humorous contact. Ghosts, per se, were very seldom frightening, she mused as her mouth formed the prayers. Even today, it was the violent event, not the mother's apparition, that truly frightened her and felt evil. Her sense of danger wasn't really from the afterlife. More often evil lay in the here and now. *We are what is to be frightened of,* she reminded herself. Tired as she was, Anna took three full rosaries to fall asleep. *But at least I'm not thinking about Stacy and Edward.*

When Anna woke up, she felt displaced. The room, usually sunny, was dark. Her view looked north and she looked out into a deep gray fog, rare for Manhattan. What time was it? Maybe the sun was still on the rise. Anna glanced at her bedside clock. It read 2:30—A.M. or P.M. she wondered, and then realized the gray murk outside her window would have to pass for day. She had slept around the clock. Raising herself on one elbow, she winced; she felt pummeled all over. It was the aftershock, she knew, of events in Connecticut—an occupational hazard. *That and events with Edward.* As her head cleared, she tuned in to the music sliding over her windowsill. Yes, Edward was playing; Edward was playing what Alan had identified as Schumann. The music's romantic melancholia matched her own. *If only Edward and I—*

Edward! She had a date with Edward in a little over an hour.

It would take her nearly that long to wash and dry her hair and she was determined this time to put her best foot forward: clean hair, fresh dress, perfume—the works—but not unless she got up now. *Now* she willed herself, but her head still spun and her body ached as if she had the flu. As Mrs. Murphy had advised her, "There's a reason they call people like us 'sensitives.'"

Sensitive she was as hot water pelted her in the shower. Sensitive she was as her very scalp hurt when she shampooed. The terry-cloth towel was rough to the touch. Excedrin might help, she decided, and a huge mug of espresso. Anna believed in caffeine nearly as fervidly as she did the afterlife.

The personal line rang and Anna decided to screen the call. She was not in the mood for her mother who might have compared Thanksgiving notes with her father, but it was Alan. "Hi, Sis, are you home or shacked up with Edward? Call me."

Maybe Alan really does have ESP about me, Anna thought. *Or maybe he's just being mean.* At four o'clock, the time of her usual Alan call, she would be meeting Edward in the lobby but with no intention of shacking up. As Edward himself had remarked, they'd gone too fast and gotten too paranoid. Now she knew better. So why did Anna recall Edward's piano touch so clearly? Why did she get a little thrill thinking of his long basketball legs and his wild carrot-colored hair? *Why, when he was undoubtedly going to prefer Stacy?*

There's no accounting for taste, his or mine, Anna lectured herself, wondering if Edward matched some inner template of which she had been unaware. And, she dared hope, could she match some picture woman of his? After much thought, she dressed carefully in a wine-colored crepe de chine vintage dress that emphasized her tiny waist. For years she had fought her looks, yearning to look tall and sleek and modern—like Stacy—but tall and sleek and modern she was not, and so in a fit of self-acceptance, she had begun to shop in vintage stores where her looks were an asset, not a liability. Once upon a time, women had had curves. And if, to most men's eyes, she looked old-fashioned? Well, she wasn't interested in most men, was she? But she was interested in Edward. *Who had been, at least momentarily, until Stacy came along, interested in me*, Anna reminded her self.

The phone shrilled again. Anna decided to screen the call. *If it's Edward and he's canceling, I don't want to know*. But this time it was Stacy, sounding contrite and just a little bit scared. "Anna, this is me, Stacy," the message ran. "I am wondering if you might be a little bit mad at me? I mean, you know the way I am and you never mentioned anything to me about an Edward and so... well, I'm sorry, that's all. I didn't mean to screw things up. Call me, okay? Oh, and I'm in a little bit of a bumpy patch with Jeffrey, and I'd really like to talk to you about it."

Not on your life, Anna thought.

When the line clicked "done," Anna played the message again just for good measure. How much, precisely, had Stacy "screwed things up"? Anna wanted to know. Had she slept with Edward or merely toyed with him until he was caught, like a cat might toy with a mouse? Or a *rat*, for that matter. *Maybe Edward was the rat. Not Stacy. Maybe both of them were.* On her supposed "date" she might soon find out. *Exactly how and why did I let Edward get under my skin?* Then she remembered: *Ah, yes. The goddamn music*.

Chapter 71

At two minutes to four, when the elevator spewed Anna out into the lobby, music was still pouring from under the door to 1E. Swooping, showy and overtly pyrotechnic, Anna took it to be Liszt. It was just a guess, and a barely educated one. Alan had given her his précis, from Edward's mouth, of each of the composers Edward was preparing for the competition. To Anna's ear, Edward's playing, while skillful, lacked the sheer untrammeled joy she heard when he played Mozart. *I wonder what he sounds like in a concert hall*, Anna speculated, considering the underwater acoustics of the marble lobby. The music stopped. The door to 1E cracked open and Edward, tousle-haired, stuck his head out.

"I didn't mean to make you wait," he said breathlessly. "But maybe I should grab a quick shower. Would you like to come in?" Edward looked mad as a hatter; his carrot hair flamed and flared around his head. He was wearing a baggy T-shirt and worn blue jeans. They hung like oversized pajamas on his lanky frame.

"I could come in," Anna allowed, and stepped through the door into Edward's studio, a single cube of space dominated by an ebony Steinway and a futon maneuvered to fit just under the piano's edge.

"Would you like to meet my fish?" Edward asked. And that's when Anna noticed the oversized goldfish swimming in a tall, cylindrical tank in a shadowy corner. "Robert and Clara," Edward introduced the fish. They were named, he explained, for Schumann and his wife, who had enjoyed a particularly happy marriage. By remembering to feed his fish, twice daily, he also remembered to check the humidifier that stabilized his piano's condition, he explained. "But I probably got them for company," he admitted with a grin. "Have a seat," Edward offered, gesturing to the futon's protruding end. "I'll just be a second." Over his shoulder, as he headed into the bathroom, he called back, "Your friend is really something."

I knew it, Anna thought miserably. *Why did I even bother to come? I'm just the sidekick, the comic relief. Stacy's the dream girl, the main event.* She felt ill at the thought.

Once Anna heard the shower running, she looked around with morbid curiosity. The walls were bare except for an old poster for Mostly Mozart at Lincoln Center and a large calendar from Wilton Office Supplies with a practice schedule neatly inked in. Anna squinted at the calendar and saw her name had been penciled in just after the afternoon's Liszt and before the evening's planned Mozart. *Like a rest*, she thought, delightedly, priding herself on one of the few musical terms she remembered from Music Appreciation 101. Then she thought about Stacy. Feeling like a snoop, she quickly scanned the future squares for Stacy's name. To her intense relief, it did not appear.

"Okay, I'm ready," Edward emerged from his bathroom fully dressed but toweling dry his flame-colored hair.

"You were talking about Stacy," Anna prodded him masochistically. *Might as well get it over with*.

"She's a real man-eater," Edward laughed. "My ex-girlfriend was that type—what's the expression? Once burned, twice shy? All we had in common, really, was heart-attack sex."

"Heart-attack sex?" Anna asked weakly, sick again with envy and the fear that she was not what Edward would consider "heart attack" material. And where did he get a hip phrase like that?

"You know the kind, don't you?" Edward himself now asked. "It's just a physical, chemical thing." Now Edward flushed.

"I thought men went for that," Anna spoke her thought aloud. "I mean, Stacy has quite a track record." *Damn it! Her jealousy was certainly showing.*

"I'll bet she does, "Edward laughed. "I mean, I was flattered at first, her wanting to confide in me. But the more time we spent together, the more I felt like I could be anybody—anybody male that is. It might sound crazy, but I felt like I was with a Venus flytrap and I was the fly." Edward glanced at her ruefully. Anna managed a weak smile.

So they had spent time together, just as she had feared. But it didn't sound like they had had sex. For once Stacy had overplayed her hand.

"This just takes a minute," Edward apologized, toweling his hair.

"I could cut your hair for you," Anna heard herself offer. *Oh, dear God!* she thought. *No wonder I am the eternal sidekick.* Still, she was skilled at cutting Alan's hair, and her father's. And Edward did need to do something about what she thought of as "that hair."

"Is it that bad?" Edward wanted to know. He was suddenly self-conscious. "I try to think of it as a trademark," he offered.

"Not bad," Anna tried to recover her tact. "Just pretty much of a showstopper and you play so well—"

"Why not let the music speak for itself?" Edward finished for her.

"Well, yes." Oh dear, they seemed to once more be treading on awfully intimate footing. And it wasn't just her. Edward loomed above her, but his eyes swept her full length. Now it was Anna's turn to feel self-conscious. *Could he really not be attracted to Stacy? Could he really be attracted to her?* The possibility seemed like Lotto odds. *Still, somebody wins at Lotto...Why not me? I like what I look like.*

"You look a little pale," Edward announced as he openly scrutinized Anna, her carefully chosen dress and freshly washed hair.

"I had sort of an accident," Anna said vaguely. She did not mention or explain about Connecticut. She was determined to leave ghosts until at least their second date, *if we get that far.*

"I thought Café Mozart," Edward offered. "If you don't mind a little walk."

Anna, who had been expecting the Starbucks at the corner of their block, accepted. Café Mozart was more a date than a mere coffee date.

Café Mozart lay sixteen blocks south of their apartment building, on 70th Street, between Columbus and Broadway. Edward set a fast pace then adjusted his long strides to match Anna's shorter ones. It was a perfect late fall afternoon. The day's overcast sky now struck Anna as autumnal and dramatic. A light breeze twirled a few fallen leaves as they passed the park holding the Museum of Natural History. Anna's hair whipped around her face as they walked. So much for the pretense of a hairstyle. She looked nearly as wild as Edward did—and Edward did look wild.

As they walked, Edward strode straight ahead with an arrow's concentrated aim. Anna stole tiny sideways glances at his profile. With his new wire-rimmed glasses, he looked both handsome and intense, but perhaps he had always looked intense, Anna corrected herself. At a changing light, he abruptly grabbed her elbow as if she were a child in danger of plunging into the street. After that, Edward walked with her arm entwined with his. *He's possessive*, Anna thought with a little thrill. *He's passionate. Hadn't they already had heart-attack sex?* She smiled to herself, laughing at the hipness of the phrase, and remembering that they had. *Not that it was just physical...*

Café Mozart was loud and overcrowded. They managed to secure a small table for two but had to lean in to hear themselves speak. They both ordered cappuccinos and Edward insisted they split a slice of Vesuvius Cake, a concoction that erupted chocolate truffle and seemed to melt on your tongue. *For a monk, he's rather worldly*, Anna caught herself thinking, and then, *But who said he was a monk? Hadn't he demolished that idea with his description of heart-attack sex?*

The café's sound system was overwhelming and Anna felt herself nearly shouting just to be heard. All around them, tables of young people yelled happily into the din. Classical music blared. *Doubtless, Mozart*, Anna thought, none too fondly.

"That's right. Me," Anna felt the words forming in her consciousness. *"I'm glad to see you're giving him another chance."*

"Leave me alone. We don't need a third party on our date," Anna thought back furiously. He might be a genius, but he *had* kept her awake. Not to mention, it was Edward he was interested in, not her.

"Draw him out," the ghost advised. *"Get him to talk to you."*

"This is terrible," Edward announced. "Not the company but the decibel level. Poor Mozart."

"Mmm." Anna wasted no sympathy on Mozart. *He's certainly got none for me.* Instead, she concentrated on the luscious chocolate cake. Conversation was clearly impossible and besides, what could she say? She certainly wasn't good at small talk. *Hooker chat*, as she thought of it derisively. A Stacy specialty.

"Come on. Speak up," Mozart urged her. *"It doesn't matter what you say. Just say something."* Anna had to smile as she saw the apparition covertly comparing itself to a bust situated on the pastry stand.

"I am much better-looking," Mozart commented to Anna who was working to screen him out of her consciousness. Like Dylan or Jeremy, he seemed determined to have her attention. *"I am better-looking,"* Mozart persisted. *"They never get me quite right."* Anna focused resolutely on Edward. Now memories of Connecticut intruded darkly before her mind's eye but she willed them away by studying his excellent bone structure.

Yes, he was actually very handsome if you ignored the carnival hair. Anna set about cutting it in her mind's eye. She would need a decent scissors but she could probably find one at the twenty-four-hour pharmacy. It would do them good to do something innocent and domestic like a haircut. It was better than being pestered by Mozart. It was by far preferable to her dwelling on Connecticut. How could she behave normally on a date when she kept thinking about how weird she secretly was? How Connecticut had just proved it? Yes, a little normalcy would be good for them. She'd had quite enough of ghosts for the moment.

"Ollie, ollie umphrey, Anna. Come back, come back wherever you are." Edward broke into her reverie. "The noise is too much. Let's get out of here," he suggested. Anna was only too glad to leave Mozart and his namesake café behind them.

Out on Columbus Avenue, it was now genuinely chill. "It's nearly December," Anna said, wrapping her coat around her.

"Don't remind me," Edward said. "I have less than forty days left."

"Left?" Anna had a sudden terror he was moving out of the city.

"Until the competition," Edward explained. "That's what I'm working toward with the Liszt, Schumann, Rachmaninoff, Bartók, Bach, Chopin and Mozart." The list was dizzying.

"I really like the Mozart," Anna ventured. "But I really don't know a thing about classical music, your whole world."

Edward took this as a cue. He had begun piano at four, before kindergarten. His parents' wealthier neighbors, the Olivers, had a good piano and Mrs. Oliver, with no children of her own, was happy to let Edward tinkle. Piano lessons had quickly followed with the Olivers stepping into the breach left by his own parents' alcoholic self-absorption.

"Your parents drank?" Anna exclaimed. "That's terrible." She thought of Edward's encounter with her and scotch. No wonder he didn't indulge too often.

Edward shrugged off her sympathy. "My father drank and had a temper. My mother put up with it—and so did we, my brother and I." They paused now at a traffic light, and Edward gathered his thoughts before continuing. The Olivers had been like a second set of parents to him. They were still, Edward explained. At the Olivers', peace and harmony had reigned while at his own house there was only chaos. Both he and his younger brother had escaped in their own ways. Edward into music; his brother into sports. There had been a music scholarship, then another, and another. Plus student loans. The Olivers continued to play a hand, and a very large one, in his affairs. In a sense, they were betting on him and Edward was determined not to let them down.

"I suppose it sounds square, but I write to them at least once a week. It seems like the least I can do for all they've done for me. Mr. Oliver is pretty deaf and has a hard time on the phone. The letters give them something concrete, like field reports."

By this point in his recitation, Edward and Anna were at the scissors display in the all-night pharmacy. Anna selected a small sharp pair and insisted on paying for it herself. "You can always use a good scissors," she assured him.

"My place is a cave," Edward spoke up as they stepped into the street. "My only good light is my piano light. Do you think we could cut my hair at your place?"

"I do have a Dust Buster," Anna volunteered, "and a good lamp, but—"

"Good then," Edward was all enthusiasm. "Your place is a lot nicer than mine."

Turning her key in the lock, she heard her professional voice starting up. "This is Anna…" *Dear God, now what to do?* She slammed the door shut again as she turned to face Edward, who loomed genially over her. "Listen," she said, "there's something we have to talk about."

"Sex?" Edward preempted her. They were still in the hallway and his deep voice carried. He spoke again in a stage whisper. "Don't worry. I'm not expecting you to just, always…I mean, that night was great but—"

Anna dragged him by the arm into her apartment. She slammed the door and dove for her answering machine in one contrary motion. She just had time to recognize Marc, the prospective house buyer, saying, "I certainly hope you've recovered. We've decided to buy the house anyway," before she could turn down his voice. When she turned around, Edward was looking at her expectantly.

"Alan said you had another job in the evenings. Is it real estate?" he queried. It was an innocent question.

"No, it's not," Anna answered sharply. She did not elaborate. Let him think she was a bitch. Better that than a whacko.

"This is very nice," Edward remarked wistfully, as if he were taking in for the first time the sunny yellow walls, the philodendrons, the needlepoint throw pillows she had so labored over. Loving hands at home and midwestern roots were both apparent.

"Very homey," Anna commented with sarcasm. What was wrong with her anyway? Was she so neurotic she couldn't bear having any male but Alan in her space?

"Where should I sit?" Edward wondered. He was standing like a maypole in the center of the room.

"Right here. Help me with this," Anna answered, moving to lug the velvet Victorian chair center stage. With surprising strength Edward hefted it to the middle of the room. Abruptly, Anna remembered the lean ropes of muscle she had felt in his back. *Does he have such flashbacks?* she wondered. The thought left her nearly paralyzed.

"Let me get you a towel and a T-shirt," Anna managed to offer. She rummaged in a bureau drawer and came up with one of Alan's, discovered under the love seat after he was gone. "Newport Jazz Festival" was blazoned in white across a navy blue ground.

"Cool," Edward said and Anna thought slang fit surprisingly well in his mouth. While Edward was in the bathroom changing, Anna's family line clicked on. It was Alan with his lame joke about shacking up with Edward again. Anna dove to turn down the volume but not before Edward, grinning, emerged from the bathroom in Alan's Newport shirt.

"Don't side with him," Anna pleaded. "Let me get you a towel." She opened the large rectangular trunk where she stored her linens. "Here."

Chastened and obedient, Edward allowed himself to be led to the chair. He was certainly getting a nice tour of her character defects, Anna reflected. Adjusting his towel tighter around his neck, Anna took a first tentative snip. A fiery ringlet fell to the floor.

As it turned out, haircuts made Edward nervous and voluble. He'd had some very bad haircuts, Anna learned, mainly at the hands of a mad Frenchman who practiced his "art" at Quick Cuts. "You're sure you know what you're doing?" Edward yelped mid-haircut. It was a little late by then.

"Alan thinks so," Anna assured him.

"I don't remember Alan's hair," Edward responded with rising paranoia.

"That's the point," Anna responded. "Right now your hair is exactly what people would remember. It looks like Bozo the Clown."

"Ouch. Do your thing," Edward muttered.

My thing, Anna felt like telling him, *is nothing you'd want to get into*. In point of fact, she wasn't very happy to be into it herself. All afternoon, as they walked Columbus Avenue, as they sat in the loud and modish Café Mozart, she had been remembering Connecticut. It seemed to her that the old lady's ghost was growing ever more vivid, her large blue topaz eyes fixing Anna with a reproving stare. She couldn't very well tell all of this to Edward. Certainly not on their first date.

What else could I have done? Anna wondered now. She snipped at Edward's hair as her thoughts darkened. *She evidently didn't see her killer and neither did I. Should I have accused the son of murder? No. Innocent until proven guilty, no matter how guilty he might seem.* Mrs. Murphy had always warned her to steer clear of legal and health matters. *Spiritualism always takes a drubbing in trials like that. Hearsay from the afterworld is not legally admissible.* No, she'd only done as she was trained.

Edward shifted in his chair. He was growing impatient and she was only halfway done. "Sit still," she reproved him. This only pressed the Play button. While Anna clipped and strategized over his hair and a heap of scarlet curls gathered on the hardwood floor, Edward told her more about his father's drinking and bad temper, more about his increased refuge at the Olivers' house. Determined not to go too fast in wooing her, he seemed to be aiming at thorough. *Well,* Anna thought, *that is one approach.*

"I used to pretend they were my real parents," Edward confessed, evidently ashamed by his lack of familial loyalty.

"Who can blame you?" Anna said, carefully snipping around his ears. They were flat, well-shaped and close to his head. "Without them your childhood would have been completely Dickensian."

"Without them I'd have been sunk," Edward agreed morosely. He was not letting himself off the hook.

"Hold still. Stop talking. I want to do the front. And you did have them, thank God." *Why am I so cross with him all of the time,* Anna chided herself.

Truth be told, Anna prided herself on her haircuts. Under her hand, both Alan and her father had undergone considerable transformations. Pre-Anna, they had both been mop-headed, intellectual geeks. Post-Anna, they displayed a certain *GQ* trendiness. Anna hoped to work the same magic with Edward. She wanted his locks to be as distinguished as his playing—or at the very least not to compete for the audience's attention.

Her professional line shrilled again. Edward made a comment about Anna's evident popularity and she allowed the muffled machine to pick up the call. Let him imagine what he would.

"And you," Edward asked, "Do you like teaching?"

Anna told him she did not particularly like teaching, although she gathered she was good at it. Children seemed to thrive under her curmudgeonly charm.

"I could thrive under it," Edward volunteered. He was a charming flirt, she realized with panic. Far from being merely a geek or a nerd, he had a sizable shot of charisma. *Well, he was a performer, after all. He had to be something of a showman.*

"This is the tricky part," Anna countered, turning aside the compliment about herself. "Could you take your glasses off for a second?"

Without his glasses and with Anna's new haircut, Edward was disconcertingly appealing. Anna carefully shaped the hair at his brow line and temples. "Now let's see it with the glasses," she demanded. Edward slipped on the new wire rims. Anna scrutinized him carefully.

"You're staring at me," Edward protested.

"Of course I'm staring at you. I'm cutting your hair." To Anna's ear, she sounded surly, even hostile, but Edward looked wonderful—and he was smiling.

"Alan said you were a handful," Edward remarked. He did not sound displeased.

Chapter 72

O nce she had shown Edward to the door—wanting desperately to kiss him, settling for a quick cowardly hug—Anna was left alone, which was bad company. *That haircut was a terrible idea*, she beat herself up. Clearly, with Edward, she was already in way over her head and moving in exactly the wrong direction. True, she had slept with him too soon, but she did not want to encourage a platonic relationship. Her feelings for him were much more libidinous than that. Instead of her Dust Buster, Anna took out a whisk broom and tenderly swept Edward's tendrils into a brown manila envelope that she labeled, "Edward." Feeling a little foolish, she created an "E" for Edward file in her file cabinet and carefully filed the envelope of Edward's shorn locks.

You have really gone around the bend, she scolded herself.

"You do like him." Mozart's voice formed in her inner ear. Caught off guard, flushing with embarrassment, Anna brushed it aside. *"You like him and he likes you. I told you so,"* Mozart persisted. He was gloating. Anna spun around. She was ready to take a broom to the obnoxious phantom but he wisely did not materialize.

"If I could have some privacy," she fumed, punching in Alan's number. Her brother answered on the second ring. "Shacked up?" he wanted to know.

"On a date anyway," Anna conceded. "We went for coffee."

"He thinks you're hot," Alan informed her, sounding dubious himself. "He was afraid to call you."

"Hot?" Anna was shocked. "You could have told me."

"Or words to that effect. I wasn't supposed to talk about him, remember?" Alan grew maddeningly vague. He launched into a long monologue on the virtues of Ella Fitzgerald, her superior phrasing, her deft touch with sentimental numbers, the way she had of making even the most shopworn material all her own. Anna listened a little numbly, filing Alan's ruminations under Jazz 101, the mock serious name she had given to this aspect of their relationship, her ongoing jazz education.

"Really, how's Edward?" Alan suddenly veered back into real conversation.

"He's OK," Anna answered warily.

"Did you tell him yet?" Alan was playing the DA.

"Tell him what?" Anna feigned ignorance.

"You know, about the ghostbusting, about how weird you actually are. I mean, he has a right to know, doesn't he?"

"Alan," Anna warned. "Don't even think of calling and telling him. He thinks he's dating this nice school teacher." *Were they "dating"?* She guessed so.

"Mmmph." Alan remained noncommittal. *He just might call Edward,* Anna realized. *He just might want to stir up trouble. After all, things could grow pretty dull in Kalamazoo, Michigan—even for someone like Alan.*

"Alan, I'll tell him. I'm just waiting for an appropriate moment. Please, Alan. Don't push me off the diving board, okay?" *Do I sound desperate?* Anna wondered. She felt a little desperate. What had happened to her happy independence? Was that all denial? She knew Stacy would think so.

"Okay, but you better get on it," Alan agreed. They hung up.

Duty called, Anna decided next, and turned her attention to

the business line. First, there was the call from Marc, confiding his decision to purchase the Connecticut house. Next, there was a message from Eleanor someone, organizing a Psychic Faire. What would Anna's fee be for an evening of messages? Money was no object. *Money was no object?* There would be a psychic, Alexander; a tarot reader, Yvette; and a medium, herself. *Damn that Harold,* Anna thought. *What was he trying to rope me into this time? What I ought to do, what I really ought to do, is just quit the ghost business cold turkey. But where would that leave me? And there is the little matter of rent.* Still, she did not feel like calling Eleanor back.

Anna had gone through spells of disenchantment before. Mrs. Murphy had told her to expect them. Normally, what she did at such a low point was call Mrs. Murphy for a pep talk. This time Anna did not feel like calling. In fact, she didn't feel like doing anything except, perhaps, going to bed and burying her mediumistic career under the covers. Which would leave her with what? A career as a substitute teacher?

At least with my mediumship, I am interesting to myself, Anna ruminated. *I may drive men away in droves, but I enjoy my company and, actually, the ghosts...well, I enjoy them, too. And I love helping with reunions.*

Now she had an unexpected problem. Edward evidently thought she was "normal" and liked her as "normal." He enjoyed her company. Exactly how long could Anna keep "normal" up? Even without Alan's help there was bound to be a blunder sooner or later.

What confessional impulse led Marc to phone me? Anna wondered as she tossed fitfully despite her cozy flannel sheets. *Why do I have to be the one who "knows" that an old lady did not die by* accident and that her son stands to profit from her death? I can't prove it. I can't get up in court and say, "Your honor, her ghost told me." No, she didn't have a leg to stand on—or a bed to sleep on, for that matter.

No matter how she pummeled the pillows, how she twisted and contorted herself for comfort, sleep eluded her. Guilt gave her insomnia. There was the old lady's ghost, for one thing, and then the dilemma of the fraud she was perpetrating on Edward, passing for "normal." The rising sun was lightening her studio as Anna finally slept. When she woke at seven-thirty, nearly late for school, Edward was already at it.

Chapter 73

Harold cornered her right after first period. He all but pinned her against a student locker. Had she called? He demanded to know. "She who?" Anna responded. Harold's friend Eleanor, that's who, the wealthy socialite throwing the Psychic Faire cocktail party.

"It could be very lucrative," Harold dangled.

"She called, but I'm not doing it," Anna retorted. "What I do is not some parlor trick and besides, I'm thinking of quitting." As soon as she said it, she knew it was true.

"You're quitting?" Harold gasped in genuine horror. "You can't quit."

"Yes, I can. I want to be normal," Anna whined. Even to herself she sounded ungrateful. A gift was a "gift" after all.

"What's so great about normal?" Harold wanted to know. "I'm normal—more or less. You tell me, what is so great about normal?"

Anna did not want to tell Harold what was so great about normal. Edward was what was so great and she had no desire to confide in Harold about Edward. No. Better to keep her personal life personal.

What would it be like, Anna wondered, *if I just let being a medium go? What if all I knew of life were what lay on its surface?* The thought gave her a brief moment of panic, like the idea of driving with her headlights off. *Maybe I should call Mrs. Murphy*, she thought. *Then again, maybe not...* Perhaps she could formally hang up her spurs. She knew what Mrs. Murphy would say about that, and she didn't want to hear it. *I'm going to be normal*, Anna resolved. *I am going to enjoy a normal romance. This is an executive decision. Mrs. Murphy and Harold do not get votes!*

Chapter 74

Dear Mr. and Mrs. Oliver,

Well, I'm a new man—or nearly. I asked Anna to have coffee with me yesterday. I suppose it was a "date." Our second, actually. Anna wanted to cut my hair and I let her. Now I know how Samson felt. Truthfully, my new haircut looks terrific, just very short. Anna said my old hair detracted from my playing. She might have been right because without it I seem to be playing better, looser than I have in some time. The neck is not bothering me much right now, knock wood. If it just stays like this until after the competition...

Mrs. Oliver, the homemade pecan fudge arrived as one delicious slab. I put it in my refrigerator where it looked a little lonely. (I eat most of my meals at that Greek diner I may have told you about.) I guess I felt sorry for it because I ate it in just two days. I know it was a week's worth but I got greedy.

I haven't heard anything about the panel of judges. Mr. Mayakovsky says Mozart is the judge. I take that to mean I am to play as I believe Mozart intended his music to be played and let the chips fall where they may.

Do I have a choice?

Sincerely yours,
Edward

Chapter 75

A nna and Edward slipped into a pattern of shared dinners at the Greek diner and shared coffees at Anna's afterward. Edward, in his attempt to be nonmodern and less terrified, was carefully filling Anna in on the details of his life pre her arrival. Anna wasn't bored. Edward told the story of his life with humor. Even the parts about his father's drinking and alcohol-fueled temper were told without bitterness. Anna caught herself admiring Edward's character. His good humor was an aphrodisiac to her.

"I'm practicing full disclosure," Edward informed her one early December night over meat loaf and mashed potatoes. "I think you should know who you're getting involved with. If, that is, you are getting involved."

It wasn't really a question, more of a shared joke. Edward had taken to laying one of his piano hands over hers while they ate dinner. It made things awkward but romantic. Anna felt awkward yet romantic herself. From behind the counter, George would often peek at them and then smile.

In the face of Edward's self-disclosure, Anna maintained her secret. Edward wasn't Roger, but she still didn't want to scare him off. Passing for normal, she felt both guilty and shrewd. In her own way, she was practicing girlish guile. She enjoyed pretending to be normal. She enjoyed having a normal romance. And she certainly enjoyed the much better than normal kiss as they stood one night under their building's awning while a light snow fell.

I really should tell him, Anna would catch herself thinking, and then, *Not now. Don't tell him now. Not yet! Not yet!* They had been seeing each other every night, and though they hadn't been back to bed, Anna had her hopes. The touch of Edward's hand on hers set off tiny tingles in other, less accessible, places. With his new haircut, Edward looked incredibly handsome to her and Harold had once again told her, with some suspicion, that she was looking really well herself.

The professional line rang and Anna was not delighted to overhear Alexander identify himself and ask for what he called a "rematch" appointment. It seemed that his late partner might have been right about the store's fortunes and now, on sober reflection, he felt they should put their heads together again so to speak. *Not with me in the middle*, Anna thought, as she shoved the machine's volume lower still.

For two weeks after that, Anna kept the volume on her professional answering machine set to "low." The messages were piling up but she didn't care. Professional suicide seemed like a good idea. She felt a sense of relief to be freed from other peoples' burdens. She realized that she had taken on helping others as a duty. Trying to be of service, she had made herself overly responsible, often booking readings when she herself was stressed. Connecticut was really just the final straw. Freedom from caretaking felt wonderful. Anna felt a truant's glee at her escape.

Sometimes in the evenings, after Edward had gone home to practice, Anna would open her window wide to the cold night air. Edward's notes came cascading over the sill then like so many silvery snowflakes, each tiny note perfectly formed and unique. Particularly when Edward played his Mozart, Anna felt herself transported to another realm. The music was truly otherworldly, and Anna felt the same thrill of discovery listening to it as she had when she first encountered her gift for talking to ghosts. After all, it was all a matter of listening and Anna's hearing was truly pitched to higher realms. It was there that she really "met" Edward.

Stacy was blessedly incommunicado, doubtless shacked up with Jeffrey again, but Harold left an argumentative message on her personal line. "You are not calling my friends back," he complained. "I have stalled Eleanor as long as I am able to. She's willing to pay you a thousand dollars for the night. And Alexander really needs your help. Do I need to mention you're my bridge to Andrew?"

A thousand dollars? Anna found herself toying with Eleanor's invitation. She knew Mrs. Murphy would disapprove, feeling she was merely "entertainment," but if she took it, she could avoid readings for quite a little while. *And it was just one night.*

That Friday Anna brought a bottle of Dewar's with her to the laundry room. She planned to ply Edward with liquor, but

Edward, also having decided the moment had come, arrived in the laundry room bearing two heavy loads of laundry and a bottle of Valpolicella. Spotting her bottle of scotch, he laughed.

"You know what they say about great minds." He hefted his bottle of wine, then set it aside.

"What do they say?" Anna asked, but Edward answered her with a kiss, then another. His kisses were a tantalizing mixture of hunger and languor. They were both subtle and insistent. They asked for more but also managed to suggest that the current kiss was also plenty. His lips nibbled playfully then drew firmer and more demanding. *Like his music. He kisses like he plays*, Anna caught herself thinking before surrendering to a wave of passion in herself.

As their lights chugged and churned, Edward and Anna exchanged kisses. By the time they were waiting for their darks to dry, their embraces were more fervid, even without the aid of alcohol, which they had somehow forgotten to drink. When their dryers clicked off, they heaped aromatic armloads into their baskets and repaired to Anna's apartment. Once there, they stripped off their clothes, scrambled into the loft bed, and fell hungrily into each other's arms.

"Is all your lingerie red?" Edward asked her.

"Yes," Anna answered. "For passion."

One more time, perhaps due to his long hours of practicing, Edward fell asleep first, his head tilted gently toward Anna's shoulder, his clipped coppery curls glinting against her naked arm. Anna slept eventually because when she heard the now familiar voice, she started awake and lay there quietly, striving not to wake Edward.

"He needs you," announced the silver-wigged apparition,

262

floating in its foppish waistcoat up near her ceiling. She all but hissed, *"Please go away!"*

"You are not my patron," the ghost replied telepathically. *"I don't need to listen to you."* Clearly, Anna was entering a battle of the wills.

"Well, I don't need you," she thought back, adding, *"and he's doing just fine without your help—or should I say your interference?"*

"You might display a little respect," retorted the ghost.

"And so might you," Anna fumed.

"Although it may not seem so to you, he might actually welcome my guidance. You might want to ask him." The ghost sounded infuriatingly sure of itself.

"Are you crazy? I am not telling him a thing about you or any other ghost for that matter." Anna was insistent.

"You're very willful." The ghost sounded peeved.

"So are you!" Anna was not about to be bullied. *"I'm not going to tell him I am talking to Mozart. He'd think I'm crazy."*

"You should just ask him. He would love to know how I want my music to be played." The ghost spoke with petulant insistence. *"He's really so much better than the rest of them—all racing through my work like it's a set of rapids. They're all interested in showing off but he's not. He actually tries to fathom my intentions. I tell you, if I had known my music was going to be immortal, I'd have left more markings. Mahler had an eye to the future. He marked everything. I was much too modest."*

"You? Modest? All the stories we hear were about your arrogance!"

"Well, I did write the whole overture to Don Giovanni *the night before we opened."* The ghost could not resist bragging.

"Exactly! Now if we could please have some privacy!" She

shifted, reluctant to wake Edward, but wanting her back to the intrusive ghost. If he was stubborn, so was she. And she simply would *not* indulge him.

"*Don't turn your back on me!*" The ghost was annoyed.

"*I will if I want to.*"

"*Yes, you're very willful, as I've said before. You're a stubborn, impudent girl and you lack respect for your elders.*"

"*You are not my elder just because you're dead!*"

"*Must you mention the obvious?*"

"*Why can't you leave us alone?*"

"*I do leave you alone. Do you notice me hanging around that terrible diner you so love?*"

"*It's a perfectly fine diner.*"

"*It's a diner.*"

"*So you are a snob.*"

"*We're not here to discuss my character defects.*" The ghost sounded grieved.

"*Why are we here?*"

"*We're both here about him. My grand, grand, grand nephew. Twice removed.*"

"*So this is nepotism?*" Anna enjoyed having scored a point.

"*You could call it that if you insist on being cynical. When he was a youngster—you remember he came from a terrible home?— he used to call on me to help him. 'Uncle Mozart' he called me. Who could resist that? I used to go to him in his dreams. Still, you know how it is. A child outgrows an invisible playmate. Edward outgrew me.*"

The ghost sounded melancholy. For the first time in their acquaintance, Anna felt sympathy for his position.

"*Now I understand,*" she said, but the ghost was gone.

Chapter 76

Dear Mr. and Mrs. Oliver,

Well, I did it again. Maybe it was overpracticing with what Mr. Mayakovsky calls my "careless posture." Maybe it was from lugging the laundry or sleeping on it funny, but the neck is gone again. I can still play, barely, and Mr. Mayakovsky is threatening me with a total layoff, which I can't afford with the competition four weeks away.

Mrs. Oliver, I am trying your suggestion of Vick's Vap-o-Rub and so far the neck still hurts and I smell like a eucalyptus plant. Is that what that stuff is made from? I've also tried your Epsom salt bath and I am signed up this afternoon for a "deep tissue" massage, which sounds sinister and is very expensive. I can play—I should say "still play"—but it's very painful and, to my ear at least, it's starting to sound that way, too.

Sorry to be so depressing.

Sincerely yours,
Edward

Chapter 77

"Westside Aquarium is my church," Anna told Tommy over a burrito at Senor Swanky's. "I hope you realize that I come there to meditate." She was and wasn't kidding him.

"I realize that. I hope you realize that I deliberately don't talk to you until you've had your quiet time."

'The fish just calm me down."

"I know what you mean. Ever since Hughie passed, I find myself looking for stuff like that."

"I've got a meditation I really like." Anna told him then about her koi pond and the calming effect it had on her nerves. "Even five minutes does the trick," she concluded.

"I could get into a koi pond," Tommy responded. "I could probably get into a lot of things you're into."

"Don't start, Tommy, okay?" Anna was alarmed by the turn the conversation was taking.

"Don't give me, 'Don't start.' You came out on this date with me of your own free will." Tommy reached for her hand. "You know you did."

"This not a date," Anna insisted. She pulled back her hand.

"Of course it is."

"Tommy, we're *friends*."

"Don't give me, 'Tommy, we're *friends*.' I know you want to jump my bones. You do, don't you?" Tommy swigged at his margarita. He eyed her over its rim.

"Are you serious?" Anna was completely at a loss.

"Cat got your tongue? Come on, Anna. I think you're hot." Tommy signaled the waiter for another drink.

"You do?" Despite herself Anna was flattered. Still, she didn't want to jump Tommy's bones. She just didn't know how to tell him that. *Be careful*, she could hear Stacy telling her.

"I think you should give it a shot. You already know the worst about me. I go through women's purses."

"Tommy, I'm flattered." Anna sipped at her Coca-Cola. For once, she wished it were something stronger.

"'Tommy, I'm flattered' is the kiss of death, the kiss-off, isn't it?" Tommy demanded.

"Maybe so." Anna admitted.

"See, listen to you. You said, 'Maybe.' You're just so nice, Anna. I could use a little nice." The waiter brought Tommy his second margarita. "A little nice would be nice."

"You deserve someone nice," Anna said carefully. "And I am flattered. But I'm not who you're looking for. You're looking for someone who's looking for you. The truth is, I'm taken."

"You certainly are!" Mozart's ghost hissed into Anna's ear. *"The last thing we need is for you to have some sort of fling—with a bi-sexual no less—and Edward to find out about it!"*

"Leave me be!" Anna willed the ghost.

"Why. You're clearly not to be trusted."

"I can be trusted!" Anna mentally defended herself.

"I don't see a ring." Tommy insisted. He grabbed for her left-hand ring finger. "See? Naked as a jaybird!"

"I don't wear one." Anna protested, yanking back her hand. "It's premature. I mean, I know I'm taken but he may not know he has taken me yet."

"Pathetic," Tommy chided. "If I took you, we both would know you'd been taken. Come on. That sounds fun, doesn't it?"

"You got yourself into this, now let's see you get yourself out," the ghost interjected.

"There's really somebody else?" Tommy's deep blue eyes fixed on her face.

"Yes." Anna sipped at her Coke. Why did she sound so tentative?

"And does he think you're hot?" Tommy's tone was teasing again, flirtatious.

"Be careful," Mozart warned. *"Laughter is the greased slide to the bedroom."*

"You should know!" Anna shot back.

"Well, does he?" Tommy repeated.

"I hope so. I think so. Oh, Tommy, I am so sorry."

"Let's not be sorry prematurely. Cheers. Here's to friends." Tommy chug-a-lugged his drink. "But if it doesn't work out, you'll call me?

"Definitely." Anna answered.

"You be careful!" the ghost hissed as it vanished.

Chapter 78

The longer Anna kept her secret life from Edward, the bigger her secret became. She had told him a ghost-free version of her childhood in Ann Arbor, a ghost-free adolescence as if there were any such thing, followed by ghost-free college years and then her ghost-free twenties. She amazed herself that, ghosts aside, she had anything to talk about. Ghosts had occupied center stage for so long that normal life seemed pale to her by comparison, although Edward seemed to find it interesting.

She told him about her father and the ice boat incident and her father's racy red roadster. He said he could picture her driving it like Nancy Drew, plucky and intrepid. *If I were really plucky and intrepid, I'd try out a few ghosts on you*, Anna thought. But she found she wasn't brave enough to risk her fragile, newfound happiness, and so she and Edward continued to spend their quiet ghost-free evenings at the Greek diner, followed by the evening's serenade, followed by bed, blissful bed, in Anna's loft. *I could see clients while he practiced*, Anna considered, then rejected the idea. *What if he quit early and I got caught? No. I can't afford the risk. Then again, right now I can't afford the rent.*

Anna gave Edward a second haircut, even shorter this time. Edward liked the haircut but he was worried about his playing. The neck brace had reappeared, although no red ringlets now crowned its snowy rim.

One night after a frequently interrupted evening's serenade, Edward arrived at Anna's apartment with tears of frustration filling his eyes.

"I can't play worth a damn," he told her. "I can't play a god-damn thing through this pain." Clearly, he was both furious and in despair. "Mr. Mayakovsky is threatening me with a layoff, and I just can't afford one."

"But do you need one?" Anna asked.

"I can't afford one now," Edward answered. "No matter what my teacher thinks."

That was the first time Anna realized how stoic he had been, how much he had suffered making his beautiful music. The competition was scant weeks away and Edward was in agony when he played. Not playing, he was in agony still. He *needed* to play. A shift in his playing habits was the long-term solution. In the short term, relaxation was the key. He needed to relax, but how could he relax about his playing? He owed it to the Olivers to be practicing, he told her. He did not say he also felt he owed it to himself.

"But couldn't you injure yourself more?" Anna asked gently. "In the larger scheme of things, doesn't your health come first?"

"Not necessarily." Edward avoided her eyes.

"But it has to!"

"Not necessarily." Now Edward's eyes flashed steel.

"I mean, you're what's important. Your health and well-being." Anna trailed off, intimidated.

"You sound like Mr. Mayakovsky," Edward snapped. "I've already got more advice than I know what to do with... Sorry. Didn't mean to bite your head off."

But he had.

Chapter 79

Harold called Anna to his office for her lunch break. He produced his famed chicken salad sandwiches on croissants. He augmented them with tiny containers of cinnamon applesauce. He offered bottles of good ginger ale. Anna accepted all of it. She had packed a lackluster peanut butter and jelly.

"You look very good," Harold said appraisingly. "A few pounds thinner. Makeup and heels. You're not really quitting, are you?" He meant, "What's going on?" She had now cancelled their standing appointment three weeks in a row.

"Come on," Harold teased. "Whence comes that rosy glow?"

"Thank you," Anna navigated the compliment by taking a large mouthful of sandwich indicating all bets were off, but Harold was not to be deterred.

"You've got a boyfriend, don't you?" he cried. "Just like Alexander saw for you. Okay, finish your sandwich then details, details."

Anna shook her head "no." Had she become a practiced enough liar to lie to Harold with his excellent nose for gossip? She doubted it.

"I have a *friend*," she ventured cautiously, feeling protective of Edward's privacy and her bond to him.

"By a 'friend,' do you mean a boyfriend or an unrequited romance?" Harold did not mince words.

"A boyfriend, I guess," Anna anted up reluctantly.

"And this boyfriend is, let me guess, a bond trader, a serial killer? No, some kind of athlete. Look at that sexy flush."

"Harold, please!" Anna protested by holding up a hand and also feeding herself the last bite of sandwich, so she couldn't answer.

"Enough about you then," Harold let her off the hook. "Even if you have, evidently, given up a promising career."

"It's just a little sabbatical," Anna assured him, wondering if that were the truth. "I'm sick of ghosts, and sometimes I mean that literally."

"Now, why would you be sick of ghosts?" Harold asked. She told Harold then about the incident in Connecticut, the way she'd come home feeling pummeled and ineffectual. The way Marc and Mallory had bought the property anyway.

"You did your job," Harold told her. "What they do about it isn't your responsibility." Harold sounded just like Mrs. Murphy.

"It feels like my responsibility," Anna answered him.

"You're disillusioned," Harold advised soothingly. "Think of all the good you've done for me and Andrew and lots of others who needed, ah, closure. If that doesn't cheer you up, think about your young man." Harold's eyes were again bright and amused. He wore his Cheshire cat smile. "Actually I've known there was someone for quite a while." His source *had* to have been Alexander, since Anna herself had told him nothing. But it seemed pointless to deny Edward's existence now.

"And what does he think of your gifts?" Harold now wanted to know. "He must find them fascinating. I know I do." *Harold sounds as bad as Stacy*, Anna thought.

"I haven't told him," Anna confessed. "I wanted to give the relationship a chance. I wanted him to think I was normal. Men usually freak out."

"You mean straight men. They're so provincial." Harold sounded a little smug.

"Harold, by definition a boyfriend is straight."

"I suppose so."

"Unless you count Tommy." Anna volunteered.

"Tommy?" Harold picked the name up like a clue. "Oh, yes. Tommy!"

"You remember. He's this very good-looking, very charming, very bisexual man who has been chasing me. It's kind of fun being chased."

"Choices, choices. Isn't that what Alexander told you?"

"Did he?"

"You know he did. So you've been playing 'normal.' That's why you haven't called Alexander back. That's why Eleanor can't get to you. Mmm." Harold tweaked a corner of his luxuriant mustache, a habit he had when he was thinking. "Maybe you underestimate him," Harold suggested.

Maybe I do. Maybe Edward wouldn't head for the hills like all her previous romances. *Maybe if I told him in my own time in my own way?* Anna decided to consider it. *But not just yet.*

"Oh, Harold," Anna murmured. "I'm afraid to tell Edward—that's his name."

"C'mon, Anna," Harold dismissed her concern. "You underestimate your appeal."

"You overestimate my courage," Anna protested. "And not everyone is as fascinated with things spiritual as you are."

"You have a gift. A rare gift. Andrew and I are very grateful. Why, you're a bridge between worlds. It's meant everything to me to know that Andrew is happy."

"He *is* happy," Anna assured him. "Death's just a doorway, Harold. It's the stepping-off place to somewhere better. It's very rare for me to meet a dissatisfied ghost."

"Then I guess you will be going back into business," Harold brusquely countered. "That Connecticut episode was just a fluke. Can I see you next Friday?"

Chapter 80

Feeling more secure in Edward's affections, not wanting to hold a needless grudge, Anna phoned Stacy and suggested they resume their regular Tuesday night supper date. Stacy sounded pathetically grateful. "Thank you for being my friend. I really didn't get it."

Stacy arrived at the Popover Café lightly dusted with snow. With her pale blonde hair and rosy cheeks, she looked angelic, like that Breck girl in the old advertisements. She quickly dispelled this image.

"I'm so glad you've forgiven me," she announced. "I really,

really didn't know."

"That's because I was keeping him one of my many secrets," Anna responded, laughing at herself. Then she noticed that her friend was not laughing with her.

"Do I look weird?" Stacy asked. She leaned across the table for Anna's scrutiny.

Anna squinted at her friend and at first detected nothing. Then she realized that Stacy's artful eye makeup concealed a shiner, a real shiner this time, not just ruined mascara.

"Is that a black eye?" she demanded.

"I've broken up with Jeffrey," Stacy informed her.

"Before or after the black eye?" Anna wanted to know. Jeffrey had always struck her as a self-centered and abusive jerk. "I could kill the son of a bitch."

"What does it matter?" Stacy asked. She began to cry in earnest, and as she did her careful makeup dissolved away, revealing a deep purple bruise the size and shape of a plum.

"What does Dr. Rich say?" Anna asked. Surely now he would come to his senses and advise her to dump Jeffrey. Or at least to keep him dumped.

"I am afraid to tell him," Stacy sniffled. "He'll think I don't have any self-esteem and he thought I was doing so well."

"Well, you're not. You look awful. Does it hurt?" Anna commiserated. She had no personal experience with male-female violence of any kind. Her parents' bickering was always rather good-spirited. They never really came to blows, even verbal ones.

"I feel awful. And stupid. I thought an open marriage was more stable than a separation. He went back to his wife. They renegotiated," Stacy blurted between sobs. She mopped at her tears with a cloth napkin. Now, her perfect nose was running, too. She daubed at that.

"But the black eye?" Anna asked. Her imagination winced at the thought of Jeffrey's explosive temper unleashed on her lovely friend.

"He was just defensive." Stacy minimized what she would later call "the incident."

"Don't make excuses for him," Anna demanded. "I'd say he has a little problem with anger management."

"That's what he said," Stacy murmured. "He felt so bad about it."

"I'll bet. You should have called the cops." Anna was serious.

"Oh, Anna. What would that have fixed?" Stacy wiped at her nose.

"What a slimeball. You should eat something."

Anna ordered Stacy her favorite, a blackened shrimp salad. She ordered herself the Waldorf, her standard. The waiter offered Stacy ice for her eye and a fresh napkin, but that only brought on another round of tears. The waiter hovered solicitously.

"Everyone is so nice to me," Stacy wailed. Even in her misery, she was attractive. Their waiter was clearly smitten. Anna hoped that soon Stacy's horde of eligible suitors would return.

"Everyone but Jeffrey was always nice to you," Anna put in. "David seemed great for a while, remember? I thought he really liked you. Remember?" David had been the longest-lived of Stacy's suitors.

"I remember that I confronted him about sex after we took that tantric workshop," Stacy sniffled. "He still calls, just to check up on me, he says." Stacy blew her nose. "Do you think maybe I was the selfish one?"

"Maybe," Anna replied. "But I actually thought you liked David.

You saw him longer than the rest of them." She hoped that Stacy was done with bad boys and slumming, and would return to the safe arms of more appropriate men.

"I *miss* him," Stacy moaned. She patted at her swollen eye.

"David?" Anna felt hope.

"No," Stacy blurted, a little ashamed. "Jeffrey."

"You probably just miss the sex," Anna ventured, thinking of Stacy's overheated descriptions. She noticed their waiter was now shamelessly eavesdropping.

"The sex!" Stacy sighed. "Oh, yes, the sex...but what is it about male artists that they all think 'genius must be served'? I guess his wife is a better geisha than I was."

Anna did not respond. She had planned to finally tell Stacy all about Edward, but now thought better of it. Her happiness seemed tactless in the face of Stacy's grief. *Let's just keep private, private*, Anna decided. Edward was, after all, a male artist and Stacy might think she, too, was in it just for the sex—which, admittedly, was wonderful. *He makes love like he makes music.* Even without prompting from Stacy, Anna flushed as she remembered... Fortunately, their salads arrived.

Chapter 81

As she turned her key in the lock, she heard Alan speaking on the family message machine. He sounded peevish—like he'd lost at chess—that he could not reach her instantly. Anna dove for the phone.

"I'm here," she said breathlessly. She *did* miss her brother.

"You're there and I'm here," Alan said gloomily. "New York is wasted on you. Did you know Branford Marsalis is playing at the Blue Note? Does Edward know?"

Anna did not. Further, she doubted that Edward knew and that, without Alan's prodding, he would ever go.

"He's a little absorbed right now," Anna told Alan. She mentioned Edward's long hours at the piano.

"New York is wasted on him, too," Alan diagnosed their apparent malaise. "How can you live there and not do things?"

"We do things," Anna answered defensively.

"We?" Alan was on to her like a cheap suit. "*We?*"

"Edward and I have been spending some time together," Anna allowed.

"I told you he had the hots for you," Alan pounced. "Have you filled him in yet on your secret life?"

"No!" Anna yelped. *Did they have to get into this?*

"Do you intend to?" Alan pressed. "Anytime in the near future?"

"That depends," Anna said carefully. *Damn Alan. He was always pushing her off the diving board.*

"Well," Alan pronounced, "I would call that a fairly large lie of omission."

"Edward thinks I'm normal," Anna protested. "I like being normal." *Normal is pretty wonderful.*

"Well, you're not normal," her brother sniped. "And as his friend, I should tell him."

"Alan! You wouldn't!" Anna yelped again, but she knew that her brother would. "Just give me a little more time and I'll tell him," she pleaded. "I just need to figure out how."

"Oh, all right. Call it your Christmas present. You are coming home, aren't you? Dad is clearly pining away for a visit from his favorite."

"How is he?" Anna asked, glad to be on more solid ground.

Their father was visibly on the mend, Alan reported. And their mother was visibly on the march. She enjoyed her temporary position as kingpin of the household. For once, their father did what she wanted. In fact, he did a lot of things she wanted, not only physical therapy but also the low-fat diet she had so long advocated to no avail. No doubt about it, Alan observed, his close shave had put him on notice and now he was toeing the line.

"So how's Edward?" Alan now wanted to know. "Is his neck okay?"

"No. I think he's in a lot of pain." Anna detailed the trickiness of Edward's neck.

"Of course he's in a lot of pain," Alan burst out. "Pain is his middle name with an injury like that, but tell him I've got fifty dollars riding on his capable shoulders."

Anna couldn't tell if her brother was kidding or not. Could he really be placing bets on Edward's handicap? Yes, she decided, he could. But who bet against him? Their father? Yes, probably. It gave him something naughty to do right under his wife's very nose. How she would hate his dragging classical music down from its pedestal.

Alan concluded his conversation with a half-hour monologue on why she should hear Branford Marsalis—the physicality of his playing, his incredible sense of propulsion and line, "almost like a drummer's," he summarized his pitch. Over her brother's voice, through her habitually open window, Anna heard Edward grappling with his worsening condition. Even to her untutored ear his playing seemed to be losing ground.

That night, Anna slept alone and it was a good thing that she did. At two-thirty by her bedside clock, Mozart's ghost appeared. This time he wafted straight toward her loft bed, determined to have her undivided attention, which he did.

"The teacher is right," the apparition began speaking aloud in its heavily inflected English. *"His playing habits are very bad. So were mine. Does that surprise you?"* Evidently the ghost wanted an actual conversation. Angrily, Anna obliged. He was, after all, talking about Edward. And she was worried about Edward.

"Yes," she relented, *"I guess it does surprise me. All we ever hear about you is how easy it all was for you. A child prodigy, et cetera."*

"Ridiculous propaganda," the ghost snorted derisively. *"Silly stories."*

"Well, it's what we hear," Anna insisted. Even she knew stories of Mozart's prodigal virtuosity, his sheer musical gifts.

"I had terrible playing habits," Mozart confessed. *"My wife had to massage my shoulders and that never really helped the playing because one thing led to another, you see. You do see. I've seen you two."*

"You spy on us?" Anna retorted hotly. *"You're nothing but a pervert, a voyeur."*

"That and a maestro," the ghost promptly corrected her. *"I take a great interest in him. If you were musical, you would understand that. Still, you could be more cooperative and quite a help to him. I wouldn't bother with you really but he is the best. I love how he plays my music. You can't imagine how often they get it wrong. He needs to change his fingering to get to the high B flat in*

the third movement."

"So what do you want from me then?" Anna asked crossly. She propped herself on one elbow and scowled across the railing at the ghost. For a fleeting instant, she had a flash of pride at her abilities. No mere voice or impression, her encounters with Mozart's ghost were nearly Technicolor in their clarity. *"I hate it when you wake me up, and you must know that I'm trying to give all this up."*

"Not yet," the ghost raised a warning finger. *"I'm not finished with you yet. Not until you help him. I want him to win."* The apparition was speaking now without sarcasm. The intensity in its tone, the power of its will, seemed somehow more pure.

"How on earth can I help him?" Anna demanded in frustration. *"I don't know a thing about music and he knows that. Actually, I think that's something he likes. He knows I love him for himself and not just for his music."*

"Of course you love him for his music," Mozart contradicted her. *"How can you separate the two?"*

"I can," she protested.

"Well, I can't," the ghost insisted. *"And furthermore, I don't want to. But I do want to help him win and that's where you come in."*

"I do? There's free will, you know." Anna did not like being bossed around.

"In your case free will is a damnable mistake. It could be so easy. I talk to you, you talk to him. Very simple. Surely even you can hear that his playing has gone off."

"Yes," Anna admitted. *"I can. I think he's in a lot of pain. He tries so hard."*

"I know how to fix it and that's where you come in." The ghost was not to be deterred.

"So I'm just convenient?" Anna bridled at the thought.

"If you love him, you'll help him," the ghost replied.

"And how do I do that?" Anna did want to help Edward.

"You will tell him," the ghost demanded, *"that you're talking to me. You will tell him that I want him to win. That I approve of his playing. That I also suffered from injuries and bad habits. You will tell him that he's just to listen for me as he plays. And relax his shoulders. And change his fingering in the third movement to reach that high B flat."*

"I can't do that," Anna said. *"I can't tell him I talk to you. Can't you understand how important he is to me? Can't you understand that he thinks I'm normal?"*

"He needs some encouragement," the ghost persisted. *"More than he can get from just you. He would be thrilled to hear from me. He would be thrilled to know he's on the right track with his interpretation."*

"But I can't tell him I talk to you. Don't you understand? He thinks I'm normal. If I tell him I talk to you, he'll think I'm crazy." Even to her own ear, Anna sounded like she was whining. And then there was the absurdity of it all, her claiming to be normal when she was sitting bolt upright in her bed, arguing with a ghost. *"Please leave me alone,"* she pleaded. *"Please let me sleep."*

"You can and you will tell him," Mozart's ghost announced imperiously. *"If you love him, you can and you will,"* it repeated. *"Or else I'll never leave you alone."* And then, abruptly, it was gone. The faintest trace of melody lingered in the air.

No one would believe me, Anna lay in bed thinking. By "no one" she meant Edward. Even if he could believe that she actually talked with ghosts, why would he believe her about Mozart's visitation? It was hard enough for her to accept a celebrity ghost.

And another thing, she thought crabbily, *what about my sleep?* She couldn't exactly doze back off in restful slumber—not after this exchange with her illustrious and obnoxious visitor. By now, she was wide awake. It was much too early to call Mrs. Murphy, and she doubted that her mentor would do anything but side with Mozart.

How could she tell Edward that she talked with ghosts? On the other hand, if she loved him and wanted to be honest, how could she not? Mozart was asking her to take much too large a leap of faith, Anna decided, not only in herself but in Edward as well.

Chapter 82

The next morning, thanks to her nocturnal visitation, Anna slept through her alarm, or she would have missed her father's call. She woke to hear his voice speaking to her on the answering machine. Throwing back her covers, she scrambled down the ladder.

"Daddy?" she grabbed for the phone and heard the answering machine disengage. "Daddy? Is that you?"

A glance at her clock told Anna she would have to call in sick. *Poor Harold, he'd have to scramble for another sub.* She was already well past tardy. It was ten-thirty in the morning. She couldn't imagine why she slept so late and then, all too clearly, she remembered.

"You there?" her father was asking. His voice had some of its robust strength back again. He continued. "Your brother tells me you've got a fellow."

"Damn Alan," Anna burst out. "I've got no privacy anymore, have I? Sorry, Daddy, I'd have told you but it's just so new."

"Too new to bring him home for Christmas?" her father wondered.

"Much too new, much too new," Anna assured him, adding, "Besides, he has a competition the first week in January and I might not be coming home myself." This was news to Anna as well as to her father. Until she heard herself say otherwise, she had assumed she was going home. Now she admitted to herself a fantasy of Christmas in New York with Edward.

"This is serious then," her father observed. "I guess he's the open-minded sort?"

Her father was trying to be tactful. Anna appreciated his consideration, but it really only made things worse.

"I haven't told him yet," she confessed miserably. "It never works out when I do."

"Ah," her father said. "I see." His tone gave the impression he considered it a considerable oversight. Of course he would. He was the one who had driven her weekly to Mrs. Murphy's. He was the one who both accepted and encouraged her special gifts.

"Don't start on me, Daddy," Anna whined. "Alan already did. He's threatening me that if I don't tell Edward, he will. I guess Alan told you the two of them are friends."

"That doesn't give your brother the right to meddle in your affairs," her father said judiciously. Anna could only hope he'd tell Alan the very same thing. Hanging up from her father, she phoned in sick. Harold was none too pleased.

"You're up all night with that boyfriend," he accused.

"Well, up all night," Anna allowed.

"At least call back Alexander today. At least call back Eleanor," Harold importuned.

"Maybe." *There is rent to consider*, Anna thought. She felt pressured from all sides.

"Hello," Alexander answered on the first ring when Anna phoned him at the shop.

"Is this Alexander?" Anna asked.

"Of course it's Alexander, there's no one else here," Alexander responded with ill temper.

"This is Anna, Harold's friend," Anna ventured.

"Ah, yes, Harold's friend. Certainly not mine," Alexander said. "I've been trying to get you for weeks, and you're only calling me back now because you need my money."

"There's rent," Anna admitted. What was the point in lying to a psychic?

"I was hoping we could do a barter. I'm a little low on cash right now," Alexander told her. "I thought you might like to know a little bit more about your love life, the way I see it going. There's a bump in the road coming, I'm afraid."

"There is?" Anna knew Alexander was reeling her in, even manipulating her, but she felt helpless to escape. Her ear pressed to the phone, she felt nearly as paralyzed as she had when she saw Isis the snake.

"I know, I know, why don't I just come up there. Everything at your convenience," Alexander sniped.

"Well, I can't come there," Anna answered. "There's that snake."

"What is it with you and snakes?" Alexander asked.

"Shouldn't you know that?" Anna sniped back. Clearly, they were not going to be fast friends.

"Harold said you could help me," Alexander suddenly changed tacks. "He said you'd be willing to see me one last time."

Damn Harold, Anna thought. *Damn Harold and his continual meddling. Why, I would be better off without him. On the other hand, I'd be broke.*

"Where do you want to meet?" Anna asked Alexander. "You've got the snake, and I've got"—she paused—"something else to consider."

"Your precious privacy? Harold told me all about you and your secrets."

"Oh, all right, just come over. But if anyone's here when you get here, zip the lip." *This is against my better judgment*, Anna thought briefly. She opened the window another few inches, craning to hear Edward at the keys. Silence greeted her ear. Silence, and a few distant sirens. *Ah, New York.*

Alexander arrived forty-five minutes later. She buzzed him up and quickly ushered him in the door. *The coast is clear right now*, Anna thought, *but how long will it stay that way?*

"Come in, sit down, let's get started," she directed, practically shoving Alexander toward the reading area.

"Nobody's going to catch us," Alexander suddenly said. "I'm not where your trouble is coming from."

"Trouble?" Anna asked. Her heart tilted in her chest. She had been braced for this.

"Trouble," Alexander repeated. "A bump. I see an estrangement, a separation. You're going to put your foot in it somehow," he concluded. "I see deceit. Yours or his. I cannot tell."

"Enough about me," Anna interrupted. "Just sit down, and let's start." She could feel a spirit ready to come through. In fact, its thoughts were circling her like planes trying to land at LaGuardia. Alexander took a seat on the love seat. *Not*, Anna noticed, *on the spring*.

"I told you so," a voice said in Anna's ear. She repeated its opening sally.

"Yes, you did," Alexander replied, chastened. "And for once you were right."

"I was always more right than wrong," the voice retorted. Wincing, Anna continued the escalation. The voice was clearly Alexander's dead partner, Jay.

"Yes, you were," Alexander unexpectedly admitted. "That's why I'm here."

"What's why you're here?" Jay demanded. Anna faithfully conveyed the question.

"I'm here to say I'm sorry, I'm here to say I've thought things over. I've had some thinking time lately—" Alexander broke off.

"Because the shop's so empty?" Jay's ghost jibed. Anna relayed the jab.

"It is empty," Alexander concurred. "Nobody's coming in. Everyone used to drop by, don't you remember?"

"I do remember," Jay said, almost fondly. Anna relayed the message and the shift in tone. *"But that was before you got that damn snake,"* Jay's ghost asserted on a rising note. Anna repeated the message emphatically. She could not have agreed more.

"But she's all I have for company," Alexander whined. "To tell you the truth, after you were gone, I was lonely."

"A snake is merely a phallic symbol, not a replacement for me," Jay's ghost hissed in Anna's ear.

That was when Anna's private line rang. It was Edward. "I

know you're not home right now, but I just wanted to tell you I'm trying to take a day off and it's driving me crazy. If you pick up your messages, maybe you could call me? Maybe I could come meet you for lunch or something. This is Edward," he added unnecessarily.

"That's him?" Alexander asked. "I told you you'd be meeting him."

"Yes, you did," Anna muttered, "But we were talking about you." The ghost was chatting in her ear. She relayed its directions to Alexander. "Jay says first of all—his name is Jay, right?"

"Right," said Alexander.

Anna continued. "Jay says first of all, you need to put in some decent track lighting. Keep the snake at home, if you have to keep it, but get it out of the store. Some plants would be nice in the front window, and crystals sell better than pentacles—those nice quartz crystals on tiny chains. The T-shirts should be pastel, not black, and the ceremonial knives should be kept out of sight, in the back. The tarot reader's not a bad idea, but you ought to try selling the *Runes* by Ralph Blum. Then people could read for themselves. The trick is to make white magic seem user-friendly. What about painting the walls a light lavender instead of black? Oh, yes, if you're lonely, get some fish. The saltwater tanks are prettiest."

To Anna's surprise, Alexander appeared to be taking in Jay's suggestions with an open mind. He had even reached for her ready paper and pen and scribbled a few notes to himself. When Anna stopped talking, he looked up, and she saw that his eyes were wet. "Is there anything you'd like to say?" she asked him.

"Just tell him he's missed," Alexander said.

"You can do that," Anna told him.

"I miss you," Alexander said into the ethers. "I miss you very much."

Out of sympathy for his financial straits, Anna did not charge Alexander for his session. Nor did she accept his offer of a barter. Already, she could feel apprehension icing up her mind like an airplane's wing. *What does he mean, he sees "a bump," "trouble"— what does he mean, an "estrangement?" We're getting along fine,* Anna thought defensively. *We are, aren't we?* Suddenly, through her window came a few halting notes. They did not float or leap with their usual buoyancy. *I could call him,* Anna thought. *We could meet for lunch. Maybe lunch would bring Edward some cheer.* She dialed the number. Edward did not answer his phone.

Eleanor, on the other hand, did. When Anna introduced herself, Eleanor laughed delightedly.

"Is there something I don't know?" Anna asked, caught off guard.

"Harold assured me you'd get back to me today," Eleanor replied. "I told him it was the nick of time. My party's tonight at nine. Your fee is a thousand dollars? I'd only need you an hour."

"Yes," Anna managed. *God bless Harold.* She could eat dinner with Edward, and then make some excuse. Her private line shrilled again. It was Edward, sounding uncharacteristically needy.

"I don't suppose I could come up and see you for a minute?" he asked.

"Of course you could," Anna answered.

When she opened the door to Edward, she nearly slammed it again in his face. The infernal ghost was right on his heels. When

Edward stepped through the doorway, so did the ghost. Anna threw him a glare.

"I'm a mess," Edward said miserably. "I can't play worth a damn. I am thinking I should not play in the competition. I'm just going to let everybody down."

"Do you see how serious this is?" The ghost demanded. *"Now he's quitting!"*

"Let me get you some mint tea," Anna offered. Edward took a seat on the love seat. The ghost followed her into her tiny kitchen.

"You can see you have to do something, can't you?" The ghost demanded. *"He needs more than a glass of iced tea. Why don't you offer him something he can grab on to? Give him some hope. Tell him about me. That would be loving."*

"No!" Anna spoke aloud.

"What?" Edward asked her from the other room.

Anna came back bearing a glass of tea which Edward took eagerly, gulping down Advil with his first swig. "I'm turning into a drug addict," he joked darkly.

"You're not really thinking of quitting are you?" Anna asked. She tried to imagine Edward without his music.

"He's dead serious. This is a catastrophe!" the ghost put in.

"If I quit, at least I won't be disgracing anyone—Mr. Mayakovsky, the Olivers—"

"It must really hurt," Anna said sympathetically.

"It's not the pain. I can live with the pain. It's how I sound that's killing me."

"And killing me!" The ghost chimed in.

"Let me give you a sandwich," Anna offered. She felt hopelessly earthbound.

"I should eat," Edward admitted. "When I'm playing I forget

to eat."

"Tuna on rye?" Anna retreated to the kitchen where the ghost blasted her again.

"Oh for God's sake. You are impossible. Can't you see that he needs something more than a sandwich?" The ghost was apoplectic. *"Stop playing house! Give him something to hold on to. Just do as I ask."*

"Leave us alone!" Anna furiously willed her visitor.

"It takes more than loving hands at home to make great music!" Anna brought Edward his sandwich on one of her prettiest plates. He took a bite, then set it aside.

"I'm not really hungry," he said miserably. "I better get back to the piano."

"Be gentle with yourself," Anna urged him. He only frowned.

"Whatever. I'll see you tonight." Edward closed the door after himself.

"Thank you for nothing," the ghost hissed. *"You're worse than Archbishop Jerome. You're worse than a Viennese audience."*

"And what is that supposed to mean?" Anna knew she was being insulted.

"They dismissed my Marriage of Figaro *and you dismiss me."*

"I do dismiss you. Scat!"

"I had to go to Prague to be appreciated. Prague!" Centuries later the ghost was still mad.

"So this is all about appreciating you?"

"It's all about appreciating music."

"For which you're the spokesman?"

"A lot of people would say so, yes." And with that, the ghost vanished.

Chapter 83

nna thought of calling Mrs. Murphy but she felt she knew what she'd be told. "Honesty is the best policy," or some close variant. She thought of calling Stacy and revealing all to her, but it seemed tactless to call now and demand an immediate answer to a complex situation. With Edward's melodies starting and stopping far below her, she found her own misery matched the sound track.

"I need to meditate," she told herself. "I need to get calm and centered."

Seating herself on the love seat, she closed her eyes and searched inward for the familiar koi pond. Instead of the serene oasis she sought, she found herself staring into Edward's tormented face. In her mind's eye, he took on the aspect of a tortured Byzantine saint. *Poor Edward!*

"How can I help him?" Anna caught herself praying. "Please guide me." But her thoughts were tumultuous and no guidance seemed forthcoming. The surface of her koi pond was muddied and rippled. No gentle fish swam beneath its surface. Anna saw only murky depths. *Why did her romance have to be so difficult? Why couldn't love be easy and fun, the way it looked in all the media?*

Her phone shrilled. Anna let the machine answer it. She heard Tommy's voice, lightly teasing her. "Anna, Anna, come out and play," the voice cajoled. On impulse, she grabbed for the receiver.

"Tommy?"

"You know my voice. That's encouraging."

"It's a distinctive voice, especially when you're trying to seduce me."

"Who said anything about a seduction? Just come out and play."

"I can't."

"Why not?"

"I just can't." Anna sounded martyred even to her own ear.

"Sure you can. You can. You can."

"I'll be right there," she breathed. "Give me about ten minutes."

Anna freshened her makeup and brushed out her hair. She threw on her tweed coat and a muffler. It was five short blocks to Westside Aquarium. She arrived breathless as if running from herself.

"Anna Banana," Tommy greeted her. He kissed her on both cheeks, then held her at arm's length. "You don't look so good," he announced. "You look worried."

"I am worried," Anna confessed. "I'm worried and I'm miserable and I need a friend."

"That bad, eh?" Tommy offered her a Reese's Peanut Butter Cup from the basket on the counter. Anna unwrapped the candy and popped it into her mouth.

"Mmm, delicious," Tommy teased. "Now tell all."

"I don't want to tell all," Anna protested.

"So give me a clue. Let me guess. Trouble with *him*."

"Not exactly."

"That was my best guess. You looked so miserable, it had to be love."

"Oh, Tommy. Why is everything so complicated?"

"What's so complicated? You like him. He, hopefully, likes you. That's happily ever after, no?" Tommy swabbed at the countertop.

"No. I don't think so..." Anna trailed off.

"Want to see the new discus? It's awesome." Tommy led the way to a nearby tank. A single large fish swam dolefully.

"It looks lonesome," Anna observed. "You ought to get it a partner."

"You do have it bad," Tommy muttered.

"What did you think," Anna asked him, "When you first found out I talked to ghosts?"

"I thought it was cool. I thought you were cool. I still think you're cool and I would be a lot less trouble than whoever he is." Tommy put a hand on her shoulder but she shrugged it off.

"Don't, Tommy. We've been through all that. We're supposed to be friends."

"All right then. As your *friend*, I think it's cool your talking to ghosts. I think anybody would think it was cool. Even *him*. That's what this is about, isn't it? You haven't told him."

"No. I keep waiting for the right time." Even to her ear, her excuse sounded lame.

"And you thought I was bad for going through your purse!" Tommy teased her.

"It's not the same," Anna protested.

"Sure it is. It's sneaky. I know that's not what you want me to say, but it is." Tommy began swiping off the fronts of the closest tanks. He began humming from Rodgers and Hammerstein.

"Any other new fish? I am changing the subject." Anna helped herself to a second Reese's Peanut Butter Cup. She savored the taste.

"Consider it changed," Tommy spoke up. "There's a new beta. Scarlet. Very dramatic."

"You're very dramatic," Anna teased.

"Tut. Tut. This is not about me."

Tommy was right. She was squarely up against her own lack of character. The issue wasn't really Edward's acceptance of her calling. It was her own. This insight only fueled her misery.

"Kack anybody recently?" she peevishly asked.

"I thought you'd never ask."

"What happened?"

"Ich. Kacked half a tank of mollies. The rest are still in sick bay."

"I ought to be in sick bay." Anna heard herself whining.

"You ought to be honest."

"Who elected you God?"

"You asked me."

"So I did. So I did."

With that Anna turned to watch the swordtails. Their numbers seemed sadly depleted. "What happened?" she asked.

"Too much ammonia," Tommy said. "I didn't want to tell you."

"So you really think I should just tell him?" Anna asked.

"What I really think is that you should stick around until I close and then come back with me to my place. We'll break your 'no drinks' rule and have a few glasses of chilled Chablis. Then I'll talk you out of that lovely vintage dress you're wearing and after you've been to bed with me everything will have a new and rosy light. Even if I do say so myself, I am terrific in bed."

"Just like that?" Anna asked.

"Just like that. Everything doesn't have to be so serious. Who said you had to suffer for love?"

"You mean you don't?"

"Not with me you don't. Come on. Go to Starbucks, get yourself a cappuccino and by the time you get back, I'll be closing."

Anna went to Starbucks where she ordered a frappucino with an extra shot of espresso. It was fattening but she was in the mood to throw caution to the winds. Of course she was. She was on her way to Tommy's. When she got back to the aquarium shop he was just triple locking the door.

"Well," he said, grinning, "You have the delighted look of a woman who is just about to be shot."

"Thanks a lot. That's very encouraging." Anna poked him in the ribs. He reached for her and enveloped her in a bear hug.

"I can't breathe!" she protested.

"Breathing is overrated. Okay, follow the leader." Jangling his keys, Tommy unlocked the door right next door. "Well, come on in," he beckoned. "Said the spider to the fly."

"You live here? Right on top of the shop? That's convenient."

"I like things to be easy."

Tommy led the way up a narrow staircase. They passed the first landing, the second landing, and the third. Just as Anna felt she couldn't climb another step, they reached the fourth landing, the very top of the stairs.

"Home sweet home," Tommy said with a flourish. He unlocked the black-lacquered door and ushered her into an apartment that was all shades of gray. The effect was oddly soothing, almost as though Tommy himself lived underwater in a fish tank filled with shadows.

"First I will take that attractive tweed coat of yours, suitable for a horse blanket."

"Thanks. I like it. I think of it as my 'walking-the-moors' coat."

"Yes. And we have so many moors."

Anna surrendered her coat and felt suddenly vulnerable and defensive without it. She took a seat on a deeply cushioned gray couch. "This place is quite the lair," she observed. Tommy had crossed to the minibar where he was opening a bottle of wine.

"You're sure you're not an alcoholic?" he asked over his shoulder.

"I think I'd know," Anna retorted.

"Good then. I am going to ply you with this Chablis. Otherwise I didn't want your drinking on my conscience."

"So you've got a conscience?"

"Oh, barely." Tommy turned, glasses in hand. He crossed to the couch and handed her a drink.

"Here's to you, Anna. Finally succumbing to my fatal charms."

"I don't like the fatal part," Anna protested, thinking of Tommy's bisexual history and the fact that Hughie had died of AIDs. "Be careful," Stacy had warned.

"Oh, that's just drama," Tommy said lightly. "I'm actually very careful and I'm glad to have you here. See how easy it is? You just sip your wine and let me have my way with you."

"Did I agree to that?"

"Of course you did. You're here."

"Only for a minute," Anna protested. "Just for one drink."

"That's what they all say," Tommy laughed. He raised his glass. "To the fine art of seduction. I actually missed my calling."

"Which is?"

"Hughie said I would have made a great courtesan. Did I say that Hughie left me this apartment?"

"What are you doing?" Anna heard Mozart's now familiar voice. *"You've got no business with this man. You're taken, remember?"*

"What are you doing? You followed me! I deserve a little privacy."

"Kiss me," Tommy instructed Anna, taking a place next to her on the couch.

"I can't kiss you," Anna protested. "You have a pierced lip and I don't know how to navigate it."

Tommy leaned over and nuzzled Anna's neck. "You'll learn. It's actually very erotic." She felt the stud in his lip as a cold tingle. She pulled back.

"What's the matter Anna Banana?" Tommy asked. "It's me. Your friend Tommy. A harmless semi-fairy."

Anna laughed at the characterization.

"She's in love with someone else. That's what's the matter!" This time the voice was louder. Sure enough, Mozart's ghost was materializing over near the minibar. His wig was slightly askew and his waistcoat was misbuttoned as if he himself had just been roused from bed. *"I admit that Edward is difficult, high strung, and a little high maintenance, but don't you think you're carrying things a step too far?"*

"Don't you think you're meddling? Leave us alone."

"Anna Banana. Cat got your tongue? Drink up. It's time for a refill." Tommy hefted the bottle.

"She's had more than enough already. She can't really handle her liquor." The ghost spoke as though Tommy could hear him.

Anna furiously thought back at the ghost. *"If you're referring to my sleeping with Edward, I'd have slept with him sober."*

"Come on. Just half a glass," Tommy coaxed.

"No thank you, thank you," Anna managed. She slid away from Tommy's circling arm. He was close to her and wore an expensive and delicious cologne. Abruptly, she found herself missing

Edward, who smelled chiefly of Dial soap. Edward, whose idea of seduction was simple self-disclosure. Edward…Oh, dear God, she really was in love with him. What on earth was she doing here with Tommy?

"Come back, come back wherever you are," Tommy cajoled her. Anna set her wineglass on the coffee table. Let the haunting be her excuse for her change of heart.

"It seems I've got a ghost for a stalker these days," Anna told Tommy. "He's here right now and he's making me a little self-conscious." Mozart smirked from the far corner. "I mean I don't think sex is a spectator sport."

"A ghost? Oh, this is getting so complicated," Tommy said with delight. "Is he scary?" He reached an arm to draw Anna close but she stiffened defensively. Mozart's ghost was shaking his be-wigged head.

"One little kiss," Tommy pleaded. "So tiny you won't even notice it?" Now Anna felt repelled by his advances. She could think only of Edward. Not for her, casual encounters. She froze in Tommy's arms. *Oh, Edward, oh, Edward. How could I?*

"Tommy. I shouldn't have come here," she blurted. "I was leading you on. I was leading myself on." Anna explained. "There really is someone else. Someone I care for—even if it's a little difficult."

"Does this mean a 'no'? I may need another glass of wine to metabolize that."

"You're very sweet," Anna went on.

"That's it. The kiss of death. Sweet! How can you look at a man with my body art, my shaved head, and my piercings and possibly detect that I'm sweet?"

"Can we get out of here? Unless I'm mistaken, you've got a

dinner date and you might want to comb your hair!" Mozart's ghost nodded his head toward Anna's coat. *"Come on. Let's get going. You're nearly late."*

Anna reached for her coat.

Chapter 84

At seven P.M., their usual time, Edward arrived at the Greek diner looking haggard and ashen. He winced as he slid into the booth. It was meat loaf night, his favorite, but his appetite was off, he told Anna, just like his playing. *You don't need to tell me,* Anna thought, *I've heard it all day.* He was popping Advil like M & Ms, Edward went on, thanks to the advice of Mr. Oliver's sports medicine guy. He'd hit bottom on acupuncture, hypnotism, and deep-tissue massage. His injury remained as implacable as ever and he, Edward, was playing like shit. Pardon his French.

"Playing like *merde*," Anna joked, then wished she hadn't. Edward was deadly earnest and actually pale with pain. He looked worse than he had at noon.

"Maybe I really should drop out," Edward was saying. "I'll only disgrace myself. I'm no good to anybody in the shape I'm in." He explained that his injury hampered free playing; that his lack of fluidity made him even more tense. "I don't have my usual control," he explained. "The tenser I get, the worse I play; the worse I play, the tenser I get. It's a vicious cycle."

"*Could* you drop out?" Anna asked. "Isn't your health the most important thing?"

"Don't start," Edward flared. "After all the hoops I've made it through, I can't stop now."

"But why not?" Anna asked.

"Because I can't, that's why not. I don't want a reputation for unreliability. An injury can be a stigma. I can't afford it. And besides...I'm *not* dropping out. I just said maybe I should."

Anna had never seen Edward so dejected—or so angry, either. She hesitated to say anything more, placing her order to George in such a half whisper that he had to tell her to please speak up. She ordered spanakopita and Greek salad, wanting something she could pick at; her appetite was off, too.

If I could have one Christmas wish, Anna thought miserably, *it would be to have Edward playing again at the height of his powers.* When she got home from her ill-advised encounter with Tommy, she had listened to Edward's music, heard it alternately soaring, limping, and straining. The notes crossing her windowsill had seemed filled with pain.

"Sorry I'm such an SOB," Edward volunteered over their tossed green salads. "I'm just miserable." He certainly looked miserable, and he sounded it as well.

"Of course you are," Anna tried to comfort him. "You're in pain." Why did everything she say sound like such a cliché? Why did she feel so powerless to help someone she loved? And she did love Edward, even if Tommy was a seductively easy alternative. She'd had a close call.

"You mean you can hear it in my playing?" Edward had never asked her such a question directly. She could tell there was no evading the issue.

"Actually, yes," she answered, feeling herself on very shaky ground.

"I knew it," Edward conceded. "I knew it wasn't just my imagination."

A miserable silence rose between them. It began as awkward and soon became unbearable.

"I wouldn't want you to lie to me," Edward finally said. "Actually, I would just hate that." He buried his face in his hands, and Anna thought for a moment that he was again hiding tears of rage and frustration. *If only I could help*, Anna thought. *If only I knew what to do.* Then she realized that perhaps she did. *"You will tell him,"* Mozart had said. *Damn Mozart.* She saw now that he was right. *What had Alexander said? A bump, a separation, an estrangement—but if I love him, do I have a choice?*

She shoved her silverware and the salt and pepper away from her as if to clear room for her thoughts. Against all her wishes and better judgment, she knew the moment of truth had come. If she loved Edward, and she now knew she did, she had no choice.

"Edward," she said, "There's something I have to tell you." At the serious tone of her voice, Edward looked up in surprise. She continued, "I have been lying to you, sort of. I mean—" She was losing her nerve, but found it again. She went on. "I am not the nice, normal young woman you take me to be."

"How could you be? You like me," Edward lamely joked. "At least I think you do. Is this a 'dear John'? If it is, just get it over with."

"Actually...I talk to ghosts," Anna blurted. "That's my job in the evenings. Not real estate, talking to the other side."

"The other side." Edward repeated the phrase flatly.

"Yes."

Her confession hung in the air. Anna felt as though she'd announced it with a megaphone. Silence loomed. Edward's meat loaf arrived, and her spanakopita. George set them down carefully, aware he was interrupting a "discussion."

"You talk to ghosts," Edward repeated. His tone was carefully neutral, as if she had said, 'Darling, there is a tarantula on your arm,' and he didn't want to upset it. He displayed no disbelief, or not of the usual sort. He was very calm—too calm. "You talk to ghosts," he said again.

"I do. I have since I was a little girl. I do it for a living actually. I was afraid to tell you." Anna blathered on. "You see, I'm a medium. That's a job, not a size," she joked nervously. "It's a gift," she rushed on. "I've had it since I was little. I talk to ghosts."

"You said that," Edward said mildly and directed his concentration toward his meat loaf. He cut his entrée into small, careful bites. He seemed to be chewing over what Anna had said.

"Ghosts," he said finally. "You mean dead people?"

"Spirits, technically, but dead people, yes. I'm kind of like a radio or a telephone." Anna shoved her spanakopita miserably across her plate.

"Why didn't I notice?"

"Because I hid it from you," Anna confessed with mounting hysteria. "Because I didn't tell you. Because I didn't—" she broke off.

"Trust me?" Edward inquired. His gaze was cool and dispassionate.

Anna flushed scarlet. He had nailed her. Of course the issue *was* one of character—or lack of character, she supposed. *Mine or his?*

302

"Well," Edward laughed. "This certainly draws things to scale. What's a little thing like a musical competition in the light of eternity?"

"But that's just it," Anna burst out. "It does matter. Mozart even thinks so. He told me he wanted you to win." Anna winced, hearing her own words.

"*Mozart* told you?" Edward tried unsuccessfully to suppress a smile. Anna knew she sounded ridiculous. Who could believe in visits by a celebrity ghost?

"Yes," she rushed on. "He's been visiting me. I'm not usually visited by celebrity ghosts, but he's been visiting me for some time now. Because of you," she added hastily.

"Because of *me*?" Edward's disbelief was palpable.

"He told me you were the best," Anna forged on. "That he loved the way you played his music and that I should tell you I'd talked to him—"

"Very interesting," Edward murmured with a touch of irony. "Anything else?"

Feeling herself increasingly damned, Anna stumbled on. "He wants you to just relax, and listen for him. And he also said he had bad playing habits, too, and that your teacher, Mayakovsky, was right about your shoulders. And change your fingering to get to the high B flat in the third movement."

"Mozart wants me to relax my shoulders and change my fingering," Edward mused. Tactfully, he displayed no sarcasm. Or perhaps, he was just being careful, now that he knew he was dining with a madwoman. Anna stared dumbly down at her plate. Of course by this point her spanakopita was cold and her Greek salad was somewhat the worse for wear. *Goddamn Mozart to Hell.* Edward was reacting pretty much as she had supposed he would: politeness mingled with incredulity. Contempt and disbelief would set in later.

"You talk to Mozart," Edward summed up. "He visits you."

"He only talks to me because of you," Anna protested. "He told me to tell you that he thinks you're the best. He likes your interpretation of his intentions. He feels you're on the right track. He feels the rest of them sound like a train wreck. He likes what you're trying. He said if he's known his music was going to be immortal, he'd have left more markings like Mahler did."

"I thought you didn't know anything about music?"

"I don't. Really, I am just repeating what he said. He told me—"

"To listen for him and to relax my shoulders and to change my fingering to get to the high B flat." Edward repeated what Anna had said. *Was he making fun of her? Yes, he probably was.*

"I think I have said enough," Anna said, moving to stand up. Her head was spinning, her face was flushing, her hands were sweating, her stomach lurched with waves of nausea. She steadied herself on the edge of the table.

"That's the deal with the two answering machines?" Edward asked. "I'd wondered about that." Yes, Anna told him, that was the deal with the two answering machines. One was her professional line.

"So you're a ghostbuster?" Edward thought he'd coined the phrase.

"That's what Alan calls me." Anna knotted her scarf around her throat. She struggled into her coat.

"Alan knows about this?" Edward was looking up at her, but he was *not* jumping to his feet. He was *not* begging her to stay. Of course he wasn't. Whatever delicate, beautiful thing had stretched between them was now broken.

"Of course he knows about this. He grew up with it. It's been happening our whole life." Even to herself, Anna sounded furious and defensive. Edward, on the other hand, seemed cool, calm and collected. Denial, Anna decided.

"Your whole life?" Edward asked incredulously. "You've always talked to ghosts?"

"Since I was five. It started at my grandmother's. I don't really want to get into it." Anna buttoned her coat. "I'm going home," she announced.

By now, Anna was red-faced and fighting back tears. She pulled on her gloves and shoved her hands into her pockets.

"Oh, Edward," she said, as she turned to leave, "I am so, so sorry."

Her tears began in the elevator and by the time she reached the safety of her apartment, they were torrential. Dressing for her nine o'clock appointment, she had to keep grabbing for Kleenex. And what should she wear? She settled on a black velvet cocktail dress she had hoped to wear to dinner sometime with Edward. Trying to repair her makeup was an uphill tricky job. Her waterproof mascara was proving something less than waterproof. Her blush was splotched. Her nose kept running. In the taxi, for once she was glad for the crosstown traffic. It gave her time to master her emotions. Or nearly.

"You okay, lady?" the driver wanted to know. No. She was not.

Chapter 85

Harold's friend Eleanor lived on Sutton Place in a duplex apartment. "Here for the party?" the doorman had inquired when she arrived promptly at nine, checking her name off on a list and guiding her toward the private elevator. *I've really done it*, Anna thought, as the elevator rose to the tenth floor. *I've botched it completely.* The door slid open, revealing an elegant black-and-white-checked foyer. A very short, very plump, very blond woman stepped toward her.

"I'm Eleanor," the woman announced, taking Anna's startled hands in hers as her two armloads of bracelets jangled like tiny bells. "I'm so glad you're here," she added, leading Anna down a long hallway hung with trophy photographs in expensive silver frames. Anna noticed many famous faces, but they passed in a blur. "You'll be reading right in here," Eleanor announced, steering Anna into a small, oak-paneled bar just to one side of a large crimson living room hung with recognizable oils. Above Anna's head, big game trophies leered down at her. Under her feet was a zebra-skin rug. *Evidently, if you were rich enough, you did not need to be politically correct. Not that I'm correct either*, Anna thought, shamefaced.

From across the living room, Alexander nodded to her from his station, a small table for two set up in one corner underneath what Anna took to be an original Monet. Alexander looked cheery and peaceful, Anna noticed. *I wonder if I look uncheery and unpeaceful*, she thought grimly, just as Eleanor seated herself in the chair beside her.

"I thought we might just start with me," she announced brightly. "What do you get for me?" Anna closed her eyes and sought to focus. From somewhere in the back recesses of the large apartment, a string quartet was playing. It sounded suspiciously like Mozart. "Do you get something?" Eleanor interrupted.

"One minute," Anna held up a warning hand. She *was* getting something. An autocratic woman's voice spoke clearly. She had an impression of someone elegant and very thin.

"Don't marry him," the voice directed.

"Don't marry him," Anna repeated. Eleanor gave a tiny gasp.

"You've done it before, and you're doing it again," the voice warned. *"Why can't you learn from experience?"* Anna repeated what she assumed to be an unwelcome message.

"Tell me," Eleanor asked at her elbow, "Ask her why she's so sure."

Anna listened, then repeated what she heard. *"The accent is bogus, the title is bogus, the man is bogus,"* she quoted. *"Of course, he's after your money."*

"Is it my mother?" Eleanor wanted to know.

"No daughter of mine should be married five times," Anna repeated the pronouncement. *"Also, he's gay."*

"It *is* Mommy," Eleanor exclaimed. "She always lectured. I could never do anything right. I still can't, evidently." She laughed lightly, as a tall, expensively dressed man stepped to her elbow.

"So, what do we have here?" he inquired.

"A medium, darling," Eleanor answered. "Anna, this is Raul; Raul, this is Anna."

"A medium? I'm a tall," Raul joked. His slithering accent sounded squarely mid-Atlantic.

"Anna was just telling me the most interesting things," Eleanor prattled on. She winked at Anna, and Anna understood then that they were conspirators—that this was the marital prospect, and that she had not told Eleanor anything she did not already suspect. *So the big Psychic Faire was just a ploy to get some guidance. Well, at least she would be well paid.*

"Pssst." Alexander was hissing in her direction. "Come here," he motioned.

"Not now," Anna called. She had just spotted Daisy, a friend of Eleanor's she recalled, who greeted her from across the room with a gay little wave. Teetering on her stilettos, Daisy crossed the room and kissed her on both cheeks. No sooner had they made contact than there was the familiar bump in her consciousness as a spirit knocked for admission.

"Love the getup," Anna heard distinctly. She repeated the compliment to Daisy who clapped her hands in delight. She was wearing a hot-pink suit. The jacket plunged. The skirt broke midthigh. The bright color became her.

"This is so much fun," Daisy enthused. "You tell Bunky that since we talked I've been doing much better." She crossed a silken leg and perched closer.

"You can tell him," Anna said. "He's right here."

"I am doing better, can you tell?" Daisy spoke to the air above Anna's head.

"You look like a million bucks and I should know," Anna repeated the ghost's appreciative remark.

"I think I'm getting the hang of things. I really do," Daisy bubbled. "Of course I know you're helping me."

"You can count on it!" Anna quoted emphatically. She fought a sudden urge to pat Daisy on a shapely knee. She reported this to Daisy who hooted with glee.

"Oh, he just loved my legs!" Daisy crowed gaily. "You tell Bunky I am still his girl. Nevermind. I'll tell him." She leaned closer and gave a girlish whisper. "Bunky, I am still your girl!" Anna faithfully reported a ripple of delight. Daisy stopped suddenly, midgiggle, to look at Anna more closely.

"Why, sweetheart! You've been crying, haven't you? Your eyes are all red. Your makeup's streaky."

"Yes, a little." Anna admitted.

"And you look ready to cry a whole lot more."

"Do I? Oh, I suppose I do. It's just that I really botched things. Totally, totally botched things."

"Man trouble?" Daisy leaned closer, patting Anna's hand. Her expensive perfume enveloped them in a little cloud of fragrance. The smell was comforting.

"I'm the one who needs a reading," Anna confessed. "I need someone to tell me what to do—or what to not do."

"What did you do?"

"Too much."

"Then don't do anything. Let him think things over. He'll be back. Of course he'll be back. You're darling."

But Anna did not feel darling. Daisy kissed her good-bye on a feverish cheek.

After Daisy's tête-à-tête, Anna glanced at her watch. Her scheduled hour was up and she had already delivered the news for which she was being so handsomely paid. *I'll just slip out*, she resolved, but as she got to her feet, Alexander furiously motioned her over. Reluctantly, she went to his side.

"Well, you're in the rapids now, aren't you?" he began. "I don't know what you did, but you sure did it. You really upset the applecart. Do you know what I am talking about?" He held up a hand as another partygoer approached his table. "This will just take a minute," he announced.

"Well, I told him I talked to ghosts," Anna confessed miserably. "I don't think he took it well. I told him what Mozart told me to say. Harold, Mozart, my father, my brother—even my friend Tommy. Everybody was all for my disclosing things. I knew it was a bad idea. I just knew it." Anna trailed off.

"Mozart?" Alexander picked the celebrated name up. "You told him you were talking to *Mozart*?" He sounded incredulous. Like Anna had done something really, really stupid.

"Yes, I'm afraid I did." Anna could feel her eyes welling up. She did not want to cry in front of Alexander. "Mozart told me to tell him. He insisted."

"He did, eh? That may have done it," Alexander pronounced.

"Thanks a lot." Anna heard her own sarcasm.

"Hey, don't shoot the messenger, but this must have been the rift I saw coming. Remember? I told you I saw—"

"Yeah, thanks—'a bump, a separation, an estrangement.'" Anna quoted bitterly.

"And I saw choices," Alexander reminded her. "Have you had to make some choices?" Anna thought of Tommy and their near affair. She hadn't so much made a choice as she had narrowly avoided a bad accident.

"Yes," she said. "I've had some choices. You were right about that."

"Well, I'm right that you're in trouble now, too."

"But what do I do now?" Anna asked.

"I'm afraid that I don't give advice," Alexander said primly. He signaled to his waiting client to step right up.

Edward did not knock on her door later that evening. Unwilling to face more rejection, Anna did not knock on his the following day. The next evening, Edward did not come to the diner at their customary time. The day after that, Santa, in the form of Harold, came to school. When it was Anna's turn for a Christmas wish, she muttered, "I wish to hell I'd kept my mouth shut, Harold." Then, she burst into tears.

"There, there," Harold tried to comfort her.

"Oh, why did I ever believe you?" Anna burst out.

Edward was not at the diner the next night, nor the night after that. With only three days left until Christmas, Anna defeated, bought a ticket home. She could at least tell Alan she'd told him so. She could at least...but Anna really couldn't do much of anything. Her depression was absolute.

On her cab ride to LaGuardia, she was blind to the passing Christmas lights. On her flight home, she declined the holiday eggnog. When Alan met her at baggage claim, she hurled herself, sobbing, into his startled arms.

"I told him," she wailed. "And now it's over."

"You had to tell him," Alan sympathized, awkwardly patting her shoulder.

"Well, I did tell him," she sobbed. "Why couldn't I listen to my own instincts? Why did I listen to you and Mozart—"

"Mozart?" A grin played across Alan's face.

"Oh, never mind." She handed Alan her carry-on bag and followed him, sniffling.

Chapter 86

"'Tis the season to be jolly," her mother woke her on Christmas morning, cheerful because her father had accompanied her to midnight mass. Anna put on her red flannel bathrobe and her outsized furry slippers and shuffled downstairs to the Christmas tree where Alan and her father were waiting. *Don't they know it is a bad time to hold Christmas?*

Anna had bought her father an elaborate carved chess set that she'd been lucky to find Christmas Eve in Ann Arbor. She gave her mother a holiday sweater—her mother loved holiday sweaters—and she gave Alan a cheap round-trip ticket to New York. Now that she and Edward were no longer seeing each other, Alan was welcome for a return engagement of indeterminate length.

From her father, Anna got a pair of white mittens with ghost faces on them. From her mother, she got the *New York Times* cookbook, as a not-so-slight hint about the dangers of Greek diners. From Alan, Anna got a hug and a small CD player. "So you can drown him out," Alan suggested—a suggestion that took Anna, one more time, straight into tears.

Christmas dinner was a forced march through holiday cheer. The turkey, the stuffing, the garlic mashed potatoes and signature cranberry-orange relish were all delicious. So was the holiday plum pudding, her mother's specialty and rightly so.

Edward did not phone on Christmas. Not that she expected him to. But she knew that he knew her parents' names. If he wanted to at all, he could easily have found her. Nor did he call the next day, or the next, and so on through New Year's Eve, which Anna spent with Alan and her parents watching the ball drop in Times Square on TV. No, Edward didn't call and Anna doubted he even thought about calling. *What were Alexander's words again? A "bump," a "separation," an "estrangement?" This is more than some "bump,"* Anna thought. *Aren't "bump," "separation," and "estrangement" three different and worsening things?*

New Year's Day came and went. Anna's depression deepened. Her hair a wild tangle, her face unscrubbed, she sat on the television room couch, huddled in her bathrobe. Her parents urged her to stay a few more days and Anna conceded rather than argue. After all, what did she have to go home to?

When her parents' phone rang on January 4, it was her brother, Alan, calling her. "Are you watching?" he wanted to know.

"Watching what?" Anna demanded. "Some stupid football game? I thought they were over with. Cartoons?" Lately, her depression had taken the form of nasty irritation with all things cheerful. *Estrangement is called "estrangement" for a reason,* Anna brooded.

Alan explained, "I've got Edward's competition on the Internet. If you want, I can tell you how to watch it." Speechless, Anna held on to the phone. *Edward!* She had a chance to see Edward, but did she want to? *Wouldn't seeing him actually make it worse? He had told her something about the competition being online. He had made fun of the idea, calling it newfangled gadgetry and beside the point. Still, she could see him.* "Are you there?" Alan yelled in her ear. "Well?" he shouted.

"I'm here," Anna said meekly. She might as well be honest. She did want to see him.

"Put Mom on, then," Alan demanded.

Anna's mother was an unlikely computer geek. She had gone back to school to pick up a few skills and once she had, there was no stopping her. Anna had confided in her mother nothing of her debacle with Edward, so now she simply said, "This friend of Alan's is in a piano competition. He wants me to watch him on the Web." Whether her mother was fooled was anybody's guess, but after talking to Alan she quickly fired up her high-speed computer, and with a few moves of her mouse there he was: *Edward in miniature. Broadcast live from the heart of Texas.*

Even as a tiny, miniature Edward, he made Anna's heart leap. No bigger than Mickey Mouse, he was still Edward, and, evidently, the man she loved. He was just launching into the Mozart. Although the computer's sound system left something to be desired, Anna could tell Edward was playing like a house on fire. *No wonder Mozart likes him*, she thought somewhat feverishly. *My God, he's playing well.*

"He's really something, isn't he?" Anna's mother observed. *Did she suspect?*

"Yes, mother, he is." Anna was close-lipped.

Feeling she was spying on his secret world—*How had Alan known Edward's competition was being broadcast online? Were they still in e-mail contact? They must be.*—Anna watched Edward play with rapt attention. *Maybe Mozart was right*, she caught herself thinking. *Maybe Edward really was the best living player of Mozart's work. He certainly was today—and his haircut looked good, too*, Anna observed with sad satisfaction. *Goddamnit*. She felt her eyes starting to burn.

Staring into the monitor, she squinted closer as the camera panned the crowd. There! Anna was certain she had caught a glimpse of Mozart.

Edward was launching into the tricky third movement. Anna had heard it played many times, but not as he was playing it today. Instead of speeding through its showy pyrotechnics, Edward was deliberately slowing down. The music seemed to deepen and develop under his touch. *Perhaps he's really playing Mozart's intention*, Anna thought with excitement. *Yes, that must be what he was doing*. On the monitor, Anna searched one more time for Mozart, but the camera was now firmly fixed on Edward, on his smooth-moving hands.

"He's just magnificent. How does Alan know him?" her mother innocently asked.

"Turn it off," she told her mother. "Just turn it off." With that, she stormed to her room, hurled herself on her childhood bed, and sobbed. Her bitter tears wet the pillow. She could have cried on for days.

It was a ringing phone that stopped her. The judges had barely had time to announce their decision before Alan was back on the line, Kalamazoo to Ann Arbor.

"What did I tell you?" Alan crowed. "He won. Put Dad on, would you? He owes me fifty bucks."

Chapter 87

Dear Mr. and Mrs. Oliver,

Thank you for your kind phone call. I agree that technology is amazing and I am glad you were able to "see" the competition on the Internet. I confess that when I first learned that the competition would be broadcast online, I thought it was just a terrible idea, a silly, modern gimmick. But modern doesn't need to mean bad, does it? And the cameras and all were really quite discreet and it all comes down to you and the keys in the long run.

Mrs. Oliver, you are quite right about the neck. It is much, much better. I had yet another expert advise me that the key was my playing habits and this was one expert I had to trust. The key was to relax my shoulders, change a fingering, stop trying so hard and believe that I was "right" as to my basic interpretation. Funny what a little timely encouragement can do.

Mrs. Oliver, you ask about my friends Alan and Anna. I am afraid Alan is back in Kalamazoo, although we are in touch by e-mail and I did tell him how to "watch." Anna is still at her parents' in Ann Arbor. I may have botched it with her again. She's a surprising woman. Alan says that if I give her time, she may come around, but I don't think Alan has a blazing love life of his own. When you met Mr. Oliver, did you know he was "the one" or did you vacillate and have doubts? Pardon such a personal question but I really have no one else to ask.

Mr. Oliver, thank you for relaying the news to my parents that I won. I don't hear from them myself. As to your question, I still don't know all of the ramifications of winning. There's the cash, of course, which I probably should just sign over to you but which does signify another year or more in New York if I am frugal. There is a set of concerts and those should yield further work. Then, too, and maybe most of all, there is the distinction—being named "the best." I thought the Korean guy they placed second really gave me a run for the money. It must have been pretty close. Still, I won and I'm glad I did. Thank you for having such faith in me and please thank Mrs. Oliver for her congratulatory box of divinity. Maybe there was a touch of "divinity" in winning.

Sincerely yours,
Edward

P.S. What I am really wondering is if you "knew" immediately that the two of you were meant for each other or if there was a figuring-it-out phase. Now that the competition is over, it seems I have time for some of life's other challenges.

Chapter 88

Anna emerged from her grief-filled holidays as from a nasty hangover. She washed her hair, made up her face and resolved to face her own turbulent feelings with more resilience and grace. She was, after all, an adult. It was time that she acted like one. *How would a woman with any self-esteem act? Act that way,* she lectured herself. With this thought in mind, she telephoned Mrs. Murphy. She'd been avoiding her for the whole vacation, not wanting to hear her cheery advertisements for the afterlife. Now, Anna thought, a visit to her might prove a tonic. At the very least, she could confide in her with safety. She borrowed her mother's sensible Volvo and drove carefully through Ann Arbor's snowy streets.

Mrs. Murphy welcomed her with open arms. "Come in. Come in. I thought perhaps you weren't speaking to me. I imagined that you must be home."

Anna allowed herself to be ushered into the welcoming foyer. She stepped out of her snowy boots and hung her tweed coat on a coat hook. She was glad to see that Mrs. Murphy had not yet taken down her Christmas tree. She had a good view of it from the velvet love seat. As she took her familiar place, a whirl of childish emotions suddenly seized her.

"I guess I wasn't speaking to you. I'm so mad I could spit," Anna started out. "You never told me how really awful it could get. You just talked about my 'privilege' and my 'gift.' You never told me it would make me a freak. I had to find that out the hard way."

"Oh, dear," Mrs. Murphy responded. She sat with her elegant hands folded serenely in her lap as if she were prepared to simply ride out the storm of Anna's emotions. "You'd better tell me what happened."

For openers, Anna told her about the experience in Connecticut, the horror of those feelings of terror and betrayal and her own guilt about letting the old lady's ghost down. Not only had the son probably killed her, he was profiting from her death, and Anna's presence had done nothing to change that. Marc and Mallory had gone right ahead and bought the house despite Anna's advice to the contrary. Mrs. Murphy hadn't prepared her for that, Anna accused.

"You're just the messenger," Mrs. Murphy gently asserted. "You report what you see and hear. You don't change things. Destiny is destiny and fate's fate. You're not supposed to play God."

"I know. I know," Anna growled miserably. It was Mrs. Murphy's standard lecture on detachment. To be frank, it was hard to practice in the trenches.

"Anything else?" Mrs. Murphy prodded. "I get the feeling you're stalling."

Now Anna launched into the real problem, her relationship

with Edward and the way it had been unfolding "perfectly" as long as she was "normal."

"He *liked* me," Anna whined, again reverting to her adolescent self. "I know he did, I could feel it."

"If he liked you, then he liked you." Mrs. Murphy's tone was soothing. "I am sure this is just a misunderstanding. Why, lovers have them all the time. You know that."

"I'm familiar with the theory," Anna groused. Then she got to her bottom line. "He liked me right up until the moment he thought I was a nutcase. Until then he thought I was fine."

"Then he only liked a part of you, my dear," Mrs. Murphy observed mildly.

"What about Mr. Murphy?" Anna now demanded. "I never thought to ask you what he thought of your gifts. Did he just accept them? Lucky you."

Mrs. Murphy offered Anna a Wurther's Original butterscotch from the crystal dish that sat between them on the marble-topped mahogany coffee table. When Anna declined, Mrs. Murphy took one herself and sucked on it thoughtfully as if she would find her answer there, in a sudden burst of flavor.

"Mr. Murphy tolerated my gifts," Mrs. Murphy spoke finally. "I wouldn't say he encouraged them, but he accepted them. After all, they went with the territory and the territory was me. He knew he had to take me as I was or not at all."

"We're at the 'not at all' part," Anna picked up her story. "I was doing well until Mozart showed up and started prodding me to tell all. I *hate* Mozart," Anna finished hotly.

"Mozart, eh? I've never had a famous ghost come through," Mrs. Murphy said, missing the point entirely. "Tell me, what was he like?"

"You're missing the point!"

"So tell me."

"Mozart? He was pushy, first of all. Very single-minded. He didn't really seem to care about me or even really about Edward except that Edward evidently got his music right and that's what he was after." She tried to convey accurately the implacable strength of Mozart's will, the way he had directed her to speak for him to Edward, let the chips fall where they may, which they certainly had.

"So your young man," Mrs. Murphy summarized, "he's missing in action?"

"No, he's not," Anna replied hotly. "He's right on the Internet winning prizes—thanks, no doubt, to Mozart's good advice."

"Mmm," Mrs. Murphy selected a second butterscotch and appeared to be mulling over Anna's complaint.

"Has Mozart been back?" she asked finally.

"So far, so good," Anna snapped. "I think his use for me is over. Thank-yous probably aren't in his nature."

"No, probably not," agreed Mrs. Murphy. "The music was the thing, wasn't it?"

Great. A fan, Anna thought. It didn't help that just then she was remembering Edward's Mozart and the spangled sky full of sound it had created right in her studio.

"So you don't really have any advice, do you?" Anna accused.

"Well, it's a privilege and a gift to be chosen as a conduit," Mrs. Murphy launched into her long familiar spiel. "You must always remember what an honor it is, although you are allowed to set up certain ground rules."

"Tell that to Mozart," Anna spat back. "He was the one calling the shots. I was the one dumb enough to listen to him." She was really having a tantrum, she realized. She was acting as young as when she'd first come to Mrs. Murphy.

"I'd love to get the chance," Mrs. Murphy answered, selecting her third butterscotch of the day. "I'd love to meet Mozart."

"Well, that makes one of us. I want to be normal," Anna burst out. "You can talk to ghosts. You've got nothing to lose being weird."

"Oh, dear," Mrs. Murphy said sadly. "We've been through all this, haven't we? You're not 'weird.' You're special. That's how to look at it."

"Will you tell that to Edward, then?" Anna gulped. To her embarrassment, her anger was melting into sorrow. Hot, familiar tears stung her eyes. Now she reached for a butterscotch to console herself.

"Remember how Isabella loved butterscotch?" Mrs. Murphy asked. Isabella was Mrs. Murphy's now deceased fox terrier. She had been a party to many of Anna and Mrs. Murphy's sessions. She *had* always loved butterscotch.

"I remember," Anna sniffled. She was noticing that Mrs. Murphy looked old and frail. Her faith might be strong, but she was not. Anna wondered just how long it would be before Mrs. Murphy herself was speaking to Anna from beyond the veil?

"Most of the time, they're good company," Mrs. Murphy mustered a final argument. "Don't you agree?"

Anna, who had spent virtually her whole life companioned by higher forces, had to agree that the spirits did take the edge off her loneliness. "Most of the time, yes, but not Mozart."

"I'll tell you what," Mrs. Murphy said unexpectedly. "I'd hold him accountable."

"Edward?" Anna asked.

"Not Edward. Mozart," her mentor replied.

Chapter 89

The ride in from LaGuardia was miserable with traffic. As the taxi made its way slowly across the Upper East Side, Anna noticed that most of the Christmas lights had been taken down and those that remained had a bedraggled air. The cab cruised across Central Park at 86th Street and pulled up neatly under the awning to her building. Anna paid the driver and hefted her single suitcase herself. She had packed lightly.

Inside the lobby there was nothing but silence and the grinding of the elevator when Anna summoned it to appear. For all the psychological distance between them, Edward might as well be caught in cyberspace, Anna thought bitterly. The door to 1E-as-in-Edward was closed and no music issued forth from beneath its sturdy door.

When Anna fit her key into the lock she wished, briefly, that she had a dog, a little Isabella perhaps, to welcome her home. Stacy had cared for her philodendrons and set her mail neatly in a pile on her reading table. She would get to that later. First, there were her professional messages to clear.

Do not think about Edward, she told herself. *That's over.*

Just as Mrs. Murphy had said, he needed to accept all of her—and, of course, he could not. *But I can*, Anna resolved. She felt a welcome spark of self-determination. *I can at least accept all of myself. I am a woman with a foot in each world. It's a gift and a privilege just as Mrs. Murphy says. I can return my professional messages and be grateful that I have them. Yes, that's where I'll start.*

Just when she had surrendered to her fate, Anna couldn't exactly say, but sometime during her visit to Mrs. Murphy, or sometime after it, perhaps on the flight home, she had reaccepted her gift. Call it fatalism perhaps. Call it a surrender. If her gift had cost her Edward, so be it. *He hadn't even tried.* Like Mrs. Murphy, Anna needed a man who at least tolerated her difference. *Is that too much to ask?* she wondered. *Evidently, for Edward it had been.*

The professional line showed twenty-one messages—a lot, but then Anna recalled the weeks of ignored messages when she was pretending to be normal. Taking out her black leather book and a pen, Anna took down names and numbers. She would certainly be solvent in the New Year, she reflected. It took her a full half hour to get all of her messages safely transcribed.

Well done, she told herself. *Just put one foot in front of the other. Do not think about Edward. Just think about work. She was lucky to have such fascinating work. She was also lucky he wasn't playing the goddamn piano. I don't need any heartbreaking sound track. I am heartbroken enough as it is.*

Also, she was exhausted. She would return her calls tomorrow, she decided. Changing into a comforting flannel nightgown, she climbed up the ladder to bed.

The bedside clock once again read two-thirty when she was awakened by a faint scrap of melody. Peering around the corner of her pillow, she saw Mozart loitering near the window, humming to himself with an air of innocent distraction.

"You!" she accused. *"What are you doing here? Or was it irresistible visiting the scene of the crime?"* Anna sat straight up in bed and hurled her pillow in Mozart's direction. He dodged it neatly.

"I came to congratulate you," Mozart announced, mustering a show of dignity. *"Job well done."* He offered Anna a bow. *What a*

fop, Anna thought. "*Congratulations*," Mozart persisted.

"*If you mean that he won, I saw it on the Internet. That's as close as Edward and I get these days.*" Anna spat her response in Mozart's direction. She cast him a baleful glance but he ignored it and prattled on.

"*He played brilliantly. He took all of my advice.*" Now the ghost was actually gloating. "*He relaxed his shoulders. He changed his fingering. Constanze and I were both thrilled. Even my father was impressed—and he's quite the taskmaster.*"

"*I figured you were there whispering in his ear,*" Anna accused. "*I saw you on my monitor.*"

"*No, no. I'm afraid coaching's not allowed. He took the advice you gave him. From me to you to him. Just like I planned. But I knew he would be glad to hear from me.*" The ghost preened himself. "*My name does carry some weight in some circles,*" he added.

"*Well, I wish I had kept my mouth shut. He used to be my boyfriend,*" Anna retorted. *Why look for sympathy where there was none? Mozart was so centered on the music there was no room for any human emotions. Maybe he'd never had them.*

"*Aha! So that's what happened!*" Mozart snapped his fingers as if a puzzle had just been solved. "*You abandoned him so he abandoned my music. I am so glad I came to speak with you.*"

"*What are you talking about?*" Anna demanded. "*He abandoned me!*" She remembered Mrs. Murphy's advice. "*I should hold you accountable,*" she threatened. Did she imagine it or did Mozart back up a little? *Do I make him a little nervous? Well, good!*

"*The music,*" Mozart explained as though he were talking to someone a little slow. "*The music, the music, the music, the music. He won the prize but now he's stopped playing my music.*" The ghost sounded desolate.

Anna remembered the evening's uncharacteristic quiet. So Edward had stopped playing? Or at least had stopped playing Mozart? Silence hung in the studio's air. Mozart sighed melodramatically. He wrung his ghostly hands in a parody of tragic woe. *"I cannot tell you how I miss the music. It must remind him of you. I shudder at the thought."*

"You have only yourself to blame!" Anna exclaimed hotly. *"It was your bright idea that I tell him everything. We were in love. We were happy. There's more to life than music."*

"That's it!" Mozart snapped his fingers again. Clearly he was onto something. Clearly, even against her own wishes, Anna was giving him information he needed. The ghost looked positively Technicolor and nearly human as he exclaimed, *"There's more to life than music! That's what my wife used to say!"*

Chapter 90

Dear Mr. and Mrs. Oliver,
Thank you for asking. I guess it's true, Mrs. Oliver, as you suggested, that everything does feel a little anti-climactic, even lonely. I guess when you have a goal and you accomplish it, it does leave a sort of emptiness in the place in your psyche where the goal was. Either that, or I'm just plain lonely.

Last night, I had a very strange dream. I dreamed I was lying in bed, but awake, and Mozart was sitting at my piano. He looked just like all the pictures of Mozart you've ever seen, just a little more vivid in the flesh. He started to play one of the piano concertos and then he broke off and turned to me. He said, "There's more to life than music, my boy," and then he winked like I might get what he meant.

When I woke up, I saw that there was a Mozart piano score still on the piano and I didn't remember leaving it there. Of course I must have.

Sincerely yours,
Edward

Chapter 91

After Mozart's departure, Anna passed an uneasy night. Some part of her was still battling with the ghost. *I should have said. I could have said...* Some part of her consciousness was monitoring the calls she had to return. Another part of her consciousness was missing Edward. She had become accustomed to his presence in her bed, the way he dove into sleep so soundly, his head resting on her cradling arm. *Damn it, damn it*, Anna had tossed and turned. *Edward was so near and yet so far from her. She could rap on his door; she could plead understanding. No, she could not. There was her pride.*

Outside the window, the January sky was a dull leaden gray—a color and condition perfectly suited to Anna's mood. There were calls to be made, of course, but Anna found she resented making them. Life could go on without Edward, that much was clear, but she didn't have to like it. *Why not go for an icy cold miserable walk in the park?* it occurred to her. *Yes, that was exactly what she would do. But first, some breakfast at the Greek diner. If I run in to him, I run in to him. Sooner or later, it's bound to happen.*

The Greek diner was jammed with early-morning diners. Anna scanned the crowd for Edward's coppery curls, but the coast was clear. The booths were full and the counter was jammed elbow to elbow. *Maybe I'll skip breakfast*, Anna thought. *I don't really have an appetite*. That was when she heard her name. The voice was Tommy's.

"So you're back!" Tommy was seated at the counter, breakfasting solo.

"I'm back," Anna confirmed. She kissed his cheek.

"I thought you might come here," Tommy gloated. "And their western omelette is great."

"I'll have to try it." Anna wasn't really in a social mood.

"Have a seat." He gestured to the stool next to him, newly vacated.

"I thought I'd just get a muffin to go," Anna demurred.

"Always hard to get," Tommy laughed. "Have it your way."

"Anna! Anna! You're back!" this time the caroling voice belonged to Harold. He made his way from the men's room straight toward Anna and Tommy.

"You take my place for a minute. I'll stand," he told Anna. He kissed her jovially on both cheeks as her mind whirled with the new variables: Harold and Tommy. Harold and Tommy having breakfast together. Harold and Tommy…

"Cat got your tongue?" Tommy teased her. "Before you wonder any further, congratulations are in order."

"That's wonderful," Anna managed.

"And of course we owe it all to you." Tommy patted Harold's hand.

"To me?" Anna was flabbergasted. "How do you owe it all to me?"

"Well, you must have noticed we had chemistry that night with the floats," Tommy said. "I mean, you were such a good sport about going out to a bar so we could get to know each other."

"I think that was your idea," Anna said. Just at the moment she didn't feel like a good sport. She felt foolish and not a little embarrassed.

"No, it was mine," Harold contradicted her. "I think I suggested the bar."

"The rest is mystery," Tommy announced gaily.

"How did I miss all this?" Anna asked.

"You went to the ladies' room and we exchanged numbers. Simple as that," Tommy explained. He didn't seem to have a shred of embarrassment. Anna felt like a spoilsport wanting to say, "But you were chasing *me!*" Harold was too happily involved to notice her discomfort. Clearly, both men expected her to be happy for them and, her shock and rue notwithstanding, she actually was.

"Anna! Anna! Over here!" This time the voice belonged to Stacy. Anna had missed her in the crowd. She was sitting in a back booth with a man Anna could almost place. Twined together, Stacy and the man shared one side of the booth.

"Duty calls," Anna told Tommy.

"Miss Popularity," he kissed her good-bye. Anna walked to the back of the diner where Stacy was waiting.

"Anna!"

"Stacy!" Anna bent to kiss her friend hello. *At least she isn't with Jeffrey.* Stacy smelled faintly of aftershave.

"Please. Join us," the man boomed out. "I'm David. We met once at the riding academy." He untangled himself sufficiently to offer a hearty handshake.

"David. Of course I remember." What Anna remembered was that David had been confronted after tantric sex. That was water long under the bridge to judge from the looks of things.

"Join us," Stacy insisted. "And tell me who that was." She patted an empty place across from her. *I don't want to join you,* Anna thought miserably. "That was just a friend," she muttered.

"Please," David insisted. "Waiter! We've added a third." *Great. Young love and company. I get to play the extra wheel.*

"C'mon, Anna. I've missed you. Who was Mr. Clean?" Stacy gave her a sunny smile. *There's no getting out of it.*

"Just a friend," Anna repeated vaguely.

"Pretty exotic," Stacy observed. "So join us."

And so it was that Anna ordered a fruit salad and a muffin. She picked away at them while Stacy and David worked their way with gusto through an order of blueberry pancakes and one of waffles with strawberries and whipped cream. *Talk about sexual appetites!*

"I'm so glad to see you," Stacy said between bites.

"Me, too," echoed David who kept one arm draped possessively around Stacy's shoulders. "Stacy tells me you were always in my corner." *Was I?* She dimly remembered taking David's part when Stacy was in the throes of her Jeffrey withdrawal.

"Yes, well. I guess I was," Anna confirmed. "When push came to shove, I guess I was in your corner," she concurred politely.

"And we're so glad you were," Stacy murmured, offering David a particularly choice strawberry.

On this tender note, Anna made her good-byes.

Chapter 92

Anna entered the park at 86th Street, just as she usually did. The colors were gone, of course, so the dead leaves clinging to the trees were as drab and dull as she felt herself. The wind was nasty. That suited her, too. She didn't even bother to tighten the muffler she'd thrown on. She nodded crossly to Charlotte, the little Westie, and her owner, familiar passersby. Regular walkers and joggers in the park often came to know each other by sight. There were only so many routes winding through the trees, and inevitably, the habitués became familiar to one another. But Anna found herself resenting any intrusions. Misery did *not* love company, and so, rather than walk the crowded perimeter of the reservoir, she chose differently.

The cinder bridle path made a looser loop around the reservoir, and she set out to accomplish it feeling a grim sense of virtue. She was alone, so at least she had her spirits for company. Her career was evidently booming. Couldn't she be satisfied with that?

No, she could not. *Damn. Damn, damn, damn!*

Steeped in self-pity, she walked on. She was just at the site of her and Edward's bike accident when she heard her name called out. "Anna, Anna, is that you?"

It was Edward's voice, and Anna numbly turned toward it. She found Edward standing a few feet behind her, his hands shoved miserably in his pockets, his face reddened and pinched from cold. His close-cropped haircut was already beginning to grow out and his copper curls spiked up alarmingly in all directions. He wore baggy runner's gear. Evidently he had replaced his biking with jogging.

"You look like a madman," Anna said crossly. "You need another haircut."

"I *feel* like a madman," Edward answered. "Can I walk with you?"

"Free world," Anna replied. She refused to meet Edward's eyes. Why should she make things easy? Edward fell in beside her, checking his loping stride to match her own. They strode furiously onward in perfect tandem.

"I don't see why you're bothering with this," Anna flared, when the tension became unbearable. "We can go right on avoiding each other. Not that I'm avoiding you like you're avoiding me." She kicked savagely at a stone in her path.

"You're the one who stormed out. You're the one who didn't answer the door when I knocked," Edward defended himself. He was half-shouting.

"You never knocked," Anna accused him. Then she remembered her absence for Eleanor's party. Hope flared. *Stop it*, she told herself. *Stop it, stop it.*

"You're mad at me, aren't you?" Edward started up again. *Mad at him? That was putting it mildly.* "I can understand that. But it was a lot to absorb and you did just vanish out to Ann Arbor."

"How did you know where I was?" Anna demanded. "Not that it was so hard to figure out."

"Alan and I e-mail," Edward answered.

Now Anna was the one who felt like a madwoman. And Edward? Despite his red pointed nose, he had never looked better. *Don't look at him*, Anna willed herself. *Looking at him will make you lose it completely.*

"Great for you and Alan," Anna sniped, realizing exactly how petty she sounded. *Why do I get to sound like the crazy one?* she wondered. *Why can't I be more sophisticated and soignée? Why can't I play it cool? What would Stacy do?*

"It was a lot to absorb. Ghosts, Mozart and everything," Edward said sensibly. He seemed bent on behaving rationally. Anna wanted to strangle him. Hadn't he abandoned their promising romance? And just when it was going so sweetly? Yes, he certainly had. *The coward. The creep. The jerk. Could jerks be so attractive? Yes, evidently they could. Don't look at him!*

"Sorry it was too much for you," Anna accused. *There! Let him deny it! Let him—*Edward grabbed her by her shoulders then, and turned her to face him. He was so much taller, she stared directly into his Adam's apple. Reluctantly, Anna looked up. Edward was looking down at her. For a moment she thought they might simply kiss, but no, Edward had something to say. He was staring wildly into her face.

"Did I say it was too much for me?" he demanded to know. He gripped her more fiercely by the shoulders. "You're the one who left the diner. You're the one who ran home. *I'm* the one who got rejected, who didn't measure up, who lacked the *scope* to take you in. That's what you decided, isn't it? I was too shallow for you. Well, actually, I took your advice—or Mozart's. I relaxed my shoulders. I changed my fingering. I trusted my gut about my interpretation. It was a tremendous help to me, more than I can tell you. In case you hadn't heard, *I won*." His piano hands did not relax their grip.

"I'm glad you won," Anna conceded. "I watched you win, actually. My mother got you on her computer. Your hair looked good." *I sound like an idiot.*

Edward held her then at arm's length as he laughed. Anna

stiffened, but still his piano hands had her firmly in their grip. *How would anyone normal act? Couldn't I please act that way?*

"You *are* laughing at me," Anna railed. *He's making fun of me. Just like he did in the laundry room. Oh, the laundry room*—Anna flushed. Edward was racked by laughter. He laughed until tears formed at the corners to his eyes. The snippy wind lashed them away. "Let me go!" Anna could feel her face reddening further. *Why do I have to blush? Idiots blush. What is it with this man?* "Let me go, I said!"

"No," Edward protested. He gripped her even more tightly. "*No.* I had a dream about Mozart."

"Mozart? I *hate* Mozart!" Anna stormed.

Edward paused to suck in a breath. He plunged on. "Mozart told me there was more to life than music."

Anna was astonished. "Mozart told you there was more to life than music?" *So Mozart wasn't such a prick after all.*

"He meant hair, I suppose," Edward joked.

"He meant me, you idiot," Anna burst out.

"There are weirder things than talking to Mozart," Edward rattled on. "Puccini claimed the music for *Madame Butterfly* was dictated to him by God. Brahms claimed the same thing. In his late period, Beethoven wrote 'for God.' And then Handel, not to mention Haydn—"

"Not to mention," Anna murmured. *Edward looked wonderful.*

"And when I was little? When I was little, *I* talked to Mozart," Edward rushed on.

"Just kiss him. Just kiss him," she clearly heard Mozart's voice. *All right, then!* She tilted up her face.

We hope you enjoyed this Hay House book.
If you would like to receive a free catalogue featuring additional
Hay House books and products, or if you would like information
about the Hay Foundation, please contact:

Hay House UK Ltd
292B Kensal Road • London W10 5BE
Tel: (44) 20 8962 1230; Fax: (44) 20 8962 1239
www.hayhouse.co.uk

***

Published and distributed in the United States of America by:
Hay House, Inc. • PO Box 5100 • Carlsbad, CA 92018-5100
Tel: (1) 760 431 7695 or (1) 800 654 5126;
Fax: (1) 760 431 6948 or (1) 800 650 5115
www.hayhouse.com

***

Published and distributed in Australia by:
Hay House Australia Ltd • 18/36 Ralph Street • Alexandria, NSW 2015
Tel: (61) 2 9669 4299, Fax: (61) 2 9669 4144
www.hayhouse.com.au

***

Published and distributed in the Republic of South Africa by:
Hay House SA (Pty) Ltd • PO Box 990 • Witkoppen 2068
Tel/Fax: (27) 11 467 8904
www.hayhouse.co.za

***

Published and distributed in India by:
Hay House Publishers India • Muskaan Complex • Plot No.3
B-2• Vasant Kunj • New Delhi - 110 070
Tel: (91) 11 41761620; Fax: (91) 11 41761630
www.hayhouse.co.in

***

Distributed in Canada by:
Raincoast • 9050 Shaughnessy St • Vancouver, BC V6P 6E5
Tel: (1) 604 323 7100
Fax: (1) 604 323 2600

***

Sign up via the Hay House UK website to receive the Hay House
online newsletter and stay informed about what's going on with your
favourite authors. You'll receive bimonthly announcements
about discounts and offers, special events, product highlights,
free excerpts, giveaways, and more!
www.hayhouse.co.uk

JOIN THE HAY HOUSE FAMILY

As the leading self-help, mind, body and spirit publisher in the UK, we'd like to welcome you to our family so that you can enjoy all the benefits our website has to offer.

 EXTRACTS from a selection of your favourite author titles

 COMPETITIONS, PRIZES & SPECIAL OFFERS Win extracts, money off, downloads and so much more

 LISTEN to a range of radio interviews and our latest audio publications

 CELEBRATE YOUR BIRTHDAY An inspiring gift will be sent your way

 LATEST NEWS Keep up with the latest news from and about our authors

 ATTEND OUR AUTHOR EVENTS Be the first to hear about our author events

 iPHONE APPS Download your favourite app for your iPhone

 HAY HOUSE INFORMATION Ask us anything, all enquiries answered

join us online at **www.hayhouse.co.uk**

292B Kensal Road, London W10 5BE
T: 020 8962 1230 E: info@hayhouse.co.uk